The Tyee's Gift

❧ Hearts Rescued With Love ❧

a novel

by
Sherry Ann Miller

A sequel to An Angel's Gift

The Tyee's Gift—Hearts Rescued With Love
Copyright © 2005 Sherry Ann Miller
All rights reserved

Published and Distributed by:

Granite Publishing and Distribution, LLC
868 North 1430 West
Orem, Utah 84057
(801) 229-9023 • Toll Free (800) 574-5779
Fax (801) 229-1924

Cover Design by: Tammie Ingram
Page Layout and Design by Myrna Varga, The Office Connection, Inc.

ISBN: 1-932280-75-8

Library of Congress Control Number: 2004117737

First Printing February 2005

10 9 8 7 6 5 4 3 2 1

Printed in the United States of America

Dedication

To Della, better known as Tiger's Belle,
who always finds a bright way to cheer me up.

To Lynda, who is the Starlight of my life,
and the sun, moon and stars to my son.

To Tracie, always my little Shnook,
who touches my heart with her unconditional love,
and her willingness to forgive my many failings.

To Diane, who is the Sunshine behind all my rainbows.
We will always be together . . .
on the porch of life . . . rocking back and forth!

To Pawneace, the Buttercup of my affection,
who returns my love in bucketfuls.

To Mindy, the Tizzie Lish of my life,
who is not only my beloved daughter,
but one of my very best friends!

To Rainy, who came with her own nickname
and endeared herself in my heart forever.

To my daughters, all seven, may you recognize
the Lord's miracles in your lives. . .
today and always.

I love you!

Mom

Prologue

*I*n a fit of anger, Abbot ripped the books from the shelf, scatter-
ing them across the cabin sole. He grabbed a velvet box from
its hiding place behind the book shelf, then went up on deck, opened
it, and removed the engagement ring and wedding band. Refusing to
look at them with any degree of fondness, as he had done in the past,
he threw both rings overboard. As the dark water swallowed the last
vestiges of hope he had for Alyssa, he acknowledged that her reasons
for calling off their engagement were his fault and his alone. Abbot
had been selfish, domineering and cruel to her. She gave him up
because she wouldn't be ridiculed or controlled. Her decision had
nothing to do with her desire to serve God. He had wanted to change
her and he had belittled her beliefs in order to accomplish it. This
realization finally crumbled what little self-esteem Abbot had left.
Slipping back through the companionway and down into the salon,
a new wave of remorse swept over him. If he could have seen himself
through her eyes a year ago, he would have known he was not the kind
of man a woman looks for when searching for a husband.

After several minutes of self-pity, he began to make order out of the chaos he'd created in the cabin of *Bridger's Child*. Sorting and stacking the books neatly, he began replacing them upon the starboard bookshelf. When he picked up the last book, it was heavier than any of the others and it fell open in his hands.

Two verses of scripture seemed to stand out from the page and grip his heart:

> "*Therefore, they must needs be chastened and tried,*
> *even as Abraham, who was commanded to offer up his*
> *only son. For all those who will not endure chastening,*
> *but deny me, cannot be sanctified.*" [D&C 101:4–5]

Shuddering, Abbot closed the book and disregarded the message he'd found. It was just a coincidence. God could not possibly be speaking to him through the scriptures.

To prove his point, he closed his eyes and allowed the book to fall open, then placed his fingers upon a page and opened his eyes to read:

> "*And the Lord said . . . Why art though wroth? And*
> *why is thy countenance fallen? If thou doest well, shalt*
> *thou not be accepted? And if thou doest not well, sin*
> *lieth at the door. . . .*" [Genesis 4:6–7]

Looking heavenward, Abbot responded coldly, "It has nothing to do with not doing well, God! I have valid reasons to be angry. You took Pa from me before I was ready! You buried him in a mountain of snow and let him die a horrible, suffocating death! Why?" It was not a prayer. Quite the opposite, it was a demand for answers. "Why didn't you warn me? Why did you forsake me, Lord, when I needed you most?"

Sorrow, unlike any he'd felt at his father's funeral and the weeks that followed, consumed him. For the first time in months, Abbot realized that all his bitterness, his domineering behavior, all the control issues with Alyssa and his abandonment of religious beliefs, had been the result of his unwillingness to let his father go. God took Sparky home, just as he'd taken Abbot's mother, Sarah Nicole, twenty-three years ago, without any regard for Abbot's feelings. When the anguish of losing both his parents could be contained no longer, Abbot sank onto the settee and wept bitterly.

Much later, his swollen eyes were drawn to the scriptures beside him, and he opened them one more time, to see what the Lord had to say. Abbot read:

> *"And Isaac brought her into his mother Sarah's tent and took Rebekah and she became his wife; and he loved her; and Isaac was comforted after his mother's death."*
> [Genesis 24:67]

Abbot Isaac Sparkleman gasped in astonishment, and hoped that God was no longer toying with him.

Chapter One

As Abbot ran along the pathway bordering the northern end of Lake Union in Seattle, a fresh June breeze, sweeping in from the north, whisked his dark, brown-black hair playfully, but he paid no attention to the wind. His arms glistened with moisture while his t-shirt clung to his well-muscled chest. Running had been good therapy for him during the past few months and had lifted him out of the depression he'd experienced after Alyssa broke their engagement a year ago.

Today he wasn't thinking about Alyssa. Anxious to locate another woman, his eyes searched ahead, but he didn't see her. A keen sense of disappointment settled in his chest. A new woman had become one of the main reasons he continued to choose Gas Works Park as a jogging site.

On several occasions, Abbot would often jog past her, fake a moment of tiredness to let her catch up to him, and then watch her as she ran past, while trying not to seem too obvious. Today, she was not running the course. His disappointment stung sharply, and he was surprised to realize this new woman had become such an important focal point in his life.

As he resumed his original course, he looked out across Lake Union and noticed a very small sailboat slip gracefully through the water toward him. A woman and a young, red-headed boy were sailing the small craft toward the park about two hundred feet from the shore. Her short, curly, auburn hair Abbot recognized immediately and he stopped, bent over as though he was winded and studied her out of the corner of his eye.

It was definitely the woman he'd been looking for, but he couldn't prevent a wrinkle of worry from creasing his forehead. Who was the young boy with her? Was she married? Was this her son? He hadn't seen a wedding ring on her finger and he had paid close attention to her left hand nearly every time they'd jogged past one another.

As Abbot straightened, a micro-burst of wind hit him square in the back on its way to the water, nearly knocking him over. Just as it passed him, the young boy stood up in the sailboat, perhaps trying to change positions for a coming-about maneuver. The jolt of air hit the sail, yanking the boom across the boat where it hit the child square in the face and knocked him overboard.

It all happened so fast, Abbot didn't have time to think. Startled, he heard the woman yell, "Cody!" Then, she dove into the icy water after the boy.

Without thinking, Abbot ran into the cold lake water, disregarding the immediate discomfort, until he was waist deep, then he dove in and swam the remaining distance between them.

Keeping his head up as he swam, he watched in amazement as the woman calmly turned the boy onto his back and listened for breath sounds. Then, she started pulling him toward the shore with little success. The small sailboat was evidently tethered to her life jacket and was headed in the opposite direction. For each stroke she took toward the shoreline, the sailboat towed her the same distance backwards. She attempted to reach the tether behind her, but holding onto the limp child at the same time made this impossible.

By the time Abbot reached them, the woman was nearly panicked. Immediately, he unfastened the tether from her vest. "Don't worry about the boat," he directed. "Can you make it to shore with the boy?"

She nodded. Her lower lip trembled, either from the icy water or her fears for Cody, or both. Holding onto the boy's life-vest neck pillow, she began swimming the two hundred feet to the water's edge.

Abbot attached the snap shackle to his belt, then pulled himself along the painter to the boat where he released the halyard. The fluttering Dacron sail fell pitifully into the cockpit and Abbot secured the halyard so the wind couldn't pick the sail back up again. Then, he followed the woman, towing the sailboat behind him with ease.

By the time he reached the shore, the woman had struggled to carry Cody as far past the shoreline as she could, then she put him down upon the grass. Abbot removed the line from his belt and pulled the sailboat up onto the black rocks. Leaving it, he joined the woman and the injured boy.

"Is he all right?" Abbot asked upon reaching them.

"He's unconscious," she gasped. "His nose is bleeding, but he's breathing okay and his heart rate is good."

"You've been able to determine all that?" He was unable to keep the surprise from his voice.

"I'm a nurse," she explained. "I assessed his condition the moment I got him ashore. We need to get him to the hospital right away." Then she moaned, as though remembering something awful. "My van is clear across the lake, near the Wooden Boat Museum."

"My Bronco is just behind that last knoll," Abbot offered, nodding back toward the rolling, green hills of Gas Works Park. "I'll drive."

An older couple, picnicking nearby, brought them a plaid picnic blanket to place over Cody's limp body. "Is there anything else we can do?" they asked.

Although the woman had tears in her eyes, she was less panicked now and seemed to glean some inner strength. She glanced back at the sailboat. "Will you tie my boat off? I'll come back for it later."

Without waiting for instructions, Abbot scooped the young boy up into his arms. He estimated Cody was about eight years old and weighed about eighty pounds. The woman had carried him as far as she could, and he was relieved that he had enough strength left to carry Cody himself.

Within minutes he had the woman seated upon the passenger seat, with Cody on her lap, the picnickers' blanket curled around him. He slipped onto the driver's seat and closed the door. As he put on his seatbelt, he asked, "Which hospital?" Before she could answer, he turned on the ignition and the white Ford Bronco roared to life.

"The University of Washington Medical Center is closest," she answered. "Do you know where that is?"

"Over on Northeast Pacific Way, right?"

She nodded and rubbed her hand across Cody's forehead.

"How's he doing?" Abbot asked as he drove out of the parking space and headed east on Northlake Way. "Shouldn't we have called the paramedics?" He was appalled to see the boy's color fading from pink to pale white, and he noticed some swelling around the bridge of Cody's nose, as well.

The woman checked Cody's pulse and counted his respirations. "Pulse is ninety, respirations are eighteen. I think he's just winded. I'm hoping he'll come around any moment." She bit her bottom lip nervously.

Just then Cody moaned. The woman sighed in relief. "Cody, honey. Can you hear me?"

"Aunt Bekah?" came his weak voice as he opened his eyes. "I can't see you good," he complained and his lips quivered.

"How many fingers am I holding up?" she asked, giving him the peace sign.

"Where?"

She looked over at Abbot and frowned. "Don't worry about it right now," she said. "We're taking you over to the University of Washington Medical Center."

"Where you work?" the child asked.

"You said you wanted me to take you there sometime." She ran her fingers through his short red hair and gave him a weak smile.

"Will I get to meet all the doctors and nurses?" Cody asked, his voice strengthening.

"Sure," she agreed, but the worried look on her face spoke volumes more than her answer.

Abbot swallowed a lump in his throat as he drove under the Interstate bridge and onto Northeast Pacific Street, then headed toward the emergency room. The moment they arrived, he said, "Wait while I get someone to help bring him in."

The woman nodded, murmuring to her nephew, "Everything's going to be just fine, Cody. You'll see."

Pushing the doors open, Abbot said to a woman sitting at a desk, "I have an injured child who needs help. *Now!*"

That was all it took. Two nurses followed him out to the Bronco, one pushing a gurney.

When the older nurse recognized Cody's aunt, she exclaimed, "Bekah! What happened?"

Bekah smiled feebly. "My nephew, Cody, got hit in the face with the boom of my sailboat."

The younger nurse said, "On your first vacation day?"

Bekah nodded as they placed Cody on the gurney. They wheeled him past Abbot and into the emergency room as Bekah explained, "We were sailing on Lake Union when. . . ."

Abbot stayed behind and parked the Ford Bronco. Then, he opened the back door and grabbed a duffle bag. Inside, he found a t-shirt and a pair of fleece sweat pants with matching jacket. After hurrying to the men's restroom, he slipped his wet shorts and shirt off and put on the fleece pants and dry t-shirt. His mind focused on Bekah and Cody as he removed his wallet, loose change, keys and cell phone from his shorts and put them in his fleece pants pockets, not even realizing that the wallet and phone were water-logged. Afterward, he returned the wet clothing to the back of the Bronco where he spread them out, hoping they might bake dry.

Carrying his jacket with him, Abbot went back into the hospital. When he arrived at the waiting room, it was empty. He looked through the windows of the two big doors leading to the emergency room, but he did not see Bekah. Though he was pleased to know her first name, he was disappointed that he was unable to be with her and Cody. Worried beyond what was normal for a perfect stranger, he paced back and forth for several minutes.

When Bekah finally joined him in the waiting room, she was wearing a weak smile and the plaid picnic blanket secured around her slender waist like a sarong.

"Nice skirt," Abbot grinned. "But you need something warm on top, too." He held his fleece jacket out and waited while she slipped her arms into the sleeves. The silver color highlighted the sparkle in her fawn-brown eyes.

"Thanks," she whispered as she zipped it up. She had to roll the sleeves up in order for her hands to gain freedom. "They're taking him to radiology for a CT scan," she told Abbot. Her dark eyes were almost gray with concern.

"Is that bad?" he wondered aloud.

"It's the first time in my career that I've wished I wasn't a nurse," she admitted. "I've never had to deal with someone from my own family being injured. And I feel responsible for Cody getting hurt. If I hadn't taken him out on the lake, he wouldn't be going through this."

"You're beating yourself up unjustly," Abbot comforted. "It wasn't your fault that you got caught in a micro-burst."

Her dark eyes widened. "Is that what it was?"

He nodded. "It hit me a second before you and nearly knocked me over. You usually can't see them coming, so there's nothing you could have done to prevent it. Moments earlier, you were both having fun, enjoying your sail."

"A micro-burst?" she questioned. "I've heard of them, but I'd never been in one before."

"They can be tricky. Just be thankful this was a small one."

She sank weakly upon a sofa. "I'm not experienced enough to have taken Cody out with me," she confessed. "I took a course last fall on sailing and really enjoyed it. But, I've had my Walker Bay for little more than a month and I've sailed by myself only three times before taking Cody out. I should have used better judgement."

"I'm sure Cody will be fine and begging to go back out again by Monday," he comforted.

She smiled. "You're probably right. Still, I know what the doctor's are looking for and if he's broken something, they may have to surgically repair it."

Abbot sat beside her and took her hand gently in his. "We'll just have to hope for the best."

"I'm a brick when it comes to taking care of other people," she confessed. "But when it comes to my own family. . . ," She hesitated as her shoulders lifted, then sagged. "I don't feel too brave right now." Her whole body shook as her eyes filled with tears. "Please, promise he'll be okay," she whispered.

How can I promise her something like that? He slipped an arm around her shoulder to comfort her, but he couldn't give her the assurance she wanted and this lack disappointed him keenly.

The woman leaned against him and asked, "Do you pray?"

Abbot hesitated. Her question caught him by surprise. It had been too long since he'd done any serious praying. "Not very often," he admitted.

"Will you pray with me?" she asked. "Please!" Her tender eyes sought comfort in his and Abbot found himself nodding.

"If that will help you." He swallowed a lump that had risen in his throat. She couldn't possibly know what she was asking. He hadn't prayed in over a year. In fact, he had only shouted at God in a fit of anger.

The woman knelt upon the floor and bowed her head. Abbot joined her. "Will you say the prayer, please?" she pleaded.

Grateful there were no other people in the waiting room, Abbot nodded, then tried to remember how to pray. A memory flashed in his mind: he recalled his father praying as he gathered his sons around him each evening at the Bar M Ranch near Vernal, Utah.

"Our Father in Heaven," Abbot began. "I thank thee for the miracle of life and recognize that I don't always live according to thy will. But Cody is in need, Father, and the blessings regarding his well-being should not be predicated upon my mistakes. Please spare Cody and restore him to full health. Bless his aunt and his family with the comfort and strength they need at this time. These things I ask in the name of Jesus Christ, Amen."

When Abbot stood, he took the woman's elbow and helped her to her feet. She looked up at him as though in awe of him. Abbot waited, looking down at her tenderly. He didn't even know her full name. Yet, her gaze made him feel protective, strong, needed. He smiled cautiously. "I'm sure he'll be fine," he comforted, not knowing why he should, when Cody's prognosis was still uncertain. "Have faith." Even as he uttered the words, he wondered, *Why should I encourage anyone, when my own faith is still sitting on a back burner?* Unable to analyze his feelings, he shrugged and said a silent prayer that his words to Bekah would be validated.

She threw her arms around his waist and held him close. "Thank you," she whispered. "I believe you."

Abbot gulped. *Now I'm in the hot seat. If Cody has serious injuries—* Then, refusing to think such thoughts, he stepped back, tilted her chin with his hand and said, "Perhaps we should introduce ourselves. My name is Abbot Sparkleman."

She blushed in surprise before she responded. "I'm Rebekah Stevens," she said. "But my friends call me Bekah." She placed her hand upon his, as he caressed her cheek. Then, she removed his hand from her face and gave him a quick, though unexpected, handshake.

"Is there someone you should call? Cody's parents, perhaps?"

"They're in Canada at a convention. Cody is staying with me while Ryan and Gail are gone. I could call their hotel and leave a message for them, but I'd rather wait until after the CT scan, when I know what's wrong."

Abbot held his hands open in a pleading gesture. "If he were my son, I'd want to know immediately. I wouldn't want my sister to wait and see before contacting me."

"I suppose you're right." She nodded.

He walked her to the telephone booth at the end of a long hall.

"I don't know how I can ever thank you enough."

"Don't worry about that," he encouraged.

Abbot waited while Rebekah dialed. She apparently had a fine memory, for she didn't have to look up any numbers, not even her calling card number, which was quite lengthy.

Then she said, "Room 318, please." After a brief hesitation, she responded. "Ask them to call Bekah when they return." She looked at Abbot with some concern in her lovely, brown eyes. "No, wait. My cell phone is in my car."

"Tell them to call—" he began, then he remembered. He pulled his cell phone from his sweat pants pocket. There was no display lit up and he realized that Lake Union had ruined it. He held it up and gave her a teasing frown.

"Tell them to call my work number and page me." Bekah spoke clearly into the receiver. "Thank you." When she hung up she said, "This way my brother, Ryan, will think I was called into work." She hesitated only for a moment, "I'm sorry about your phone."

"It's insured," said Abbot. "Don't worry about it." Then, to change the subject, he asked, "How about some food? Are you hungry?"

"I couldn't eat anything. I'm too worried about Cody."

"I'm surprised they didn't let you go with him for his tests."

"Standard protocol," she explained. "From experience, we've found that children over six usually behave more bravely when the family isn't around to hinder their emotional strength."

"Will they let you see him when his tests are done?" he queried, walking her back to the waiting room. When they arrived, three others had taken up empty seats in their absence.

"Yes."

"You know, I wanted to be a surgeon, once."

"Really?"

"Until the third day into anatomy class. That's when I knew that I wouldn't be able to do it. I had planned to tell my family over Christmas that year, but my father was killed in an avalanche two days earlier and I never got the chance." He winced with the memory, unable to prevent himself from doing so. His father dying was one of the most difficult periods in his life, and Abbot had spent a great deal of time blaming God for taking him home too early.

"I'm sorry to hear that," Bekah offered. Then, as though sensing that it was a painful topic for him, she said, "Anatomy class never bothered me. Neither does the trauma or the blood I see in the ER. Unless it's my own, or someone I love. Most of the time I'm glad I chose nursing as my career. But not today," she admitted. "I'm afraid Cody's experience has drained all my reserves."

He sank down onto a sofa and asked her to join him. When Bekah sat beside him, she picked up a magazine from an end table. While she read, Abbot toyed with a magazine of his own, but he found himself looking at Bekah Stevens over the top of the pages.

Rebekah had somber, brown eyes that darkened when she was frightened and lightened when she smiled. Her auburn hair was cut short, pixie-style and curled all over her head, especially when it was wet. She had long, dark eyelashes, high cheekbones and beautifully bronzed skin, evidence of spending a lot of time in the sun.

Abbot hadn't had much time for sunshine, even on those rare days when Seattle weather allowed it. He'd thrown himself into his new job and additional university schooling with all the vigor he could.

Too many thoughts of Alyssa Mae Kendall and what might have been had plagued him last summer and fall. After seeing his brother, Ed, at Christmas and realizing how much Ed loved Alyssa, Abbot had reconciled himself to their upcoming marriage.

With a smile on his lips he realized that tomorrow was their wedding day, and he wasn't feeling jealous in the least. Looking at Rebekah, he realized she was probably a good part of the reason why.

Abbot noticed the magazine she was reading droop steadily until it fell onto her lap, startling her. She had almost dozed off. He put an arm around her shoulder and whispered, "Go ahead and rest. I'll wake you when Cody comes back."

"I'm sorry," she mumbled. "On the job I handle stress fine. But now, I'm totally wiped out."

"Don't worry about it," he encouraged her. "I promise I won't bite you."

"I know," she admitted with a timid smile. She leaned against him, resting her head on his shoulder. Within minutes she was fast asleep.

Abbot looked at the other people in the waiting room: an older woman knitting; a businessman with an attaché case; a younger man in torn jeans and faded flannel shirt. They no doubt thought he and Bekah were sweethearts. He doubted any of them had the slightest idea that they'd barely been introduced half an hour ago.

His chest swelled with satisfaction as he realized she felt comfortable enough with him to fall asleep against his shoulder. It gave him a sense of elation he had not felt in a long, long time.

Allowing his thoughts to drift back to Alyssa, he recalled that his former fiancée had never really been comfortable with him. Why she'd ever agreed to marry him Abbot still didn't understand, except as his brother, Ed, pointed out: Alyssa was an impulsive woman who hadn't thought through the consequences of her actions.

Abbot had received a letter from Alyssa last year. It was written in September, added to in October and mailed in November. The letter was quite lengthy, but he hadn't answered it. In addition to her apology, Alyssa explained how she'd come to love his brother. Although Abbot knew that she'd fallen in love with his brother, Ed, the moment he saw them kissing in Mountain Meadow almost a year ago, seeing the words on paper had further irritated him and brought a flood of feelings back that he thought he'd buried.

He'd thrown the letter away, vowing to disown his brother completely. But last Christmas, Ed turned up in Seattle for a surprise visit. They'd talked about Alyssa and what had happened with her affections. Fortunately, Abbot was able to forgive Ed and Alyssa. By late December, Abbot was engrossed in his job as assistant administrator and lead archaeologist for the Museum of Natural History, funded in part by the University of Washington. It was a job he could sink his teeth into and he had done so with a vengeance. Perhaps that was part of the reason why, when Ed and he talked about Alyssa, it didn't sting as smartly as it would have four months earlier.

Ed pleaded with him to come to the wedding; he wanted Abbot to be one of his best men. But Abbot had declined the invitation. It would be like rubbing salt into an open wound. However, when Ed left they were finally on good terms. Had it not been Alyssa who had stolen Ed's heart, Abbot would have been happier for his brother.

By this time tomorrow his brother and former fiancée would be married and very likely getting ready to stand in line for their reception back in Maeser, Utah. Tomorrow night, they would be honeymooning somewhere, but for the first time in months, Abbot realized, the thought didn't bother him.

Abbot wouldn't have been able to go to the wedding ceremony, but that was entirely his own fault. He'd dropped out of church more than a year ago. Although he used to attend his meetings sporadically, he hadn't gone at all since he broke up with Alyssa. In fact, for a long time he'd blamed the church as one of the main reasons why she broke their engagement. Alyssa wanted a temple wedding and at that time, he wasn't ready for one, in fact, he'd doubted the temple was the right place for him to ever marry.

Besides, he'd wanted intimacy and she wasn't ready for that, either. His motives had been self-serving and he'd finally realized it last September. Abbot hadn't been concerned with Alyssa's feelings, only with his own. The remorse he felt, when he finally acknowledged that their breaking up had more to do with his selfishness, rather than with her determination to choose God's way over his own, had been overwhelming. When it finally sank into his thick skull just how much at fault he'd been in their relationship, he was devastated.

But when the remorse ended, resolve replaced the sorrow in his heart. He'd learned a valuable lesson: relationships are like two-way streets. In order to become the kind of man a woman would want to marry, he would have to be willing to give everything to the relationship. His father, Sparky, once said that in a good, working partnership, both parties should meet the needs of the other and when they did, the union would be on solid ground. In his own selfish state, Abbot had wanted to take and to rule; he'd been unwilling to give anything in return. When he looked back upon it, he was ashamed at how selfish he'd been.

In silence, he reiterated his unspoken vow. *Never will I put my needs above the needs of the woman I love, especially now Bekah Stevens is snuggled up next to me.* Although his primary motive for helping Bekah were strictly out of concern for her nephew, he admitted that he rather enjoyed the position he was in at the moment.

Eagerly, he turned his attention back to Bekah, hoping she would sleep a little longer, hoping he could comfort her the rest of the day if she needed him. Abbot enjoyed the feel of her head on his shoulder and relished the complete trust she put in him to protect her. Eager to learn more about Bekah, he waited patiently while she slept, committing to memory every feature of her beautiful face, from her long, curled eyelashes to her delicate chin.

An elderly woman was knitting an afghan opposite him and the look on her face reminded him that he should also be feeling some anguish over Cody. However, when he'd prayed earlier and again when he'd told Bekah that her nephew would be fine, he'd sensed a warm, comforting feeling in his chest that gave him the courage to believe it. The sensation surprised him, particularly because he hadn't had that special kind of inspiration for several years, since before his pa died. Recognizing it as the prompting of the Holy Ghost, he was astonished that his Father in Heaven was still mindful of him. After all, Abbot had not been paying much attention to Him lately.

Just then a doctor came through the swinging doors into the waiting room. Abbot sat up a little straighter and gently lifted Bekah's head in the process. "Here comes the doctor," he whispered.

She opened her sleepy eyes, then looked fearfully at the doctor approaching them.

Abbot stood up and held his hand out to help her stand.

Taking it eagerly, she asked, "How is he?"

The doctor smiled. "His CT scan looks good. We couldn't find anything broken."

Bekah almost went limp, but Abbot put his arm around her to support her. "Then he—he's going to be okay?" she stammered.

Nodding, the doctor said, "He was unconscious for, what did you say, about fifteen minutes?"

Bekah nodded.

"That's quite a while. I think we should admit him for tonight, just to be sure. But his vision is clearing and he's responsive and alert."

"May I see him now?" she asked.

"Certainly. He's back in room eight."

Bekah threw her arms around Abbot's neck. "Thank you," she cried, tears streaming down her cheeks. "He's going to be okay."

Abbot hugged her back and silently thanked God for the miracle that He had afforded Cody. When she released him, he shook the doctor's hand vigorously.

"It's nice to know there are good Samaritans out there," the doctor said.

"Thank you," said Abbot, unsure that he wanted any praise for what he'd done. Helping a woman with an injured child had been a natural instinct. It hadn't taken any conscious effort on his part. In his heart he wondered, *Natural instinct or spiritual prompting?*

The doctor turned back to Bekah. "Good luck."

As though luck had anything to do with it. The whole day had been planned out by a higher power than man's. His thoughts surprised him; it had been a long time since he'd had such strong, inspirational sensations and for a moment he basked in them.

Abbot turned his attention back to Bekah. She stepped toward the emergency room doors, then turned back and took Abbot's hand.

"Come with me," she encouraged.

"If you're sure," he hesitated.

"I don't often take to strangers," she admitted. "But in my heart you'll never be a stranger."

Timidly, Abbot allowed Bekah to lead him back to the gurney where Cody was resting. The child's coloring was still a little pale, but his blue eyes were bright and clear. "Hi," said Bekah. "How are you feeling, buddy?"

"My nose hurts," said the eight-year-old.

"I didn't introduce you to Abbot," Bekah said. "He's the man who drove us here."

"Hi," said Cody, shyness evident in his voice.

"Abbot swam out to us. He rescued both of us," explained Bekah.

Bold azure eyes looked at Abbot in amazement. "You did?" came the timid inquiry.

"Well," Abbot blushed. "I just happened to be in the right place at the right time."

"Wow!" Cody exclaimed. "That makes you my tyee! I never had one before."

"Your tyee?" Abbot wasn't certain he wanted that kind of title added to his name.

"Yes," Bekah explained. "Tyee is a Kwakwala word, it means 'elder brother.' It's usually reserved for a male who does a brave or courageous deed, or one who takes a prominent position in the namima."

Abbot gave her a smile. "Meaning family, right?" He wondered whether or not to tell her that he already knew the terms she and Cody were using.

"You know about the namima?" she questioned.

Abbot had no choice but to confess. "I work for the Museum of Natural History here in Seattle. Although I'm more familiar with Native American artifacts, I have learned a few things about their family relationships."

A delighted grin wandered across Cody's face as quickly as one did across Bekah's. "See!" The young boy beamed with pride. Excitement strained from his voice as he mustered strength and declared, "I told you he was my tyee!"

Chapter Two

As Cody talked to his parents on the telephone early that evening, Abbot and Bekah stepped away from the hospital bed to converse without disturbing him.

"I'm glad you're both feeling better," he said. "You had me worried."

Bekah put her forehead against his chest and felt his heart beating against it. "Thank you for giving me your strength," she whispered, hoping he wouldn't think her too forward. "I needed you there for us. I still need you with me." *There, I've said it. I've made my confession.*

When she looked up at him and studied his response in the emerald of his wide, alluring eyes, the expression she found gave her confidence. Giving him a shy smile, she continued, "I hope that I haven't upset you. I don't even know if you're married or engaged or–?" She left the sentence open, hoping he would finish it. To her secret delight, Abbot gave her a look of total astonishment.

"I'm not married," he admitted. "And I'm not engaged."

"That's good." She stood on tiptoe and placed a quick kiss on his cheek. "Because right now I need you to be my support system." She felt the color rush to her cheeks. It wasn't like her to be so bold and it surprised her to learn that her feelings for Abbot were already strong.

"Dad wants to talk to you," said Cody, interrupting them.

Bekah stepped back to the bed and took the telephone from Cody's hand. "Yes," she spoke into the receiver.

"Bekah, we're going to catch the next Victoria Clipper. I think it leaves in about an hour. We'll be there as quick as we can." Her brother's voice sounded worried.

"He's going to be okay," she reminded. "But I'm glad you're coming anyway."

"We'll take a cab from the terminal once we reach Seattle," said Ryan. "Hang on, Sis. We're coming."

When she said goodbye, she replaced the receiver and moved a chair closer to Abbot as he resumed a child's card game with Cody.

"Abbot says he's just like Indiana Jones," said the precocious child. "He and I are going to find Chief Taquinna's secret cave when I grow up."

Abbot shook his head. "I said, 'we'll see,' Cody. That isn't definitive."

Cody scrunched up his mouth, then grinned from ear to ear. "But," he reminded, "a lot can happen to change your mind by the time I grow up."

Bekah watched them bantering comments back and forth and smiled. Abbot was one of the nicest men she'd ever met. Not at all like Barry, whom she'd dated off and on for the past few months. Barry's universe revolved around himself. *And Barry is an atheist,* she silently remembered. *He couldn't be the man in Grandma Lili's dream.*

Her mind wandered back over the past few weeks. She had secretly been hoping that Abbot would introduce himself, or that she would work up the courage to introduce herself. Every weekday at 3:45 P.M., he could be found jogging along the path that led around the perimeter of Gas Works Park, a rolling hill of green grass and antique bronze art pieces nestled at the north end of Lake Union in the heart of Seattle. And every weekday, she would join him, either behind or in front, hoping for an opportunity to say more than just, "Hi. I see you're at it again."

When she'd waved to Abbot earlier that afternoon from out on the lake, she had hoped she could somehow invite Abbot aboard with her and Cody.

"So can we, huh?" asked Cody, this time in a louder tone so Bekah finally heard him.

"Can we what, buddy?" she asked, blinking in surprise. She could tell Abbot was stifling a smile, so she shook her head and explained, "I guess I'm still in shock."

"Can we go look for Chief Taquinna's cave together?" Cody asked impatiently. "I'm out of school for the whole summer and it's boring most of the time."

"Oh, Cody! We mustn't impose on Abbot's time." Scolding Cody wasn't her strong suit and she was sure Abbot could see right through the ruse.

"I have three days sick leave coming," said Abbot. "I'd be happy to join you. Cody tells me the cave is supposed to be somewhere near the Hoh River. Is that right?"

"Rumors," she admitted hesitantly. "Years ago one of our ancestors told the story that someone had stolen some of Chief Taquinna's prize possessions, including a totem pole that was quite tall, and hidden them in a cave near the Hoh River. No one's ever found it."

"That doesn't mean we can't look," suggested Abbot. "It might be a fun expedition."

Cody grinned from ear to ear! "An expedition!" he repeated with enthusiasm.

Abbot smiled and it made his emerald eyes sparkle at her, warming her heart. "We'll see," she conceded at last.

"Great!" exclaimed Cody. "See, I told you she'd want to go with us."

"That you did," Abbot admitted. He reached out and took Bekah's hand in his. "Tell me a little about your ancestry," he coaxed. "It really helps me with my line of work."

His hand was warm and comforting somehow. She enjoyed the feeling immensely. But his request disturbed her and Bekah hesitated. She'd never told anyone about her ancestry. Uncertain how people would react, she normally didn't offer such private information.

"Please," he said in a soft, husky tone. "I promise to treat the information with respect and honor."

Since Abbot's interest seemed genuine, she smiled shyly and said, "Chief Taquinna governed the Kwakiutl from the 1780's until around 1830 when he died. He was my seventh great granduncle. My Native American Taquinna ancestry comes through his sister, Rebekah. Each of the first-born granddaughters in her lineage have been named Rebekah Taquinna, usually with a third given name and then their father's surname. For example, my grandmother's name is Rebekah Taquinna Lili Parker-Kirk, but most people knew her as Lili. My mother's name is Rebekah Taquinna Charity Kirk-Stevens, wife of Kyle Stevens, but she's known as Charity. My parents named me Rebekah Taquinna Stevens."

Abbot asked, "Why not Rebekah Taquinna and a third given name like the others?"

"When my mother was a young girl, someone teased her about her name. They told her people should only have a first and second given name and then the surname. She vowed she would never name her daughter with three given names, although she received a lot of ridicule from her tyee when she parted with this family tradition."

"Are your parents living?" he asked.

"They're in Europe on their retirement trip. They won't be home until December. It's a trip they've planned and saved for all their lives."

"Sounds great," he admitted. "Retirement and traveling to foreign lands."

"We miss them, but they plan to live in my brother's condo when they return, so they'll be nearby come Christmas. My brother, Ryan, and his wife, Gail, are Cody's parents. They're in the process of building a new home. Hopefully, it will be finished by the time our parents return, or it's liable to get crowded over there."

"I guess I'll have to depend on you to tell me your mother's family legends, then. Are there any stories about Chief Taquinna that are passed down from one generation to another?" Abbot asked, apparently fascinated by her history.

"Only what is found in books. Remember, in the late 1800's and early 1900's, the Native Americans were forbidden to relate their stories. Our language was outlawed and we were forced to learn English. Children were taken away from their parents and sent to schools far away to learn the ways of the white settlers." Bekah certainly didn't want him to think for a moment that she condoned the treatment her ancestors had received. However, she also knew what little blood that was left in her was not enough to keep her allegiance strictly geared toward her Native American ancestors.

"So you're Kwakiutl?" asked Abbot.

"I'm one-sixteenth Kwakiutl and one-sixteenth Quileute. Otherwise, I'm as American as you are."

She could tell her answer surprised him, so she explained. "The division in my blood line began with my second great grandmother, who was full-blooded Kwakiutl. The story is told that she fell in love with a full-blooded Quileute, which was forbidden. When their love was discovered, she was told she could either give up the man she loved and receive a Kwakiutl husband of the chief's choosing, or shame her family by joining with the Quileute. She chose the latter and married her sweetheart, who took her away from Nootka Sound, never to return. Later, while living with the Quileute near the Hoh River, she was told about the cave and the things hidden within it. She always wanted to find Chief Taquinna's belongings. She knew that if she restored the articles back to the Kwakiutl, her shame could be erased. But she never found them."

Cody grinned. "Someday I'm going to find the cave and bring the two tribes together so they can live in peace."

"They already live in peace," Bekah told her young nephew. "These old stories are like fairy tales. They please us while we're listening to them, but they're no more real than the mythical spirit people who change into animals."

"I can believe if I want to," insisted Cody with a defiant tilt of his chin. "They're just as real as Santa Claus, aren't they?"

Bekah had to smile at his stubborn streak. "You're still a child, Cody," she murmured. "You can believe anything you like."

Cody folded his arms with satisfaction and leaned back against the pillow. As he listened to them talk, his eyes grew heavy with sleepiness.

"It's fascinating," said Abbot. "So if you're one-eighth Native American, what's the remaining seven-eighths?"

"English, Welsh and Irish. One ancestor came to America in 1620 with the Mayflower. I understand there are thousands of New England ancestors way back. My father's family came from Wales in the 1800's. His mother was Irish, a red-head. I suppose that's where young Cody gets his red locks. Probably my auburn hair, as well."

"It surprises me that you know so much about your ancestors," said Abbot. "Is there a designated genealogist in your family?"

Bekah laughed easily. "No. But the Native Americans keep their lineage recorded almost religiously. That's why a person's ancestral line can be traced back on their totem poles, which was the original reason for totem poles in the first place."

"Why do you suppose they keep these records so carefully?" he asked.

"Legend says that long, long ago, after the earth was purged of all iniquity, the great white spirit came out of the sky and told our people to keep a record of their ancestors. This legend has been passed down for centuries," she explained.

Abbot said, "Do you know there's a book you can read that will give a fuller account of the great white spirit's visit to the Americas?"

"No!" Bekah opened her eyes wide in surprise. "I would give anything to get a copy. Do you know where I might find one?"

He smiled as though he had a little secret that he hadn't shared with her. "Maybe when I get to know you better, I'll tell you," he teased.

She punched him in the arm.

"Ow!" he moaned playfully. "Is that anyway to treat the man who just rescued you?"

His complaint stirred Cody almost into wakefulness. Bekah put a finger up to her lips. "Shhh. Don't wake him."

Abbot stood up and took her by the hand. "While he's sleeping, why don't we resume our conversation in the cafeteria?"

Bekah hesitated. She couldn't leave Cody's side until his parents arrived, but she didn't want to disappoint Abbot.

As though he'd read her thoughts, he said, "Or I could go get a sandwich for you and bring it back. You haven't eaten since—when?"

"Since lunch," she admitted.

He glanced at his watch. "That was eight hours ago, right?"

Bekah nodded. "Rye or wheat bread, no mayo and no chips," she suggested, grateful he was willing to let her stay with Cody. She shrugged. "I'm trying to stick to healthy foods."

"I should have known." He rolled his eyes. "Then don't be shocked when I come back with something for myself that you'll no doubt find disgusting."

As he turned and walked out through the door, Bekah sighed wistfully. Abbot was a refreshing change in the direction her life had been heading. He was tender and kind, compassionate and caring. His every thought seemed to be motivated by her well-being, rather than his own. She was beginning to like him and she hoped that he might be doing the same.

Looking upon Cody's sleeping face, Bekah hoped she could have a child as sweet as her nephew, someday. She was already twenty-six and had recently begun to feel that it was time to tackle more than just her own solitary world. She found herself longing for a husband and family lately, and her feelings surprised her. A few years ago, she doubted she would ever find the man with whom she would want to settle down. But things in her life had changed. She had changed.

Family was now more important to her than ever before. And religion. She'd felt a longing to find some kind of religion in which to believe. Somehow, she knew that God existed, somewhere. She wanted to find Him and learn whether or not He was pleased with what little she'd accomplished in her life. Laughing to herself, Bekah realized she was so very different from the woman who graduated from nursing school four years ago. Back then she'd been ready to take on the world. Instead, she'd ended up working four, ten-hour days a week at the University of Washington Medical Center, doing everything from emptying bedpans to assisting trauma patients in the emergency room. She liked the fast pace and the three days off every week. But, working Sundays had been a real disappointment. Although she had enough seniority by now to request Sundays off, she hadn't exercised that option. To be truthful, Bekah didn't have anything better to do on the Sabbath than take care of patients. Lately, she'd felt like something was missing in her life and as she had evaluated it, the only conclusion she could come up with that made any sense was that she should be attending church on Sundays . . . somewhere!

Her mother had a firm belief in God, but her father was a little reluctant to commit himself on the issue. Although Charity Stevens had read diligently to her two children from the Bible, she'd never taken them to a formal church. Bekah had never wondered why until lately.

By the time Abbot returned, she felt her stomach rumbling, emphasizing how hungry she really was. He smiled as he gave her a turkey sandwich on rye bread loaded with sprouts, onions and mustard, a glass of milk and a dinner salad with several packets of salad dressing. She liked his smile most of all.

"I didn't know whether you liked ranch, thousand island or bleu cheese, so I got them all," he said with a grin.

She opened the thousand island and squeezed all the contents onto her salad. "I have to admit, I haven't given up salad dressing, yet," she confessed.

For himself, Abbot had a polish hot dog smothered with sauerkraut, a large order of french fries and a glass of milk.

As she ate, she noticed he had a healthy appetite. He finished the polish hot dog with gusto and started dipping the french fries in fry sauce as he ate them.

"I don't know how I'm ever going to repay you for all you've done for me," Bekah said. "Not only for your time, but for your ruined cell phone, your shorts and shoes and now for supper.

Abbot swallowed a mouthful of french fries, then wiped his lips with a napkin before he said, "I told you the phone is insured. My shorts

and shoes get more wear and tear jogging than they'll ever get swimming. And supper wasn't that much. As for my time, I think it's been
well-spent. Who else could I have been with today that would have
kept my interest more than you and Cody have?"

"At least let me take you to dinner sometime," she suggested. "Or
fix dinner for you."

"Tell you what," Abbot bargained, drinking some of his milk.
"Maybe we can take a picnic over to Gas Works Park and watch the
duck dodges sometime."

"That would be fun! I've never seen them."

"I get that privilege every week through the summer because I live
near Gove's Cove on Lake Union."

"Do you have a houseboat there?"

"No, I'm living aboard my uh—" He hesitated a moment before
continuing, as though he were trying to decide just how to define whose
boat he was living on. Finally he said, "It's my . . . sister's husband's
sailboat. They said I can stay as long as I want, or at least until they're
ready for it again. I don't plan on living there forever. I'm still trying
to decide if I want to settle in the Northwest or not. Until that time
comes, I'll just keeping living aboard."

"What kind of boat is it?"

"It's a Cabo Rico 38."

"Cutter or sloop?"

"I think it's a cutter. I've never sailed it by myself."

Bekah laughed. "And here I thought we were going to have
something in common."

"I want to learn," he amended, rather quickly she thought, smiling
to herself. "But I'm afraid if the boom came around on Bridger's Child
and hit me in the face, like yours did to Cody earlier, I may not survive
it. That thing must weigh a hundred and fifty pounds."

"Doesn't it have a boom break or a preventer?"

Abbot laughed freely. "I don't have a clue. My brother-in-law, Joshua Bridger Clark owns it. He was the captain when we brought it down from Friday Harbor and put it in a slip on the west side of Lake Union, but I've not moved it out of the slip since he put it there. I pay a waste disposal service to come around once a week and drain the holding tank and I fill up the water tanks every Saturday. Oh, yes. I check the dock lines every day, sometimes twice a day, to make sure there's no chance she's going to get loose. Other than that, I'm afraid I'm not well-versed in nautical terms and I haven't an ounce of sailing ability."

"All you do is just live there?" she asked with a quirky smile.

"That's right," he grinned. "And wise enough not to pretend otherwise. I could never have taken Cody out on that sailboat because I wouldn't know the first thing about how to sail it."

"Yet, you live on a sailboat." She was surprised to learn of his living arrangements.

"It's cheap. I'm saving a lot of money in apartment rent. Josh says that lake water doesn't permit the undergrowth that salt water does and he's glad to know someone is taking care of it. Besides, my sister's having twins in another month or two. She and Josh don't plan to use *Bridger's Child* again until next summer. So until then, I have full use of it."

"Would they mind if you took it out?"

"Took it out where?" he asked with a crinkled frown.

Bekah laughed at him. "Took it out of the slip, sailed it around."

"No. Josh said I could sail her anywhere between the northern tip of Vancouver Island and as far south as San Diego if I wanted. But she's not insured to go any farther than a hundred miles offshore."

"Have you ever wanted to take her out sailing?"

"Maybe if I had some competent deck hands, but by myself, never."

Bekah mulled his response over in her mind for a few moments. "Well, then I know what I want to do to repay you."

"You don't have to—" he began.

Bekah interrupted. "I *want* to do this," she insisted. "I want to teach you sailing basics in my sailboat. Then when you feel confident, I want to help you take *Bridger's Child* out for a sail on Lake Union."

Abbot gulped and gave her a forlorn look.

"It'll be fun!" she exclaimed. "Besides, it would help me a lot if I could teach you because that's a sure-fire way to learn my own skills better."

"Couldn't we just take a class together?" he teased.

Bekah placed her forehead against his and stared into his deep green eyes. "Mr. Sparkleman! You're not afraid of one woman in a tiny little sailboat, are you?" she asked.

He didn't remove his forehead from hers when he answered, "Miss Stevens, I know I can handle a tiny, little sailboat, but I'm not so sure about the woman."

She leaned back and punched him playfully in the arm. "I'm not that bad, at least not when I'm by myself."

"My point, precisely," Abbot teased.

❦ ❧

They spent the rest of the night at the Medical Center, talking quietly while Cody slept. Bekah did more than her share of giggling. Amused by Abbot's good nature, she found that they got along well together, almost as though they were made for one another. Abbot was good company for her and kept her easily entertained.

She was surprised to learn that he had his master's degree in archaeology and was currently working on his doctorate in the same field while he held down a full time job at the museum. Although he loved his job, he also hoped that one day he would be able to get some hands-on experience at a native artifact dig site.

Around two in the morning, Ryan and Gail Stevens arrived from Victoria. Introductions were made and Bekah was finally able to relax and relinquish the care of her young charge to his more capable parents. After saying good-bye to her brother and his wife at the Medical Center, they walked to the parking garage and found Abbot's Bronco waiting where he'd left it.

"Mmm," said Bekah when Abbot opened the door for her. "Nice fishy smell in here. I guess I'll need to get your Bronco cleaned out, as well."

"It's not that bad," he insisted. But the wrinkle in his nose said otherwise.

Abbot slid onto the driver's seat and started the engine. Within minutes he'd wound his way across the 11th Avenue bridge and through the quiet streets of Seattle toward the south end of Lake Union, where Bekah's silver Dodge caravan awaited them, with a small boat trailer hitched to the back.

Bekah was unusually quiet. She didn't want the evening to end. She had enjoyed Abbot's company so much she'd forgotten they would have to part sometime. "Thanks, Abbot," she said. "You've been a treasure."

"Don't say goodnight just yet," he insisted. "We still need to get your boat picked up and—"

"But it's late and you're probably tired."

"Tomorrow's Saturday. I'll have plenty of time to sleep in."

From the tone of his voice she could easily tell that he wasn't taking no for an answer. More relieved than she could ever tell him, she said, "Thanks. Do you want to follow me over there?"

"I'll be right behind you every rotation of the wheels."

Bekah pulled her key out of her shorts pocket and opened the door. Within a few minutes she drove the caravan out of the parking lot and along West Lake Avenue towards the Fremont bridge. Soon she parked the Dodge near Gas Works Park. The gate to the parking lot was already closed and locked.

"It's going to be a grunt," she told Abbot, locking the van door after she got out, "getting the boat over here. I forgot that they close everything up overnight."

Together they stepped around the barrier and started walking toward the park. A bright light illuminated them from behind and they turned to see a police car with a spot light focused on them.

"Uh-oh," said Abbot. "Foiled again. Maybe they'll be understanding."

"Do you think?" she asked.

Simultaneously they held their hands high above their heads and walked toward the police car. As they neared it, the officer inside the car bellowed, "That's close enough."

"Officer," said Abbot. "We've just come to pick up this woman's sailboat. There was an accident today and—"

"How's your son?" asked the officer as he got out of the police car and came toward them, his shoulders relaxed, his hands swinging at his sides.

"My nephew is much better, thank you," said Bekah. "Nothing broken. But they're keeping him overnight at the Medical Center for observation."

"We put your Walker Bay over there," said the officer pointing toward the large dumpsters. "Out of sight. Had a dickens of a time keeping people from walking off with it, so we attached it with a short chain. I'll release it for you."

"Thank you," said Bekah. "I had no idea it would cause you so many problems."

"You were pretty smart, putting that name behind the rub rail. Otherwise, two or three people would have talked us out of it by now."

"Pink Lady?" she asked.

"Yes." He grinned. "Whew! You don't know how many false names people have given to claim your boat."

"Pink Lady?" questioned Abbot with a quizzical glance. "What does that mean?"

"My brother's been teaching me how to troll," she explained. "I kept forgetting what the diver was called that I was supposed to buy and put on my line. I finally wrote it there so I wouldn't forget it."

The officer laughed. "We had a bet going. Everyone's tried to guess why you'd put that name under there. Turns out we were all wrong!"

Abbot and the officer carried the Walker Bay to the trailer and then he waved good-bye to them. "Glad we could help," he insisted when Bekah tried to thank him again.

Bekah took hold of her car door to get in, but Abbot stopped her. "Do you have a safe place to park this thing?" he asked.

"Yes."

"Well, if you don't mind, I'd like to follow you home, make sure you're safe before I leave you alone."

"That's sweet," she said. "Thank you."

"You're welcome."

Then he turned and went back to the Ford Bronco while Bekah climbed into the caravan. Within minutes she was driving north, up the hill on Wallingford. When she finally reached her condo, an eight-story building on Woodlawn Avenue that overlooked Green Lake, she signaled for Abbot to pull alongside her.

When the Bronco was beside the Dodge, she rolled her window down and said, "If you follow me in quickly, the door won't stop you and it automatically lets you out without any codes. You can walk me to my condo if you'd like."

"I'll be right behind you," he agreed.

Bekah pressed the buttons on the security system and waited for the doors to open, then she drove down beneath the condos to the parking garage, with Abbot following closely. She pulled forward near two empty stalls and stopped.

Abbot got out and came forward. "I don't know how to back the trailer in yet," she confessed. "I usually just unhitch it and push it back by hand."

He smiled. "Allow me to teach you," he said. "And we'll be even."

"What?"

"You know a man living in a sailboat whose never sailed it and I know a woman with a trailer whose never backed it up."

It took her about fifteen tries to get it right, but Abbot was finally able to teach her how to back the trailer up so that it would fit perfectly beside her caravan. She was so pleased with herself when she stepped out of the vehicle that she gave him a quick embrace. "Thanks!" she exclaimed.

"You're welcome. Now let's get you safely to your door," he suggested.

Bekah took his hand in hers and led the way. When they reached the open elevator they stepped inside. She pressed the button marked 'eight,' the doors whisked shut and the elevator made a sudden lurch on its way to the top floor. "I'm in eighty-six," she stated. "There are six condos on each floor, with the pool and sauna on the main. Each condo has two parking stalls, but if we need more parking there's a big parking pad north of the condos for extras."

"Were they expensive?" he asked. Then, "Sorry, guess that's none of my business."

"They weren't that bad four years ago when I bought mine. They've gone up in price, though, from what I understand."

"I was looking at those condos over on Alaska Way, the ones that look out on Puget Sound. But whoa! Are they really worth it? I could buy a house for less."

"So you are thinking of staying?" she asked thoughtfully.

"Maybe," he shrugged. "I'm liking Seattle more and more all the time."

Bekah smiled. "Do you want to come in for a while?" she asked shyly.

To her surprise, Abbot stopped. He looked at her seriously, as though he was contemplating how to answer her. "Not tonight," he replied. "It's late. And we're both tired."

Bekah was disappointed. "I wasn't inviting you in for the reason you may have assumed," she informed him. "I just hoped we could talk a while longer."

"Not tonight," he said again. "The way I'm feeling about you, my coming in would not be in your best interest."

Bekah blushed as she gave him a warm smile. "Oh," she murmured, finally understanding his motives. Then, "By all means, go home to *Bridger's Child*, Abbot."

Chapter Three

*B*ekah stripped off her damp clothing and climbed into the shower. She doubted she could sleep and hoped the warm, soothing water would lull her into forgetfulness. Now that the crises with Cody was over, she found she was unable to forget about Abbot.

Having never felt so comfortable with any other man before, Bekah wondered if Abbot was the special man that Grandmother Lili had dreamed about. Searching back through her memory bank, she recalled a time almost ten years ago shortly before Lili died. Her grandmother told her she had a dream one night wherein she saw all of her grand-children gathered together for a party, as well as all the people they had married. As Grandmother Lili shared the experience with Bekah, she said that an extraordinary tyee would come into her life one day and become the father of Bekah's many children.

Grandmother Lili counseled with each of her grandchildren and so far everything she told them had come true. Ryan was supposed to marry a woman with blonde hair and exceedingly clear blue eyes named Gail and they were to have a son with hair the color of the red cedar bark and a daughter with Ryan's dark brown eyes. Bekah's cousin, Robyn, was to marry a serious man with blonde hair and blue eyes, and together they would have identical twins. Several other cousins were told how their future spouses and their children would look. So far, most of Grandmother's predictions had been validated. Three events remained that had not come true, yet: the twins for Robyn, who was pregnant at that very moment, whether with twins or not was still unknown; Ryan's wife, Gail, was supposed to conceive and have a little girl; and Bekah's portion of Grandmother's dream had not happened, either. The rest of Grandmother Lili's visions for the other grandchildren had been fulfilled.

Her grandmother had not described Bekah's husband-to-be in physical terms, nor given him a name. Not at all. She said Bekah's husband would hold the keys that would unlock the windows of Heaven, allowing her family to enter together into the realm of God.

Bekah was the last person Grandmother Lili spoke to before she died. She had asked for her youngest grandchild specifically and Bekah had hastened to her bedside. Lili had gathered Bekah to her bosom and whispered words that were embedded in Bekah's heart forever: *"The man you are to marry will know God and will talk with the spirits. They will whisper to him and he will listen to them. He will pray mighty prayers and they will be granted. After you meet him, he will go on a long journey to the home of the ancient ones. You must be patient and wait for him. When he returns, he will take you to a lofty, white mansion where a man with a gold trumpet stands on a tall pinnacle. Together, you and your tyee will preserve the unity of our namima, and lead them out of darkness all the way back to Chief Taquinna."* When Grandmother finished speaking these words she smiled, closed her eyes and took her own journey to the home of the ancient ones.

Bekah was barely sixteen when this experience occurred and she never forgot it, which explained why Bekah had decided that Barry was not the one she should be dating. She had only learned two weeks ago that Barry didn't believe in God at all. He only believed in law and justice in the world in which he lived, and he had no faith that there was anything beyond this life. Barry was a high-profile, corporate attorney, with a plush office in the heart of downtown Seattle. Although he was basically a decent person, he was also self-centered. She realized now that Barry could not possibly be the person about whom her grandmother had spoken.

But Abbot . . . he was different. He knew how to pray and his prayers were answered. She recalled him telling her about a book that gave the accounting of the Great White Spirit's visit to America. These two pieces of information about Abbot had kindled a flame within her heart. It was a new beginning for Bekah, and she wanted to do everything she could to make sure that she would not lose Abbot. He might very well be the man that her grandmother saw in her dreams, ten years earlier.

❧ ❧

Abbot was up by eight the next morning. He watched the rain splatter on the starboard deck outside one of the sailing vessel's portholes for a few minutes. The weather was not unusual for Seattle, and he wondered if he should expect it to rain most of the day. He flipped on the VHF to the weather channel. A monotone male voice droned, "—for Seattle and Puget Sound, cooler with a chance of rain. Temperature sixty-nine degrees and the relative humidity, ninety-four percent."

As he listened, he stepped into the head and turned on the faucet where he brushed his teeth, shaved and combed his hair. Afterward, he poured sweetened cereal into a bowl with milk and ate it down hungrily. By the time he'd finished, the weather report was beginning to repeat itself, so he turned it off.

Abbot loved the smell of the rain. He opened the companionway, stepped up a few stairs and stuck his head through the opening. The burgundy canvas dodger protected the forward half of the cockpit from inclement weather, allowing the live-aboard to enjoy the rain without having to mop it up afterwards. Inhaling deeply, he savored the fresh, clean scent. It was different from the rain in the Uinta mountains where he'd been raised on the Bar M Ranch. There, the rain had an earthy green smell, but here in Seattle it was a salty clean that tickled his nostrils and kept his lungs moistened.

Stepping back down into the cabin, he pulled on a clean pair of dockers and a khaki-colored shirt, slipped on a pair of loafers and loaded his pockets with change and keys.

His wallet was finally dry. He had emptied it and left it open on a towel overnight. Now, he put his driver's license, employment and credit cards and cash back into it.

A photo of Alyssa had been damaged when he'd ended up in the lake yesterday. Abbot studied it for a minute, then tossed it into the wastebasket. *You're marrying my brother today,* he spoke silently to his former fiancée, though she was more than nine-hundred miles away. *And you know what? I'm glad you are. I don't think we were meant for each other, anyway.* For the first time in months, he actually meant it.

I'd better call Ed and congratulate him before he leaves for the temple. Then, Abbot remembered his cell phone. One of the items of business for the day would have to be a new cell phone, then a belated call to the Bar M Ranch. He knew Ed was still hoping he would change his mind and show up for the reception. Though he wished them well, Abbot was not leaving Seattle now, for anyone.

Although he'd not slept much he didn't feel tired. Thoughts of Bekah had wandered through his mind from the moment he left her condo door. She had him so filled with hope, it almost frightened him.

Had she been offended when he refused to go into her condo unit with her last night? He was still kicking himself for that one! She said she wasn't inviting him in for any other reason but to talk. Had he revealed too much of his true feelings by turning her down the way he had? No, it was best that he had declined her offer. He knew how quickly his emotions got out of control and he wasn't going to risk an ugly situation with Bekah. He cared too much for her to do that.

Abbot had once tried to force his affection on Alyssa and that had backfired on him. Besides, it took him six months before he gathered enough courage to kiss Alyssa and another year before he felt confident enough to propose.

He admitted, only to himself, that he was painfully shy around women. When he got to the other side, he was going to ask God why He'd made him so awkward around the fairer sex that it took years before he felt comfortable with one of them.

However, he smiled to himself, he hadn't felt uncomfortable with Bekah yesterday. She'd slept against his shoulder, she'd kissed his cheek, held his hand. *I even held hers!*

Recalling their foreheads touching as they bantered conversation about, he had felt at ease, like he'd known Bekah all his life. She had a way about her that made him want to be a better man. Recognizing that he had faults in his character had not come easily to him and no one, not even Alyssa, had caused a change in his heart like Bekah had.

The prayer he offered yesterday was a perfect example of how Bekah affected him. He had felt the prompting of the spirit, telling him that Cody would be all right. Because of this divine inspiration, he'd been able to comfort Bekah.

He recalled some of the sweet sensations of the spirit he'd known years earlier: at his baptism; the day he received the gift of the Holy Ghost; when his father, Sparky, had ordained him to the Aaronic Priesthood; and again, right before he left for college, when he was ordained to the Melchizedek Priesthood.

In his mind, he saw images of past church meetings, many of which he'd deliberately missed as a teenager. But he also recalled, when he was a young boy, how he had stood and borne fervent testimony of Jesus Christ.

Recalling how his mother had visited him from across the veil when he was just fourteen years old, Abbot remembered he had desperately missed her and wished he could be with her for a while. When he'd prayed and asked God to send his mother back to help him through that dark time, she came almost immediately. She'd brushed the hair off his forehead and put a lullaby in his heart. All night long she'd comforted him as he'd poured out his feelings to her. That was no dream, it was as real to him as Bekah putting her forehead against his chest yesterday.

Recalling these sweet memories, he thought about the spiritual side of his life and realized that his father's death had hurt him more than he had ever revealed. The double funeral for his pa and Mont, with Kayla in a wheel chair and all the trauma his family faced that Christmas, still haunted him. He hadn't understood how God could be a kind and loving Father, yet still allow such a tragedy to happen. He could have dealt with Mont dying, though he loved Mont as if he were his own father. He could have held up knowing Kayla's injuries were serious. Even learning about Tom's role in the brutalization of Morning Sun could be endured and forgiven. But to lose Pa . . . Abbot wasn't prepared when Sparky died, and all Abbot's inclination toward spiritual matters died with him.

For the past two and a half years, Abbot refused to acknowledge that a God who could authorize so many bad things to happen all at once had any place left in his life.

Unwilling to allow all his true feelings to surface, Abbot had blamed his attitude on misinterpretations of the scriptures, on the priesthood brethren, on people's 'holier than thou' attitudes. But the truth kept staring him in the face and a scripture kept burning into his mind . . . *and if thou doest not well, sin lieth at the door.* [Genesis 4:7]

Humbled by the experiences he'd received yesterday, and the Lord's willingness to bless Cody, regardless of Abbot's shortcomings, he felt divinely fortunate. Humility drove him to his knees, and for the first time since his father died, Abbot wept as he prayed with all his heart for forgiveness, for the Lord's continuing patience with him, and for guidance to help him accomplish the tasks which God had sent him to Earth to do. Then Abbot did something he'd never done before. He promised God that he would follow Him and obey Him for the rest of his life.

When at last he arose from the teak-and-holly cabin sole, Abbot felt the spirit so strong in *Bridger's Child* it nearly overpowered him. Again, he sank to his knees and asked God what he could do that day to show his gratitude. Afterward, a thought about Cody came filtering into his mind, and he stood up, put his wallet in his pocket and climbed out through the companionway. Within minutes he was headed toward the University of Washington Medical Center, anxious to see how his young friend had fared through the night.

❧ ❧

The telephone ringing jarred Bekah awake. She reached across the bed and grabbed the receiver, only to mumble a sleepy, "Hello."

"Are you still in bed?" came Abbot's unmistakable voice.

Bekah sat up with a start and finger-combed her short, auburn curls as she answered. "What time is it?"

"Ten," said Abbot. "They're taking Cody home within the hour and I hoped you might be up here to wish him well."

"You're at the Medical Center?"

"That's right," he chuckled. "How did you guess?"

"What a sweet man you are," she murmured.

"Anyway, Cody was just telling me that the doctors want him to rest for a day or two, then he should be able to resume his normal activities."

"That's wonderful. I guess I'll see him when he gets home."

"You will?"

"They live below me, down on the sixth floor. At least, they will until their new house is finished."

"Cody didn't tell me that," Abbot offered.

"He's a kid!" she defended.

"He's serious about going on an expedition to find Taquinna's Cave," Abbot said quietly.

"I'm sure he is," Bekah responded, rolling over and sinking back into the comfortable pillows.

"So am I," Abbot added. "I'm going to make arrangements to take some time off while you're still on vacation. Your brother and his wife want to go with us and I think it would be fun. Would you like to go?"

"I don't know why not. Ryan has a motor home and I've gone with them quite a number of times. Have you got a trailer or something?"

"No, but I like tent-camping. Perhaps it's time I made an investment in some camping gear."

"When did you want to go?"

"When do you have to be back to work?"

"Two weeks from Monday."

"We can leave a week from Monday and spend six days trying to find Taquinna's cave."

"Six days? I thought you only had three sick days coming."

"I'll only have to take two extra ones. I've already found a replacement, so don't worry about it."

"Abbot, I. . . ." She hesitated. He was moving faster than she'd expected and the prospect thrilled her. "Thank you for thinking of us."

"The trip is for Cody," he insisted. "Having his family along is a bonus."

"It'll be fun," she admitted. "Cody's going to become your best friend."

"Well, I was sort of hoping you'd take that position."

Bekah couldn't suppress a surprised giggle. "I could try," she admitted.

"Then how about spending the day with me?"

"The whole day?"

"Well, after we sit down with Ryan, Gail and Cody to plan out our trip. Perhaps you'd help me go shopping for that camping gear I was talking about."

"When will you be here?"

"By one. Ryan and Gail invited me to lunch and gave me permission to invite you, as well."

"Sounds great," said Bekah. "I'll see you then."

When she hung up, Bekah grinned from ear to ear. Then she dashed into the bathroom to prepare for the day.

Her hair took forever. She'd gone to bed with it wet last night, after her late shower, and now it didn't want to cooperate. Even a curling iron failed to control it. Finally, she soaked it down, stuck a few large rollers in it to tame it a little and worked on her makeup. Fortunately, by the time she'd finished making her bed and cleaning her apartment, her hair had dried. This time it didn't take long at all to comb it into place and mist it.

When the telephone rang, she looked at the caller i.d. and noted it was Ryan's number. "Hi!" she said into the mouthpiece.

"We're home. Cody's doing fine. Do you think Abbot will like hot dogs on the barbecue or should I think of something more formal?" Gail's verbalized train of thought came rapidly through the receiver.

"He ate one last night, so I know he likes them." Bekah couldn't stifle a giggle as she pictured the gears rolling around in Gail's mind.

"Oh, if he had it last night, he might not want it today. What about deviled eggs and crab dip. No, I don't have any crab left over. I know. Hamburgers. Does he like beef? Because we could do turkey burgers."

"Gail, I don't know what he likes to eat, other than hot dogs and french fries."

"But he's your friend—"

"I only just met him yesterday."

"I know, but isn't he the jogger? Cody said you knew him from jogging."

"We met yesterday."

"But isn't he the same jogger you were talking about last week, the one you wanted to introduce yourself to, but didn't quite know how to do it? We talked about him for hours last week, didn't we?"

"Not hours," Bekah corrected. "I asked for a few suggestions on introduction clauses. We spent maybe three minutes on the subject."

"Oh."

When Gail didn't say any more, Bekah knew she'd offended her. "I'm sorry, I'm as keyed up as you are, but I'm trying to remain calm."

"It's making you grouchy."

"No, Gail. It's making me cautious. I don't want to scare him off after our first real date together."

"You couldn't do that. The men you date just keep coming back. All the time. Wish I'd had that many fish on my line when I was your age."

Bekah laughed. "Ryan was the only one you wanted to nibble at the hook," she reminded.

Gail giggled in return. "What about salad?"

"Salad would be good."

"Good plan," said Gail. "Okay. I gotta' go. See you soon."

Bekah smiled as she hung up the receiver. Her sister-in-law was a flighty woman, except when it came to who had claim on her affection. She could be swayed from one thought to another like a hummingbird going from flower to flower, but when it came to protecting her family and close friends, she was strong and steady.

When the phone rang again, almost immediately after she'd hung it up, Bekah picked it up without even looking at the caller i.d., thinking it was Gail again.

"Hard rolls and apple juice," she said into the receiver.

"Is that an invitation?" asked a familiar male voice.

"Barry!" Bekah exclaimed. "I thought it was Gail."

"Is she preparing dinner for anyone special?" he asked.

"For Cody," Bekah insisted. "He was injured in a boating accident yesterday and they just brought him home a few minutes ago."

"And she can't ask Cody what he wants for dinner?"

"Well, he's. . . ." She didn't know how to respond.

"You never were very good at lying, Bekah. Which is why you're a nurse and not a corporate attorney."

She could hear the sarcasm in his voice without any effort. "Sorry," she said. "The man who helped rescue Cody was invited to lunch."

"I see, that sounds more truthful. Do you like him?"

"Not that it's any of your business," she complained.

"This doesn't mean that we can't negotiate time schedules. He hasn't had the pre-nuptial agreement written up yet, right?"

Bekah hesitated. "I'm not sure I like you prying."

Barry laughed. "Trust me, Bekah. I'm only looking out for your best interests."

She almost laughed, but was able to suppress it before he heard anything. The only time Barry had worried about her best interests was when it concerned himself.

"What did you want?" she asked, finding the tone of her voice a little harsher than normal. She didn't want to be rude, but it was time to bring their relationship to its conclusion.

"Direct, I like that."

"Well?"

"I was calling to confirm about next Sunday afternoon."

"What about it?"

"Did you forget?"

"Refresh my memory."

"A week from tomorrow. You were going to accompany me to Sand Point for the annual charity auction."

"Oh, I'm sorry, Barry. It must have slipped my mind."

"You promised," he reminded, his voice taut, as though he was talking to a small child. "I'll pick you up at—"

"At four?" she asked, hoping she'd remembered the time, at least.

"Good girl. And by the way, you know it's formal, don't you?"

"Yes, Barry. I'll see you then. Bye." Bekah hung up before he could ridicule her any further. What she ever saw in him to begin with, she couldn't imagine.

Reluctantly admitting defeat, she knew she would have to keep her date with Barry, though now she really didn't want to. If Abbot asked her out for that day, she would have to tell him no. The thought disturbed her and she fretted about it, wondering how to let him down without taking hope away from him. "Why, Abbot, I'd love to, but I promised a friend I'd—No, that won't work."

She was just beginning her fifteenth rendition when the doorbell rang. It felt as though her heart slipped up into her throat as she looked through the peep hole and saw Abbot standing in the hall. He was holding a small paint can and a fine-tipped brush in one hand.

Bekah opened the door immediately. "Hi!" she exclaimed, happier to see him than she'd expected. They'd only been apart eight and a half hours. *Eight hours, thirty-seven minutes!* she reminded herself, glancing at her watch.

"A neighbor of yours let me in the building as they were going out. Hope you don't mind."

"Not at all," she answered, awestruck as he stood before her in the hallway. He was handsome, she had to admit. And spiritual. Was he the tyee who would rescue her family from darkness?

"A gift," he said as he grinned and handed her the paint can and the brush. "To put your boat's name on properly."

Bekah stepped on tip-toe and kissed his cheek, secretly delighting in the blush that spread on his face. "Thanks! But I don't know what to name it."

"I thought you already had," he suggested with a wink.

"Pink Lady?"

He shrugged. "Or not. It's up to you."

"I like the lady part," she admitted. "But it should be 'something lady', or 'lady something.' Just not pink. It's not my favorite color."

"Aquamarine is," said Abbot, glancing over her shoulder into the living room. "At least, if what I see of your condo is any indication."

"Oh! My manners! Come on in!" She took his hand and pulled him easily into the living room.

Bright aquamarine and lime green in fluid-looking spirals covered the pillows resting on a pale, silver gray sofa. Peach-colored curtains with splashes of the same colors hung from both ends of the sliding glass doors. The carpet was a pale blue sea-foam. Textured pictures of the sea, with colors that matched the pillows, hung on one wall. A

Bentwood rocker and oak end-tables with smoked glass inlays accompanied the sofa.

Beyond the living room, a dining room held a sturdy oak and glass table, with matching oak chairs. The kitchen to the left was cozy and efficient, with built-in appliances and canisters that resembled seashells.

"Well?" Bekah asked. "Do you approve?"

"My compliments to your decorator. I wonder if she has a knack with teak and holly."

"Oh, no!" she exclaimed. "Decorating isn't my strong suit. My mother gave me her sofa when she redecorated her house. The dining room table came from an uncle's garage, with the glass broken out. I restored it and replaced the glass with a piece of strong plexiglass. The end tables I found at a garage sale. But the kitchen appliances were all new when I moved in."

"Hmm, quite a flare for creative furnishing. That should come in handy."

"It's not that I couldn't afford better," she said, though why she felt the need to explain she didn't understand. "But I like fixing things up and I also like saving money. It's a fetish with me."

"Then I'm glad you're helping me pick out my camping gear. No doubt you'll know where all the bargains are."

❦ ❧

Before the day was over, Bekah had dragged Abbot all over the bargain shops in Fremont, Ballard and northern Seattle. But they'd found some great prices on excellent camping equipment. He was now the proud owner of a four-man spring-bar tent, sleeping bag, air mattress, camping table with chairs, Dutch oven, skillet, lanterns, cookstove, assorted enamel pans and dishes and a utensil kit.

Abbot finally remembered he needed another cell phone just before the stores closed. By quickly driving to the nearest Sprint store, they were able to squeak in, just in time. The number would be different, and his old number cancelled, but a year or two was the life expectancy on cell phones, anyway.

When he slid behind the driver's seat of the Bronco, he looked across at Bekah and could not believe his good fortune at having met her, at having spent the day with her. *Good fortune or great blessing?* A warm feeling in his chest told him it was the latter.

"It's nearly nine," he said. "Are you hungry?"

"Yes, but I'd like to take you to dinner, to repay you for yesterday."

"I don't think so," he refused the invitation. "I'm going to hold you to your promise of teaching me how to sail. That will be payment enough."

She gave him an alluring smile and he couldn't help adding, "Besides, if you pay for dinner tonight, you won't be obligated to see me anymore."

"Abbot!" she complained. "Even if I wasn't going to teach you how to sail, I would still want to see you again."

"You would?" he asked, pleased to hear her say it.

"Of course. I enjoy your company."

"Thank you," was his response. "The feeling is mutual."

He was silent a few minutes, giving her time to consider his confession regarding his feelings. Then he said, "Is Chandler's Crab House all right?"

"I love Chandler's!" she enthused.

It didn't take long to get there. A quick swing around Eastlake Avenue to Fairview and they were leaving the Bronco with the valet.

"We'll probably never get in," she informed him.

He grinned. "I made the reservation right after I talked with you this morning."

"How did you know I like seafood?"

"I figured that any woman who lives in Seattle on purpose has to like fish."

After they were seated near the big windows that overlooked Lake Union, Abbot was glad he'd chosen Chandler's. The lights of the city sprinkled the serene surface of the lake with myriads of color, making it sparkle like diamonds on a velvet backdrop.

Abbot ordered the fresh Dungeness crab, while Bekah chose blackened snapper. When the waiter asked about their beverage, Abbot chose milk and was glad when Bekah followed his example.

Since he'd made a sacred promise to his Father in Heaven that morning, he had no intentions of breaking it.

"You don't like living in Seattle?" Bekah asked the moment the waiter left.

"I like some things about it," Abbot responded. "The rain, the fish, the Fourth of July fireworks over Lake Union."

"But?"

He heard the hesitancy in her voice and tried to explain his feelings. "I grew up in the mountains with no one around me for the first eighteen years of my life but blue sky, three brothers, Pa, Mont, Kayla and Morning Sun. Pa or Mont took us into school by pickup truck and when the snow was too deep, they home-schooled us until they got the roads cleared. In the schools I attended, there were very few classmates, less than I see every day at the museum. There are more people living on my dock here in Seattle than on the entire Bar M Ranch. If I decide to stay, I'll want to find a place away from the city, with a little more elbow room."

"It must have been a culture shock when you finally went to college," she observed, her eyes focused on his, as though her very existence depended on the words he spoke to her. He was flattered by her attention, but he was also a little worried about it.

"One insignificant young man against several thousand students," he agreed. "Yes, it was intimidating. But I met a remarkable man my third year there and we became good friends. He helped me realize my potential for dealing with the world at large."

"What about girlfriends?" she asked, as though it were the most natural question in the world.

Abbot cringed. "I was engaged once. But I wasn't ready for marriage and my fiancée noticed that fact four months into our engagement and broke it off."

"And now?"

Avoiding the path she obviously wanted him to travel, he said, "She fell in love with my brother. Today is their wedding day."

Bekah straightened and stared curiously at him. "Does that bother you?"

He laughed a little nervously. "Obviously not," he finally answered. "Otherwise, I don't think I'd be sitting here with you."

She smiled at hearing his response. "But you didn't attend the wedding?"

"It was in Utah. I couldn't make it."

"Oh, Abbot!" she moaned. "I kept you from going to Utah yesterday. Why didn't you say something?"

He shook his head and held his hands up to protest. "I hadn't planned on going from the beginning. My brother knew that." Reaching out, he took her hands in his across the table.

"And he didn't mind?"

"He tried to talk me into it, but I wouldn't budge. Now I'm glad I stayed here. Otherwise, I wouldn't have met you."

Her delicious smile told him his remark had hit a nerve. "I'm glad you stayed, too," she confessed. "But I have something I need to tell you. It's been bothering me and I really want to be honest with you."

Abbot worried, thinking she was going to tell him she had a steady male companion, or. . . ? As nonchalant as he could manage, he released her hands and sat up straighter in the chair. "Oh?"

Bekah studied him for a moment, as though she were trying to weigh what she wanted to say. *Risk versus consequence*, he worried. Finally she gazed steadily at him and said, "For the past two weeks I've been trying to decide on a good way to introduce myself. I'd seen you jogging nearly every day and I was impressed. Yesterday I deliberately chose the time and the place to sail with Cody, hoping that you would see us. When I waved at you, I'd wanted to sail over and ask if you wanted to join us. I thought that you wouldn't think I was too forward if I had Cody with me." She exhaled sharply, as though she'd just unburdened herself from something terrible.

"Whew!" he exclaimed. "For a minute there, I thought you were going to tell me you were engaged or something."

"No."

Her dark eyes reflected sorrow and Abbot didn't quite know what else to say. He was relieved and elated at her confession, but he didn't want to scare her off by announcing exactly how he was feeling about her. Finally, he decided that a glimpse into his heart couldn't hurt at this point. "I could make a similar confession, Bekah. It would be just as true."

Her satisfied smile told him he'd responded correctly. Unexpectedly, she blushed, and he felt the color rising in his own face as well.

"I hoped you were feeling the same way," she said boldly. "I have no intention of letting you slip away, Abbot. Besides, you're my tyee now," she reminded.

"I know that's supposed to be a grand privilege, Bekah," he said huskily, "but I really don't want to be considered your elder brother."

"The tyee is usually a chief," she explained, her voice trembling slightly. "My grandmother told me that there is no greater honor than to be chief."

"What are the chief's responsibilities?" Abbot asked. He wanted to be considered her special friend, with the hope in his heart that more might develop from their friendship.

"In ancient times, the chief was served by his namima. Today it is different. The chief is the one who serves most. He has the right to spiritual guidance and he oversees the affairs of his little family. If you were my tyee, you would have to decide whom I could date and where I should live. You would also have to make the final decision regarding whom I should marry."

Abbot smiled. "Hmm," he mused aloud. "Maybe I won't mind being your tyee after all."

Chapter Four

Rain pellets crashed against the cabin top with vengeance, sounding like machine gun fire. Although it was a sound to which Abbot had grown accustomed, there was something different about it. He opened his sleepy eyes and lifted his head, listening for the subtle differences. It was pitch black and he couldn't see anything. But a muffled voice seemed to be coming from the closed hatch above him. His weary fingers searched the book shelf on both sides of the v-berth until his hand closed around the flashlight. With his thumb, he pushed the 'on' button and was glad the batteries still had some life left in them. Splaying the light across the smoky glass hatch door directly above his head, he saw someone's hand beating a pattern against it.

"What the—?" He leaned back, startled, then stared up at the hatchway glass.

A familiar face pressed against the pane and Abbot sat bolt upright in bed. "Hans?" he questioned. Then, he realized Hans was drenched from the torrential downpour, outside. "Hans!"

Abbot rolled over, doing a backwards somersault out of the v-berth. His feet touched the warm cabin sole and he took six large steps toward the companionway stairs. Unlocking the inside latch, he slid the top back, then started removing the teak door boards. "Hans!" he called.

Two dripping figures came from the deck, both tall and lean, both all too familiar. "It's about time you woke up!" Hans grumbled. "We've been out here twenty minutes trying to get your attention." He almost had to shout to make himself heard above the roaring wind and pelting rain.

"Come in!" Abbot said at once, stepping back down into the cabin as Hans entered. The boots following him Abbot recognized immediately. "Tom? Is that really you, Tom?"

"Yep," came a gruff voice. "Tarnation, Abbot! Don't you never hear nothin' when yer sleepin'?"

Abbot grabbed a couple towels from a cupboard and gave one to each man. But before they had a chance to dry off, he grabbed them and hugged them fiercely, giving them a bear's pat upon their backs. "Why didn't you call me?" he asked. "I would have been up for you. Did you drive up?"

"Plane," said Hans, rubbing his wet chestnut hair with the towel vigorously.

"I would have picked you up at the airport if I'd known," said Abbot.

"You didn't answer your boat phone or your cell phone," Hans explained.

Abbot finger-combed his brown-black hair as he remembered. "I keep the boat phone plugged into the computer full time and I fried the cell phone in the lake Friday afternoon. I didn't get the new one until late last night. It's a new number, anyway. You don't have it yet."

"What'd you do?" Tom asked. "Drop it overboard?"

"No," Abbot smiled broadly. "I was rescuing a damsel in distress and I forgot it was in my pocket when I dove in after her."

"A likely story," drawled Tom.

"What are you doing here?" Abbot asked, his curiosity getting the better of him.

"We thought you was up here sulkin' over the weddin' yesterday," Tom explained, "but I guess we was wrong."

"Actually, I spent the day with Bekah, the damsel in distress that I mentioned," Abbot responded quickly. "I meant to call Ed and wish him well, but my phone . . . you know. Then, I got busy with Bekah and the day slipped by before I realized. I'll try to call him later today." He looked at his watch and noted that it was only four in the morning. "What did you guys do, take the midnight special?"

"Something like that," Hans nodded.

"And we're beat," Tom added. "You got room fer us to crash here?"

"Sure. But I don't have any extra blankets."

"We brought our sleeping bags," said Hans. "I know how little storage space there is on a sailing vessel."

"I'll go get 'em," said Tom.

"Let me help," Hans and Abbot offered simultaneously.

Tom chuckled a deep, husky laugh that vibrated his whole body. "Naw, you two polecats just settle down. I'll be right back."

As Tom's cowboy boots scuffed the companionway steps, Abbot's eyes opened wide. After Tom had left, Abbot said, "I wonder if my spare pair of deck shoes will fit him." He slipped into the forward cabin to find them.

"I hope so," Hans agreed. "And I also hope Grandfather Hansen didn't roll over in his grave just then. This was his boat, you know."

"Yes, I've thought about that nearly every day I've lived here. I'm pretty conscientious when it comes to your grandpa's third love and I've tried to keep it up the way he would have wanted."

"It looks great," Hans said, taking a soft-bristled brush from the sink and scouring off the scuff marks Tom had made with his boots. "We're going to have to get him boat oriented in a hurry."

Abbot handed Hans the pair of deck shoes.

Nodding, Hans took the white-soled shoes and headed up the companionway stairs. "No reason to let this become a problem," he insisted.

Abbot followed, watched Hans go in the direction of the parking lot, then he looked forward at the deck. The rain was coming down like rapid-fire bullets, but it was too dark to tell whether or not the deck would need to be scoured as well.

"Inviting Tom onto a sailing vessel is like inviting a tiger to a tea party," he moaned softly. Within a few minutes the two men returned and Abbot was relieved to see his deck shoes on Tom's feet, while the cowboy boots were nowhere to be seen.

Evidently, Tom noticed Abbot's reaction and growled, "How in tarnation was I supposed to know? I ain't never been on no gentleman's boat before."

Abbot laughed. "A mountain man all the way through, aren't you, Tom?"

"And proud of it!" his brother stated. He swept his dusty-blonde hair back with his long fingers. His hands were huge, larger than most men's, and he was the tallest of the Sparkleman boys, six-foot three inches. His hazel eyes were guarded by long, pale lashes and his lean, lank body was well-muscled. Tom wasn't afraid of work and it showed in his sinewy arms. "Left my hat on the airplane!" he grumbled. "Don't know where my mind was."

"I'd say on the stewardess with the beautiful red hair," observed Hans, dryly.

"Maybe," Tom replied. "Which sofa do you want me to sleep on?"

"Take the port settee," said Abbot. "It pulls out and you can sleep diagonally if you want. It gives you a little more room."

"The what?" asked Tom.

Abbot smiled. "The left sofa, Tom. Port settee is boat-speak."

Tom nodded, rolled out his sleeping bag and placed its opening closest to the galley. "Hope I learn all that boat-speak stuff before I have to go to the bathroom," he mumbled. "Otherwise. . . ." He left the sentence open.

Without thinking, Abbot said, "The head is forward."

"What?" asked Tom. He gave Abbot a bewildered expression, then moved the sleeping bag so that the opening was now facing forward. "But if I put my head at this end, I'll bump it on that fold-up table you got there."

Abbot and Hans laughed.

"Maybe we should cover the basics," Hans suggested.

Perplexed, Tom nodded in agreement. "Maybe so."

"You want to?" Hans asked Abbot.

"No. I learned from the best. Go to it." He was thinking about the two weeks he'd spent on Hans' boat, well over a year ago. Hans had a 49' Hallberg-Rassey Ketch moored in San Diego. The first time Abbot was on board, Hans gave him a detailed rendition of nautical terminology. It didn't take long.

"Very well," said Hans, facing the v-berth. "The basics. When facing forward on a boat, the left side is called port, the right side, starboard."

Tom stood up and faced Hans. He held out his left hand. "Port," he said.

Hans turned him around one hundred and eighty degrees so that Tom was facing the same direction as Hans. "Facing forward. . . ." he said.

Tom's face lit up. "Got it. Port on the left, starboard on the right."

"Very good. Now, you're facing toward the bow: The bow is the pointed, forward end of a boat. Aft is the stern."

"After's the stern what?" Now Tom seemed completely confused.

Abbot could stifle his laughter no longer. He laughed so hard he had tears of laughter rolling down his face. "It seems to me you're trying to teach a polecat how to sip tea with Queen Elizabeth."

"It took you a while to learn, Abbot," reminded Hans. "Give Tom a chance. He'll get it soon enough."

By the twinkle of humor in Hans' eyes, Abbot could tell that Hans was straining to prevent himself from laughing as well.

When the rain had nearly been wrung from the clouds overhead and the sun had begun to change them from black to light, pale gray, Tom and Hans almost had the nautical terms figured out.

"Sole?" Hans inquired.

"Yer standin' on it," Tom barked in return.

"Head?"

"Where yer backside belongs."

"Galley?"

"Includes the kitchen sink."

"V-berth?"

"Where Abbot sleeps."

"Settee?"

"The sofas."

"Quarter berth?"

"Where yer sleeping."

Hans arched an eyebrow.

Tom growled, "The smallest bed in the house."

"Cabin," corrected Hans.

"House!" Tom insisted.

Hans sighed wearily. "And the 'bow' is?"

"The nose."

"Aft?"

"As far behind the nose as yer can git."

"Stern?"

"Same thing."

Hans hesitated.

"Are you done yet?" asked Tom. "Because my backside needs to meet up with the head and my head needs to settee a spell."

Hans finally allowed himself to laugh. "Yes, I'm just as tired as you are."

"Good!" said Tom, then he opened the door to the head and went inside. Ten seconds later he opened the door and poked his head out to growl at them. "Yer kiddin'! Right?" His gruff voice held a mixture of dismay and disbelief.

"What?" Abbot asked.

"The sign in here that reads: *Don't put anything into the head unless you have eaten it first!*"

The astonished look on Tom's face as he realized the sign was not a joke, caused a new ripple of laughter. It was all Abbot could do not to end up on the cabin sole, where Hans was laughing and rolling back and forth.

❧ ❧

By noon, while Hans and Tom were still catching up on their sleep, Abbot took a quick shower and dressed in a business suit, thankful that his current occupation dictated that he wear one every day. He'd purchased a nice assortment when he was hired by the museum, and now, they would also come in handy for Sunday services. Resolute in his determination to put his life right with the Lord, Abbot taped a note to the microwave in the galley and left *Bridger's Child* to attend his first church meeting in almost a year.

A little nervous when he arrived, he was grateful he had the foresight to look up the location and meeting times on the church's internet site. At twenty minutes to one, he was walking through the double doors of the Seattle North Third Ward building.

Several members welcomed him. After shaking hands and giving his name, Abbot asked for the executive secretary. An elderly man was pointed out to him and Abbot approached and gave his name, address and phone number, then made an appointment to see the bishop the following Sunday at seven in the evening. Satisfied that he had done the right thing, he attended Priesthood, Sunday School and Sacrament meetings.

It was the first time in perhaps a decade that he didn't have the desire to duck out halfway through the meetings and go somewhere else. Amazingly, it was also the first time in many Sacrament meetings that he felt the spirit of the Holy Ghost descend upon him, filling his bosom with warmth, his heart with love and his mind with enlightenment. When the meetings were over, Abbot left carrying a feeling of peace within himself, with the world and with his Father in Heaven. It was a sensation that he hadn't had in a very long time.

He hadn't made arrangements to see Bekah today and now he wondered if she would be available. Last night he'd only told her that he'd call her. Would he be pushing the relationship too much if they spent time together today as well? Missing her more than he dared admit, even to himself, he removed the cell phone from his pocket and dialed her number.

After four rings, her voice mail answered for her. *"If it's important, you'll leave a message. And if you don't, how will I know you called? Think about it."*

He waited for the beep, then said, "Bekah, it's Abbot. I know it's short notice, but if you're available later today, call me."

❧ ❧

"Gove's Cove," Bekah murmured to herself. "Ah! There it is." She parked her Dodge caravan, got out, locked it and stuffed the key back inside her pocket.

Searching the parking lot, she didn't see Abbot's white Bronco anywhere. But she knew that there was a parking garage a block or two south of her and she hoped that he parked in there. She should have telephoned first, but he hadn't given her his new number to memorize and when she called information earlier in the day, his number was not yet available. Of course, it had been nearly nine o'clock last night when he bought his new phone, so she doubted the computer operators would have his number processed until Monday.

The rain finally stopped an hour ago, but there were puddles everywhere. Darker cumulonimbus clouds were still headed her way, but perhaps they'd have an hour or two before another deluge descended upon them this evening. Stepping over the puddles carefully, she headed toward the steep stairs that would take her down to the waterfront.

Walking past an open door on her way to the docks, she noticed a man at a desk inside. The office was cluttered with photos of sailing vessels and power boats for sale. She stepped inside.

"May I help you?" the man asked.

"I'm looking for Abbot Sparkleman. He lives aboard a—"

"*Bridger's Child?*" the man interrupted.

Bekah nodded.

"Straight ahead, take the first turn left and the next right. Go all the way to the end. You can't miss her."

Bekah thanked the man and followed his instructions. When she saw a beautiful sailing vessel at the end of the dock, she hoped it was the one Abbot told her about. The bright work was meticulous, with smooth lines and a pulpit that stretched out over the bow a good three feet. A little symbol, CR38, identified the boat near the stern on the port side, which was facing her. Quickly she walked the length of the dock and turned right at the very end where she could plainly see the name painted on the stern: *Bridger's Child.*

She sighed in relief, then removed her shoes and stepped aboard. The companionway hatch was slid back about six inches, and no boat owner would leave their vessel unsecured while they were away, not in Seattle. Tapping on the cabin top she called out, "Hello! Abbot! Are you down there?"

She heard some movement and waited for a moment. It didn't take long. Soon a man with chestnut hair and bold, blue eyes slid the hatch completely open and poked his head through the opening.

"He's not home," said Hans. "May I help you?"

"I didn't realize he was sharing the boat with anyone," she said, confused to find someone other than Abbot at home.

"He didn't know we were coming. We arrived around four this morning."

"We?" she asked.

"Tom's still sleeping. He's Abbot's brother."

"Oh." Still a little confused, she queried. "And you are?"

"Hans Bridger Clark, at your service." He removed the teak door boards and stepped out through the companionway. "And you?"

"Bekah Stevens." She reached out and accepted his offered hand. "Abbot told me about you. Didn't you and he go to college together?"

"Yes. Are you the damsel in distress that Abbot told us about?"

"The same." As she nodded, her auburn curls bounced about her head.

"Sit down," said Hans. "We didn't get the full story. It was late and we were all tired."

Bekah sat opposite him on the port cockpit bench. Just as she was about to speak, she heard a husky voice say, "Wait up!"

Hans gave her a tender smile. "That's Tom."

"Abbot's brother?"

A gangly-looking man came climbing out through the companionway, finger-combing his dusty-blonde hair with one hand and holding onto the hand grip with the other. "Eee-gads! Don't this boat never hold still?" he asked.

"Tom, this is Bekah Stevens," Hans introduced them.

"Pleased to meet you, Miss Stevens. Sorry I ain't too decent yet, havin' just woke up and all," he drawled as he tucked his shirt into his western jeans.

"What brings you both to Seattle?" she asked.

"Aw, we was worried how Abbot was handling yester—" He stopped mid-word as Hans' blue eyes warned him off that subject.

"It's okay," Bekah responded, aware of what Hans was trying to do. "Abbot told me about Alyssa marrying Ed yesterday while we were at dinner last night."

"He was okay with it?" asked Tom.

Not that it really should concern you, she thought with a smile. *Cozy family.* "I asked him the very same question," she answered. "He said, 'Obviously not.' That was good enough for me."

Tom gave her a wide grin. She was impressed with his deep hazel eyes and his lean, angular features, though she couldn't see any family resemblance between the two brothers.

"You were about to tell us how Abbot ended up rescuing you and your nephew," reminded Hans.

Within a few minutes, Bekah gave the two men as much information as she felt necessary to satisfy their curiosity.

Then Hans said, "Is anyone hungry? I was about to raid Abbot's ice box when you arrived, Miss Stevens."

"Please, call me Bekah," she told him.

"I like Bekah," said Tom, letting the name roll off his tongue as though it gave him some secret little pleasure.

"I like her, too," Hans teased.

"Aw, you know what I was sayin'," grumbled Tom.

While Hans laughed openly, Bekah suppressed her laughter.

"You know, a fella' could git fed up with you makin' fun of him all the time," he complained to Hans.

"I apologize," said Hans.

Tom nodded his approval.

Then Hans slipped below and started looking through the ice box. "Eggs," he called up to them. "Bread. A toaster. Guess we're in business."

"Nothing for me," Bekah told him.

"So how is Cody doing today?" Tom asked her.

"He's running around like it never happened," she replied.

"Ain't that just like a kid?!" he exclaimed.

"Yes." She gave him a smile and sat back, enjoying the feel of a fresh breeze coming that would precede the next rain squall. The scent of salt and city hung heavily in the air, however, and she was surprised at how quickly the city smells took over after a rainstorm. "Do you know when Abbot will be back?" she asked, wondering whether she should stay or go.

"I didn't even know he'd gone," said Tom. "But, I guess he didn't need to sleep as long as we did."

Hans evidently heard their conversation and looked up at them from the galley. "He left a note. Said he would be at church if we needed him and to call his cell phone number."

"Did he say when he would be coming back?" she asked.

"No. But church only lasts three hours and I've been up for one. So he couldn't be more than a couple hours. Though I expect that he should be coming in anytime now."

"What makes you say that?" questioned Bekah.

"I haven't heard of any wards that start their meetings any later than two. That would mean five at the latest and it's almost that now. . . oh, there he is!"

"Where?" Bekah wanted to know.

"Coming down the dock."

She gave him a quizzical expression and he explained. "Through the galley porthole. Look behind you."

Bekah turned. Just seeing Abbot walking toward her made her heart flutter. Dressed in a suit and tie, he looked like a model straight out of an Armani commercial. When he noticed her sitting in the cockpit, Abbot's eyes lit up and a broad smile wandered across his handsome face.

"Hi!" she said in her brightest voice.

"I just left a message on your voice mail!" he exclaimed. "Then I come home to find you sitting in my cockpit."

"I was going to call," she explained. "But I couldn't remember your number."

He gave her a secret smile. When she arched an eyebrow he said, "I thought with your photographic memory you never forgot phone numbers."

Bekah blushed. "I normally do, but for some reason, I don't remember you giving me yours."

He reached into his jacket pocket and pulled out a card and an ink pen, then wrote his new cell phone number down for her. As he handed the card to her, his fingers touched hers and she felt a tingling sensation that made her tremble inside. *Wait a minute! That's never happened before!* Certain that her face was crimson, she took the card and whispered, "Thanks."

Abbot stepped up on the deck where a welcome mat greeted new arrivals. From there, he removed his dress shoes and came aboard, sitting next to Bekah in the cockpit. After putting his shoes up on the cabin top, beneath the dodger, he put an arm about Bekah's shoulder and gave her a little squeeze. "I missed you."

"Me, too," she murmured.

"That's my cue," said Tom.

"No, don't go," Abbot said. "I don't plan on doing anymore than giving Bekah a little hug. Stay and visit with us."

Tom looked hesitantly at her, so Bekah followed Abbot's lead. "Do stay, Tom." Though her heart whispered, *Goodbye, Tom.*

"I thought Ed said that you met a sweet little filly from Texas territory who wanted you to manage her filling station while you got better acquainted," said Abbot. "What happened?"

"We broke up." Tom nodded, looking a little dejected.

"I'm sorry," Abbot comforted. "I know it's been hard for you."

Tom straightened. "I been sober for thirty months now and I'm finally off probation."

"That's great," Abbot told him as he reached across and squeezed Tom's knee. "Keep it up, Tom. Good things are bound to come your way."

Tom frowned. "I keep thinking that. Then, WHAM! I bite the dust again."

Bekah wasn't certain she liked the way the conversation was headed, but she felt at a loss as to how to change it.

Finally Tom looked at her. "We got yer wheels spinnin' now, don't we Bekah?"

"I was—" she stopped mid-sentence. Barry was right, she wasn't very good at lying at all. Why did she even bother? "I was a little curious," she admitted.

"Go ahead and tell her," Tom said to Abbot. "She's bound to hear it sooner or later."

Abbot frowned. It was apparent that he didn't like the topic either, but he turned to Bekah and said, matter-of-factly, "Let's just say that Tom let his drinking get the better of him one time, and leave it at that, shall we?"

"And I been sober for thirty months!" Tom added for the second time. "I ain't never touchin' alcohol again, it's the devil's tool!"

"None of us are," Abbot comforted. "Tom, we're all in this together. You know you can count on any of us. When times get tough, that's when family sticks together."

Tom nodded. "Yeah, I know. The Sparkleman boys, we always stick together."

"And Kayla, too," Abbot insisted. "She's just as much our sister as we are brothers in my eyes."

"Mine, too," Tom confessed. "Sorry if I get a little down once in a while. I don't understand why people can't just forget. The man who did those things is as dead as Pa. He ain't never comin' back."

Abbot moved from Bekah's side and sat next to Tom, putting his arm around him, hugging him like a tender father would hug a repentant son. The scene touched Bekah more than she realized, and she found it necessary to fight down a few tears.

"Omelettes are ready," said Hans through the companionway. "Come and eat, Tom."

Tom stood and gave Bekah a weak smile. "Sorry," he apologized.

"It takes a long time to heal old wounds."

Bekah stood, gave Tom a little squeeze and kissed him on the cheek. "As long as you have family and friends, you'll be okay."

He blushed and scampered down the companionway steps, obviously embarrassed.

"Do you want to go for a walk?" asked Abbot.

Bekah nodded. She stepped off the boat and put her shoes on. The rest of the afternoon the two of them walked the docks and talked about Cody and sailing lessons and everything in between. When she finally arrived home at dusk, Bekah realized it didn't really matter what they'd talked about. The only thing of importance to her was that she'd never felt so at ease around any man before Abbot.

Chapter Five

"Okay," said Bekah as she steadied herself in the center of her Walker Bay sailboat. "First things first." She picked up a rope and said to Abbot. "What is this?"

He had to smile at her because she was being so serious. "A rope."

"Wrong. The first thing you need to know about sailing is that when a rope is used in connection with a boat it changes names, depending on what it is used for. Right now, this is a line."

"Why is the rope a line?"

"Because it's aboard a boat."

"I see," he answered. She was so cute he didn't have the nerve to tell her he already knew that much.

"If I attach this line to the bow of my boat, it is no longer called a line, it is called a painter."

Abbot nodded. Hans smiled. Tom just gave her a look that indicated he didn't know what in blazes she was talking about.

"But if I attach this line to the head of the sail, it is no longer called a line, it is called a halyard."

"Gotcha," said Abbot. *Knew that, too.*

"Tom, hand me that rope over there." She pointed to a loop of rope she had left on the pavement.

There they were, in the parking lot at Gas Works Park north of Lake Union, and Bekah was demonstrating the critical points of sail terminology for Abbot, Hans and Tom. Having agreed to meet them there each weekday afternoon at 4:30, this was their first day of instructions. Abbot was pleased, however, that she'd spent time jogging with him before sailing lessons. It gave him extra time with her to which Tom and Hans were not privy.

"How come this is a rope and that one ain't?" asked Tom, pointing to the line she'd just used.

"In sailing terminology, the rope you're holding onto is not being used for anything nautical. It's not holding the boat to a dock or securing the boat in any way, so it's actually a rope. Now, bring it to me."

Tom gave her a curious tilt of his mouth as he handed her the rope.

"Since I am standing in the boat, Tom, you gave me a rope, but I received a line. The moment that rope comes on board, it's a line."

Abbot couldn't prevent a smile from escaping onto his face at the serious manner in which Bekah was teaching her class. And he couldn't help feeling his heart drawing closer to hers, either.

"If that don't beat all!" exclaimed Tom.

"Concentrate," Bekah said. "Here's where it gets tricky. I already put a line on the head of the sail."

"That's the top again, ain't it?" Tom asked.

She nodded. "And the foot of the sail is the bottom. But what is this edge called that is closest to and runs the length of the mast?"

Tom scratched the back of his head, bumping his Stetson forward as he did so. "Beats me."

"That's the luff," Abbot answered.

"What's love got to do with it?" Tom teased.

"Be serious!" Bekah warned them both.

When they were still, she continued. "Now the foot of the sail travels along the boom until—"

"What's the boom again?" asked Tom.

"It's the pole at the foot of the sail," Abbot answered.

"Aw, shucks!" teased Tom. "I thought the boom was how the mast sounded when it realized the sail luffed it."

Hans and Abbot both started laughing, but Bekah was evidently taking her job too seriously. "Doesn't anyone around here know how to pay attention?"

"That's just the problem," said Tom. "Yer so dang cute, Bekah, no one here can concentrate on rope-speak. Everythin's coming out woman-speak!"

Clearly exasperated, Bekah glared at Tom and said, "Are you sure you didn't fall off the wagon today, Tom?"

Her question threw Abbot for a loop. Had she pushed his brother too far? He was relieved when Tom gave her a mischievous grin and said, "Ain't no need fer liquor when yer around, Bekah. Yer enough woman to intoxicate all three of us."

"That's it!" laughed Abbot. "Time for a break."

Bekah jumped down from the boat as it rested in the trailer well. She punched Tom playfully and said, "Better watch yourself, Cowboy. Some woman's going to come along and knock your hat off." With her remark, she quickly reached up and grabbed his hat, then sent it soaring toward the green grass like a frisbee.

"Not my hat, Bekah. I told you, no one touches my hat," he moaned as he hurried after it.

"Especially when it's brand new and he's breaking it in," whispered Abbot.

She leaned back against him unexpectedly, then grabbed his hands and pulled his arms around her so he had no choice but to hold her in that position. He was not disappointed. He'd never met a woman quite like Bekah before. Her playful ways, her teasing, tenderness and empathy amazed him. She filled his heart with unexpected feelings of completeness. It was almost as if they'd known each other forever.

"Mmm," she murmured, leaning back against him, pulling his arms tighter around her. "You feel nice."

Bekah's encouragement and the knowledge that she was enjoying him holding her like that gave him the courage he needed to blow softly against her ear and kiss her neck in a trail that led up to her forehead. She turned into his arms and he saw passion in her eyes that startled him. Pulling his head toward hers, she gave him a trail of her own kisses, from his neck up to his lips. Sirens went off in his head, stars circled in his mind. His heart pounded so fiercely he thought it might burst right out of his chest.

The sweetness of that first kiss lingered with Abbot for hours afterward. For the rest of the day he couldn't concentrate on anything else that happened. Vaguely aware that Tom had given up teasing her after retrieving his hat, Abbot went through the motions of learning all that Bekah taught. When he climbed into the v-berth that night, he realized that no one else had ever touched his mind or his heart like Bekah had during that one moment they shared a kiss in the parking lot at Gas Works Park.

While Abbot spent his days at work the rest of the week, Hans took Tom on a sight-seeing trip of Seattle and the surrounding areas. The workweek was grueling and the museum was busier than it had been for months, due mostly to the tourist season, now in full swing. Abbot much preferred the fall, winter and spring, when the attendees were less numerous. Although his assignments didn't usually have anything to do with tour groups or discussions, the summer season forced him out of the research library and into the thronging crowds.

Afternoons, however, could not have been more enjoyable, because Bekah taught him how to sail her Walker Bay. The smile on her face as the wind filled the Dacron sail and pushed the little boat around Lake Union brightened his spirit like nothing else could. Her patience with him seemed to have no boundaries and for this Abbot was grateful.

Hans taught Tom the same basic skills, using the dinghy that served as a tender for *Bridger's Child*. Though rigging the inflatable dinghy with a sail proved a little tricky, until Hans purchased a kit designed for that very purpose. When Tom fell overboard, both men had to dive in and save him. It was the first time that Abbot realized his brother didn't know how to swim. After that experience, no one would let Tom in a boat unless he wore a life preserver, and he didn't complain about wearing one, either.

Bekah made Abbot joyful; she helped him love life more than any person he'd ever known. When they tipped the sailboat over, she was the first one to laugh and the last one to give up trying to get back into it. He also discovered that she had the most dulcet tones when she giggled; it sounded like heaven's music to his ears.

Abbot had invited Bekah to attend the annual museum banquet, which was being held in the governor's honor this year. A live band would be playing softly in one corner of the assembly hall, while tables would be set up around the perimeter. He looked forward to it with great anticipation and had rented a tuxedo for the affair.

Abbot had also invited Tom and Hans to join them, though seeing Tom in a tuxedo was more like picturing a tiger in a straightjacket. Smiling to himself, he thought, *I guess they're here to stay.* He had dropped them off at the center prior to picking up Bekah.

After he drove over to her condo, he made certain his bow-tie was straight, his tuxedo shirt was tucked smoothly beneath the cummerbund and his hair combed neatly. Then, he grabbed the ivory-colored roses with aquamarine and cream-colored ribbon streamers from the car seat. Wanting this evening to be perfect, he offered a quick prayer, stepped up to the front door and pressed the keypad. Then he waited.

A few seconds later he heard her voice. "Abbot?"

"That's right."

"Come on up."

A loud buzzing noise indicated the front door could be opened. He pushed against it and walked down the hall to the elevator. Soon, he was standing outside Bekah's condo door, a lump in his throat. Although she had helped him overcome a lot of his shyness during the week, this was a special evening and he was partly responsible for it. All week long he'd pushed his staff and worked alongside them to make the evening perfect.

When Bekah opened the door, she was wearing a cream-colored, floor length satin cloak over a gown made of a soft aquamarine and silver fabric. Her hair was perfectly curled, her face so beautiful his heart almost stopped beating, completely. "Hi," he said, "I hope these will match your dress satisfactorily. The florist couldn't find any flowers that were aquamarine."

Bekah took the posy of roses from him, parted the satin cloak and compared the creamy colors to the delicate fabric of her dress. "Perfect," she whispered with a smile. "Thank you."

He offered her his arm. "You look lovely."

"I could say the same thing about you."

He gave her a teasing scowl. "Lovely?" he questioned.

"Devastating," she amended.

The thought that he had that much affect on her made his heart begin beating faster, once again. "Shall we?" he asked.

After some effort at getting Bekah up onto the leather passenger seat without damaging her cloak or gown, Abbot slid onto the driver's seat and fastened his seatbelt. "Sorry you have to climb up so high to get in my Bronco. I still wish I'd rented a limo," he apologized.

"As I told you last week, limousines are expensive and frivolous," she reminded.

"Your protest earlier is the only reason why I didn't," he told her. "Though I wish now that I hadn't listened to you."

Within minutes they were whisking east on NE-45th Street toward the campus. "Thank you," he said as they drove along.

"For?" she questioned.

"For teaching me how to sail, for allowing me to share part of your life with you."

"Is this a goodbye speech?" she asked.

"Of course not." *Why had she thought that?*

"I was teasing," she confessed. "Oh, Abbot, sometimes you take life too seriously."

"I'm sorry. I don't mean to."

She smiled at him, reached her arm across and rubbed his shoulder. "I've enjoyed being with you."

"I know we've spent every possible moment together the past nine days," he began timidly. Why did he feel so uptight tonight? He couldn't understand what had changed. This was the same woman with whom he'd shared those nine days, the same woman he'd kissed a dozen times since they first met. Why should tonight be any different? Then, he realized why his feelings were disrupting him. He wanted to ask her if she would go to church meetings with him, yet he wasn't even sure if she knew that he was a Latter Day Saint.

"Yes?" she questioned, studying him closely.

"I wondered if you were going to be busy tomorrow afternoon?" he felt his heart pound nervously.

She hesitated before she answered and gave a little sigh. Abbot panicked. Perhaps he'd been taking unfair advantage of her time. She'd never indicated that she wanted to be anywhere else but with him. He wondered if she was dating someone else, as well. They'd never discussed it and he'd just assumed that he was the only man in her life right now.

"I have a previous engagement," she finally responded.

"Oh," his voice almost growled but he was able to keep it under control. "Another time, perhaps," he added quickly. *Too quickly!*

"Of course."

When she didn't say anymore, he asked, "Will you be late getting in? I could call you if you'd like."

"I can't imagine I'll be much past eight. We could go for a stroll around Green Lake."

I'll wait up all night if I have to, he groaned to himself.

When he didn't respond, she reminded him, "You will have my undivided attention all next week."

"That's right. Cody's quest for the cave of Chief Taquinna."

"He's so excited to go, he's been calling me every morning."

"I hope he won't be too disappointed when we don't find it."

"I doubt he'll ever forget the experience, regardless. You're giving him a rare gift, Abbot. He's never had a tyee as his best friend."

Abbot smiled and felt himself loosening up a little. Perhaps she was attending her own Sunday services, or had a family activity to attend. The fact that she hadn't offered any information as to what her previous engagement was, still left him wondering, but he shouldn't automatically assume that she was seeing someone else. Maybe she could attend church with him next week. *But don't push her. Take your time. See what develops during the camping trip.*

When they arrived at the cultural center, Abbot escorted her into the large foyer and toward the assembly hall. Bekah had never looked more lovely he decided, as he put a hand on the small of her back, allowing her to lead the way to their table.

Hans and Tom gallantly stood up as they arrived, though Tom's demeanor reminded him of a polecat in a petticoat. At first, his eyes took in the environment, the soft music coming from the orchestra, the white satin table coverings, muted lighting, tea-rose candles at each table.

"Abbot, everything looks lovely," she murmured in his ear as he helped her out of her satin cloak.

As he looked down at Bekah, his heart did a resounding thud inside his chest. It felt like his head was going to spin around and twist itself off. His mouth dropped open and he gasped. Bekah was wearing an aquamarine and silver-threaded, backless dress that shimmered when she walked and hugged her curves beautifully. *Backless is an understatement!* The dress hung past her waist in the back, revealing far more than he wanted anyone, not even himself, to see. Embarrassed, his painful shyness around women came crashing down around him and her dress was the reason for it! Abbot wouldn't be able to dance with Bekah tonight, for he would never touch her bare back and he obviously couldn't put his hand on the fabric below it. Nor would he permit any other man to dance with her. A knot of panic seeped into his heart as he realized several of the men nearby were ogling her with admiration and lust in their eyes. It annoyed him and he felt uneasy. But, how could he tell her? The last time he tried to tell a woman how she should look, it came back and bit him.

Tom gave a low, cat-call whistle as Abbot held a chair out for her. Abbot scowled at him and Tom took the hint immediately.

Hans, on the other hand, seemed genuinely amused at the affect Bekah's evening gown was having on him. Abbot glared at him. But, like the Cheshire cat, Hans gave Abbot a wistful smile, then ignored him.

Having completely forgotten where he was and why, Abbot could scarcely concentrate. When all the tables in the assembly hall were full, the administrator introduced the governor, whom they were supposed to be honoring. Abbot stood and clapped, as did most of the guests. When Bekah stood, however, Abbot wanted to beg her to sit back down.

She leaned seductively against him, her bare back just inches from his fingers. He wanted to touch her, to stroke her back gently, caressingly, but strong as those feelings were, after his promises to his Father in Heaven, he would never touch her unless he married her first. *Marry her? I hardly know her! Amend that! I don't know her at all!*

Abbot didn't want the other men in the room to look at her the way that they were, either. To solve the problem, Abbot stepped behind her, curled his arms around her and covered her bare back with his chest. She leaned against him and he didn't know whether to be relieved, because now he couldn't see what he didn't want anyone else to see, or concerned because he didn't feel the position they were in was appropriate for a man who'd just placed his life back in God's hands with the promise that he was going to walk the straight and narrow path. Caught between a rock and a hard place, as his pa used to say, Abbot didn't know whether he was going to be crushed into oblivion, or just bruised really bad. Saying a silent prayer, Abbot asked for divine inspiration. *Just tell me what to do, and I'll obey you, Father.* When the answer came, Abbot realized that the consequences may cost him his relationship with Bekah, but he had no choice.

Whispering to Hans, he said, "Will you and Abbot take a cab back? I've got something I have to do."

Hans nodded and returned his attention to the program. The governor stood and basked in the applause for a moment, then raised his hands, indicating that the audience should sit down. Then the administrator announced that the meal could be served. Immediately, the clapping subsided and people started talking with one another.

Abbot released Bekah and picked up her cloak. "Bekah," he said, "we need to leave. I hope you won't mind."

"Of course not," she said. "I noticed you were a little pale. Are you not feeling well?"

"No," he admitted and his answer was absolutely truthful. What he was about to do made no rational sense in the world, but he'd made a promise to forsake the worldly and cling to the spiritual. If it meant he had to offend Bekah for the Lord's sake, he would do so, although he prayed with every ounce of strength he had that she would under-stand.

He held her cloak out for her and made certain that she was properly covered before he led her from the assembly hall. When they were outside the doors, he took her hand and led her in silence toward the reflecting pool which was, fortunately, abandoned by that time of night. The rain had stopped earlier in the day, but there were still a few damp spots on the pavement. As they walked, Bekah remained silent, as though she was waiting for him to begin.

Shuffling his feet, he hesitated, praying that the Lord would give him the right words. Finally he said, "I'm not ill, Bekah. Not physically, at least. There are some things about me that you need to understand. I would never hurt you and I would never do anything that I felt would not be in your best interest. I hope you know that by now."

"Of course," she murmured. "What is it?"

"Let me begin by telling you something about Alyssa," he sug-gested.

"Oh?"

He heard the concern in her voice but he brushed it aside. "When we were dating and engaged, I mentioned a few times that I liked her hair a certain way. She thought I was trying to control her. I suppose I was."

When she didn't respond other than to study his face as they walked along, he continued. "Then one day she wanted to do what she felt in her heart God wanted her to do. At the time, it made me angry. I accused her of trying to control *me*. But she informed me that I had my free agency to do as I pleased, however she chose to follow the Lord. At the time, I was angry with her. I acted foolishly and she called off the wedding. Afterward I blamed God for all the problems in our relationship. In retrospect, I realize that she was right. The problems we were having came because I was too blind to see God's hand at work in her life. I was the problem."

"And now?" Bekah prodded, giving him her complete attention.

"Recently I've been trying to return to the way I believe God wants me to be. I'm not always successful, but at least I'm trying. I believe that God is mindful of me, that He really cares what happens to me, but now I'm a little confused because He's asked me to say something to you that may cause you to act the way I did when I turned my back on Alyssa and the Lord."

"What is it?" she asked as she stopped and faced him, her eyes searching his inexorably.

Her expression frightened him and he feared the worst from her. How could he go through this again, especially when he knew he was in the right this time? Finally he lowered his voice and said huskily, "I'm uncomfortable when you wear the dress you're wearing."

She arched an eyebrow, as if in disbelief. "What, exactly, don't you like about my dress?" she asked, her voice a little more brittle than he wanted to hear.

"I feel uncomfortable when your back is exposed all the way down to your waist." He blew out a gasp of air. *Whew! All right, Lord. I said it!*

Unexpectedly she threw her arms around him and hugged him tightly. "You are the sweetest man!" she exclaimed. "Take me home right now and I'll change. I have another dress that's a little more modest. Perhaps you'll like that one."

"You—you're not mad?" he stammered.

"Abbot, I've never had a man care so much about me before. I only wore this dress because I wanted to 'wow' you. I didn't realize it would offend you or I would never have worn it."

"I'm not saying the dress didn't have the affect that you wanted. You're a lovely woman, but where I'm concerned, you don't need anything like that dress to impress me. It's just that, I don't feel comfortable with you 'wowing' every other man on planet earth, as well. Besides, I've promised God that I will wait until I marry before I allow those intimate feelings to surface again."

Bekah giggled as she snuggled right up against him. "Abbot Isaac Sparkleman, you are a most peculiar man!"

"I hope that's good," he admitted. "Because right now I'd like to go back to my old ways, but I don't think God would appreciate it."

"Abbot, you are absolutely the best!"

He couldn't believe his good fortune. Having expected her to dump him like yesterday's newspaper, he certainly had no clue she would react this way. A warm feeling spread through him and he realized, once again, that God was mindful of him in ways he could not yet begin to fathom.

Tenderly he kissed her forehead and said, "Come on. I'll take you back to your condo."

"We'll never get back in time for the banquet," she conceded. "They'll have finished before we do."

"Then we'll stop by that Chinese place on forty-fifth and pick up something. While you're changing, I'll prepare a banquet of our own."

And he did. While Bekah was changing in her bedroom, he was hustling around her tidy kitchen, finding dishes, candles, grape juice, ice, stemware. By the time she returned he had a tea towel draped over his arm and the table set to perfection. The soft glow of candles, a romantic symphony coming from her CD player, a potpourri of steaming cinnamon and cloves on the stove, chicken chow mein, sweet and sour pork with rice and fortune cookies for dessert, were ready to make their evening a memorable one.

When Bekah entered the dining room, the cream-colored dress she wore was exquisitely beautiful, with tiny cap-sleeves, fitted waistline and fairly modest neckline. *Though she'll not be able to wear it after she goes to the temple with me,* he thought for a moment. The thought startled him almost as much as the aquamarine dress had earlier. Was he already thinking about marrying her? Had he fallen so hopelessly in love with her that marriage was the only 'next step.'

He smiled as he pulled out the chair for her to be seated, then slid it closer to the table for her. "I like your dress," he said, though his heart sang, *Will you marry me?*

After he poured the grape juice into their goblets, he sat down opposite her and said, "Will you mind if I offer a word of prayer?"

"Of course not."

Abbot bowed his head. "Our Father in Heaven, as we come before thee this evening, we are indeed thankful for all the many blessings which thou doth provide for us. We're thankful to know that thou art mindful of us in our tribulations as well as in our times of joy and happiness. We ask thee to bless this food which we are about to eat that it might nourish us. And bless us with thy spirit, that we might always know to choose the good over the evil. These things we ask, in the name of Jesus Christ. Amen."

"Amen," whispered Bekah. Then she said, "I have an attraction for men who know God and converse with Him."

He smiled. "Then perhaps I stand a chance of finding a little place in your heart."

"Just a tiny, little place," she teased.

"It's a start," he grinned. "But I warn you. Let me have a tiny, little place and I'll want to expand my living quarters."

Halfway through their meal, they were laughing as they recalled Tom falling overboard at sailing lessons. Intoxicated with the feelings he was having for Bekah, Abbot unsteadily reached for the grape juice at exactly the same moment she did. Their hands collided and his, being the larger, bumped both goblets of grape juice onto the table where it splattered and splashed towards her.

Bekah scooted back, but not in time to prevent the purple liquid from staining the skirt of her cream-colored evening gown.

"You must not like this one, either," she moaned.

Abbot stood up and grabbed a kitchen towel. "I am sorry," he apologized as he began to blot the juice from her lap.

She took the towel from him and said, "It's all right, really."

"I'll buy you a new dress," he offered.

"Don't worry about it, Abbot. My parents used to say, 'It's not a meal without a spill.' Now we've gotten the spill over with."

He smiled, though he did feel terrible about ruining her gown. "Perhaps if you put it in cold water right away?"

She stood up, then noticed his clothing. The white shirt and jacket were splotched with grape juice. "I think we should call it a draw," she laughed. "What do you think?"

Abbot looked down. The satin white jacket and shirt would no doubt be ruined. He gave her a quirky frown in response.

Bekah started giggling and couldn't stop for several minutes. Laughter filled his spirit up, as well and soon he was laughing with her.

When their cheeks hurt and their sides ached, another peal of laughter would permeate the dining room.

When they were finally able to stop, Bekah slipped back to her bedroom to change while Abbot tried to make some order out of the mess he'd made. Unable to get all the stains out of his jacket and shirt, he turned his attention to the dining room floor. Unfortunately, the carpet stain simply wouldn't come out, no matter how much cold water he threw at it.

Returning to the living room dressed in aquamarine sweat pants and a cream-colored t-shirt, she found him down on his knees, scrubbing under the table.

"I'm sorry," he apologized. "But you're going to have to add some splashes of lavender to your decor, buy a replacement carpet piece, or put a big rug over it."

"It's okay," she said. "Really, just leave it."

"It's not in my nature to leave things undone," Abbot responded. "At least, not anymore," he amended.

"I've learned that. But Abbot, don't worry. I'm sure I'll think of something."

He crawled out from under the table. "All right."

"Come sit with me on the sofa," she suggested.

Abbot hesitated. "No, thanks anyway. Dinner was wonderful, what we were able to eat of it, but I've made enough mistakes for one night, don't you think?"

Bekah smiled and walked directly over to him where she wrapped her arms around his waist and snuggled up against his chest.

"Bekah, you'll ruin your t-shirt," he warned. Although he'd removed the jacket, he still had damp grape juice on his shirt and cummerbund.

"Shhh," she whispered. "I don't care about the grape juice and

I'm not going to seduce you. Just hold me for a minute, okay?"

Abbot timidly put his arms around her, fulfilling her request. They stood in the quiet of her dining room for several minutes, just holding one another, until she was comforted enough to release him.

She tilted her head back and said, "Just one kiss, kind sir, before you go."

Smiling, Abbot complied with her wishes, but he also made certain it was a kiss that wouldn't make him ache for her all the way back to *Bridger's Child.*

❧ ❧

On Sunday, Bekah hummed a little tune as she contemplated her date with Barry scheduled for later that day. This would be their last one, she vowed merrily, as she brushed her teeth. In times past, whenever she had to tell a man that she wasn't interested, it came at a personal sacrifice. She always worried if she was doing the right thing, making the correct choice. Would she regret it later? Today, however, she didn't feel those concerns in her heart for two definitive reasons: She had decided even before she met Abbot that Barry could not be the man she was looking for because of his erroneous belief system. She felt in her heart that Abbot may be the right man for her.

This final date with Barry was also one in which she had nothing to wear. Barry had said the charity affair was formal attire. Unless she wore the aquamarine backless gown that Abbot didn't want her to wear, she would have to go in a skirt and blouse. The corporate attorney would never approve of that.

Finding a dress shop open that carried formal wear during the middle of the week, or even Saturday, would not have been a problem. But this was Sunday and, contrary to popular belief, Seattle was not as modernized as some might think. After several telephone calls, she'd come up empty-handed.

Although she'd tried on several formals belonging to her sister-in-law, Gail, none of them fit her right and all three were almost as immodest as her backless gown. A moral dilemma assailed her. If Abbot hadn't spilled the grape juice, she could wear the cream-colored gown, but now that was impossible.

She thought about calling Barry to cancel, but she had no logical reason that he would believe to back her up; he could recognize a lie and point it out to her with no qualms whatsoever.

With a weary sigh, she decided the only thing she could do was to wear the backless dress today, and donate it to the Salvation Army, tomorrow. Although she hadn't told Abbot that she would never wear it again, in her heart she felt that God would know and this would betray Abbot's confidence in her. Still, she loved the fabric and color of the gown. Admitting that it was, perhaps, a little too risque, she wondered if it would be possible to alter it somehow.

Then an idea occurred to her. She rinsed her mouth, blotted it dry with a towel, and located the floor-length aquamarine slip that matched the gown. Assessing her options carefully, she decided that a black slip would serve the same purpose, while the aquamarine slip could be cut and fit as a loosely-draped insert across the back. It took a bit of scrambling and some help from Gail to make it all work, but by the time they were done, she couldn't tell the gown from an original design.

With only a few minutes to spare, Bekah dashed back upstairs and finished getting ready for Barry, thankful she'd taken the extra time to please Abbot, though he would likely never know about it.

She was still struggling with the side zipper when the front doorbell rang. She pressed the door release to buzz Barry through, then managed to get the zipper up before he rang the condo bell.

Peeking through the peep hole, she saw that Barry had a wrist corsage in his hands as he waited for her to open the door. For a moment she wanted to run back to her bedroom and refuse to answer. But, this was their last date and if she could make that clear enough to him today, she would never have to go through this again.

Over the years Bekah had learned how to discourage men, or encourage them as necessary. *Barry will be no different!* she determined with a fierceness that startled her.

"Hi, Barry," she said sweetly as she opened the door.

"Nice dress," he smiled back at her, his straight white teeth flashing.

"Thank you." She took the box he offered and opened it. "Red roses," she murmured. Dismayed that he'd not bothered to find out what she was wearing, so he could match her dress with his flowers, she thought wryly, *How original!* "Thank you," she said, slipping the flowered band over her wrist as she forced herself to remain unconcerned.

"How long do you think we'll be?" she asked, picking up her cloak from the sofa.

"I doubt you'll need that," he said without answering her question. "The weather forecast was for warm, sunny skies."

"You're probably right." *Why does he make me feel like a juvenile?* she wondered as she left her cloak and tucked the key to her condo into a small folded handbag. "I'm ready."

"Always on time, too," he noted. "You're in good humor today."

Bekah's lips curled at the corners mischievously, and she realized the expression wasn't wasted on him when his eyes almost danced in surprise. *Until you take me home, dear Barry.*

On her best behavior, Bekah enjoyed the evening as she rubbed shoulders with the wealthy socialites who frequented Sand Point Country Club. A sumptuous buffet that guests could dine from all afternoon and evening, graced two long tables under pavilions, with every gastronomic delight known to man: ice sculptures; hors d'oeuvres and salads of every variety; smoked salmon and cod; cream and tomato based shellfish soups; several different cracker assortments; vegetable and cheese trays; shrimp and crab; a dozen different bread variations; and free-flowing wine and champagne served by men in black pants, white shirts and forest-green cummerbunds who carried trays of the beverages on one hand and a shoulder.

The auction didn't begin until almost six, and by that time Bekah had been introduced to no less than a thousand guests, Barry knowing most of them on a first name basis. His repertoire of acquaintances seemed to know no bounds. He was the perfect gentleman throughout the evening and she did her best to keep up a pleasant facade, complementing his style with a graciousness that seemed to flatter him. Proceeds were to benefit the new children's hospital being built in Seattle and the items for the auction were priceless pieces of artwork donated by members of the country club and other elite benefactors throughout the city.

Bekah was quite pleased to learn how the upper class lived, and of their generous beneficence. Although there was a 'stuffed shirt' or two, most of the people she met were genuinely thrilled to participate in raising funds for such a worthy cause.

By the time they got in the car to go home, Bekah's cheeks hurt from maintaining a perpetual smile for almost five hours. Since it was after nine, she worried that Abbot had telephoned and not found her home.

The sun had already set behind the Olympic mountain range and stars were beginning to give forth their light. A sliver of the moon could be seen in the eastern sky and the evening was warm and humid.

"You surprise me," Barry said huskily as he parked his gold Lexus in front of her condo and turned to face her. "I've never seen you quite so charming before."

"I've made a special effort just for you," she said sweetly, "because

I wanted our last date to be a memorable one."

"Our last date?" he asked, the surprise evident in his voice. "Why?"

"It's not your fault, Barry," she explained. "You're a good man. The problem is all me. I have expectations that are rather difficult to meet."

"What were you expecting" he asked, almost sardonically she thought.

Inhaling with the relief her next words would bring, she couldn't hold back the moisture in her eyes as she whispered, "Someone who knows God and speaks to him like a son would speak to his caring father." Until that very moment, she didn't realize just how good those few words would make her feel.

Barry laughed scornfully. "Have it your way, Bekah. But, when you fail to find this rare commodity, call me . . . if I'm still available."

"I think I already have," she confessed.

His eyes darkened and a muscle along his jaw twitched. *Oops! Perhaps that would have been better left unsaid.* Forcing herself to remain calm, she allowed only a quiet, serene demeanor to surface.

He parked the Lexus in front of her condo and asked, "Do I know him?"

"No." Her fingers sought for the handle, but before she could open the car door, Barry left the driver's seat, came around to her side and was holding out his hand to help her out of the Lexus.

She stood up, prepared to take his arm and be escorted to the condo entry, but he placed both hands against the roof, pinning her between them. Watching his face warily, she wondered if Barry might be the one man who wouldn't give up without a fight. After all, that's what he did for a living.

"May I kiss you goodbye?" he asked after studying her dark eyes almost as cautiously as she had studied him.

His politeness threw her off guard. It was a move she hadn't expected. Before she had time to consider the question thoroughly, Barry pulled her towards him and placed his lips against hers. His arms went around her back, pressing her close to him as his lips hungrily sought hers, as though he wanted to compel her to respond. Closing her eyes, stiffening, keeping her arms rigidly at her sides, she forced her mind to focus on something other than Barry's kiss: The sounds of the evening, the crickets chirping, an approaching car, the squealing of tires on pavement, the smell of burned rubber and exhaust fumes; anything but what Barry was trying, unsuccessfully, to do to her emotions.

Knowing she could never love a man who didn't believe in God gave her courage and helped her get through that moment of sheer torture. When he was thoroughly finished kissing her, he withdrew and blew out a ragged breath.

Then, as though he finally realized he had stirred nothing emotional within her by his passionate embrace, he grabbed her arm and yanked her away from the car.

His fingers gripped her tightly and she winced. "Barry! You're hurting me!"

In response to her complaint, he tightened his grip and nearly dragged her to the condo's front door.

"Goodbye!" he snapped, his voice grating against her fragile nerves. Then he turned, stomped back to the Lexus and drove away.

Chapter Six

$\mathcal{S}$quealing his Bronco down the street past Bekah's condo, Abbot turned the corner onto Kenwood Place and skidded the four-wheel drive over to East Green Lake Way, then headed south through Wallingford.

His hands trembled as he strived to gain control of his emotions. Bekah had told him she'd be home by eight and when he finally finished a lengthy discussion with his bishop, it was after nine. It hadn't occurred to him that she would return to the condo as late as she had, or he wouldn't have driven by after his meeting with Bishop Jackson.

Abbot's only plan was to see if the lights were on in Bekah's condo. If not, he would assume it was too late to call her and she was in bed. If so, he planned to call her from his cell phone and see if she still wanted to take that stroll around Green Lake. Certainly, his intentions had not been to spy on her, or find her in another man's arms.

Nor had he imagined that she would ever wear the aquamarine, backless evening gown, the same one that plunged daringly past her waist in the back. He'd made his discomfort about that dress more than clear to her. Although she hadn't said she would never wear the dress again, Abbot felt betrayed. Recalling their conversation from the night before, she'd told him she had only worn the dress to 'wow' him. It had apparently had its devastating affect on someone else, tonight.

The thought of another man caressing her bare back while kissing her passionately, left a bitter taste in his mouth and an ache inside his chest.

Fortunately, he'd had the presence of mind not to hang around and see her final reaction to the man's kiss. *At least it wasn't my brother this time!* Thoughts of Alyssa kissing Ed in Mountain Meadow last summer swept through his mind, leaving in its wake a quaking terror inside him. Why would Bekah let another man kiss her when she and Abbot had grown so close the past ten days? *Why?*

He wasn't certain she'd welcomed the kiss because she hadn't put her arms around the man; they'd remained at her sides, as though she'd not cared one way or the other that he was kissing her. But, why allow the kiss at all?

If he'd seen her struggle, or push the man away, Abbot would have stopped and helped her. But she hadn't struggled. She'd remained still and straight.

Confused and bewildered, Abbot drove the Bronco back to the parking lot near Gove's Cove on West Lake Avenue and parked it. Knowing he should call Bekah, he just couldn't bring himself to do it. He was afraid that if he did phone her, he would cancel the trip to the Hoh river and for Cody's sake, that was something he couldn't do, either.

When he stepped up onto the deck of *Bridger's Child*, he slipped off his shoes and climbed down the companionway. Tom and Hans had loaded the cockpit with newly purchased camping gear and were sitting in the salon swapping cattle drive tales while Tom polished his revered cowboy boots.

"How did it go?" Hans questioned.

"Don't ask," said Abbot. He frowned and bit his lower lip until it hurt.

"Yer bishop's interview went poorly?" This from Tom as he put a gleaming boot down on the cabin sole and picked up the other boot to polish it.

Abbot's ears heard the question, but his mind only picked up the word, bishop. "Bishop Jackson seemed like a pleasing man."

"Then what shouldn't we ask about?" queried Hans.

"Bekah," sighed Abbot as he sank down upon the settee, moving a bag of tent poles out of the way, and rested his elbows on his knees, his head in his hands, feeling nauseous.

"Oh, no!" exclaimed Hans. "Not again."

"I thought everythin' was going good fer the two of you," said Tom. "After the dress thing last night and the romantic dinner party."

"I drove by her condo before coming home," Abbot confessed.

Hans arched an eyebrow as if to ask why, but he didn't voice his concern.

Tom's tactfulness didn't prevent him from expressing his opinion. "Didn't we talk about this?" he barked. "Why in blazes do you ask my advice, then ignore it? I told you she probably had another date! You ain't got the good sense God give a jack rabbit!" When he had finished ranting, Tom added curiously, "What happened?"

Abbot ran his fingers through his hair and groaned. "She was standing beside a car wearing that backless dress and some man was kissing her. From what I saw, his hands were just as busy as his lips. I didn't wait around to see how she liked it."

Tom gave a low whistle. "Yep, another Sparkleman bites the dust. What is it with us brothers and women?" he asked. "The only one of us men to git hitched without a trial is Will. Guess the rest of us are just too dang cantankerous!"

"You know," said Hans, "my role as cupid ended when Ed and

Alyssa married. I've done my tour of duty in that regard."

"And I ain't playing cupid fer nobody!" Tom growled. "I gave you my best advice and you didn't listen. Now yer on yer own!"

Abbot's cell phone rang and he pulled it out of his suit coat pocket and looked at the caller i.d. "It's Bekah."

"You gonna' answer it?" Tom asked.

Nodding, Abbot pressed a button and said, "Hello."

"Abbot, it's me."

Regardless how irritated he was with her actions, he couldn't bring himself to be rude to her. He cared too much about her to do that. Unlike his reaction to Alyssa kissing Ed, Abbot wasn't willing to walk away and never look back. "Hi," he said, though he knew his voice sounded somewhat brittle.

"I thought you were going to call me," she reminded.

"Sorry, I guess I got sidetracked."

"Is everything all right?" Bekah questioned.

"Sure. Why?"

"You sound upset."

"I'm not feeling well."

"I'm sorry. Is there anything I can do?"

"No."

"Are we still meeting at Royal Brougham and Alaska Way at eight in the morning ?"

"Sure," he agreed. "That's about the only way we can get on the same ferry."

"Okay. I'll see you then."

"Sure. Bye."

When he replaced the receiver, he didn't know whether to be relieved they were still going, or disappointed. How was he going to spend the week with Bekah and her family without his emotions completely unraveling?

All other images of the past ten days they'd spent together had been erased from his memory bank by that one startling image he had of her now. *She was kissing another man while wearing that revealing, backless dress!*

ᷧ ᷧ

By eight-ten in the morning, Abbot was a nervous wreck. He hadn't slept most of the night and now he was just plain irritable. Hans and Tom were both careful in what they said, or did, for fear he'd snap at them.

They were parked under the highway overpass along the waterfront, waiting for Ryan's motor home to pull up, but so far the twenty-four foot class C Jamboree Rally had not arrived. Hans was watching Abbot pace back and forth, while Tom was snoozing in the back seat.

The roaring of cars overhead echoed around him and the taste of the salty air lingered on his lips regardless how often Abbot licked them. An impenetrable fog had settled in overnight and visibility was less than a hundred yards. *What a morning to leave!* he thought to himself.

Hans stepped out of the Bronco. "Why don't you call them?" he asked. "Doesn't Bekah have a cell phone?"

Abbot pulled his phone from his jacket pocket and handed it to Hans. "Go ahead," he suggested. "Just hit redial."

"You already tried?" he asked.

"No." Abbot glared at him. "But I almost did!"

Hans shrugged and pressed the redial button. After a few minutes, Hans said, "There's no answer."

"Where are they?" Abbot asked.

A honk answered the question before Hans could as out of the dense fog came a tan-colored Jamboree. Abbot waved as Ryan pulled the motor home ahead of them. Then, he hopped back up in the Bronco, as did Hans, and they followed the motor home onto Alaska Way, toward the ferry terminal. Westbound ferry traffic during the week was usually not too busy and they arrived just in time to be directed onto the 8:20 A.M. ferry.

The clanking of the dock guard as they drove over it and onto the ferry always gave Abbot a little shiver. It was a disconcerting thought to realize that one thin metal plank was all that separated his Bronco from the icy-cold water of Puget Sound. A woman with an orange vest directed them to the left and up to the second floor parking area, while the motor home was directed to the first level in the center, where taller rigs were parked. When he had set the brakes and locked the Bronco, he, Tom and Hans joined Bekah and her brother's family upstairs on the passenger level.

Cody ran straight for Abbot the moment he saw him. "Abbot!" he yelled, jumping into Abbot's open arms.

"How's my buddy?" Abbot asked, hugging him fiercely.

"I'm doing great!" exclaimed Cody.

Although the child still had two black eyes, the bruises were fading to a brownish yellow and would probably be completely gone by the end of the week. Cody's red hair contrasted as it stuck out from beneath a blue baseball and his bright eyes were more azure than Abbot remembered.

Introductions were quickly made and then they went outside on the forward deck to wait for the ferry to move ahead. After a brief intercom announcement regarding the safety of passengers, a whistle blew and the ferry started forward with a gentle, smooth motion.

Abbot made no effort to stand next to Bekah or resume the casual, comfortable relationship they had enjoyed before Sunday night. Until he could decipher her motives for last night, which was all he could picture in his mind when he looked at her, he had decided a little distancing may be best for both of them.

Hans took the edge off the awkwardness of the situation by asking Bekah to give him a tour of the ferry, directing her attention to other areas of interest.

Cody took Abbot by the hand and made it known immediately that Abbot and he would be joined at the hip for the duration of their expedition.

Seagulls cawed overhead as they spread their wings and rode on the forward airfoil which the ferry created in its momentum across Puget Sound. The water was flat and calm, like deep-green, polished glass. Thick fog built up a fine sheen of water vapor on their faces and it was cold enough to feel like they would soon freeze if they didn't dry them off.

Abbot removed a clean handkerchief from his pocket and wiped Cody's face with it. "There, does that help?"

Through chattering teeth, Cody stammered. "Ye—yes."

Tom stood beside Cody while Ryan and Gail went indoors, following Hans' and Bekah's example. It was simply too cold to remain outdoors, but Cody wasn't budging.

Using his hat to keep some of the wind off his face, Tom remained steadfast with them. After a little while Cody tugged on Tom's shirt sleeve. "Can I ask you something?"

"Yep," Tom drawled. He squatted down until he was eye level with young Cody.

"Are you a real cowboy?" asked the precocious child.

"Yep."

"You got a real gun?"

"Yep."

"How about a horse?"

"Yep."

Cody was thoughtful for a moment. Then he asked, "Do you like it?"

"Best time of my life is sittin' in a saddle ridin' across Porcupine Ridge up at the Bar M Ranch."

"Where's that?" He wrinkled his nose as though he was trying to see around what little swelling remained there.

"That's where Abbot and I grew up. High in the Uinta mountain range, the Bar M Ranch's got Black Angus beef cattle grazin' in the meadows in the summer and a couple of corrals nearby for roundin' up calves. It's got ranch hands lassoin' and brandin' steers and a campfire going all day and most of the night to chase away mosquiters. There's an old ranch hand named Marcus who makes the best dang pancakes this side of heaven."

Cody's azure blue eyes widened with each new tidbit of information Tom gave him. With a captive audience, Tom wasn't going to back down now. Abbot had to smile at Tom's eagerness to tell tall tales to the young boy. He'd never seen Tom take such an interest in a child before and it pleased him somehow, knowing what Tom had been through and how far he'd come on his journey back.

"Really?" Cody wondered in a breathless, awestruck tone.

"Yep. And there's an old moo-cow called Bess that gets milked every mornin' and every night. And there's a big garden with fresh peas in the spring and mouth-waterin' tomatoes in the fall. And there's black bears around with their bear-cubs, so you have to be real careful."

"Real bears?" asked Cody. "Did you ever see one?"

"Seen plenty," said Tom. "But Hans seen one up real close one time. A big old mama bear who thought he was gonna' bother her cubs, and she got real ornery with him."

Abbot cleared his throat, hoping Tom would change the subject.

Tom nodded almost imperceptibly and Abbot realized Tom was well aware of what he was doing. Tilting his Stetson back off his forehead, Tom stared into Cody's deep blue eyes and said, "But, the best thing about the Bar M Ranch is that our family still lives there. And whenever we go back to Utah, we can always go to the Bar M Ranch and call it home."

Someone slipped a hand into Abbot's unexpectedly and he almost cringed. He knew who it was without even looking, so he tried his best to keep his attention focused on Tom and Cody.

"Abbot and me, we got two other brothers," Tom drawled. "Did you know that?"

"No," said Cody. "Who are they?"

"Our oldest brother is Ed. He's the foreman at the Bar M Ranch. . . ."

Bekah tugged on Abbot's hand, turning her toward him so that he had no choice but to look down at her. "Hi," she said, giving him a bright smile. "Remember me."

Abbot nodded, but he didn't dare say anything to her for fear he wouldn't be able to keep his emotions under control. *I love her too much to risk saying something that would drive us further apart than we are!* When he realized what thoughts were tumbling around in his head and his heart, he was astounded. Searching deep inside, he pulled the pieces of his heart back together and tried to hold them in place while the cementing power of his love set up, praying every instant that she would not break his heart. As he looked down at her lovely brown eyes he knew that whatever reasons she may have had for wearing the dress, whatever motivated her to kiss another man, he loved her anyway. Somehow, he would have to find a way to understand her actions. If he could do that and come to terms with it, he might be able to forgive her.

"Are you speaking to me today?" she asked, breaking into his thoughts.

"Sure I am."

She squeezed his hand and his heart started racing. *Oh, boy! I am in trouble this time!* he thought as he realized that just having her fingers entwined with his made his head swim. How could she do this to him and to someone else, in less than twelve hours? His memory of seeing her with the other man flashed in front of his eyes, along with a big, red, imaginary banner that read: Danger! Danger! Danger!

Abbot pulled his hand free and walked away from her before he was unable to control the feelings pounding inside him. Without saying another word, he left Tom, Cody and Bekah standing on the forward deck as he sought the safety of the Bronco one level down. Climbing inside, he yanked the door shut and found that he was shaking. A few minutes later Hans was at the passenger side, joining him.

His throat felt like it was closing off and he was having difficulty breathing. Could he go through losing another woman? How could he have fallen in love with someone who wasn't willing to make him the only man in her life . . . for the second time? He folded his hands in front of him and bowed his head.

Hans whispered, "Would you rather be alone?"

"No," Abbot rasped. "I think I need a blessing."

"I can't help you there," said Hans. "I'm only a priest."

"What?" Abbot asked. "You joined the church?"

"Last January," Hans confessed.

"I thought you were just being polite when you went to church with us yesterday." He was astounded.

"No, I was showing the Lord whose side I'm on." Hans gave him a weak smile.

"Why didn't you tell me sooner?" Abbot asked.

"If you'll recall, last time we were together you were blaming God and the church for every calamity that had befallen you. I was waiting to see how you felt about the church you once despised, before I told you."

"I was wrong," Abbot admitted. "About everything. About the church, about God, about Alyssa, even about you, it seems. I thought you were the last man on earth who would ever join us."

Hans smiled. "You say 'us' as though you finally belong."

"You remember the things I said on your boat more than a year ago?" Abbot asked.

"Of course," Hans responded.

"Well, I was wrong. God is a kind and wise Father. In the past few weeks he's shown me nothing but compassion and love. He was there for me all along, but I was past feeling. I hope you can forgive me for all the things I said in the past, Hans. I was tortured by my father's untimely death and ended up blaming God for everything."

"Forgiveness seems to come easy for me," Hans said. "But if you need a blessing, I'm sure we can find someone who can give you one."

"Can Tom?" Abbot asked. "I'm always worried about asking him anything personal. I know he wasn't excommunicated because his was a crime committed under the influence and it's been two and a half years, but what is his status in the church? Do you know?"

"No. I didn't think it was right to question him."

The intercom interrupted them, advising passengers to return to their vehicles because the ferry was landing at Bainbridge Island.

Hans shook his head. "Maybe we should mention that you aren't feeling well and that you'd like a blessing. He'll either volunteer or suggest we find someone. That'll at least give us a clue and will remedy your need either way."

Abbot nodded. "I blew it up there," he said. "Bekah wanted to hold my hand. I pulled free and walked away. What must she be thinking?"

"Tom told her you weren't feeling well, so she came to me and asked that I come check on you," Hans confessed.

"I'm not sick," Abbot admitted. "At least not physically."

"I've seen what happens to the men in your family when they're lovesick," Hans confided. "You've got it as bad as Ed did last summer."

"Then, it's a good thing he married Alyssa," said Abbot. "Because this feeling is the worst I've ever had."

"For all of us," Hans teased.

When they saw Tom approaching, Hans said, "Trade me places. It'll be safer if I drive today."

By the time Hans drove the Bronco off the ferry, across Bainbridge Island and over the Agate Pass bridge, the traffic had thinned out enough that the two vehicles could maneuver to the side of the road and park. Scotch Broom, with its tiny yellow blossoms, grew profusely along the roadway, along with green blackberries, huge pine trees intermingled with lots of alder.

The minute Hans parked the Bronco, Bekah stepped from the motor home and came over to the passenger side door. Abbot rolled the window down and looked at her with a rather forlorn smile.

"You are a little pale," said Bekah as she stared into his green eyes. She put her hand against his cheek and then his forehead, "But you're cold and clammy. Did you pick up a flu bug?"

"I don't know," he said weakly as his heart kicked into a fierce pounding sensation inside his chest.

"Why don't you go on ahead?" Hans suggested. "We're going to stop in Poulsbo for a bit, see if we can get some assistance for him."

"Do you think you can find a doctor on such short notice?" she asked. "Wouldn't it be better to go back to your own doctor in Seattle? We can do the expedition another time."

"I'm not going to disappoint Cody," said Abbot with conviction.

"We'll meet you up at the Hoh Rain Forest campground this evening, Bekah. I should be feeling better by then."

"Do you want me to ride with you?"

Abbot shook his head. "No."

"You'll find us cowpokes like to do our suffering in private." Tom offered, giving Bekah a tip of his hat.

But she wouldn't back down. "Then you two tagging along may not be too good for him. Why don't you both ride in the motor home and I'll drive the Bronco."

"No!" Abbot growled. "Just go, Bekah! We'll see you up there tonight."

Stepping backward, her eyes widened and her lower lip trembled. Abbot's heart lurched. More tenderly, he said, "Bekah, I'm sorry. I didn't mean to yell at you. Please, let us deal with the problem I'm having and we'll see you up there tonight."

She looked at him curiously for a moment, as if she were trying to understand. Then, she returned to the window where she placed her hand against his cheek. "All right," she finally agreed. "But I don't like it one bit!" Pivoting around, she left the Bronco and hurried back to the motor home.

After it pulled away, all three men exhaled in frustration.

"You sure do like to put yer women to the test, don't you?" asked Tom from the back seat.

"And your brother and your friend," suggested Hans.

They found a telephone booth at the Thriftway market in Poulsbo, where they stopped and looked up the nearest church to them. It was up on Northeast Mesford, which they learned was not far from where they were. After trying the phone number to no avail, they drove up to the red brick building hoping they would find someone there. A Toyota was in the parking lot so they went around to all the doors and knocked. After a long wait, an elderly gentleman came walking down the hall toward them.

He opened the door and asked, "May I help you?"

Abbot had never felt more desperate. "Is it possible to find someone who can give me a special blessing?" he asked.

The man's eyes opened wide. "So that's why I felt inspired to come in today."

"What?" Tom's mouth dropped open.

"I'm Bishop Parmally from Poulsbo Second Ward." He shook their hands vigorously and was introduced to each of them. Then, he led them down the hall to his office. As they walked along, the bishop explained, "This morning I was arriving at work when I had a feeling I was supposed to come over here. I've been kneeling in my office for quite a while." Pulling the door closed behind them, he indicated that they should sit down. "I had about decided to go back to work."

"Thank you for waiting for us," said Abbot. "And thank you for listening to the spirit."

"Would you like me to call someone to assist, or will one of you. . . ?

Since Tom had indicated in the Bronco that they should find someone to give Abbot his blessing, they were surprised when he said, "I can anoint, but I ain't ready to do the sealing yet. Not fer my own brother, anyhow."

Bishop Parmally beamed. "Yes, that's what I thought. I had a feeling that one of you could assist me." Directly to Hans he said, "Don't worry Brother Clark, it won't be much longer before you'll be able to do this."

"Thanks, Tom," Abbot said, giving him a smile he hoped his brother understood. He couldn't have been more proud.

"Now, then," said the bishop. "Is there a special reason for this blessing?"

"It's personal," said Abbot. "The Lord knows what's going on inside me, but I'd really rather not get into it."

The bishop stood. "Then, let's get on our knees first and ask the Lord to direct us. Brother Clark, would you offer the prayer for us?"

As the four men knelt around the bishop's desk, Hans cleared his throat, then hesitated for a few minutes before beginning: "Our Father who art in Heaven, Hallowed be thy name. As we, four of thy lowly sons, kneel before thee this day, we are thankful for the priesthood and for the opportunities it gives us to serve thee and promote thy gospel here upon the earth. We stand in need of thy guidance and thy inspiration, Father and recognize that these gifts cometh only from thee. Bless Bishop Parmally and Brother Tom Sparkleman as they participate in the holy ordinance of bestowing a special blessing this day, that they will be led by thee, that their words will be thy words and that all those things which Brother Abbot stands in need of will be granted unto him. These favors and blessings we ask, in the name of Jesus Christ. Amen."

When they stood, Abbot noticed there were tears in Tom's eyes and he couldn't help feeling compassion for his brother. The bishop opened a drawer, pulled out a vial of consecrated oil and handed it to Tom. As Tom took it, his hands were shaking. "I ain't never done this before," he whispered hoarsely.

It took a few moments to explain the procedure and with the Lord's assistance Tom was able to do the anointing.

Afterward, the bishop sealed the anointing and gave Abbot the blessing for which he stood in need: "Brother Abbot, you have come down a long and treacherous journey, yet your Father in Heaven has walked with you every step of the way, even when you did things that displeased Him. He has never left your side and has waited all day, every day, for you to come unto Him. Your earthly parents have watched over you, as well, and have been mindful of you. Indeed, you have a great ancestral stadium filled with people who love you and who are cheering for you as you have progressed in the gospel. They have wept for you when you've set your foot on another path. Always be mindful that your cheering section in Heaven is great, and you will know, if you remember your ancestors, that you have a divine mission to fulfill. Your earthly parents, who now live beyond the veil, have worried about you, Brother Abbot. Our ancestor angels weep for us because they love us. They are very near, yet we do not prepare ourselves sufficiently to realize it.

"Today your heart is troubled and the feelings which you are having are hard for you to bear. You have experienced something that troubles you greatly. But, the Lord would say, trust those you love the most, Brother Abbot, for this will bring you great happiness and joy, not only in this life, but in the next as well. Your life's mission is not yet complete and you will have many trials. Through them all, you will have the Lord's guidance, if you will seek Him diligently. Remember to fulfill the missions for which the Lord has sent you to the earth, regardless of the personal costs in terms of careers or appointments. If you forsake all and serve God, hidden treasures of great joy shall be yours. These blessings I seal upon you and any others the Lord sees fit to bestow upon you, in the name of Jesus Christ. Amen."

When Abbot stood and shook the bishop's hand, he noticed tears in the older man's eyes. Tom wiped quickly at his face with his hands, obviously hoping Abbot had not seen. Hans, who was filled with the spirit of the Lord, had a glow about him that Abbot had never noticed before.

"Thank you," Abbot said to all three of them. "Thank you."

By the time they headed west towards the coast, they were singing church hymns and feasting upon the spirit of the Lord, three brothers in the gospel, three brothers united in their hearts.

The fog had cleared and the sky was a clear azure-blue, the air humid and warm. Dense forests on both sides of the road seemed to close in and place them in a deep tunnel. When the forest moved into the background, leaving fields and houses in front of them, they realized they had reached Sequim, where they stopped across from the LDS meeting house at a restaurant for lunch. Afterward, they resumed their journey west past Port Angeles, then around Lake Crescent. Long before highway 101 curved south, they were in the Olympic National Forest, where Sitka spruce and towering Douglas fir shadowed the road and made their journey quite enjoyable.

After an hour of singing, their voices grew hoarse, and they ceased altogether. Abbot drove while his brother slept. He turned on the radio, but was unable to get anything except static. Humming *A Poor Wayfaring Man of Grief* because he couldn't remember all the words, Abbot thought about his blessings. One of the first considered was Hans, who had hummed with him for a while, but soon joined Tom in slumber. Kayla's brother-in-law was certainly one of the finest friends a man could ever have.

Tom had certainly surprised him, as well. Recalling those days after Pa died, when the bishop had his hands full just taking care of the Sparkleman and Clark clan, he remembered how repentant Tom had been. At the time, Abbot had been so blinded by anger about his father's death that he hadn't given Tom any support at all, during those first few months. Unfortunately, Tom had to spend a few weeks in jail and twenty-four months on probation. It would have gone a lot worse if Morning Sun hadn't refused to press charges. She even refused to identify Tom as her attacker. That held a lot of weight with the judge. Also, if Ed and the bishop hadn't pressed the judge to go lenient on Tom, due to his inebriation at the time of the crime, it could have been a lot worse for him. With Ed's empathy, encouragement and a lot of prayers, the high council brethren had decided it would serve no useful purpose to strip Tom of his church membership when Tom had been so drunk he couldn't even remember what he'd done and thought it had all been some horrible nightmare. The brethren felt that because Tom had sinned while under the influence, he had been incapable of rational thought or behavior. His church membership was not revoked, but he was disfellowshipped for a full year. During that time, Abbot learned that Tom had weekly interviews with the bishop, as well as monthly interviews with the stake president. Abbot was absent during a good share of Tom's repentance process, but his brothers, Ed and Will, usually brought Abbot up to date, if he inquired. Now the feelings he had for Tom filled him with joy and peace. They were both back on the path toward celestial goals.

Abbot considered the words of Bishop Parmally that morning. Twice the bishop had told him to trust the people he loved the most. When Abbot wondered if he was talking about Bekah, a feeling spread through him like none he'd ever had, and he knew that he should trust Bekah because he loved her more than he ever thought it was possible to love another human being.

He reflected for a moment on the differences in his feelings for Alyssa and Bekah. Smiling to himself, he realized he hadn't been in love with Alyssa at all. He'd been 'in lust' with her, but it couldn't have been love.

Whenever he was with Bekah, he wanted to be a better person. She had given him her trust and he didn't want to disappoint her. He loved her with all his heart and he would learn to trust her because the Lord said that he should.

If only he could get up enough courage to talk to her about last night and the man who had kissed her. But, if he told her that he saw her, what would she think? That he'd been spying? That he was stalking her? Although those were not the reasons why he'd driven past her condo, would he damage the fragile threads of trust between them if he told her? These were questions for which he had no answers.

Chapter Seven

ekah stepped quickly from the path and found a precarious route down the bank to the Hoh River. Having arrived around three in the afternoon, over an hour ago, she was worried about Abbot. After helping Ryan and Gail level out the motor home and put a roast with potatoes in the oven for dinner, she'd told them she needed to be alone for a while, suspecting they were just as glad to have some time without her, since she'd been moody ever since Abbot told her to go on ahead.

The Sitka spruce and towering red cedar trees, some of them centuries old, were covered in a thick, dense moss that hung in streamers from their ancient branches. Ferns, the size of bushel baskets, grew everywhere, and she found it difficult to pick her way through them to reach the river. Even the rocks at the water's edge were covered with moss, which was not unusual for an area that gets over twelve feet of rain annually.

The heavy scent of decaying wood and wet undergrowth assailed her nostrils and she found herself sneezing a couple of times in order to adjust to the musky smell. She could hear the gray jay birds chattering playfully. The woodpecker's rat-a-tat-tat-tat sounded clearly through the forest as it made a home in one of the trees nearby. A black-tailed deer, feeding at the water's edge, sprang away the moment it heard her coming, with a sure-footedness Bekah certainly didn't feel.

The glacier-fed Hoh River, with its caramel-colored water, rich with minerals, lapped near her feet and she sat down upon a mossy boulder and watched as though mesmerized by the swirling eddies. The color of the water was unusual; white water her brother had said. Although she could understand why it was called that, because of the glacier melt that filled it, she could see that it wasn't white at all, more like a buttery caramel.

Her heart was heavy as she contemplated what was wrong with Abbot. He'd been cold and unreachable and she wondered if he was really ill, or just plain tired of her. After all, she'd practically forced herself on him from the very beginning. When he'd barked at her earlier that morning, saying he wanted her to go ahead without him, he'd hurt her deeply. His actions were difficult to accept because she cared so much about him.

She'd thought Abbot was feeling the same way about her. But, when she recalled their relationship, she realized that she had been the forward party, not him. Yes, he'd responded willingly enough whenever she kissed him, but he wouldn't allow himself to be alone with her for very long and that annoyed her. What did he think she was going to do to him? Had he left early Saturday night because he didn't want to spend time alone with her? Finally realizing she was more confused than hurt, she wondered if he might be feeling the same.

Perhaps she was pushing him too fast, too soon. Wondering if she should back off a little and give him some space, she shook her head because she simply did not know what to do where Abbot was concerned.

Laying on her side, she dipped her fingers into the swirling river water, surprised to discover that it wasn't as frigid as she had expected;

perhaps the minerals had something to do with that. Propping her head up with her hand, she loved the feel of the silky-cream water against her palm. Sitting upright, Bekah slipped off her tennis shoes and stockings, rolled up her pant legs and placed her feet in the cool liquid, enjoying the soothing affect it had on her temperament, as well.

How long she sat there she didn't know, for she was lost in thought about the man who meant so much to her, the man her grandmother had dreamed about, wondering in her heart if Abbot was one and the same. When she could see the glow of sunset filtering ever so faintly through the thick forest, she wondered why Abbot had not yet arrived.

Standing up in the stream, she turned around and found the man whom she loved, leaning against a tree, watching her. She was so startled, her foot slipped off the rock she was standing on and she fell over backwards in the Hoh River, clothes and all.

Abbot stepped over to her and helped her up, laughing as he said, "You just can't stay out of the water, can you, Bekah?"

"How long have you been there?" she asked, ignoring his question entirely. She wrung the edges of her shirt out and tried to squeeze some of the water from her pant legs.

"Maybe an hour." He shrugged and gave her an adoring smile.

"Why didn't you make your presence known sooner?" she demanded.

"I didn't want to disturb you, though I thought about it a few times. But it looked to me like you had a lot on your mind."

"I didn't even hear you come."

"My point, precisely."

She sat on a boulder and pulled her dry stockings over her wet feet, then put her shoes back on, lacing them up tightly.

"Are you feeling better?" she finally asked.

"Much," came his response. "I'm sorry I was a little out of it this morning. Will you forgive me?"

"You hurt my feelings," she confessed.

"I know," he said, taking her hand and helping her up to the path. "But, I can only say I'm sorry so many times before you either believe me or cast me off."

"Cast you off?" she asked, fear growing in her heart. "Is that what you're expecting me to do?"

"I wouldn't blame you." His voice was deep and husky. "I treated you poorly and if you can't forgive me, then I'll have no one to blame but myself."

She wrapped her arms around his waist, regardless of her wet clothing and ignoring the inner warnings that she shouldn't be too forward. "Oh, Abbot! I can forgive you easily if you can forgive me."

"Have you done something for which you need forgiveness?" he asked.

"I've been overly sensitive and I took offense when I shouldn't have."

"Oh," he nodded, but she sensed something in him that made her feel he was expecting more of a confession than she'd given. Then he said, "I forgive you for those two things and more."

"What more?" she wanted to know.

He waited before answering as his arms held her close to him and he gazed at her as though weighing his answer cautiously. Finally he said, "I trust you, Bekah, so let's just enjoy what we have going for us right now and build upon it, shall we?"

Leaning her head back, she hoped that he would kiss her, but he just looked deeply into her eyes as his green ones smoldered. She felt a tenseness in him that hadn't been present two days ago. When he released her, the disappointment she felt was painful, but he took her hand and walked with her along the path back toward the campsite.

Just before they arrived at the motor home, she asked, "You found a doctor, then? Is it a virus?"

He laughed. "I wasn't physically ill, Bekah. I needed a special blessing and I had to find someone who could give it to me."

"A special blessing?" she asked.

Abbot nodded. "I'm a member of the Church of Jesus Christ of Latter Day Saints. In our church, there are men who have authority to act in God's name. This authority is called the Melchizedek Priesthood. When someone needs a special blessing, they ask for a priesthood bearer to give them one. That's what I needed today."

"And you found a priesthood bearer to do that?"

"Yes," he answered. "I did."

"Would you share the blessing with me?"

He hesitated, as though searching his mind before responding to her question.

Why are you debating how to answer me? Why can't you share all your feelings with me, like you used to? Why can't we go back to comfortable and casual, Abbot? Her heart felt heavy inside her chest.

Finally he said, "I was told to trust those people whom I love most."

"And that helped you?" she was confused by what he'd told her.

"Yes," he responded. "It helped me more than I can say."

While Abbot went inside the tent, Bekah surveyed the changes made to the campsite. Hans and Tom had set up a four-man, spring-bar tent next to the motor home and they had lanterns strung across the airspace over the picnic table with a rope. A campfire was roaring hot. A pile of firewood, enough for several days, was stacked near the fire and covered with a heavy plastic tarp. Sitting logs were placed conveniently around the campfire to accommodate all of them. They'd made a hand-washing station with a gallon jug strung on a short rope between two branches, with a hand towel and a bar of soap-on-a-rope hanging next to it. A clothesline was set up at the far side of their campsite. Pots of burning citronella candles were placed in a row down the table center, which was also spread with a red and white checked vinyl tablecloth. Marshmallow roasting sticks had been whittled and a bag of marshmallows, chocolate candy bars and graham crackers sat in the middle of the table. Two burning candles were also placed not far from the front door of their tent. A utensil holder made with pockets and heavy canvas was stretched and tied between two branches nearest the fire, for easy access while cooking outdoors.

"My, aren't you boys the clever ones," she said with admiration.

"Tom's the one to praise," suggested Hans as he sauntered from the tent. Abbot followed him carrying a heavy blanket.

Bekah looked to Tom for an explanation while Abbot wrapped the blanket around her and sat beside her on one of the campfire logs. "Thanks," she said.

Tom gave her an ear-to-ear smile. "You may know how to teach sailing school," he said with a wink, "but when it comes to mountain country, Bekah, us good ole' boys should be able to return the favor."

"I'll bet you could," she grinned. "But where did you get the dry firewood?"

"Bought it over in that city we passed, the one named after silverware," said Tom.

"Forks," said Abbot.

When Bekah giggled, Tom explained, "I been wonderin' when we'd locate Knife and Spoon, but guess they ain't got no cities named like that."

"Why did you buy firewood?" Bekah asked Tom, changing the subject. "I thought you guys would gather your own."

"Abbot warned us that they don't call this a rain forest for nothin'," Tom replied.

"And what's that roasting in the coals by the fire?" she asked, observing several blackened aluminum packets and a dutch oven.

"Gail said she had a roast baking in the oven inside her motor home, so I put on a pot of sweet beans and some corn on the cob. It's just about ready, too." Tom tipped his hat to her, obviously pleased with himself.

Ryan, Cody and Gail came walking toward them as they returned from a hiking trail known as the Hall of Mosses. When Cody saw Abbot he ran straight for him and threw his arms around him. "Did you throw up yet?" he asked. "I always feel better after I do that."

Abbot gave him a quick hug. "No, but I feel a lot better now. I apologize for not being much fun on the ferry this morning."

"Aw, that's okay," Cody said as a wide grin wandered across his freckled face. "Aunt Bekah was the only one that minded. But, I finally told her that when a man is sick he just wants to be left alone. Isn't that right, Abbot?"

"Sometimes, buddy," agreed Abbot.

"Did you hear that, Aunt Bekah? Abbot called me buddy, just like you and Dad do."

She had to smile at her nephew. The precocious child had won more than her own affection. "Yes and I'm glad because you make a pretty good buddy for all of us." Tousling his hair she looked over at Gail. "How was your hike?"

"It was a beautiful trek!" she exclaimed. "You've got to see it sometime. The trees are covered more with moss than they are here and the branches bend over the trail like old friends, shaking hands. How is the roast coming?"

"I just got back," Bekah confessed, feeling a twinge of guilt.

"I'm sure it'll be fine," Gail insisted. "I put it on two-fifty so it would never burn. And beef roast is something that improves with time in a slow oven."

"Beans and corn are about ready if you ladies want to bring on the meat and potatoes," offered Tom.

"It doesn't take two of us to carry out one roasting pan," insisted Gail. "Let me get it."

Bekah wasn't about to leave Abbot . She gave Gail a silent *Thank you* with her lips.

Within a few minutes they were all seated at the table, ready to eat, when Abbot stopped them. "If you don't mind," he said, "since this is my expedition, I would like to ask your permission that we have a blessing on our food at every meal. Would that be all right with everyone?"

Ryan's eyebrows raised, but he nodded quickly and smiled at Bekah. After everyone else had bowed their heads he mouthed the words to her: *Is he the one from Grandmother's dream?*

Bekah gave her brother a secretive smile and bowed her head.

Abbot's voice came through rich and mellow on the early evening air as he offered a prayer for them. "Our Father in Heaven, we thank thee for this food which we are about to partake. Wilt thou bless it, that we might be strengthened and nourished? We thank thee for the Stevens family and for Tom and Hans . . . for their friendship. Wilt thou watch over them and protect them on this expedition? Our hearts are filled with gratefulness to thee for our many blessings and we recognize thy hand in all of them. If there are any among us who have needs for which we have not asked, wilt thou bless them according to the desires of their hearts, if it be thy will? These favors and blessings we ask in the name of Jesus Christ. Amen."

Everyone said a hearty, "Amen," in response, while Bekah sat dreamily looking across the table at Abbot. His words had touched her heart, as they had at the Medical Center the day Cody was injured. Hadn't Abbot said that he didn't pray very often? How could his prayers sound so natural and normal if he hadn't had a lot of practice?

Then she recalled what he'd told her on their way back to the motor home. He was a member of the Church of Jesus Christ of Latter-day Saints. Perhaps he'd learned to pray from the ministers in his church.

Inhaling deeply, Bekah felt warm and tingling sensations spreading through her as she basked in the beauty of Abbot's prayer. *Is he the one, Grandmother?* she asked. *Is Abbot the man from your dreams?* Although she could not hear it audibly, she felt her grandmother's voice inside her heart, giving her a resounding, "Yes."

The only problem with receiving such a startling revelation was that Bekah harbored a deep and abiding fear that she would not be able to win Abbot's heart. Sensing a hesitancy in him tonight, she wondered if he was expecting something more from her, or from himself.

Bekah was not naive in the ways a woman wins a man's affection, but with Abbot she hadn't had to play those silly mind games or use body language in even its simplest form. What they shared last week had been genuine and carefree. He was the only man with whom she'd ever felt completely comfortable. Why had he changed? What was keeping them apart? Would she have to lure him with flirtatious, meaningless gestures? No! Refusing to go back to the way she was before she met Abbot, she would have to find a way to help him recapture the feelings he'd had two days ago.

Her life now fell into two time slots: before Abbot . . . and after. The realization made her see how small and shallow her actions had once been. Before Abbot she'd dated dozens of men, teasing and enticing them like salmon to the hook, until she learned whether or not they could possibly be the man from Grandmother Lili's dream. Perhaps a few hearts had been bruised along the way, but never hers and never theirs for very long because she'd rarely given a man time to get that close. Her signature performance, always enacted during her last date with the men she had relinquished through the years, would have received rave reviews had Hollywood been aware of it. She always gave the men in her life one last, exceptionally special date, going to the extra effort to please them, wanting their final evening together to be memorable, perhaps even intoxicating. But, like the native chinook, when the evening drew to an end, she did exactly as she'd done with Barry, put them on her catch and release program. Until Abbot she hadn't found a man who could possibly meet the exact requirements embedded in Bekah's heart by Grandmother Lili.

After Abbot, there was no reason to entice or allure. In a moment of panic, she had asked him if he prayed, hoping beyond all hope that he would be the one for whom she had sought the past ten years. The words kindled by her grandmother had been ignited when he spoke with God like a son speaks to his father. After Abbot, Bekah felt at peace, as though she had been lost at sea and finally found the beacon of light that would lead her home. There had been no conscious effort on her part to win him over. No need to jig the bait or set the hook. With Abbot, she had no need to put on false provocations. Like the comfortable quilt wrapped around her, Abbot had given her warmth, endurance and purpose. There was nothing shallow or base about their relationship, no hidden messages or reasons to withhold from one another all their feelings, hopes and dreams. Until today.

Bekah looked across the table and watched as Abbot crunched into his corn with gusto. He and Tom were having a contest to see who could eat the kernals off the cob the fastest. Since the corn was scalding hot, they were both having a difficult time, while Cody, Hans and Ryan were laughing, and Gail was trying hard not to laugh.

Absorbed in her own feelings, Bekah had failed to notice that their race had even begun. Tucking her concerns in the deepest recesses of her heart for another time, she smiled and began cheering for Abbot to win. Abbot . . . her hero, her tyee, her chief.

❦ ❧

Abbot walked along the darkened road that led around the campsites at Hoh Rainforest, with a flashlight in one hand and Bekah's delicate hand in the other. Although it was nearly midnight, neither one of them had been able to sleep. Suggesting they go on this walk had been Bekah's idea, though he could have told her it may not have been the wisest. Quiet time in the campground began at ten-thirty. Now they could only whisper, if they talked at all.

A dank fog had rolled in off the coast. The mist was so thick, Abbot could see the puffy billows of moisture move around them as they walked through it. The dampness sank into their clothing and onto their faces, beading up quickly until it dripped in tiny rivulets off their chins. Inhaling deeply, he savored the salty wetness inside his lungs and enjoyed the cleansing effect that it had.

They walked the outside perimeter of the road, looking for the next campsite in the flashlight's beam as it tried to penetrate the moisture. If there had been stars out tonight, or a moon, they wouldn't have known it, for they couldn't even see the tops of the trees, or more than twenty feet ahead of them.

Bekah was silent for a long time, and Abbot certainly had nothing that he felt he could say that would ease the somber mood that had come over them. She'd been quiet and reflective through most of dinner, participating in conversation for only a few moments when he'd tried, unsuccessfully, to win against Tom in the corn-eating contest. Later she'd helped Tom and Gail clean up while he and Cody played glow-in-the-dark frisbee and Hans got a complete mechanical tour of Ryan's motor home.

The six adults and Cody roasted marshmallows after the dishes were done and it got too foggy and dark to see the frisbees, but Bekah hadn't eaten any dessert. She'd helped Cody make a campfire S'More with roasted marshmallow, chocolate and graham crackers, and giggled as she watched him drip melted chocolate down his chin. When Ryan, Gail and Cody retired for the night, she sat around the campfire and listened to Tom and Hans tell their interminable cattle drive stories. The only one that seemed to catch her attention was Hans' retelling of the time he was attacked by a black bear up at the Bar M Ranch. Otherwise, Bekah had been silent and contemplative all evening, and Abbot had noticed her watching, studying him when she thought he wasn't looking.

Little did she know that he was paying attention to her out of the corner of his eye, ever alert to her mood and her melancholy, for which he felt solely responsible. He sensed on more than one occasion, as they walked along, that she wanted him to kiss her. But, every time he thought he should, the picture of her kissing someone else the night before came floating into his mind and he couldn't suppress the image, though he tried fiercely.

Bishop Parmally had told him to trust those whom he loved most. There was no one in the entire world he loved more than Bekah. She was the one he was supposed to trust. And he was trying his best to trust her. Abbot just couldn't erase the images from his mind about where her lips had been last night while she was 'wowing' another man with her backless dress. Praying silently for understanding, he pleaded with the Lord to release him from the torment that seemed to be overpowering his ability to trust her.

They'd walked nearly the entire route before Bekah finally broke the silence. "Abbot, something has come between us," she whispered. "I don't know what it is and I want you to tell me."

Squeezing his eyes shut for a minute, Abbot stopped and moved his head back and forth, trying to release the tension in his neck. *I can't answer that! She's got to be willing to give it up, so I can trust her again.* When the thought struck him with such force he couldn't deny it any longer, he said, "I can only tell you that I want to trust you, Bekah."

"But you think that you can't?" she asked

He dropped her hand and lifted his arm up around her shoulder. "I want to," he insisted. "I really do."

"But you don't." Although it was too dark to see all the contours of her face, he knew that she was pouting, that her lower lip was trembling like it had earlier that day when he'd barked at her.

"I—" He stopped. Refusing to tell her that he'd seen her outside her condo, he feared that she would accuse him of spying on her, he sucked in a big breath, then blew it out slowly. "Bekah, for more than two years I spent my life cursing God because He took my father away from me before I was ready to say goodbye. During that entire time a scripture from Genesis 4:7 kept running through my mind, that says, '. . . and if thou doest not well, sin lieth at the door.' That scripture haunted me for months until I finally realized that all my problems I had brought upon myself by being disobedient to God. At the Medical Center that day when you asked me to pray with you, it was the first time I'd prayed in almost a year. I wanted to help Cody with all my heart, and I knew I had authority to do that. For the first time in years I felt the spirit of God upon me and I wanted to keep that feeling with me always, because of you. When I'm with you, I have this driving conviction that I want to be a better man than I am. I also have a feeling that I have more to do in this life than I've done so far. You make me want to do everything I can do to stand approved in God's eyes and in your own."

She sniffed and he realized she was crying.

Gently he pulled her against his chest, close to him and kissed her forehead to comfort her. "I'm sorry," he said, "I didn't mean to make you cry. I'm just trying to say that I hope you have similar feelings about me."

"I do," she confessed. "Truly I do, Abbot. I look back upon who I was before I met you and I don't like what I see. I want to be a better person because I've known you. I just don't know what I've done wrong that's upset you."

"Don't worry about that now," he whispered, as he put his hand on her cheek and felt the dampness upon them. Certain that it was her tears and not just the night's heavy mist, he wiped the moisture away with his fingertips and said, "No more tears, Bekah. Please, not tonight."

She nodded and leaned her head back, looking up at him in the dark. He didn't need cupid to tell him that she wanted him to kiss her, but as he leaned down to brush his lips against hers, the images he was trying to eradicate from his mind assailed him once again and he shuddered. As he did so, she stiffened in his arms and he knew that she had sensed his uneasiness.

Suddenly, Bekah pulled away. "Let's go back," she suggested, then she pivoted and started walking away from him.

"Bekah," Abbot moaned. "Don't go."

Turning back, she took his hand and tugged him along behind her as she walked quickly toward their camp. "I'm not leaving you," she insisted. "I'm taking you with me."

By the time they reached the camp, Abbot felt more miserable than he had before they left. He walked Bekah to the motor home door and told her goodnight, then waited outside until he heard her lock the door securely. Then, he went over to the tent and unzipped it, removed his shoes and carried them inside where he stepped carefully past Hans and Tom, then removed his pants and climbed into the sleeping bag.

When he'd turned off the flashlight he heard Tom's gruff voice ask him, "Well?"

Abbot sighed and decided that would be answer enough.

"Tarnation!" growled Tom.

"You didn't make any progress at all?" came Hans voice from the other side of the tent.

"Naw!" Tom answered for Abbot. "It's the Sparkleman curse. That's a fact!"

"It's nothing of the kind," said Abbot. "It's me. I just can't get those images out of my head, that's all."

"But you trust her?" questioned Hans.

"You gotta' trust her," insisted Tom, "otherwise you won't git all those blessings you was promised."

"I know," Abbot replied. "I know."

❧ ❧

Bekah climbed into bed after brushing her hair vigorously. Cody was asleep on a bed created in the space where the table had been, while Ryan and Gail were sleeping on the queen-size bed over the cab. Her bedroom was at the rear of the motor home, a three-quarter sized cubby-hole opposite the bathroom. She pulled the curtain around the perimeter for privacy then laid back against the pillows.

Abbot told her earlier in the day that he trusted her, but tonight he said he wanted to trust her. First he did, but now he was trying to trust her. His statements confused Bekah.

One thing was perfectly clear in her mind: he didn't want to kiss her. She'd felt him shudder and had hoped he had done so out of desire. But, when she realized it went deeper than that, she didn't know what to think. What had she done to make him react that way?

And why did he distrust her?

Searching through her memory banks, she couldn't think of anything she'd done since meeting Abbot that he didn't know about, with exception of her date with Barry.

Closing her eyes, she tried to remember if she'd told him why she couldn't see him Sunday afternoon. Had she mentioned that she had a date? Certain she had said only that she had a previous engagement, she began to realize that perhaps he had put one and one together and come up with two. It had to be the date with Barry.

Having prayed only a few times in her life and then as her parents had taught her, she remembered the few prayers she'd heard Abbot offer and decided it was time to see if God was listening. Scooting up on her knees, she bowed her head and folded her hands in her lap. "Heavenly Father," she began in a tiny whisper that no one could hear but herself, "Thank you for sending Abbot to me. Help me to know how to tell him about Barry without making our problems any worse than they are. I love him and I don't want to lose him over a man like Barry who doesn't even believe in you. Please God. I know I haven't paid much attention to you, but I've been waiting for the man from Grandma's dream to teach me how. I wanted to get it right. Please God, otherwise how can Grandma's vision come true? Everything else from her dream has come true: Ryan marrying Gail and having Cody; all my cousins and their spouses. I feel in my heart that Abbot is the man in Grandma's dream. How can we possibly get over what's holding us apart without your help? Please, God. In the name of Jesus Christ. Amen."

When she was finished she climbed back into bed and spent the better part of the night enacting different scenarios for telling Abbot about Barry, to see which one felt the best. Unfortunately, by morning she hadn't come up with anything. Either God hadn't answered her, or Bekah just wasn't listening.

Chapter Eight

Early Tuesday morning, Gail and Ryan had a delicious hobo breakfast ready, along with scrambled eggs, toast and juice. As Bekah opened her packet she found sausage and fried potatoes cooked together with some onion and green pepper. "Aren't you the clever ones?" she asked as she bit hungrily into the eggs. Realizing she hadn't eaten much last night, or most of yesterday for that matter, she felt starved and it didn't take long to eat most of it.

Abbot, Tom and Hans had already eaten and had an assembly line going on the other side of the table, making sandwiches, slipping them into small, plastic bags and stacking them up for further distribution. When they finally had all the sandwiches made, they put them in brown bags, along with oranges, apples, bags of potato chips and cookies. Everyone was given a backpack with two water bottles and their lunch. They made certain that everyone had a rain poncho, a whistle, a bear bell, a small first aid kit, dry stockings, mosquito repellent, sun block, a few candy bars, a compass, a fluorescent orange vest, some kind of hat and a walking stick.

Each person had been instructed to wear their clothing in layers and Bekah had complied by putting on shorts first, then a long pair of jeans, a t-shirt and a long-sleeved burgundy-colored blouse. The fluorescent orange vest clashed with her blouse, but it didn't mismatch as poorly as Tom's red-plaid flannel shirt, so she immediately dismissed her concerns.

When they were ready to go, Abbot asked them all to stand in a line for inspection. As he walked past each one he straightened their packs, if necessary and made a great show of being the leader of the expedition. Finally, he stopped in front of Cody and squatted down to eye level with him. In a deep, resonating voice he said, "Young man, are you the assistant expedition leader today?"

Cody couldn't suppress a giggle as he answered, "Yes, Indy, I am!"

"Then why are you wearing a baseball cap on an expedition?" Abbot asked with grave seriousness.

Cody's eyes widened and he removed the hat immediately. "But, you said we all had to wear hats," he complained. "This is the only one I have."

"Cowboy Tom," barked Abbot. "Did I or did I not order a new hat for my assistant?"

"Yep!" Tom grinned widely.

"Where is it?" demanded Abbot in a stern, yet playful tone.

Tom pulled a hand out from behind his back and held out a dark brown leather hat shaped exactly like the hat Indiana Jones wore. "Right here, Indy!" He handed it quickly to Abbot, then stepped back in line.

Resting the hat on Cody's red hair, Abbot said, "To avoid confusion and chaos during this expedition, I hereby place this hat on young Cody's head and name him Indiana Cody, partner and buddy to all of us. Therefore, the men and women in this company shall address me as Abbot and my assistant as Indy or Cody, or whatever happens to seem appropriate at the time."

Simultaneously, everyone said, "Yes, sir!"

Bekah couldn't suppress a wide smile as she watched Cody's reactions to Abbot's serious demeanor. A wide grin wandered across Cody's face from ear to ear and his eyes lit up like sparklers. The young boy would have memories built in his heart this week that would last him a lifetime.

"At ease," said Abbot.

Each member of the group relaxed a little in their stance, but still maintained their lineup. Continuing, Abbot said, "Every successful expedition has a plan and ours is no exception. We are about to spend four days searching for the cave of Chief Taquinna and it will be a hard and difficult journey. There are seven of us, so we should be able to cover a lot of territory each day."

As Abbot talked, he paced back and forth like a drill sergeant. The expression on Cody's face was worth the efforts he and the rest of them were going through for him. Bekah could easily see that Cody was taking the entire expedition with absolute trust and sincerity.

Continuing, Abbot instructed, "Since everyone has been given a rough map of the Hoh river, which begins at a glacier high in the Olympic mountains twenty-five miles east of here and empties into the Pacific ocean twenty-four miles west of here, we have a lot of ground to cover. In considering the probability that the Taquinna's totem pole was carried fifty miles up a mountain, I have concluded that this feat would have been highly unlikely. It is possible, however, that they could have carried it several miles up the mountainside, so my plan is this: we shall search each day going westerly, following the Hoh River until it empties into the Pacific. We have four days to cover twenty-five miles. That means we must cover six and a quarter miles every day. We will spread out, putting three of us on one side of the river and three on the other, with a distance between each person of fifty paces. Remember that caves are dangerous places, so if you find one, blow your whistle and wait until the rest of us join you before venturing into it."

"It's eight o'clock now. If we hike until one and stop for lunch, we should be able to hike another five hours after lunch. Since Ryan and Hans already took the Bronco over six miles down the road, we'll have transportation to get everyone back to camp by evening when we're too tired to walk the distance."

Abbot stopped pacing and studied each and every face in the group, then he stopped, resting his eyes on Cody. "Is everyone ready?"

A resounding, "Yes!" was the immediate response.

"Very well. Since this expedition is such an important one, we should begin it every day with a word of prayer. Tom, I believe it's your turn this morning."

Cody pouted and Abbot held up a finger before Tom could begin. "However, I think Cody may want to volunteer."

Bold blue eyes looked up at their leader as Cody said, "Sure!"

Abbot nodded, giving Cody permission to proceed. Everyone bowed their heads and folded their arms. Timidly, Cody said, "Will you help me?"

Abbot looked at Ryan, as though asking permission. Ryan said, "You do much better than I can. Go for it."

Lowering himself to his knees, Abbot put an arm around Cody and said, "Just repeat what I say."

Cody nodded. His voice lowered to a whisper as he suddenly became a little shy. But he persevered and as Abbot whispered in Cody's ear, the child repeated the words. His tender voice was sweet and innocent and touched them all as he said: "Heavenly Father. Thank you for all our blessings. Please bless us on this expedition. Give us safety and strength. In the name of Jesus Christ. Amen."

When they were finished, Cody looked into Abbot's eyes and said, "We didn't ask to find the cave."

"No," said Abbot, "because God knows the intents in our hearts already. When we pray to Him, He already understands the special blessings that we want. What we ask for is not nearly as important as letting God know we care about Him enough to include Him in our lives."

"Then how does He know when we haven't told Him?" Cody asked.

"God created all the earth, the trees and grass, the animals, fish and birds and He created us. We are His children. Do your parents always know what's best for you?"

Cody nodded and Bekah could see a moment of understanding between the boy and his special friend.

"God is our parent also. He looks inside our hearts to see what we are feeling and inside our minds to hear what we are thinking. Then He gives us only what He knows is best for us," Abbot explained.

"Okay!" exclaimed Cody. He looked heavenward and called out with a child's pure trust, "Heavenly Father! Can you see in my heart that I love you?"

Abbot gave him a quick hug as Bekah blinked back a few tears. She looked over at Ryan and saw that her brother was having difficulty keeping his emotions under control as well.

Then she noticed that Gail, unabashed, had tears streaming down her cheeks.

Ryan lifted his head and nodded toward Abbot. Bekah focused her attention back to him as he mouthed the words, *Is he the one?*

Happily, Bekah nodded her head and gave him a smile of relief that she had waited ten years to share with him.

❧   ❦

As they began their journey, they had to climb over boulders, wade through damp, decaying timber and side-step ferns almost as tall as

Cody. A thick, dense, green moss seemed to cover everything from the tree trunks and branches to the pebbles and stones. Their world for the next several hours was drenched in various shades of green. Occasionally, a glimpse of the red cedar bark or the Sitka spruce would show through the moss, but the majority of the forest was lathered with emeralds and greens in shades so numerous it was impossible to count them all.

Raucous jay birds made a screeching sound, as though warning them they were in violation of trespassing through their personal property.

Traveling downstream had been his best idea yet, Abbot decided, as he noticed the weariness on Bekah's and Gail's faces. The men were stronger and more likely to hide how tired they were. But, Cody's energy knew no boundaries. Skipping over larger rocks, turning flat rocks onto their backsides, lifting fallen branches, wiggling through narrow gaps between fallen logs and sharp boulders, balancing across nurse logs while trying not to step on the saplings they nursed, swinging from hanging vines, Cody's curiosity and energy never ceased. He had started a rock collection that already filled Abbot's, Tom's and Bekah's pockets and would have filled their backpacks if they hadn't insisted he only collect rocks that were unusually pretty, or especially unique. *If we could only bottle his energy and sell it, we'd all be rich!*

Smiling at Bekah in response to a timid smile she gave him, Abbot asked across the fifty foot gap separating them, "Does he ever slow down?"

"At bedtime," she replied. "And occasionally for an exciting video."

"Shhh," whispered Cody. "Look!" He pointed several hundred feet below them where a black-tailed deer was drinking from the Hoh River.

Abbot pulled out a camera from a bag attached to his waist and whispered, "Do you think you can be quiet enough to approach it?"

Cody nodded and started a silent quest. When he was just a few feet from the deer, Abbot started taking photographs. The deer looked up at Cody curiously and the boy took another step towards it. Suddenly, the deer bolted away, leaving a disappointed child behind it. "He's scared of me," the boy offered.

"You know," said Abbot, "Tom is the mountain man in our family. I've seen him walk right up to deer before, with an apple in his hand and feed it. Perhaps you'd like to have him teach you how."

"Really?" asked Cody. "Do you think he could?"

"If anyone can, it'll be Tom," Abbot suggested. "I was always too busy reading to learn all the camping and wildlife secrets that Tom learned growing up at the Bar M."

"Cool!" exclaimed Cody. "Can I go with him this afternoon."

"May I," Bekah suggested.

"You want to go with Tom, too?" asked Cody, misunderstanding her.

Abbot burst out laughing as he saw a blush of color in Bekah's cheeks.

"No, I meant that you should try to use correct English."

"Oh, yeah," said Cody. "May I go with Tom?"

"If you'd like to," Abbot answered. "Provided it's all right with your parents."

"They like Tom," Cody giggled as he confided, "But they like you best because of Dad's grandma. She had a dream about you."

"Cody!" Bekah admonished as she slipped her long-sleeved burgundy-colored shirt off and tied it around her waist with the sleeves. The pale lemon t-shirt she'd worn underneath it highlighted her auburn hair.

Flashing his blue eyes at her, alarmed at her reprimand, he apologized. "Ooh, sorry Aunt Bekah."

Abbot didn't pursue the topic at the moment, but he planned on asking Bekah later on. If her grandmother had a dream about him, he'd like to know more details.

Getting Cody off the hook, he bent over and lifted up the end of a stump that was laying on its side, covered in soft, velvety moss. "Look," he said to the boy. "How many snails can you count?"

Cody squatted down and started counting them as he touched each one with his fingertip. "One, two, three. . . ." By the time he'd finished, he announced, "Seven."

"Are you getting hungry?" Abbot asked.

He rubbed his stomach. "Starving to death! Can we eat now?"

Abbot smiled and tousled the boy's red hair. Then, he blew his whistle and waited for the others to gather around them. They had to wait a few minutes for Ryan, Gail and Hans, who were on the other side of the river. When they couldn't find an easy area to cross, they said they'd eat lunch where they were.

Ryan waved to Cody and asked, "How you doing, buddy?"

"Great! Dad, can I walk with Tom this afternoon? Abbot says he knows how to feed apples to deer. I'm going to ask him to teach me how."

"Sure," Ryan answered. "But don't make a nuisance of yourself, okay?"

"You always say that, but I never do," Cody responded.

Then the child turned and walked over to Tom, who was sitting on a fallen log next to Abbot and Bekah. "Is that okay with you, Tom?"

The cowboy lifted his Stetson and swept his dusty-blonde hair back with his long fingers. "Sure thing, Indy," he said as he put the hat back on his head. "You want to sit by me to eat yer lunch?"

"Yep!" Cody answered in a deep drawl, imitating Tom's husky voice.

Abbot couldn't prevent a laugh from escaping. "He's a precocious child," he said to Bekah, as he opened his lunch sack and pulled out a tuna fish sandwich smothered with dill pickles and lettuce. It was a little soggy, but it still tasted good to him.

Bekah waited to respond until she'd finished swallowing a bite of her sandwich. "We never know what to expect from Cody. At his school he's in the gifted student program. He has a keen memory and is able to mimic nearly every thing he hears."

Cody evidently had been listening to his aunt's praise, for he cupped his hands together and made a screeching sound like the gray jays they'd been listening to all morning.

"Pretty good, Indy," said Abbot.

"I can make all kinds of sounds," beamed Cody. "Do you want to hear?"

"You'd better eat your lunch first," Bekah suggested. "Otherwise, we'll have to wait on you before we can resume the expedition."

"Okay," he said, ripping open his paper bag. The apple fell out from the torn space and rolled down the hill. Cody jumped down to retrieve it, knocking the sack off his lap, but Tom grabbed it up before anything else rolled away.

Tom stood up. "I got an idea," he said in his deep voice. "We need to find you a table top where you won't have so much trouble." He looked around and spotted a flattened boulder about fifteen feet away. Walking over to it, he put the sack down on the flat space, tore the sack all the way open and spread it out like a place mat on top of the rock. "There you go, Indy. You can sit on the ground to eat yer lunch."

"Thanks," said Cody as he folded his legs and sat down quickly, placing the apple next to the orange on the brown paper. Tom sat beside him and began eating his own lunch, while Cody took his sandwich out of the plastic bag and started munching away at it. Before long, they were both involved in a conversation about apples and black-tailed deer.

Abbot finished his sandwich and started peeling an orange. As he did so, he noticed that Bekah had grown quiet and he looked at her curiously. If he could only decipher what was going on inside her mind, he might catch a glimpse of how she really felt about him.

Recalling their conversation at midnight as they'd walked around the campground, he wondered if she even had a clue why he was having a difficult time forcing himself to trust her.

Although he'd finally fallen into a restless sleep after retiring to the tent, he hadn't done so without seeing in his mind the image of Bekah leaning against the gold Lexus, a strange man pulling her close to him and kissing her soundly. As he'd done last night, Abbot tried to imagine why she hadn't put her arms around the man, why she'd left them rigidly at her sides. He rolled around ideas in his head as to why she'd not actually responded to the man's embrace. Had she not wanted it? Was she frightened, or was she just waiting for him to warm her up before she gave him any real encouragement?

Had she invited him into the condo afterward? The thought made him tremble inside and he forced his mind to push such images away. If only he understood her motivation. . . .

She wiped her lips on a napkin and left the rest of her lunch in the bag. Sipping on a water bottle, she swallowed several times, then pressed the seal down and put her lunch away. When she was done, she looked at him as though trying to debate how to talk to him.

"Just say it straight out, Bekah," he encouraged. "We shouldn't keep secrets from one another."

Her eyes widened in surprise. "I don't intend to," she answered. "I was just thinking that this would be a good time to talk to you about Barry."

"Oh?" he asked in a choked whisper. A lump seemed to grow in his throat as he realized the 'man' now had a name. Barry. He wondered if he really wanted to hear what she had to say. Perhaps he would regret hearing the truth.

"Before you and I met the day of Cody's accident, I had been dating Barry Lee Grady."

"The corporate attorney from Grady and York?" he questioned.

"You've heard of him?" she asked with surprise.

"His picture is plastered on billboards all around Seattle," Abbot explained. "I've never met him, but he has a great advertising campaign."

She shook her head. "Yes, I guess he does."

"Go on," Abbot encouraged.

"He invited me about a month earlier to attend the Sand Point Country Club's annual charity auction. It's a formal affair where expensive art pieces are auctioned off with the proceeds going to the children's hospital. At the time, I'd never even met you and I told him I would go with him. The auction was last Sunday, which is why I wasn't able to spend time with you that day."

"I see," he said, hoping she'd elaborate.

"Abbot, I don't want Barry to come between us. He means nothing to me, other than a man I dated a few times before I met you." Her dark brown eyes bored into his as though pleading with him to understand.

"Did you enjoy the auction?" he asked, still uncertain about the kiss and the dress.

"It was all right. I have to confess that whenever I've had to tell a man that I didn't want to date him anymore, I've made a special effort to make our last date a memorable one. I don't like to part with hard feelings," she explained.

"Did he enjoy the evening?" Abbot asked. The closer she came to telling him the entire truth, the more he feared it.

"Until he brought me home," she admitted. "While we were sitting in his car, I told him that we'd shared our last date together."

"And?" A knot grew in the pit of his stomach.

"When I stepped out of the car, he pinned me there and said he wanted to kiss me goodbye. He took me by surprise. Usually, I get the cold-shoulder treatment when turning a man out to pasture. I tried to remain calm and think about it, but he didn't wait for an answer."

"So he kissed you goodnight?" Abbot asked, feeling the knot in his stomach beginning to ease a little.

She nodded. "I just stood there like a statue, waiting for him to finish. When he realized he wasn't getting any response from me, he grabbed my elbow and almost dragged me to over to the condo door. Then he left."

"Did he hurt you?" Anger welled up, as Abbot tried to force down the image of Barry Grady dragging Bekah anywhere.

"He left some bruises," she admitted, "where his fingers squeezed me like a vise." She lifted her arm to show him.

Abbot frowned as he looked at the delicate skin with three round bruises on the inside of her elbow. "That neanderthal!" he snapped. "Somebody ought to wring his neck!"

Bekah gave him a timid smile. "That's why I called you Sunday night, rather than waiting for you to call me. I wanted to ask you to come over, but you said you weren't feeling well."

Abbot was surprised and pleased that he was the one she had called, but he also felt bitterly disappointed with himself because he'd been cold and hostile to her when she telephoned that night.

Her smile brightened. "And," she said triumphantly, "you'll be very happy to know that you no longer have to worry about my backless dress."

"Oh?" he asked as he recalled exactly how she looked in it and how her attempt to 'wow' him had set him on edge.

"I took the slip that matches it and went down to Gail's. She and I designed a draped insert from the slip's fabric, then sewed it into the back of the dress. Not only is it modest, it looks just like something out of Vogue Magazine!" Her bright smile filled his heart with gratitude.

"You altered it?" he asked in amazement.

"Well, I couldn't very well wear it to the auction without doing something to it," she admitted. "Oh, Abbot, I was desperate. The cream gown was ruined and all of Gail's formals looked terrible on me, plus they were all too short and some were less modest than my aquamarine dress. I must have called twenty shops, thinking I'd go buy a new one, but none were open. Besides, you know that I couldn't possibly give it away. It's my favorite color and, other than the back, you have to admit it looks good on me."

Abbot laughed and put his arm around her shoulder, letting her lean her head against him. "I can just see you panicking about that dress. And, I'd forgotten how clever you are at remodeling things."

"Is that what's been standing between us?" she asked, throwing him completely off guard.

His heart lurched. She had given him what he needed to trust her completely, but how could he expect her to trust him when he had his own secret. Realizing he would have to suffer the consequences of his actions, he confessed, "That's part of it, Bekah. But, the other part is my own guilt. You see, I'd gone to see my bishop, Sunday evening, and I didn't get out of our meeting until after nine. You said you'd be home by eight, and I thought, I'll drive by and see if your light was on. If it was, I planned to stop in to see you, and if not, I'd go on back to the boat and get some rest."

"Oh," she moaned, putting her hand over her mouth in surprise. "You saw something!"

"I saw Barry kissing you, with his hands wrapped around your back. I didn't know you'd altered your dress. You told me that you'd worn

it to 'wow' me. I . . . I jumped to all the wrong conclusions, Bekah."
He looked tenderly at her face, studying her expression, hoping she
believed him, hoping she understood.

She reached her hand up and pulled his face nearer hers where
she brushed her lips tenderly against his. "I'm sorry," she whispered,
her breath warm against his mouth.

That was all the encouragement Abbot needed. He pulled her
close, their sack lunches falling to the ground as he kissed her with
passion and love and absolute trust.

The sound of people clapping was the only thing that stopped
them. Abbot withdrew, his face growing crimson as he realized they'd
given their families a show worth watching.

Then he did something completely out of character, something
that only love could have motivated him to do. He stood up and bowed
like a true gentleman. As their family cheered and laughed and clapped,
Abbot took Bekah's hand, pulled her up from the log bench and kissed
her once again, this time with all the longing of a man who has finally
found love. A man who would not risk losing that love for anything
in the world.

❦   ❧

Much later, after seven exhausted expedition members climbed
into their own beds to recuperate from a strenuous hike, Bekah thanked
God for answering her prayer. She had no doubt that the influence of
something spiritual and calming had given her the courage to tell Abbot
he need never fear, where her heart was concerned.

Abbot's demeanor the rest of the day had been carefree and
content as he had been before her date with Barry. The sensation of
his kisses lingered on Bekah's lips, warm enough to comfort her all night
long.

They'd had no further reason to hold anything back. Although neither had confessed love to the other, she knew in her heart that Abbot was beginning to feel the same toward her as she was toward him. She wanted nothing more than to see her grandmother's dream realized. How grateful she was for all that had transpired.

As she recalled their conversations before the incident with Barry, chronologically from that moment until now, Bekah also realized something very important.

Yesterday when Abbot first arrived at the Hoh River, he'd told her that he trusted her. A short while later, he said that in his blessing he was instructed to trust those whom he loved the most. His words had been carefully selected, though she hadn't made the connection until that very moment. Had she recognized his guarded message earlier, she may have had the courage to tell him she loved him back.

Last night when they walked through the campground together, Abbot said, "I want to trust you." His words still stung inside her chest. How he must have struggled after seeing her with Barry, then receiving a blessing telling him to trust whom he loved most.

What was this Melchizedek Priesthood, of which Abbot had spoken? When would he begin sharing with her the mysteries of his belief in God and his ability to ask that his prayers be answered? If authority from God came through this priesthood, did Abbot have it for himself? When he said he knew he had authority to ask for Cody's injuries to heal, during his prayer after the accident, was he speaking of the Melchizedek Priesthood, which gave a person authority from God? These were all questions that needed answers, and Bekah hoped that Abbot would soon give them to her.

# Chapter Nine

By Friday, Cody was beginning to tire of walking downhill all day, searching for something that was not to be found. Knowing it was their last day and they would likely reach the Pacific Ocean before evening, Abbot tried to think of something that would perk up the boy's spirits. Arising extra early he walked away from camp, toward the Hoh River, where he knelt in the mossy grass and offered up a prayer of thanksgiving, a prayer of hope for young Cody.

When he felt a tiny hand upon his shoulder, he closed his prayer quickly and looked up to see Cody standing beside him, bare-footed and still wearing his pajamas, with an apple in his hand. Bekah stood behind him, her camera slung over her shoulder. "Shhh," Cody whispered. "Look!"

Searching down river, then up, Abbot spotted a black-tailed deer several hundred yards upstream. "Let's go," whispered Abbot, lifting Cody up onto his shoulders as he stood and smiled at Bekah.

She went up on tiptoe and gave him a quick kiss. "Good morning."

"Shhh," said Cody. "Aunt Bekah!"

"Sorry," she whispered.

Abbot grinned as he watched her suppress a giggle, then he turned his attention to the deer. It was a beautiful doe, with a buff-brown coat, and black around the tip of the tail and on the hind legs near the hooves.

Cautiously and quietly as he could manage with a boy on his shoulders, Abbot walked upstream toward the unsuspecting deer. Bekah followed, her video camera rolling. He pulled out his pocket knife and cut the apple into quarters as they walked from one thick moss pad to another. Then, he handed the apple pieces to Cody, wiped the knife off on his jeans and put it back. When they were within twenty feet of the deer, Abbot slowly lowered Cody down.

The deer was facing the opposite direction, drinking at a little pool filled by the Hoh River. Ever so quietly, Cody started forward, careful to put his feet only on the mossiest places to prevent making any sound. When he was within five feet of the doe he stopped and held out his hands, then remained as still as a statue.

Bekah continued filming, but followed Cody's example. Completely in freeze-frame positions, they waited.

A minute passed, then two and three. Still the deer didn't notice them. Cody glanced at Abbot, as though wanting to ask him what to do next. But, from what Tom had been teaching him, they shouldn't be moving at all. Abbot quickly shook his head and looked sternly at the boy. Cody froze, as though remembering the six or eight times Tom had almost fed a deer during their expeditions, by holding completely still, sometimes for half an hour or more, with an apple sliced in his big hands.

When seven minutes stretched into ten, Abbot was able to appreciate the patience his brother had. But, Tom had taught Cody well, for the child remained immoveable, holding his hands out with two apple quarters in each of them, which certainly spoke volumes regarding Cody's potential.

Just when Abbot was beginning to think the doe was deaf or blind, she turned, looked curiously at Cody and blinked. She sniffed the air a moment, as though cautious and worried something was wrong. Apparently she liked the aroma of fresh apple, for she turned slightly, her front hooves a mere two or three feet from Cody.

For a moment Abbot panicked, thinking the deer might bite his young friend. It took every ounce of strength he had not to scare the deer off. He would never be forgiven if he ruined Cody's one chance of doing what Tom had been trying to do all week.

Cautiously, the deer sniffed at the apple pieces, while her eyes watched the apple-bearer warily. Apparently deciding this child was no threat to her, she nibbled at a piece of apple until she took it firmly away from Cody's hand. His mouth curved up in a smile that stretched clear across his freckled face. The deer, convinced that this was an offering she couldn't resist, ate the remaining apple, then turned and drank some water from the Hoh River. The only sound was a very faint humming from Bekah's camera. When the deer finished, she looked back at Cody one more time, then bounced away, disappearing into the forest as though she'd never been present at all.

When she was gone, Cody started jumping up and down, laughing and squealing, "I did it! I did it, Abbot! I'm gonna go tell Tom!"

Before Abbot could protest, Cody sprinted bare-footed up toward the road, his voice echoing throughout the campground, "Tom! Wake up!"

Bekah laughed as she filmed Cody's race, then finally stopped when he went through a thicket of trees and out of sight.

Abbot beamed. It was a proud moment for all of them. "I'm sure glad you brought your camera."

"Cody told me to," she responded. "I was just getting dressed when I heard him open the motor home door. He told me he was going to go look for deer and if I wanted to get a picture, this would probably be my only chance."

"Tom told him deer are best seen early morning or late evening when they're awake."

"I'm sorry if we interrupted your prayer," she said as he took her hand on their journey back to their campsite.

"I was just finishing."

"Do you often get up this early to pray?"

"I wanted Cody to have something memorable for his last day here, since every day so far has been a bust for him."

"It seems your prayer was answered," she said in amazement. "Rather quickly."

Abbot smiled. "So it was. I hadn't expected him to feed a deer, but I was hoping he might find some garnet-colored stones today down on the beach when we get there. Or, some sea creature that will catch his attention and make him feel like it has been a worthwhile trip."

"He already does feel that way," she comforted. "Last night he said his prayer before he went to bed, the way you've been teaching him. He thanked God for giving him the best expedition ever."

Abbot beamed. "Your brother and sister have been great about our prayers," he said. "And so have you. It's surprised me, because most people aren't as open-minded as you are."

Snuggling up against him, she confessed, "Grandma Lili told us you were coming."

"Oh?" Taking her in his arms, he couldn't resist the temptation to kiss her soundly. When he finished, he asked, "Is this what Cody was trying to tell me last Tuesday when he said your grandmother had a dream about me?"

Bekah blushed. "She told us someone would come to our family who would know God and would talk with the spirits. Grandma said the spirits would whisper to him and he would listen to them."

"And you think that someone is me?" he asked.

"Maybe."

"Is there anything else your grandmother dreamed about me?"

"She said you will pray mighty prayers and they will be answered."

"If you believe all that, doesn't that put me in a pretty bad position?"

"Why?"

"What if I don't do all those things? What if I fail?"

"You haven't so far," she said, giving him a delicious smile.

Abbot shook his head. "No wonder I have such strong feelings to become a better person when I'm around you."

"That's a two-way street," she murmured. "You make me feel the same way."

"Good," he said. Then, he released her and took her hand. "We'd better see if Cody has awakened the entire camp."

When they arrived, they found Tom and Hans making a huge fire.

"What's this?" Bekah asked. "That won't die down for hours."

"Tom's specialty," Abbot explained. "They're making an in-earth dinner.

"What's that?"

Tom winked at her. "First we dig a big, deep pit. Then we build two roarin' fires with lots of small, split wood, about the thickness of a barbecue brick, but longer. One fire in the pit and one on the side."

Abbot pointed to the pit fire and enjoyed the surprised expression on her face when she realized there was a pit. She apparently hadn't seen it.

"Oh!" she exclaimed. "What's it for?"

"Impatient gal, ain't she?" Tom asked.

"So I'm learning," Abbot admitted.

She punched him playfully. "Hey! I did pretty good filming today. Ten whole minutes of standing stiff and still like the royal guard."

"That doesn't count. Cody can motivate all of us to do anything for him," reminded Abbot.

"Ahem!" said Tom. "Gettin' back to my dinner. I'm gonna brown a sliced sirloin roast in a dutch oven. After it's just barely cooked, I'm gonna smother it with onions, taters, carrots and a package of au jus with some water. Then, I'll put a sheet of aluminum foil over the pan and the lid on top of that. Another sheet or two of foil, to keep any coals from getting in and then I'll put the dutch oven down in the pit, making sure it's got plenty of coals. That's the secret to any in-earth dinner," he said with a tip of his Stetson. "Two secrets, actually. The meat should be thinly sliced, no more than a quarter inch thick and there's gotta be lots of coals. Some people use charcoal bricks, but I like it the old fashioned way."

"Then what?" she asked.

"I put hot coals all around the dutch oven and a bunch on top. Then I bury the entire thing in dirt. Since yer soil up here is always soakin' wet, I'm using more coals than I normally would. Wet soil does a good job at steamin', but it cools down quickly, so you gotta use more than you think you'll ever need."

"That's it?" Bekah questioned.

"Unless our cowpoke friend wants me to make it for him," suggested Hans as he began slicing the sirloin roast.

"I think I could make it a little easier, if I'd made it," suggested Bekah.

"How?" asked Tom, jutting out his chin in defiance.

Bekah gave him a mischievous grin. "I'd have asked the butcher to slice it for me."

Abbot and Hans both laughed, but Tom gave a patronizing frown. "Where I come from, Bekah, I *am* the butcher."

&s èa

For Abbot and his adult companions, it was another tiring day. But for Cody, who bounced from boulder to nurse log to moss patch, gathering rocks for his collection, examining snails and looking for the ever present jumping mouse, it was another day for exploration and rock hunting.

By three in the afternoon, the expedition members arrived at a stretch of beach between the Hoh Indian Reservation and Ruby Beach. North of them lay the wild Hoh River, while south was the Ruby River, a branch off the Hoh that meandered behind some bleached driftwood logs and then emptied in the Pacific Ocean.

They walked south along the beach as Cody stripped down to his shorts and t-shirt and played in the tide pools, searching for garnet-colored stones, and studying starfish the size of serving platters.

Ruby Beach is quite a tourist attraction on its own, with a wide, pebbly beach and several tall sea stacks, some standing fifty feet tall with pine trees growing atop them. Another had a hole that went straight through it, big enough for Tom to stand upright, with room to spare. The south branch of the Hoh, which they crossed as it journeyed to the sea, was appropriately named the Ruby River because of its deep, clear ruby/amber color, tinted from all the minerals that had leached out of the ground from higher elevation.

Driftwood formed a tremendous graveyard of twisted logs, bleached by the salt and the sun, that stood in odd formations, wherever the tide happened to drop them, reminding Abbot of the power and majesty of the unconquerable ocean.

When Cody had spent his energy gathering stones and shells, they started walking up to the Bronco, where they'd left it earlier at the Ruby Beach parking lot.

"You're not disappointed, are you?" Abbot asked Cody.

"About what?" came the response as bold, azure eyes gazed curiously at him from the passenger seat. "We found a whole bunch of cool rocks and I got to feed a deer and there was a huge starfish and lots of shells and . . ."

"Slow down," came Ryan's plea from the back seat.

They were crammed into the Bronco like sardines. Tom and Hans behind the back seat, scrunched up with their knees almost at their chests. Bekah, Ryan and Gail on the two back seats, sharing two seat belts, which wasn't too difficult because both women were fairly thin, while Cody rode up front with Abbot, always with Abbot, his tyee.

"What?" asked Cody innocently.

"Remember what we told you about your collections."

"I remember," said Cody. "I can't take it all home with me. I have to leave some of it for the next kids who come to the Hoh Rain Forest."

"That is a good idea," encouraged Abbot. "Besides, Indiana Jones never kept any of the treasures he found. He always donated them to a museum."

"Do I have to give them to a museum?" asked Cody.

Everyone laughed. "No," said Ryan. "But, only keep the ones that you think are the most special."

"Okay," Cody sighed. "I'll try."

By the time they reached the camp, it was nearing five. Everyone was starving and they were anxious to have something more hearty than hot dogs, Cody's favorite and the mainstay of their evening meals for the past three nights, because the adults were all too exhausted to cook anything. All week long, the women had a couple of side dishes made ahead to complement the meat, making their hot dog dinner less boring. Cody hadn't minded, because he loved nothing more than sticking frankfurters on a stick and roasting them. At least he was having a great time, and that was the main purpose for the expedition.

Tonight's dinner would be entirely different. While Tom began to dig out the dutch oven he'd put in the ground that morning, Gail made a tossed salad and Ryan gathered the plates, silverware and glasses to set the table. Hans and Cody had gone over to the visitors center before it closed to purchase a souvenir since Hans was the only adult with enough strength left to walk that far.

Bekah and Abbot had clean-up tonight, so they'd gone down to the river for a brief respite. When they'd finally found a comfortable boulder big enough for both of them, they stripped off their hiking boots and socks and slipped their weary feet into the cool water.

"Ooh," Bekah moaned. "That feels so good."

"Mine, too," Abbot agreed.

"I've been looking forward to this moment all week long," she confessed.

"Why?"

"I am worn out. This hasn't been a vacation, it's been an exercise in endurance," she complained.

"No one twisted your arm to hike with us every day," he pointed out as he tousled her hair playfully. "You could have stayed up at the motor home and rested."

"And disappointed Cody?" she asked.

Abbot smiled. "Cody's expressions and antics have certainly made the trip worthwhile to me."

"This has been a lesson in love," she told him. "There are not too many men in this world who would take a whole week off work just to take a child and his family on a quest to fulfill the child's lifelong dream."

"His father would have, one day."

"I doubt it," she admitted. "Gail and I practically had to force him to take off this time. With owning his own business and having plenty of employees, it's really not a problem for him, but in his mind, it is. You've done something I doubt Ryan would have ever found the time to do without your organization and encouragement."

"Ryan hasn't been disappointed," Abbot observed. "He's been easy to get along with and he's enjoyed Cody every bit as much as the rest of us have."

"He's done those things for you," she murmured. "Because he believes you're the tyee our grandmother dreamed about."

"I'd like to meet her," said Abbot. "And learn what else she's been dreaming about."

Bekah's eyes widened. "She died ten years ago."

"Oh, I'm sorry. I didn't realize." Then as this information sank in, he asked, "You've remembered a dream she had more than ten years ago?"

"A few weeks before she died, she called us all together. I was just sixteen and quite impressionable. She told us she had a dream and it was so real for her that she considered it a vision given to her from the Great Spirit. Everything that she told us has come true except Robyn's twins, Gail and Ryan's daughter and the tyee who would know God and talk to the spirits, the tyee who would pray and have his prayers answered. My whole family has been waiting for the tyee to come for a long time now."

"And you believe that's who I am?"

She hesitated as though uncertain how to answer.

Abbot sensed the battle going on within her. "If it is me, how will I know?"

She leaned against him and rested her head on his shoulder. He put his arm around her and held her there, enjoying the feel of her. Bekah leaned her head back and looked deeply into his eyes. Abbot sensed she wanted to tell him something, but was preventing herself from doing so. What could he tell her that would convince her she could trust him with her grandmother's dream? When the answer came so clearly through the inspiration of the Holy Ghost, he knew he would have to act on it. His voice deepened huskily as he said, "I love you, Bekah. I want to marry you."

Her eyes widened and her lips formed a smile that gave him her response before her mouth could. "I want to marry you, too."

His lips found hers willing and she responded with such astounding sensations of love, passion and conviction, it took his breath away.

When he finally released her, she said, "You can know you are the man from Grandma Lili's dream because the day she died, she called me to her deathbed and held me in her arms. These are some of her dying words to me: *The man you are to marry will know God and will talk with the spirits. They will whisper to him and he will listen to them. He will pray mighty prayers and they will be answered.* She spoke other words as well, but these few have been the driving force behind my wanting to find you. I have searched for you every day since then. Now that we've finally met and know that we love each other, Abbot, I don't think I can ever let you leave me." Tears filled Bekah's eyes.

"I have no plans to go anywhere without you," Abbot said, cradling her in his arms. For a long time they clung to one another, content that they had finally found each other.

After a while, she said, "When do you want to marry me?"

"I can't marry you right away if we are to marry the way God wants us to marry."

"Why not?"

"I want to get married in a temple. The only way I can marry you there is if you join my faith."

"I'll join right now, Abbot. Just tell me what to do and I'll become a member tonight."

"It's a little more complicated than that. You can't become a member just because you love me. You must also love the Lord, which I'm sure you do. But in addition, you must know His gospel and understand all His precepts before you can be baptized into my faith.

That will take time. We'll need to get some missionaries to teach you." He kissed her forehead, hoping she could learn the gospel is true for herself, not for his sake.

Tears slipped down Bekah's cheeks as she said, "Abbot, I don't need these teachings to know that your way is God's way. Grandmother told me that you would know God. For ten years I've waited for you to come and show me God's way. Her words are embedded in my heart. I prayed the other night and asked Grandmother if you are the tyee of whom she spoke and I heard her whisper in my heart that you are. That is all I need to know to join your faith."

He smiled at her naiveté, yet loved her for it. "I will feel better about your joining if I know that you understand completely what it means to be a Latter Day Saint. If you take the missionary lessons, read the Book of Mormon, pray about it and still feel that you want to be baptized, then I will be thrilled beyond what I can express."

"Okay," she whispered against his neck as she snuggled to him. "But, as soon as I'm baptized, then we can be married, right?"

"No." He shook his head. "There is a one year waiting period before a new member can be married in the temple."

"Why do we have to be married in a temple?"

Concern etched lines on his forehead. "Bekah, in my religion, the temple is the only place on the earth where a couple can be married forever. It's not a civil ceremony and it isn't a marriage that only lasts until one or the other person dies. It's an eternal union. It's where we are sealed as husband and wife forever, even after we die."

"Where is this temple?" she asked, as though uncertain that she wanted to marry him there.

"There's one in Bellevue. There are several in Utah and California. Bekah, there are temples nearly everywhere now. Last I heard there were over a hundred of them."

"But I have to wait a whole year?" she asked.

"I'm sorry, sweetheart. The only other way is to marry you first, then wait the year with you until your year is up. Then we could be sealed in the temple."

"Why can't we do that ?" Her voice faltered, as though she were crying.

He felt her lip tremble against his neck and pulled back to kiss her tears away as he tried to explain. "Bekah, the day after I met you I promised the Lord that I wouldn't spend my life doing things my way anymore. I promised Him that I would marry in the temple, that I would pay my tithes and pray often. How can I expect Him to bless me if I don't keep my promises?"

"But," she complained as new tears replaced the ones he'd kissed away. "Why can't we marry as soon as I'm a member? Then we can go to the temple in a year. You'd still be marrying me in the temple in a year, either way. I don't understand why we should wait. I don't think I can do it, Abbot. How can I live without you near me?"

"Bekah, I want to marry you now, but I—"

"Please, Abbot. Don't make me wait. I can't," she sobbed. "I just can't."

His heart caught in his throat. What was he to do? If he forced her to wait a year before they married, could she do it?

Hasty, jumbled thoughts came tumbling into his mind. *Why wait? I could marry her in Forks, tomorrow, on our way back to Seattle. We could be on our honeymoon tomorrow night. She doesn't need to be a member just to marry her. We can be sealed in the temple a year from now. Just do it.*

"Abbot, please," begged Bekah.

Fearful of the feelings he was having and the thoughts besetting him, Abbot released her and stood up, walked out into the Hoh River and sat down in the deepest part of it, wedging his back against a large boulder so he wouldn't get swept away.

Bekah stood up and pouted. "That's not the answer I wanted."

"You can't expect me to think clearly when we're sitting that close and clinging that tightly, Bekah," he defended, grateful he'd had the presence of mind to cool down a little.

"I'm not coming out there," she insisted.

"I didn't ask you to."

"Abbot Isaac Sparkleman, do you want to marry me or don't you?"

"My physical side says yes. Right now. My spiritual side says no, not until I can take you to the temple. How can you expect me to allow my physical side to rule, when you've made such a clear point of how strong my spiritual side should be? You're the one who's waited ten years to find your spiritual giant and now that I know it's me, I have to live up to your grandmother's expectations."

The look on her face told him he'd finally found the avenue to convince her they should wait.

"Does this temple have a statue of a man on top of it with a golden trumpet?" she asked.

Her question surprised him. He stood up and walked over to her. Shivering, Abbot took Bekah in his arms and held her close, warming himself against her. "Yes, it does," he answered. "Have you seen it?"

"No. But Grandmother Lili said you would marry me in a lofty, white mansion where a man with a gold trumpet stands on a tall pinnacle."

"Then we have to wait out that year, Bekah." He gave her a lopsided grin and picked her up into his arms.

"Why??" she demanded, though he could see a glimmer of softening in her fawn-brown eyes.

"Because you just described the Washington Temple."

Chapter Ten

"**A**re you nuts?" Ryan asked Bekah as he talked with her later that evening in the motor home. Gail and Cody were snuggled up together on the bed over the cab, sound asleep. "You should have told him everything Grandma Lili said!"

"I don't have to," Bekah insisted. "He's convinced we have to wait the year out, no matter what."

"But there's more to her dream, Bekah, and if he doesn't know it, how is he supposed to do everything that Grandma said he would?" he demanded.

"Ryan, I'm not going to tell him. He's *my* fiancé, so butt out!"

"If you don't tell him, I will," he snapped.

"If you tell him, I'll never speak to you again!"

Ryan stood up and glared at her, but Bekah was more obstinate than any other member of Grandmother Lili's family. She stood and glared right back, not allowing a muscle to twitch or an eyelash to flutter.

After several minutes at an absolute impasse, Ryan acquiesced and sank wearily back onto the bench. "You are the most stubborn woman I've ever met."

"Perhaps his journey isn't what we think," Bekah said softly when she finally sat down, trying not to give him anything triumphant in her demeanor that would insult him.

"Grandmother said he would go to the home of the ancient ones for a long time," Ryan pointed out, though Bekah could tell he was weakening.

"We don't know exactly where he will go," she insisted. "And a year *is* a long time. How do we know how long Grandmother meant?"

"How will Abbot know that he is supposed to take this journey?" asked Ryan. "Unless you tell him about it."

"Let God worry about that part."

"I'm sure God will," said Ryan. "God rests upon Abbot's shoulders. Perhaps He will punish you for not telling Abbot everything."

Ryan stood up and turned away from her. He lifted sleeping Cody off the bed above the cab and placed him on the bed where Bekah had been sitting. Bekah pulled the blankets up over her nephew and kissed him.

"I will pray that He won't," Bekah offered. "He answered me once already. Perhaps he will understand that I can't bear for Abbot to leave when I've barely just found him after searching for ten long years."

Ryan gave her a quick kiss on the cheek and a hug. "Bekah, I think you should tell Abbot everything. I fear for you, if you don't. Remember when Robyn refused to believe and married Paul, what happened?"

"God wouldn't take Abbot away from me like that. Not like that, Ryan."

"He took Paul. Only later did Robyn find the man with the tattoo on his left wrist, the man who would have Quileute blood in him."

"If God wants Abbot to leave me, it won't be forever. Grandmother said he would come back and marry me. Surely God is powerful enough to tell Abbot where he is to go without my help."

Her brother just sighed wearily. "Goodnight, Bekah."

After her brother had gone to sleep, Bekah remained awake in her bed, having pulled the curtains around the bed's perimeter for privacy. Her brother might be right, and she may have to tell Abbot all of Grandmother's dream, eventually. But not yet. Couldn't they spend some time together first? She offered a prayer, pleading with God to tell Abbot, Himself, for she didn't think she had the courage to do it for Him.

When she finally fell asleep, she found herself in a terrible nightmare from which she thought she'd never awaken. In her dream she saw Abbot aboard *Bridger's Child*. The boat was sailing out toward the sea, while she remained in Seattle. At the back of the vessel a tiny fishing hook was embedded into the fiberglass. The hook was attached to a line on a fishing pole that she was reeling in. Yet no matter how hard she tried to bring Abbot back to her, the boat just kept sailing away, far, far away.

ఴ ఴ

Everyone slept late, Saturday morning, except Cody. Abbot knew he would awaken early, and when he heard the motor home door open, he sat up, unzipped the sleeping bag and slipped on his pants. Grabbing his shoes, he stepped past Tom and Hans, who were sleeping soundly, and left the tent.

Cody was lifting a heavy bucket onto the campsite table. Abbot put on his shoes then walked over to where his young friend was busy sorting rocks.

"Good morning," said Abbot. "You're up early."

"Yeah. Dad said I have to take care of this before we leave today," came the response. Abbot thought he heard a touch of sadness in Cody's voice.

"Do you need some help?"

"No. A man's gotta do what a man's gotta do." said Cody, but his deep voice mimicked Tom's.

Abbot smiled. "I'll bet Tom's going to miss you."

"Yep." Cody imitated.

Cody laid his rocks out in rows, categorized by color, then by size. His methodical mind hinted at what possibilities awaited him as he grew to manhood, and Abbot was, once again, astounded by Cody's potential.

"I'll head over to the restroom. Will you be okay?"

"Yep." The voice was the same, but this answer came from the direction of the tent.

Abbot looked around to see Tom pulling on his cowboy boots.

"I'll keep an eye on him until you git back," Tom volunteered.

"Thanks," said Abbot.

When he returned, he was surprised to see that young Cody had all of his rocks spread out on the table, with large rocks at one end, graduating to small. Tom was helping him sort them.

"Your turn," Abbot said, sitting down beside Cody. "Have you decided which ones you want to keep yet?" he asked.

Tom swept his hair back with his long fingers and put his Stetson on, then headed in the direction of the restrooms.

"Only one," said Cody. "Tom said it might be worth something."

"Why, is it gold?"

"No." He reached into his pocket, pulled out a flat piece of stone and gave it to Abbot.

The rock was smooth, except for four worn spots, as though someone had painstakingly rubbed indentations in it to hold some kind of rope in place. When it occurred to him what it might be, Abbot's heart quickened. "When did you find this?" he asked.

"Yesterday morning," Cody said. "Why? Do you think it came from the cave?"

"It's similar to a weight," Abbot explained. "The Ozette dig site had a few like these."

"A weight?" asked Cody. "Like a paper weight, like the one on Dad's desk?"

"No. They were used as a fishing sinker, primarily by the Northwest tribes."

"Cool!" Cody exclaimed. "Is it valuable?"

"I don't know," Abbot said. "It would be nice if we could figure out just where you found it."

"That's easy," said Cody. "Right after we stopped for lunch yesterday, we crossed that one big log that had lots of baby trees growing on it. You remember. You call those kind, nurse logs."

"You found it near that log?" asked Abbot.

"No. But, that's where I remember, because that was when I went way over by Tom, only he wasn't looking for the cave."

"He wasn't?"

"No. He was scolding some raven bird that kept flying at him."

"A raven bird? Yes, he mentioned that later," said Abbot, recalling Bekah's irritation about the crow. It seems a Native American custom by some tribes is to distrust the presence of a raven or a crow. Back to Cody, Abbot asked, "Did you find the stone there?"

"No. I passed Tom up and went pretty far away. There was another stone I wanted to get, but it was too big to carry. It had some strange stuff on it."

"What kind of stuff?"

"It was probably just some baby stuff," said Cody matter-of-factly.

"Why do you say that?"

"Because I couldn't read none of it, and I'm a good reader. I'm in the gifted class at school, you know."

"Do you remember what the writing looked like?"

Cody jumped down and walked around the table. "I'll show you."

Abbot followed him down to the river where Cody looked for a small stick. Along the bank, where the soil was soft and smooth, Cody drew some lines and circles that looked very much like hieroglyphics. Abbot's heart began to pound oddly. "Are you sure that's what you saw?"

"There were some funny lines like this," he said and drew a squiggle above one of the circles. "And some things that looked like a tent with feet on it, like this." He drew a capital A without the middle line, then put little marks from the stem up, outside each one.

"How big a stone was it?" Abbot asked.

Cody held his hands out and measured off about fifteen inches square. "Is it something really important?" he asked, his eyes widening. "I thought about telling you, but Aunt Bekah had already yelled at me for running off . . . twice!"

By this time, Abbot's attention was excitedly geared toward Cody's discovery. "We ought to wake the others and go look at it. What do you think?"

"Sure!" came the excited answer as Cody turned and raced up the hill toward their camp site. "Tom! Guess what?"

Tom gave a wide grin, "What?" he asked.

Cody showed Tom his Native American fishing weight and told him quickly about this new discovery.

By the time Abbot arrived back at camp, Cody had awakened the entire expedition. Hans was coming out of the tent, Tom was looking at Cody's rock collection, Gail was apparently still inside the motor home and Bekah was putting on her boots at the camp site table.

Ryan was just getting ready to scold young Cody. Before the child received a sharp reprimand, Abbot called, "Did you wake everyone like I told you to, Cody?"

"Sure did!"

Abbot smiled. "Good morning," he said to the frowning faces awaiting him. "Cody may have stumbled onto something yesterday that deserves further investigation. How many of you want to go with us?"

Hans smiled wanly. "All right," he almost moaned. "I'll go."

"I'm gonna go." said Tom.

Bekah smiled. "Count me in!"

Ryan raised an eyebrow. "Anyone mind if Gail and I stay behind?"

"It's okay, Dad!" said Ryan. "I know you're getting old by now. You probably need your rest."

Ryan frowned, but didn't let the child discourage him. "Anyone else object?"

"We'll keep an eye on Cody," Bekah encouraged.

Then Ryan gave them a mischievous smile, opened the motor home door and called inside. "Hey, Gail! Wake up! We're going to get some time alone!"

They heard her giggle as Ryan stepped up and pulled the door shut behind him.

Within minutes the five explorers were headed down the Hoh River road to highway 101, then due west toward Ruby beach. Estimating how far they'd walked by noon, Abbot pulled over to the side of the road, as far off as he could get and said, "We'll start here. If anyone sees a big nurse log, blow your whistle. We'll try to spot it first, then see if young Cody can find his hieroglyphic stone for us."

Walking past Sitka spruce, western hemlock, red cedar and Douglas fir, they soon found themselves in a forest of moss-laden trees that made their world a profusion of varying shades of green. Since

Tom, Bekah and Abbot had been on the northern side of the Ruby River yesterday, they soon found a narrow place where they could cross safely.

Once across the Ruby River, they began the walk down, spreading out at fifty paces each, with Cody chattering happily between them as he got into the spirit of the expedition again. About an hour of westward trekking later, Abbot was beginning to think he'd parked the Bronco too far west, when he heard Tom and Bekah yelling, "There it is!"

Hans joined Tom as Cody grabbed Abbot's hand and led him over to the big nurse log in question. A colonnade of Sitka spruce stood in a row as a result of their getting a start on this particular nurse log. The spruce were about two feet tall and the log beneath them was already beginning to crumble and decay.

"Is this the one?" asked Abbot.

Cody nodded his head. "And Tom was just over there."

"That's right," said Tom. "I was bein' dive-bombed by a black raven. Say, maybe he was tryin' to scare us away." He winked, as Cody's eyes got big and round.

They walked due north at least a hundred paces. "Farther than this, Cody?" asked Bekah. Her tone was sharp and Abbot could tell she was growing weary of this game.

Cody shivered, as though worried he would be scolded.

Abbot squatted down to eye level with the child. "Cody, no one is mad at you. Perhaps Chief Taquinna was leading you to find that stone. Search inside your memory and see if you can visualize the stone you saw and where it is."

"Okay," Cody said as he closed his eyes and searched his mind for the right location. "It's down there!" He pointed to a group of rocks about a quarter mile down the steep grade.

Shuddering, Abbot realized they hadn't watched him close enough yesterday. Not just Tom, all of them. He offered a quick prayer in his heart, thanking the Lord for taking over the job for them when they should have acted more responsibly. Perhaps they were all tired by the time they'd reached this point. After all, they'd been doing nothing but searching and downhill hiking for four solid days.

Cody skipped ahead, slithering under a fallen tree, jumping over a boulder, leading them through an emerald world where the smell of moss and decaying wood assailed their nostrils, where gray jays chattered and the jumping mouse occasionally surprised them, where the warmth of the sunshine overhead could hardly penetrate the thick, dense forest. Finally Cody squealed, "There it is!"

Soon, they were all gathered around Cody as he pointed to a flat stone, about fifteen inches square. But it wasn't really flat, as Cody had described it, rather it was like a mortar box, fifteen inches cubed. It had an indented portion, like a lid, that seemed to be sealed by time. Astounded, Abbot realized that if the top of the box had been lacking its old hieroglyphics, faintly embedded in the lid, he would never have recognized it for what it was, a repository for some kind of ancient record.

Hans rubbed his fingers over the few curious markings in the lid. "Abbot, this was recently unearthed by a small slide, there's still mud embedded in some of these indentations."

Abbot stepped back, examining the terrain. It certainly appeared that a fairly recent mudslide, perhaps within the last year or two, had swept past the area where they were standing, taking a good chunk of earth with it. The soil, although grassy, had a definite thinness to it that other areas did not have. In the slide's path, the stone box had apparently been uncovered, or had been too heavy to slide any farther down the hill. Abbot walked uphill several hundred feet where an indentation in the land's structure indicated the position from which the slide had started. On the way, he noticed a dark overhang where the slide had washed away the soil around an opening of some kind, perhaps a cave. Before he told Cody about it, he thought he'd better be certain what it was. The boy's hopes were already in the clouds.

"It apparently started here," he called down to them, as he placed himself exactly at an indent where lush green grass grew thickly, with a distinct separation zone where soil four fathoms deep had fallen away, leaving a wide, gaping ledge. Pacing the distance off, he rejoined them at the box. "About three hundred feet," he said. "Somewhere between this point and three hundred feet east, that box was buried. Judging by the depth of the slide, it couldn't have been buried more than forty feet deep."

Hans stood up. "Calculating two feet of accumulative soil from decay and erosion per hundred years and a depth of forty feet . . . this box could have been placed here as far back as two thousand years ago, maybe longer.

Tom tipped his Stetson back off his head and exclaimed, "I'll be a one-eyed polecat!"

Bekah stepped over to Abbot and gripped his hand tightly. "What is it really?" she asked.

He heard the concern, and something bordering on fear, in her voice. How could he comfort her when he didn't know what her concerns were, nor anything, for certain, about what they'd just discovered? A strange burning sensation began in his chest and spread outward. "Something that's been missing for a long, long time," Abbot whispered as the words formed in his heart.

Hans looked up at him curiously. "Are you thinking what I'm thinking?" he asked.

Abbot nodded. Hoping Hans understood the significance of a find such as this, he said, "We need to find out who owns this land. Does your satellite phone have a locator in it?"

"Yes," Hans replied

"Lock our location into it."

Hans was already removing the phone from his backpack. He dialed a number and read out the coordinates.

"Does anyone have a pencil?" asked Tom.

"We don't want it written down, we want it memorized." said Abbot.

Cody spoke up. "I can memorize, too."

Bekah shook her head. "No, Cody," she said. "You and I should go over near the nurse log and watch for raven. If he sees us, he may tell his friends we're here. They may come and take the box away."

"But Aunt Bekah," the boy complained. "I can memorize real good."

Abbot was surprised by her story, but he acquiesced to her wishes. For some reason she didn't want Cody or herself involved in this. "You heard your aunt," he said. "Watch closely for the raven and warn us if he comes near."

When they were out of hearing distance, the three men committed to memory the coordinates locked into Hans' cell phone. When they were all satisfied that each one knew the location, Hans pressed the button on his satellite phone marked clear.

Abbot removed his orange vest, and took a pocket knife from his pants pocket. Then, he started cutting his vest into strips. "Tom, take these and mark a path out to highway 101." He gave him the keys to the Bronco. "Take Bekah and Cody back to the motor home. By the time you get back, we'll be at the road. Give us an hour leeway. Hans and I will stay here and see if there's anything we're missing."

The lanky cowboy nodded. "You gotta tell her goodbye, first. I gotta suspicion you won't be leavin' this place anytime soon."

"All right. Take Cody, but only go out of hearing range. I'll talk to Bekah in private. She's evidently got some misgivings about what we're doing. I'll send her over to you shortly."

Tom nodded. Together, he and Abbot joined Cody and Bekah.

The expression on her face was one of concern mixed with fear, a reaction Abbot had not expected.

From a squatting position, so he could be eye level with him, Abbot rested a hand on Cody's shoulder as he said, "I'm really proud of you, Cody. Not only have you been a great buddy to me, but you found something that is very important. It's something so special that only adults are strong enough and wise enough to take care of it. So I'm sending you with Tom and Bekah back to the van.

"Why?" Cody asked, his azure eyes widening in alarm.

"We're worried that if someone else finds it, they may take it away, or destroy it."

"Who would do that?" the young boy asked.

"Raven would," Bekah insisted.

"Why do we have to go?" Cody wanted to know.

"Because we need you out of harms way before anyone else comes," said Abbot. "It's my responsibility to make sure you and Bekah are safe. The only way I can do that is to send you back to your dad and mom."

Cody's lower lip trembled as he threw his arms around Abbot's neck. "I love you, tyee," he said.

A lump formed in Abbot's throat. "I love you, too, buddy," he whispered.

"Hey, partner," said Tom to the young boy. "Abbot thinks that old raven might come in from the river, like he did yesterday. Why don't we mosey on over there and see if we can shoo him away, while yer Aunt Bekah says goodbye to Abbot, okay?"

"Aw, she just wants to kiss him," said Cody in a grown up manner. He giggled, then reverted back to Tom's first topic. "We won't let raven get by us, will we, Tom?"

"Naw," drawled Tom. "We sure won't."

When they were out of hearing range, Bekah whirled on Abbot. The outrage in her eyes was readily apparent, but her tone was worse. "What's this all about?" she demanded.

"I don't know yet," Abbot admitted. "It may be nothing, but it has all the earmarks of a historical find of astounding significance."

"What is that stone?"

"I think it's a burial box, used to store ancient records."

"Why are you taking it?"

"I'm not!" he exclaimed as he suddenly realized why she was so upset. "Don't you know by now that this is what I do? I'm an archaeologist, Bekah. A find of this magnitude has to be protected. If word got out about this before the proper authorities were called in, there would be a thousand people camped down here within a few hours."

"How will you protect it?"

Although her voice softened a little, he could still see the uneasiness in her eyes. "Bekah," he pleaded. "Trust me."

She folded her arms and glared, apparently unconvinced.

In exasperation, Abbot explained, "First we'll find out who owns the property. If at all possible, we'll purchase it. If not, we'll take the matter up with the governor and with the tribal council. They'll place a quarantine on the site until it can be examined by professionals. If it proves to be of any historical significance, the site will be deemed a state or tribal trust and the property owner will be compensated for the value of the land."

"Then what will happen?"

"If there are other artifacts around, we'll find them. It might become a major dig site, similar to Ozette."

"Where will you be?" Her question targeted his heart.

Abbot looked down at her, unwilling to tell her the truth, yet knowing that he must. Finally he said, "I'll be here."

"Why?" she demanded. "What can you do here?"

"It's my first dig site, Bekah. It's important to me to see this project through."

"How long will that take?" she asked.

"It could take years," he admitted.

Tears formed in her eyes. "What about us?" she asked as they slipped effortlessly down her cheeks.

Abbot smiled, realizing the second reason why she'd been so concerned. "Don't they need nurses in Forks?" he asked.

She blinked, then wiped her tears away. "Yes," she said. "I suppose they do."

"Bekah, I'm not abandoning you. But someone has to protect this discovery until it can be properly channeled. Hey, they may not even let me work it. But if there's a chance that I could, I want that chance. That doesn't mean that I don't want you near me. And if Forks doesn't need a nurse, surely Port Angeles does."

Wrapping her arms about his waist, she gave him a gentle squeeze. "Please call me every night," she whispered against his chest. "You know I work Sunday through Wednesday, right?"

He nodded. "Ten hour shifts, five to three. I'll be back soon, hopefully by Thursday. By then, I'll know more about what's going on out here, okay?"

Bekah tilted her head up and studied his face. He could still see something akin to fear in her eyes, though he wasn't sure what it meant. "What is it?" he asked tenderly.

For an answer, she gave him a bright smile and replaced the look with commitment. "Nothing," she said. "I'm just going to miss you, that's all."

"Then, let this keep you warm until I get there," he said.

He bent his head and gave her a warm and tender kiss that deepened quickly as both realized they were about to embark on a journey that may separate them for quite a long time.

When he finally released her, Abbot's emotions felt raw and vulnerable. It could be several days before he'd see her again. With one long embrace, he held her in his arms and curled his fingers in her short, auburn hair. "I love you, Bekah. Don't lose sight of that, all right?"

"I won't," she said as she slipped away. "And I won't say goodbye, either"

Unsteadily, Abbot turned and made his way back to Hans. Glancing at his watch, he noted that it was after noon. The heavy fog of days gone by had no power today and had already dissipated. What sky he could see in brief glimpses between the towering trees, was blue and bright, though the sun could scarcely penetrate the forest walls.

Refusing to turn around and watch Bekah go back with Tom, mainly because he was worried what affect it would have on him, he gave Hans a smile and a shrug.

"What was her problem?" asked Hans when Abbot arrived beside him.

"I think she was worried we wouldn't see one another anymore," he answered. "And she might have had some concerns about what we plan to do about this box."

"I've been studying it," said Hans, disregarding Bekah immediately. "and it's definitely been sealed with something."

Abbot wished he could dismiss Bekah just as easily, but the thought of her going back to Seattle and him remaining behind, sent shivers up his spine. It was something he'd never thought would ever happen. Then, turning to the task at hand, he asked, "Can you identify it?"

"No. We're going to need some high-tech equipment, that's for sure."

"The museum can probably arrange something," Abbot offered. As an afterthought, he said, "You know, if some teenagers happen upon this thing, it'll be busted open and desecrated."

"I know," Hans agreed. "We'll have to locate the property owner and set up a watch until we get some government or tribal sanctions for it."

"If it's as old as we think it is," said Abbot, "the tribal councils may not be able to help us. It may fall under the United States jurisdiction."

"Let's find the owner first," Hans reiterated. "It may be that this is something the Admiral could really sink his teeth into."

"Oh?"

"He once told me that he had wanted to be an archaeologist. Instead, he went into the military at the insistence of his father. He said if he'd had a choice, he'd have chosen the former."

"You never told me that before."

"I didn't know last time we were together. The Admiral and I had quite a nice visit last winter aboard the *Bridge*. After Grandma died, Mother went to New York to meet with a publisher. She was able to sign a contract for Grandma's book, which should come out this year sometime. Meanwhile, the Admiral and I went sailing out to Catalina Island. There were a number of things I learned on that voyage that I didn't know before."

"If your father can possibly be of any usefulness here, he's got my vote."

"Shall we start laying out a rough grid?" asked Hans.

"Too soon and no string. Besides, there was something I noticed earlier when I walked up the hill. Perhaps you'd care to join me?"

Hans arched an eyebrow curiously. "What?"

"I think I may have spotted a cave up there," he grinned.

"Without telling Cody?" Hans asked in surprise.

"I would have told him, but Bekah seemed bent on getting the kid away from here. You know, for a thoroughly modern, sophisticated woman with only one-sixteenth Native American blood in her, she sure can let some of those old superstitions bother her. Sometimes the legends she was taught from the cradle seem to inhibit her rational thought. They instill some sort of fear in her that's not healthy. Besides, I'm guessing it's not Chief Taquinna's cave after all."

"Let's go find out," suggested Hans.

Chapter Eleven

*N*early a hundred feet below the point where the mudslide originated, a flat rock protruded about thirty feet from the embankment on the north side. The natural landscape had been clearly altered by a slide that began at one point and widened in a two hundred foot swath, overturning trees and leaving a barren path in its wake. Now, perhaps a year or two later, the area was covered with thickening grass and a few traces of moss along ridges and exposed rocks, but it certainly did not have the lush greenery of the neighboring areas around it.

Daylight easily reached the boulder-strewn stretch of land, the sun overhead making the earth steam around them. For the first time in a week, Abbot and Hans had removed their outer, long-sleeved shirts and left them behind, with their backpacks, which now rested near the flat, protruding stone.

After removing some rope and flashlights from their backpacks, the two men stretched out on their bellies and nosed their way further beneath the rock, scooping out clumps of soil and rock as they tried to discern just how far back the cave went. With no more than a foot of crawling space, the going was tedious.

Abbot was leading, with Hans not far behind, though Hans had finally stopped and was now holding his flashlight so Abbot could see. Having tied their ropes together and the trailing end to a fallen tree outside the entrance, they dragged it along a good hundred feet into the narrow cave until the rope tightened. Hans stayed with the rope, giving light to Abbot.

When he realized the light was not penetrating sufficiently enough for him to see clearly, Abbot stopped. "This isn't going to work," he said, his breathing labored and weary. It had taken them over two hours to make as much progress as they had. "We're going to need a lot more gear than we have.

"Tom's no doubt waiting for us," said Hans. "It's nearly three."

"If I know Tom, he's on the trail right now, headed toward us. His patience level has always been pretty thin."

Abbot scooted backwards, his t-shirt soiled and dirt rubbing against his chest. There was no way he could turn around.

"I've got my end of the rope tied to a boulder near your left foot," said Hans. "Tie it to your belt when you get back to it."

"All right," Abbot grunted as he struggled to maneuver in the narrow space.

"Could you see an end at all?" Hans asked from far behind him.

"Negative. The only thing for certain is that the cave follows a northeasterly curve and seems to open up a little, farther in."

As they progressed steadily backwards, they were glad the digging process was unnecessary, having dug what they'd had to on the way into the cave.

"You fella's gonna come out?" came Tom's deep, booming voice. He was waiting at the entrance to the cave.

"What did I tell you?" said Abbot.

Within another twenty minutes, they were outside of the cave brushing off the damp soil from their shirts and pants.

Abbot stripped off his t-shirt and the silver chain that he wore, glistened in the hot afternoon sun. A delicate ring with an unusual jade stone set in a leaf and filigree pattern was attached to it,. On the inside of the ring were the initials: EDS + SNT. Examining the ring carefully, Abbot noticed that his journey into the cave had not been a good idea for the ring. One of the filigrees was bent and it was covered with minute chunks of wet soil. He slid the chain off his neck and used his thermos to pour some water over it. Then, using the shirt tail of his long-sleeved shirt, he cleaned the ring until the silver gleamed once again.

"Still wearing Ma's ring?" Tom asked.

"I rarely ever take it off," responded Abbot, straightening the bent filigree with his fingers.

Tom pulled out his wallet and flipped it open. "I still carry Pa's driver's license with me," he confessed. "I never let it out of my possession."

Abbot smiled. "Sentimental fools, aren't we?"

Hans was buttoning his long-sleeved shirt, having removed his stained t-shirt the same time as Abbot. To Tom he said, "I thought you were going to stay with the car."

"I waited an hour. Maybe a few minutes past. But I know Abbot. When he gets his mind on something, until he satisfies his curiosity, he stays with it. I'm surprised you both came out of the cave this early."

"We ran out of rope," Abbot responded.

Tom grinned and removed his Stetson, then swept his dusty-blonde hair back with his long fingers and replaced the hat. "Yep. That's what I figured."

Abbot noticed that Tom had brought a sleeping bag and a backpack filled with cooking essentials and water. "Are you planning on moving in?" he asked.

Tom nodded. "The way I see it, you both got some work to do that I ain't cut out fer. Hans will want to git on up to Forks, find out who owns this property, likely buy it up." He winked at Abbot, "And you gotta git on back to Seattle and see yer sweet little filly and talk to yer boss for some time to work out here. If I know yer mind at all, Abbot, yer just itchin' fer this to become a major dig site."

"You know me pretty well," Abbot observed as he put the silver chain back over his head, letting the delicate jade and silver ring dangle in the vicinity of his heart. Then he slipped his arms into the long sleeves of his shirt and buttoned it up.

"So you're planning on staying?" questioned Hans.

"Yep. That's where my line of work comes in handy. "I got me enough food and gear for four days. If you ain't back by Wednesday I may have to mosey on out and hitch a ride to Forks where I can stock up."

"That's generous of you, Tom," said Abbot. "Since I'd rather not leave the site unattended, I'll be back by Wednesday. That's a promise."

"She didn't say it," Tom added, "but Bekah was still steamin' when I got her and Cody back to the motor home. I expect her ruffled feathers need some additional soothin'."

Abbot eyed his brother curiously. He thought he'd placated Bekah before she left. Hoping his brother hadn't said something that would have upset her, he stuffed the flashlight into his backpack and swung it over one shoulder as he said, "Let's get going. Thanks, Tom."

He reached his hand out to shake Tom's hand, but the tall, lanky cowboy pulled him closer and gave him a big bear hug. "I'm sure I didn't offend, Bekah," Tom whispered. "She was steamin' before I even opened my mouth. Mostly I just talked to Cody on the way back because her temperament was not too kindly."

Nodding, Abbot rolled the rope up as he started walking south toward the Ruby River and then highway 101.

Hans retrieved the satellite phone from his backpack and handed it to Tom. "I'll call you when we know what we're doing. If you need something, call Abbot's cell phone number."

Abbot turned. "I'm going to pick up a satellite phone as soon as I can. I'll call you to give you the number."

Tom nodded. "You don't need to worry about me. I'm in my element."

Smiling, Abbot stuffed the coiled rope into his backpack and waved to his brother. "Come on, Hans."

His friend turned and headed toward him. When he'd caught up to Abbot, he said, "You're anxious to get back to Bekah."

"She's upset by all this, but her fear seems to go deeper than that. It as though she's afraid I'm going to abandon her somehow. We need to talk it out." Almost stumbling over a thick root that lay in his path, Abbot caught himself and paid closer attention to where his feet were going.

"Ryan told me his grandmother had a dream about you," offered Hans. "Did you know that?"

"Bekah mentioned it," he admitted.

"Did she tell you any specifics?"

"From what she said, I believe her grandmother did see me in her dream."

"Because of the man with the gold trumpet?"

"Exactly," Abbot responded.

Fortunately, Tom had marked the trail well, tying fluorescent orange pieces of vest fabric methodically to branches every fifty paces, giving them an easily defined route. All were approximately eye level, in a fairly straight line, all the way back to where he'd parked the Bronco.

During the next half hour, Hans and Abbot developed a game

plan. Hans would be dropped off in Forks, buy a used car, then do whatever he could that afternoon to determine the owner of the property. Afterward, Hans would come to Seattle for Sunday services, then assist Abbot on Monday with negotiations at the museum and whatever else might be entailed in acquiring rights to the property.

Abbot would telephone Bekah as soon as he arrived back at *Bridger's Child*. Then, he'd attend to his Sunday meetings with Hans and arrange for missionaries that same evening at Bekah's condo. Hopefully, he would get back to Seattle in time to see her before she went to bed.

Arriving in Forks around two in the afternoon, they stopped at West Marine and picked up satellite telephones for both of them. Then, Abbot drove Hans over to a used car dealer, where Hans purchased a Jeep Cherokee. When Abbot was certain Hans would have decent transportation, he left him in Forks, and headed toward Seattle.

He made the nine-ten ferry from Bainbridge Island that evening. Once aboard, Abbot parked the Bronco and secured the brake. Then, he locked the car and headed up to the aft passenger deck, outside the big dining hall.

The sunset was brilliant, with hues of pink and purple touching the puffy clouds all around him. Abbot was surprised at how dry the air seemed. When he'd left Seattle six full days ago, the humidity in the misty fog had to be in the ninety percentile. Now the air was almost free of moisture and with that aridity, came a clearness that was unusual for Puget Sound.

Abbot's thoughts turned to Bekah and her anger at their discovery, although he couldn't imagine her reasons. He said a prayer in his heart that Bekah would still be up when he finally arrived back home.

It was after six in the evening when Bekah returned to her condo in Seattle and stepped inside. After securing the locks she leaned back against the door and sank to the floor, her mind torn between sheer exhaustion and unquenchable fear. Wrapping her arms around her knees, she rested her head against them and tried to focus.

The trip back with Ryan, Gail and Cody had been interminably long, especially since Cody blurted out the news to his parents the moment they'd returned with Tom in the Bronco.

For the first hour or two on their journey home, Ryan and Gail had quizzed her about Abbot and what they'd found. Several times Ryan had raised an eyebrow as though he wanted to probe deeper, but Cody didn't give them a moment to talk, for which she was grateful.

In desperation, Bekah finally persuaded them to let her take Cody back to the three-quarter bed where she had spent the past five nights, to take a nap. Although she wasn't able to sleep much, her nephew took full advantage of the opportunity. Having run at full speed almost their entire trip, he was more exhausted than any of them. Remaining with him until he finally awakened near Poulsbo had given Bekah the opportunity to avoid Ryan's penetrating questions.

Now that she was finally alone in her condo, she could more fully explore the feelings in her heart and in her mind regarding what had happened near the Hoh River, and the importance Abbot had placed upon finding the stone box.

An ancient record could be found inside, he'd told her. The words terrified her. Ancient record . . . would the secrets locked inside that box have anything to do with Grandmother Lili's dream?

Her brother had insisted that Abbot should have been told the entire dream. But how could she tell him that he was supposed to go on a long journey to the home of the ancient ones? Couldn't the ancient ones be the people whose records might be waiting inside the box they'd found? Why would he have to go away? Wouldn't it make more sense for Abbot to stay in Washington? And if he was to go away, why couldn't she move and live near Abbot while they waited their year to marry in the temple?

Bekah's mind wandered back through the past two weeks. She'd finally found the man in her grandmother's dream. The only problem was, Bekah didn't want to let him go. After spending ten years searching for him, then to have to give him up while he leaves her to pursue some strange journey, the whole idea made her nauseous with fear. Ten years to find him, two weeks to love him and a long time to miss him. And, what was she supposed to do with him gone? *No! I won't do it! Grandmother, I can't give him up now that I've found him. I just can't.*

How long she sat there in a crumpled heap by the floor, Bekah didn't know. Dark shadows had already spread across the floor from the dining room window when she finally realized how late it was getting.

Affirmative action was the first order of business she decided, as she tried to pull herself together. How soon could she join the church? Her year of waiting for a temple wedding couldn't even begin until she was baptized.

Deciding that she must telephone the missionaries herself and begin learning what she must in order for Abbot to baptize her, she stood and went into the kitchen. Just as her hand was about to touch the receiver, the telephone rang. She glanced at the caller i.d. and noticed that it was Abbot's cell phone.

Immediately, she put the receiver to her ear. "Abbot?" she asked, her voice a mixture of joy and relief.

"Were you resting?" came the tender, husky voice that she'd grown to love.

Bekah glanced at her watch. *Nine-fifteen.* "No. Where are you?"

"At *Bridger's Child*," came his answer.

"You're back in Seattle?"

"Yes. Bekah, I don't like the way we left things. May I see you tonight?"

Her heart raced, her voice became giddy, like a young school girl as she exclaimed, "Of course, Abbot. Come right over." She was so excited she replaced the receiver without saying goodbye. Immediately, she dialed his number. When he answered she said, "Sorry. I didn't mean to hang up on you like that."

Abbot laughed. "That's good. I was beginning to wonder."

"Fifteen minutes?" she asked.

"That's fine. I'll leave right now."

"Bye, Abbot."

"I love you, Bekah. Bye."

Her heart sang all the way down the hall, through the bedroom and into the shower as she removed her clothing and scrubbed down quickly, then toweled herself dry and slipped into a pair of cream-colored shorts with a matching blouse that had tiny jade beads stitched into a dream catcher pattern on the front. After blowing her hair dry, she softened the curls with a large curling iron and put on a little makeup. Before she had a chance to apply some perfume, she heard the buzzer.

Stepping quickly to the door, she pressed a button and asked, "Abbot?"

"Yes," he answered.

"I'll buzz you through." She pressed the door release button and knew that she had only a minute before he would be knocking. Bekah dashed down to her bedroom, slipped on a pair of sandals and gave her neck a sparse drop or two of her favorite fragrance, lilac mist.

Then, the doorbell rang.

Bekah raced to answer it, but just before her fingers touched the knob, she told herself, *Composure, Bekah! Don't let him know you're* ruffled. But as quickly as the thought arrived, she suppressed it. This wasn't just any man she was welcoming home. This was Abbot! She yanked the door open and didn't give him any warning as she went bursting through the doorway and into his strong arms. Tears, left unshed throughout the day, filled her eyes. For several minutes all she could do was snuggle up against him and weep for joy. Abbot was home.

He held her for a few moments, whispering soothing words of comfort. "It's okay," he whispered tenderly. "I'm here. I'm not abandoning you." When she was finally able to compose herself, he asked, "Are you going to invite me in or are we going to stand out here in the hall all night?"

Bekah drew back and noticed that his smile swept from ear to ear across his handsome face. His bright, emerald eyes glistened and his brown-black hair was combed neatly; musky cologne, mingled with his own male scent, made her skin tingle. He had cleaned up since she last saw him, and he looked sharp in his docker pants and nautical print shirt.

Then, she remembered his question and laughed. "Yes, come in." Taking his hand, she led him into the living room and closed the door behind him.

Abbot sat down on the silver-cushioned sofa and pulled her down beside him. "So, you really missed me, hmm?" he asked, and a look of amusement mixed with love stirred the colors in his eyes.

Bekah nodded. "I thought you weren't coming at all, or at least not for a long time."

"I won't know that for certain until we can secure the site and get the proper authorities to aid in our investigation," he explained. "Since we can't do anything until Monday, I wanted to spend some time with you before I get too involved in the project."

"I think I'll call in and rearrange my schedule," she suggested.

"Can you?" he questioned. "Because I'd like to take you to church with me tomorrow, if that's possible."

A feeling of determination came over Bekah that she could neither analyze nor explain. "Let me call my supervisor."

Abbot nodded his agreement and Bekah stood. She walked over to the telephone and dialed the number. Finally, she heard a male voice answer, "ER, this is Chris."

"Hi, Chris. It's Bekah Stevens."

"Bekah! Say, aren't you due back tomorrow?"

"I am, but I'd like to trade with someone if that's possible."

"Hang on, I'll check."

She heard the line click as she was placed on hold, then relaxing music for a few minutes.

Abbot stood and walked over to her where he wrapped his arms around her, pulling her back against his chest. Bekah was so flustered she could hardly concentrate.

Finally, she heard a male voice answer again. "Kim wants the extra time and won't trade, but he'll take your shift if you want to give up ten hours."

"Yes," Bekah said without hesitation. "Tell him thanks."

"You'll be in on Monday?" came the response.

"Absolutely."

When she hung up, she leaned back against Abbot, wishing they were married already, wishing he would never have to leave her again. Then, she turned and snuggled close to him as he held her in his arms. "What time's church?" she asked, surprised to find her emotions so evident in her voice.

"At one," he answered as he stepped back, distancing them a foot or two.

Bekah was disappointed, but she knew his feelings regarding

intimacy prior to marriage and she wasn't going to attempt to persuade him, otherwise. This high moral standard was one of the things she admired about Abbot, so she would have to get used to the idea that intimacy would only come when they were married. It was going to be a long, miserable year for her, and she secretly hoped he would feel just as anguished. In the world she lived in, most people consummate their love when they become engaged. In his world, that just wasn't going to happen. And Bekah would do nothing to upset the spiritual balance in his life. That was one of the reasons she'd been drawn to Abbot in the first place. For ten years she'd longed to find the man who knew God and prayed to him. Now that she'd found him, she wasn't going to let her own physical desires hinder his spiritual progression, or her own.

"Well?" he asked.

Bekah pulled herself out of her thoughts and asked, "What?"

"Does this mean you're going to go with me?"

"To church?"

"Of course."

Bekah nodded. Then, she took his hand and led him back to the sofa where they sat down and faced each other. "Tell me everything you've been up to since this morning."

"We found a cave not too far east of the stone box."

"Chief Taquinna's cave?" she asked, surprised at their discovery.

"It's too soon to know for certain," he explained. "So far it's only a narrow, cramped opening that tunnels back in about sixty feet. Hans and I slithered that far into it on our bellies."

"Did you find anything?"

"Not yet, but we'll go back in when we have better equipment."

"Cody will be so excited. He'll want to go explore it right away."

"Maybe Ryan will let us bring him back sometime."

"If you told Ryan you were going to walk on water, he'd believe you," she confided. "You've won him over."

"I didn't set out to win anyone over," he insisted, "except you."

"Now that you've done that, what's next on your agenda?"

He looked tenderly at her, as though debating how to ask her something. Whenever he did this, it puzzled her and made her wonder why he didn't just ask her outright. Why play the fish out when it was already well-hooked? Why not just bring her aboard? "Abbot, what is it?" she queried.

"I was about to ask the same question," he admitted. "What frightens you so about the box we found, Bekah?"

She stiffened, unable to prevent herself from doing so. Without answering, she changed the subject. "When will I get to meet the missionaries and start learning about your faith?"

Abbot persisted. "Why won't you talk about this?"

Bekah turned away stubbornly. "It doesn't matter. It's what you want to do and I want you to be happy. If digging up ancient things does that, then that's what I want."

"What frightens you?" he asked, sensitive to the feelings inside her regarding his quest.

"I won't tell you," she replied. "I'll never tell you, so don't ask me anymore."

"Bekah, we can't let this come between us. Without trust, what kind of relationship will we have?"

"If you want to know, then you must ask God for answers," she said resolutely. "You will not get them from me." Standing, Bekah walked toward the sliding glass door, opened it and stepped out onto the balcony. The fresh night air felt cool to her skin, as a gentle breeze whisked her curls around her face. The smell of a late-night barbecue from one of the balconies below her wafted up and she could almost taste the succulent steak cooking there, but it had no affect on her appetite. Bekah's stomach rumbled, but not from hunger.

Abbot had sensed she was frightened of his working on an archaeological project so far away from her. But she could never tell him why she feared it.

From where she stood, she could see across the street and above the roofs below her eighth-story condo to Green Lake, a small body of inland water, about the size of a football field, where it lay north of Seattle, past Wallingford. The park benches that rested on the green grass could easily be seen below the park lights and were scattered about the lush setting, reminding her that she and Abbot had never walked around it yet, though it used to be one of her favorite places to jog, until she happened one day to expand her horizons and go to Gas Works Park at Lake Union to run. Had she not done so, she doubted she would ever have met the tyee from Grandmother's dream.

Abbot's hands on her shoulders brought her back to him. She turned and looked up at him, loving his nearness, loving him.

"I won't ask again," he said, his tone defeated. "But, when you're ready to tell me, I'll listen."

Bekah thought about his words long after he'd gone back to *Bridger's Child*. She knew he was disappointed with her, but she was determined not to believe that portion of Grandmother Lili's dream. Abbot could not leave her because she wasn't strong enough to survive a lengthy separation. She'd waited ten years already.

Chapter Twelve

*S*unday would be the last respite Abbot had before his duties increased in speed and momentum. Soon he would have little time to himself, or for Bekah. They enjoyed fast and testimony meeting at church that afternoon and invited the missionaries to come and teach Bekah the basic discussions, preparatory to her baptism. When Ryan and Gail heard they were coming, they wanted to join, and Abbot would not deny them.

When the missionaries arrived at Bekah's apartment, they were surprised to see not only Bekah and Abbot there, but Ryan, Gail and Cody, as well. The lesson was remarkably well presented and appointments were made for the rest of the week.

Hans telephoned late Sunday night to tell him that he'd been able to sign an earnest agreement to purchase several hundred acres of land that included the landslide area where the box lay waiting. Hans would sign the final contract Monday and asked Abbot to wait until the land was legally in their possession before telling the administrator at the museum about it. Abbot didn't ask for details, but he expected the Admiral had a great deal to do with it.

On Monday, Abbot went through the motions of work, but he

couldn't concentrate on anything but Bekah and the archaeological project.

By the time he got off work and stopped by the jeweler, he was late meeting Bekah for their run. She had already finished and was sitting on a bench at Gas Works Park when he arrived.

It had been overcast most of the day and now a light drizzle began to fall. Abbot opened the umbrella he'd brought with him and approached her from the west end of the park. When she saw him coming, she stood and ran over to him, kissing him vigorously.

"Where were you?" she asked when she finally released him.

"I'm sorry," he apologized. "I had something more important to do today." Then he gave her a mischievous grin.

"Something more important than be with me?" Her eyes widened in surprise when he nodded.

"Come here," he said. Taking her hand, he led her back to the bench and sat her down upon it, holding the umbrella so she wouldn't get too wet. A thunderous applause came from the dark cumulonimbus clouds that were swiftly moving in and the rain began pelting them with a vengeance. Abbot was determined, however, that no thunderstorm was going to deter him from what he felt was one of the most necessary things he could do right now.

"Don't you think it's getting a little too wet to be out here?" she asked.

"No. I didn't do this right last week and I'm determined it's going to be done today or I'll die trying."

"Sounds serious."

Abbot knelt upon the ground with one knee and pulled the jewelry box from his pants pocket. He could feel the wet grass soak into his pant leg. His hair was plastered on top of his head by the driving rain, but he was not deterred. Just before he opened the box, he said, "Rebekah Taquinna Stevens, will you marry me?"

She laughed and her voice was music to his ears. "I will, Abbot Sparkleman."

"Abbot Isaac Sparkleman," he corrected.

She beamed, then ignoring his correction she asked, "When?"

"You know when."

"Promise me," she suddenly demanded, "that it won't be any longer than one year from the day of my baptism."

Surprised by her request, he hesitated. "What makes you so insecure about this?"

A thunderous roar from above seemed to rattle the very air surrounding them. "Abbot, can we resume this conversation in the car?" she asked.

He laughed and stood up, brushing the mud from his knee. Taking the engagement ring from the box, he slipped it on her finger and said, "I promise, Bekah. One year after your baptism, I will put your wedding band on this same finger and marry you in the Washington temple."

She threw her arms around his neck and hugged him with such fervor she almost crushed the breath from him. "I'm going to hold you to that promise, Abbot Isaac Sparkleman."

Then they raced one another to her caravan. "Where's your Bronco?" she asked.

"I took a taxi today."

"Why?"

"I haven't had time to unload the Bronco. Besides, I may need to load it right back up again. I didn't think you'd mind if we spent the rest of the afternoon together. At least until your missionary appointment."

"You're not staying for it?"

"I am," he answered. "But then, I'll need to take a cab back to *Bridger's Child*. Hans is supposed to call me tonight."

"Can't he reach your cell phone?"

"I left both of them back on the boat."

"Abbot Sparkleman, where is your mind today?" she asked. "You've never been without your cell phone since the day we bought it."

"My mind is on you!" he reminded her with an eager kiss.

Later, he was astounded to answer the door to her condo and find an entire crowd of people arriving for the missionary discussions. "Um, Bekah," he said. "Did you invite more guests for tonight?"

"Ryan was going to call my cousins, why?" she asked as she came into the living room from the kitchen, where she was cleaning up their supper dishes.

A woman answered her. "We were just over at Ryan's condo. He told us to tell you he'll be right over."

Abbot understood her message. He opened the door wide as he said, "Come in. I'm sure we'll find room for you."

Bekah stepped across the space and started hugging and kissing men and women he'd never met before. "Robyn! You're looking good!" She patted Robyn's rounded belly. "Let's see, due August 30th, right?"

The oval face of the older woman smiled at her. "Twins!" she said, "Just as Grandma Lili promised."

"Twins!" Bekah exclaimed. "I'm so happy for both of you! It couldn't happen to a more deserving couple."

Introductions were made and soon everyone was admiring the diamond ring on Bekah's finger. When Ryan, Gail and Cody arrived, Abbot sat back in a corner watching in amazement as this miracle unfolded.

When the missionaries knocked on the door, they were astounded to find not the four people they were expecting, but eleven additional investigators. It was missionary heaven and they'd been invited to a smorgasbord.

After the discussion and everyone left, Abbot approached the subject of Grandmother Lili's dream from another angle. He was drying dishes after serving everyone cake and ice cream. "Bekah, when your grandmother was describing her dream to your cousins, do you remember all of it?"

"Of course," Bekah answered as she washed another dish, rinsed it and put it in the dish drainer. "She said she was at a big family party, walking around and getting introduced to all the new family members. She described in detail what my cousins' spouses looked like and some of what their lineage was and she told us how many children everyone had at the time."

"And all of it has come true?" he asked.

"Well, we haven't had the big family party yet," she admitted. "We've been waiting for you to show up."

"Your whole family?"

"Of course. Most of what Grandmother saw has already happened."

"The twins that she saw," he said. "Did she see them born?"

"They were running around with the other children. So when Robyn announced she was having twins, I certainly wasn't surprised."

"What hasn't happened yet?"

"Gail is supposed to be pregnant at the party . . . with a daughter."

"But she hadn't had the daughter when your grandmother had the dream."

"No, Grandmother said that her spirit escort told her the baby would be a girl."

"Have they been trying for another child?"

"Ever since Cody was two."

"Your grandmother had quite a vision," he said, his voice and his heart filled with awe and admiration.

"Is it any wonder that when my cousins learned I had met you, that they came to learn of your religion? We've all been waiting for you, Abbot. All of us, not just me. It's been a long, long time. Everyone expected me to find you much sooner than this."

He shook his head. "A remarkable woman, your grandmother."

She finished putting the last dish in the drainer, and Abbot picked it up to dry it, but she removed it from his hands, then snuggled up against him. "I think that the big family party grandmother saw was our wedding reception because I had on an exquisitely beautiful white gown and it was held in a lovely garden. The house that Ryan's having built has a huge back yard with pines bordering it. And Gail has such a green thumb, she'll turn it into the garden of Eden in no time. I was hoping we could have our reception there next June."

"Sounds good to me," he said, hugging her to him.

How he loved the feel of her as she rubbed his back. The scent of her hair always tantalized him, yet it was her tender spirit that he was learning to love most about her. She might be an excellent nurse and a modern, sophisticated woman, but because of her child-like faith, he'd recognized her as one of God's chosen daughters.

Had she not turned his heart back to God, he doubted he would ever have realized the importance that he now felt in following the right path. His chest filled with tender feelings for Bekah. He stepped back and took her hand in his, admiring how the ring looked on her finger.

She smiled as she watched him, and with her other hand she stroked his cheek. "I have a question I want to ask," she said, "but I don't want to offend you."

"You can ask me anything," he whispered huskily.

She hesitated as a timid expression stole onto her face.

"Anything!" he reiterated. "Bekah, I have no secrets from you."

"Then what is this?" she asked, her hand slipping under his collar and lifting out the silver chain with the jade and silver ring.

He gave her a serious look as he said, "It was my mother's ring. She died when I was a child and my father kept the ring in his wallet until the day he died. He gave it to her when they were sweethearts in high school. Look, he had their initials carved into it."

Bekah looked at the underside of the silver ring. "EDS plus SNT," she whispered in wonderment.

"Edward Davis Sparkleman plus Sarah Nicole Timothy." He smiled as he remembered, "Pa always called her Sarah Nicole. I didn't realize until years after she died that Sarah and Nicole were two separate names, I thought she was one of those lucky women who had a four-syllable name." He hesitated for a moment, relishing the sweet memory. Then he said, "When Pa died in an avalanche two and a half years ago, my brothers found the ring tucked inside his wallet. I, being the youngest, had very little to remember my mother by, so they gave her ring to me. I put it on this chain, and it's hardly been off my neck ever since."

He studied her wide, oval eyes and realized she was fighting to keep her tears at bay. After she managed to do so, she confessed, "I wondered if it was the ring you gave to Alyssa, when you proposed to her."

Abbot exhaled, disappointed that she would think something like that. "No," he said with determination. "I tossed that ring overboard long ago."

"Wasn't that rather expensive?" she asked.

"At the time, I'd just learned Alyssa had accepted my brother's proposal and I was angry. You'd be shocked at what I can throw away when I'm angry."

She smiled at his confession. "I hope I never see you that angry."

"Fortunately, I've learned to control my temper a little better. Anyway, hindsight tells me it would have been better to sell Alyssa's ring or pawn it." He shrugged. "I guess it was one of those *I'm through with you!* gestures."

"Abbot, tell me about Alyssa," Bekah requested. "Since you proposed, I've been wondering how I measure up."

He smiled. "You have nothing to worry about," he said persuasively, "because I love you with all my heart and soul."

"What's different between us?"

He took her out on the balcony and looked out over the houses. The rain was nothing more than a light misty drizzle. "You can see Green Lake from here," he noticed aloud. "It's a beautiful lake and certainly one to enjoy and be desired. But in my mind, Bekah, you're the ocean. Alyssa was only the lake."

Her eyes lit up and the corners of her mouth curled as she smiled. "What a sweet thing to say."

"I can do better than that," he explained as he put his arms around her waist and pulled her close to him. "Alyssa was the stepping stone to someone far better. She dumped me because I couldn't give my life to God and I deserved it. Alyssa's giving me up sent me fleeing to Friday Harbor. The San Juans are one of the most beautiful group of Islands in America and I've learned to love the area. While I was there, I met Scott T. Hamilton, a fellow sailor acquainted with Josh and Kayla and a relative of the museum administrator. He gave me a good reference on Josh's recommendation, and told me that the administrator was looking for an assistant. That brought me to Seattle, where I found you. In reality, I owe Alyssa the biggest thank you. If I'd married her, I don't know where I'd be now, but I know that we wouldn't have been happy. The way I look at it, God was using me to bring Alyssa to Ed. My stubborn cowpoke brother wouldn't go looking for her on his own. And because I did that, albeit unknowingly, God gave me one of His greatest blessings in return. He gave me . . . you. And you gave God back to me."

Bekah melted against him. "I've never met anyone like you," she murmured.

"I can say the same thing about you," he whispered as his lips brushed her forehead with light kisses.

"Then, tell me about your family. You have three brothers and one sister," she said, "but I don't know much about them, except for Tom."

"Kayla's not actually related to us by blood. Her father and mine were best friends. Mont owned the Bar M Ranch and Pa managed it for him. Pa and Mont had known each other since school and they were best men at each other's weddings. Mont and his wife had Kayla, but when she was about a year old, her mother died. Pa helped him through it. When Mont was finally able to reconcile himself to losing his wife, he built a log cabin across the meadow from his lodge for Pa and our family. That's where I was born, their fourth son. When I was four, my mother died from cancer. Neither Pa nor Mont remarried and Kayla grew up with us boys as though we were sister and brothers. I always thought she was my sister until I was a teenager and found out Ed planned to marry her. Boy! That was a shock!"

"But he didn't?"

"No. Kayla wanted to be a scientist and a sailor and she couldn't do either of those things at the Bar M. She finally moved to California, got her doctorate and started working for some big company in San Diego, where she met Joshua Bridger Clark."

"That's Hans' twin, right?"

"Identical twin," Abbot corrected, as he recalled how very much alike the two brothers look. "Anyway, Kayla married Josh. That threw Ed for a loop because he still had feelings for Kayla, even though she'd told him she felt more like his sister than his sweetheart, even when they were engaged."

"I'd like to meet Josh and Kayla."

"You will. They're expecting twins soon, so I doubt they'll come up here this year. But next summer with the twins, well, I can't imagine they'll miss our wedding."

"What is your other brother's name?" she asked.

"William Davis Sparkleman, but we call him Will. He and Melanie got married about a year ago. Their first child is due sometime this summer."

"Does he work at the Bar M Ranch?"

"No. He runs a river rafting company for his father-in-law up at Dutch John. That's at the southern end of Flaming Gorge. I expect he'll take over the business when Melanie's dad retires because she's an only child and her father dotes on her."

"It sounds like you have a great family," she said.

Abbot yawned. "And I promised Hans I'd be there for his call tonight. I'd better call a cab."

"I can drive you back," Bekah objected.

"I don't want you out at night on my account. This is Seattle."

She arched an eyebrow and gave him a stubborn frown. "And just where were you the past ten years since I got my driver's license?"

Abbot backed down. He wasn't going to get in a fight with her tonight. "All right," he agreed. "Shall we go?"

Within a half hour they were kissing goodbye at *Bridger's Child.* When he finally said goodnight, he wondered how he was ever going to keep their relationship at a safe distance so they could get to the temple in a year.

He stepped up onto *Bridger's Child,* slipped off his shoes and unlocked the companionway door, then slid the hatch back and removed the door boards. Soon he was taking a cold shower in the stall adjacent to the head, grateful that the Cabo Rico 38 had one: It was a shower temperature of choice. When he was thoroughly chilled, he slipped into his pajamas and checked the messages on his telephones.

Hans' messages on the cell phone sounded urgent. "Where are you? I've been trying to reach you since noon. Call me."

Dialing the number, Abbot waited a few seconds for Hans to pick up. The background noise he heard sounded as though Hans was driving the car.

"It's about time," came Hans' answer.

No hello, how are you? "Good to hear you missed me," Abbot said.

"Did you talk to your boss yet?" Hans asked.

"You told me not to until you called."

"I've been calling all afternoon."

"I left my phones home."

"Both of them?"

"Sorry."

"Here's the plan. I'm on my way back to Seattle. In the morning I'll go in with you to the museum and we'll talk to Mr. Hamilton together."

"Did you get the contract signed?" asked Abbot.

"Yes. The owner is in failing health, without heirs. He's also friends of the Quileute and Hoh nations. I had to stipulate in the agreement that all artifacts found on the property would be preserved according to current archaeological standards and that someone from the museum would head up the project. I gave him your name and it seems he's heard of you through some PR work you did last December for the Native American Potlatch Benefit."

"Yes, that project was phenomenally successful," Abbot admitted. "It was the first real opportunity Mr. Hamilton gave me to prove my worth."

"With the property ownership in our hands, I've gone to an attorney and established the Cody Owen Stevens Antiquities Trust, COSAT for short, designating the trust as the beneficiary. I just have to file the documents tomorrow in court. Then, it'll be a matter of public record. I wanted Mr. Hamilton in on the project before it goes public. The press will hear of it sooner or later, and we should have our documentation in order before that."

"What about funding?" Abbot asked, amazed at how much Hans had already accomplished. Of course, Hans came from a very wealthy family, with a fund from his grandfather that would ensure financial stability for the next dozen generations.

Hans answered, "The Admiral wants to get in on the ground floor and he's flying up Thursday afternoon. I'd like to take him out to the site and draw up some preliminary plans. But he says whatever we need, he and Mother will manage the funding. He's got rich, powerful friends all over the globe. I'm certain that money will be the least of our problems." Hans laughed, and it sounded like an echo over the airwaves.

"How's Tom?"

"I packed in another few days of food, some extra rope and batteries. He's doing well. Surprisingly, he's become a fisherman in our absence. He shared his catch with me before I left this evening."

"Always resourceful," Abbot admitted. He hadn't seen any fishing gear, but he knew Tom well enough to realize he'd probably built a trap. There were plenty of traps in the stream that flowed across the meadow when they were growing up and Tom built most of them.

"Another interesting thing," said Hans, interrupting his thoughts.

"What?"

"If we'd have driven down the old oil road north of the river, we'd have only had to go about a half mile to the site, rather than the three miles we walked coming in from the south. It shouldn't be too tough putting a decent road into the project at all."

"That figures," said Abbot. "What about the Governor? I'm not sure what the protocol dictates."

"The Admiral said he'd deal with the Governor."

"What do you suppose he meant by that?" Abbot asked.

"If I know the Admiral, it means a media circus for a few days."

"Do we want that kind of publicity?"

"Yes," answered Hans. "Trust me on this one, Abbot. Without the Admiral, we'd never have the political backing to get the project off the ground."

"All right," said Abbot. "But I'm going to head on out there on Wednesday, regardless what Hamilton says tomorrow. We need to get some photos taken and a complete computer setup to document every single aspect of the dig."

"The Admiral will ship us all the electronics we need. But, photos for how the site looks right now is going to be of real benefit once we begin."

"I hear the excitement straining from your voice, Hans," Abbot accused. "Tell me you're not at least half as anxious as I am to begin."

"Well," came the belabored response. "Perhaps a little."

Abbot laughed. "I thought so, you scoundrel."

"Hey! I'm naming you as the overseer, what more do you want?"

"I want you to be co-manager with me, Hans."

"I promised Mr. Ridgely that you'd head up the project and I can't go against my word."

"Very well," said Abbot. "But in my mind, you're the second in command."

"For now, Indy," came the casual response.

"How far away are you?" Abbot asked.

"I'm almost to Port Angeles. I should just make one of the last ferries."

"I'm not going to wait up, then."

"Leave the door unlatched, will you?"

"Sure, just don't wake me."

"Say," Hans interjected just before Abbot was going to hang up.

"What?"

"How's Bekah?"

"Great! She accepted my formal proposal today and is now wearing my ring."

"Did you get the fear issue worked out?"

"No. She won't give it up and I'm clueless what she's so worried about."

"Maybe with time," suggested Hans.

"Maybe," Abbot agreed. Though how long it would take her, he had no idea.

When Abbot hung up, he was astounded at all the changes taking place in his life. All were a direct result of his having met Bekah. He'd fallen in love, gotten engaged and found an ancient treasure. In his heart he had to give God the credit. For the first time in his life, he could see the Lord's hand moving him into position to receive blessings. Silently, he acknowledged his gratitude to his Maker.

For as long as Abbot could remember, he'd wanted to work on an archaeological dig site and now he would get the opportunity. He knelt upon the cabin sole and offered his heart-felt thoughts in prayer. "Father in Heaven, I have been richly blessed. Thou hast opened up the windows of heaven and poured me out blessings so great I scarcely know how to contain them. I thank thee for Bekah, Father. She is the product of Thy divine inspiration. Bless her that her heart will be softened and her fears will be eased. Ever since we found the stone box, she's been afraid of something. She's also worried that I'm going to abandon her. Lord, help her to know I would never leave her."

He stopped. For a few minutes, he couldn't go on. A thought had entered his mind and warmed his heart, yet he didn't quite understand it. After a time, the feeling passed, so he continued.

"Thank Thee for allowing us to find the stone box. I feel certain that there is something of great worth inside it. I'm not speaking from a material standpoint. It may contain ancient writings, perhaps from some ancient tribes who inhabited these areas. If it does, it will become one of the greatest scientific discoveries of our time. As far as we know, these northwestern nations had no written language from an archaeologist's or linguistic's standpoint. Help me to be ever mindful of the sacred trust Thou hath placed in my hands. I recognize the value of such records would far outweigh any material gain possible. Help me be true to Thee in all that I do with this project.

"Perhaps my mission in life is to work on this project and solve some of the mysteries that—" Again he was assailed by a powerful, warm feeling inside his chest, but he didn't understand what it was. "Help me, Lord, to understand what Thou wouldst have me do. Guide me, that I may know Thy will."

Abbot ended his prayer and stood up. The feelings that he'd had were strong, but he didn't know what the Lord wanted from him. For several long minutes he pondered the sensations he'd received, but he shook his head in abject futility because he did not comprehend them.

Finally, he gave up and decided to check in with Tom. When he dialed the satellite phone number, it rang several times before Tom answered it.

"Yep!" came the gruff voice of his brother.

"I heard you've been fishing on private property," Abbot teased.

"Owned by the Cody Stevens Antiquities Trust," Tom growled back.

"Down, boy!" exclaimed Abbot. "I was only teasing."

"I'm glad yer just teasin', 'cause I'm mad as a grizzly in a bear trap."

"Why?" Abbot questioned.

"I thought I was bein' real helpful this afternoon. Hans left me two hundred feet of rope and some fresh batteries and what not. I tied the rope to my belt and the other end to that tree outside yer cave, then I went in. Got about a hundred feet or so into the cave, where it opens up real wide and saw some things that'll make your hair stand on end. Some Indian stuff, I think."

A knot grew in the pit of Abbot's stomach. "What do you mean you think? Either you saw something or you didn't."

"I dropped my dang flashlight! It rolled down into a crevice where I can't reach it. The light went out, too. I had to crawl all the way back in the dark. It's just a good thing I tied myself onto that rope, like you fellas did Saturday, or I'd likely be in there still."

Abbot laughed. "That's why you're mad?"

"Yep. Dumbest thing this ol' polecat's done in a long time."

"It could have been worse. You could have fallen in some crevice. Don't go back in unless someone's there to back you up, Tom," scolded Abbot.

"Aw, I was plannin' on thumbin' a ride into Forks tomorrow for another flashlight, or one of them cave helmets that have a light on 'em."

"No. I'll be there on Wednesday and I'll bring plenty of gear."

"If you insist, little brother."

"I may be your younger brother, Tom. But you don't want to mess with me on this one. I've lost enough family members for one lifetime!"

"All right," Tom defended. "You can dish it out, but you can't take it, can you?"

"I'm sorry," Abbot apologized. "But, I care too much about my family to take any risks on this project."

"I understand, boss," came the gruff reply.

"Anything else you want to share?" Abbot asked.

"Best dang trout I ever tasted."

Abbot laughed. "I'll see you Wednesday night. You might want to flag some markers north of you to the old oil road that runs down to the Hoh reservation."

"Yep! Hans and me already done that."

"Did he think about *No Trespassing* signs?"

"Yep."

"Good. Wednesday then."

"You're the boss, little brother."

❧   ❦

"Is that you, Hans?" Abbot asked, sitting up as he heard the door boards being removed. He glanced at his watch, it was well after midnight.

"I thought you were going to be asleep," Hans answered as he came down the companionway steps. Turning back around, he replaced the boards and secured the interior latch.

"I couldn't sleep after I talked to Tom. You'll never guess what's happened." Abbot slung his legs off the front v-berth and padded across the cabin sole.

"Hmm?" Hans asked, apparently too tired to care.

Abbot stood across the galley counter from him, watching Hans get a glass of water. Refusing to answer until Hans showed some real interest, he waited. He knew Hans was tired, but now the poor man was daft.

After Hans drank the water, he turned his attention to Abbot. "Why did you say you waited up for me?" he asked, yawning and stretching.

"Oh, nothing," said Abbot as he turned and walked nonchalantly toward the v-berth. "Just Tom discovering a room full of artifacts inside the cave," he said softly as though it were an insignificant bit of trivia.

"That's nice," Hans mumbled absently. Then he stopped.

Abbot turned around quickly and watched his friend's reaction. He'd been waiting for this all night and he wasn't going to miss a second of it.

"What did you say?" Hans questioned as a puzzled wrinkle sank into his forehead.

"Tom found a room full of native artifacts in our cave."

"When? How? What kind? How many? Abbot!"

Abbot just smiled and waited for the rapid-fire questions to end. When Hans had finished, he sighed elaborately, "We don't know. Tom dropped his flashlight down a crevice and had to abandon his search."

"If you're joking with me—" Hans growled threateningly.

Abbot sank wearily on the starboard settee. "Unfortunately, it's true."

"I can't even go back over there until Thursday when the Admiral arrives. Is he going after another flashlight?" Hans removed a shoe and dropped it to the floor.

"No. I told him not to go in the cave again unless one of us is with him. He's liable to get completely lost."

"Good point." Hans removed his other shoe. "Well, there's nothing I can do until Thursday." The sleepiness in his voice made him sound dazed and confused.

"But, I'm going back first thing Wednesday," Abbot insisted, "No matter what Hamilton has to say about it. I don't even care, at this point, if he fires me."

"Mmm hmm," mumbled Hans as though his mind had already taken a nap.

"I really don't want to lose my job," continued Abbot. "But this is the opportunity of a lifetime."

"Night," Hans moaned as he fell over on the port settee, sound asleep.

Abbot covered him up with a blanket and climbed back into the v-berth where he doubted he would ever be able to rest until after he'd explored the cave more thoroughly himself.

Almost a full hour later, he heard Hans' sleepy voice ask, "Did you say Tom went into the cave, or was I dreaming?"

"You were dreaming," Abbot answered. Then, he chuckled as he heard the rustling of the blanket and a contented snoring sound coming from the salon.

Chapter Thirteen

When Abbot walked into the museum administrator's, with Hans at his side, he was once again impressed with the grandeur of it: fine gold lettering on the door; plush hand-woven carpet; red cedar furnishings and finely woven basketry wall hangings, handcrafted by Native American artisans. The expansive room was a masterpiece, a blend of ancient American and modern contemporary art forms.

Randall Hamilton, a stocky man in his early sixties, had a dashing smile and a shock of white hair surrounding a balding spot on the back of his round head. "Come in, Abbot," said Randall, as he arose and greeted Abbot with a warm handshake.

"Good morning, sir," Abbot returned the smile and directed him to his friend. "This is my associate, Hans Bridger Clark."

"My yes, I do believe I've heard about you from associates of your brother, Joshua Bridger Clark."

"Word travels fast," said Hans. "I'm happy to meet you, Mr. Hamilton."

"Randall, please, gentlemen." He motioned for them to sit down and then turned his attention to Abbot. "Splendid banquet for the Governor," he praised. "Though I didn't see you around after the meal."

"I had an unexpected emergency," Abbot responded.

"Nothing serious, I hope."

"No. As a matter of fact, I could probably have returned, but it would have been too late to do anything more than participate in the last dance and bid everyone goodnight."

"No matter, you have trained the staff remarkably well, Abbot. I've been very impressed, indeed."

"Thank you, sir."

"Before we get into details, may I have a word with you in private?" Randall asked, giving Abbot a conspiratorial smile.

Red flags went off in Abbot's mind as he nodded. What was this all about? Randall Hamilton had never had any qualms about speaking in front of anyone who happened to be nearby and now he was asking for privacy?

Hans stood immediately. "Sorry," he said. "I'll be right outside, when you're ready." He walked over to the door and pulled it closed as he went out.

Abbot's attention turned back to his employer. Had he done something wrong? He searched his mind, worrying.

The older man said, "No need to squirm, Abbot, I'm not inclined to reprimand you. Though I must say, I was certainly surprised when I received the governor's telephone call this morning."

"Yes, sir," Abbot said, hoping it sounded like he knew all about the governor's purpose for calling.

"An archaeological discovery and you hadn't mentioned a word to me," said Randall. "No matter, I'm not the kind to take offense. I'm certain there's a perfectly logical explanation."

"Yes, sir," Abbot responded. *The Admiral works fast, I see.* At least he now understood why the man wanted privacy. He didn't know Hans was part of the project, as well.

"If I'd known your extra days off last week would be spent in the field, I would have told you to keep track of the actual time and reimburse you for it, son."

"My associate, Hans—" Abbot began.

"Come now," said Randall. "I know that Admiral Bridger Clark is his father and that is precisely why I sent Mr. Clark out. This is between the two of us, Abbot. You've shown some remarkable initiative and I'm prepared to offer you a proposition."

"Oh?" Abbot gulped, a little leery of Randall Hamilton's domineering manner.

"Yes, my entire life's work is founded here in Washington. I was with the Ozette excavation from the very beginning. Everything I've lived for, with exception of my family, is wrapped up in this building. I lobbied for it, I gathered every single penny that went into the construction. This was my dream. Now I'm old, I have no son to share it with. Some miraculous power brought you to me, after I'd had several disappointing years with other young men I'd hoped could take over after me."

"What are you getting at, exactly?" Abbot asked, a little confused.

"I'm preparing my retirement papers," Randall confided. "I had hoped you would want to take over when I'm gone." He hesitated and studied Abbot's reaction like a tyee would study his namima.

"I'm flattered," Abbot finally said, exhaling slowly.

"Your salary would double, your duties would be less demanding. Instead of being the glue that holds everything together you would only have to delegate where the glue should be put. This would make more judicious use of your time, son, giving you options, such as spending more time in the field, at various dig sites of your choosing."

Abbot gulped. He hoped he didn't appear as flustered as he felt. "I . . . don't know what to say."

"Say yes, of course," encouraged Randall.

For some unknown reason, Abbot couldn't answer right away. He tried to analyze his feelings, but he only knew that he should stall. "I'd like some time to think about it, sir."

Randall nodded, arched an eyebrow precariously and said, "I intend to hand in my resignation by August thirtieth. It would give me great honor to present your name at the same time, as my final recommendation for my replacement."

"Thank you, sir," said Abbot. He stood and shook the older man's hand. "I will give you my answer by that date."

"Good!" Randall sat down and rubbed his hands together. "Make sure you clock your time from last week," he encouraged. "I insist."

"Yes, I will." Abbot was speechless.

Randall pressed the intercom button. "Miss Giles, please send Mr. Clark back in, would you?"

When Hans rejoined them, Randall turned to him and said, "Your father is apparently a very good friend of the Governor, Mr. Clark."

"I'm not surprised," Hans said, though Abbot recognized a little amazement on Hans' face.

"I'm prepared to lobby for museum funds to back the Cody Stevens Antiquities Trust by thirty percent. The Governor has assured me that the state will match whatever we put into the project. But your father will have to find someone to cover the remaining forty percent. Is that understood?"

"The Admiral works fast, doesn't he?" asked Abbot.

"That he does," said Hans. "That he does."

"I presume, Abbot, that you would like to request a transfer to the field for a period of no less than, shall we say two months?" Randall asked.

Calculating quickly, Abbot realized that would give him the time he needed to make a decision regarding his appointment to administrator. He smiled. "That would be just about right, sir."

"The governor has invited the three of us to a luncheon at his mansion this afternoon. I accepted for all of us, I hope you don't mind. And we've scheduled a press conference for tomorrow morning at ten. Am I moving things along fast enough for you, Abbot?" the older man asked.

Abbot hedged. It would make a late start on getting over to the project tomorrow, but it was a necessary evil in terms of their obtaining adequate funding.

Suddenly, Randall laughed. "I can almost see those wheels working," he said. "You're debating whether or not to take time away from your new project so you can pump up the COSAT's bank account. Your enthusiasm for the project shows clearly in your eyes, son. You remind me of myself when we first started digging at Ozette."

❧   ❧

Abbot arrived at Bekah's condo after her relatives this time; he'd been busy with Hans at the state supreme court getting signatures and documents obtained. A quick luncheon at the Governor's mansion around two that same day, and a promise to pledge state funds tomorrow morning during the press conference, was the highlight of the day. Now it was Bekah's turn, and Cody's, whom Abbot planned to include. After all, it was Cody's discovery, not theirs.

"Sorry I'm late," he said, giving her a quick kiss. Then, he whispered in her ear, "Keep Ryan, Gail and Cody here after the missionary discussions. We need to talk."

She gave him a curious smile, then took his hand and led him inside. After a brief hello to each of her family members and new introductions, *Yikes! There's three more tonight!* he sat beside Bekah on the floor and held her hand while the missionaries began their lesson.

It took quite a while for all their questions to be answered, longer than the night before and Abbot felt the tension tightening at the back of his neck. He wanted to feast upon the spirit of the meeting, and he recognized that it was strong that night, but his mind was so filled with the importance of what had happened today that he could hardly contain himself.

When the benediction was offered and cookies for the relatives had been served, the family started filing out one by one. It seemed to take forever. Finally, Abbot went back to the restroom and washed his face with cold water. He was steaming with anxiety.

A knock came at the door. "Everyone's gone but my brother's family," Bekah said.

"I'll be right out." As he dried his face, he said, "I need to speak with Ryan and Gail first."

"I'll take Cody down to their condo and get him ready for bed, then bring him back. Will that work?"

He opened the door. "Thanks."

"What's going on?" she asked.

"The project," he answered, giving her a quick kiss. When she wanted to linger there, he laughed. "Later, honey. Right now, there's business to attend to."

She gave him a lop-sided smile, and he hoped it meant she was getting over some of her fears. He followed her into the living room.

"Hey, buddy, let's run downstairs a minute, okay?"

"Aw, you just don't want me to hear all the good stuff."

Abbot saw the disappointment in Cody's eyes. "Stay," he said. "It's okay, Cody. I just need to ask your parents' permission for something. Then I'll explain it to you."

"Okay!" squealed Cody. "You hear that, Aunt Bekah? I get to be a grownup!"

Bekah nodded and started talking to him about what kind of pet he planned to get when they moved into their new house.

Meanwhile, Abbot stepped over to the dining room and whispered to Gail and Ryan, "I'd like your permission to present Cody to the Governor tomorrow morning at a press conference, as the boy who found a priceless treasure near the Hoh River. Is that all right?"

"The Governor?" Gail asked. "Really?"

Abbot nodded and was pleased to see them both agreeable.

When they rejoined Bekah and Cody, Abbot sat the young boy down on the coffee table, then he sat directly in front of him on the sofa. "We need to have a man-to-man talk," Abbot began.

"It's about that big rock, isn't it?" asked Cody.

"Yes, it is."

"It's really important, isn't it?" Cody said as his lower lip trembled.

"It is probably one of the most important discoveries of the century," Abbot confided. "It's so important, the Governor wants to me to announce it at a press conference tomorrow morning. There'll be newspaper, magazine and television reporters from all over."

"Are you gonna'?" Cody asked timidly.

"Not without you there, buddy. You're the one who found it and you're the one who deserves the credit. What do you say?"

"You want me to go with you?" came the curious response.

"You didn't doubt my integrity for a minute, did you?"

"Integrity's a pretty big word," said the boy. "I don't know what it means, but I was thinking you wouldn't remember me when you got famous."

"Cody, you're the famous one. Without you, how could we have found anything?"

"You mean it?" Cody asked.

Abbot took Cody into his arms and hugged him like a father to his son. "I absolutely mean it. I won't go to the press conference without you. In fact, we're naming the project after you. It will be called the Cody Stevens Antiquities Trust. Will you come?"

He held Cody away and studied his expression for a moment. The eyes of this small boy seemed to fill his whole face as the magnitude of what was happening sank into him.

"Sure!" said Cody after several stunned moments. "Long as you're there."

"Together," Abbot insisted.

"Buddies forever!" Cody squealed, throwing his arms around Abbot's neck and squeezing him tightly.

"There's something else I want to tell you."

Cody sat back down, almost reverently Abbot noticed.

"We found a cave not too far from the box."

"Chief Taquinna's cave?" The boys blue eyes widened in amazement.

"I don't think so. I think this cave may be older than Taquinna."

"But it's important, right?" Cody asked.

"It might turn out to be important, we'll have to see."

"Cool!" Cody exclaimed. "Can I go see it?"

"Not yet. It's very dangerous right now. We have to wait until we make certain it's safe for people to enter."

"How long will that take?" A frown wrinkled its way across his freckled face.

"I don't know, buddy. But when we determine that it is safe, you'll be the first to know."

Ryan tousled his son's red hair. "If you're going to meet the Governor tomorrow morning, we'd better get you to bed."

"Will you bring him to the mansion about nine o'clock?" Abbot asked. "The press conference is at ten, but we'll need to run through some questions and answers first, to prime him."

"Of course."

When the Stevens returned to their condo, Abbot was still sitting on the sofa. He took Bekah's hand in his as she sat beside him. "You haven't said a word about all this."

"What's there to say?" she asked flippantly.

"We're not going to have a problem about this, are we?"

"It doesn't matter what I think," she said. "You're going ahead regardless of how I feel."

"If I understood why you're upset about the project, perhaps I'd reconsider. But you've given me no explanation at all." He tried to pull her close but she backed off and stood up, keeping her back to him.

"If I asked you not to take the project anywhere, just walk away right now, would you?" came her question.

Difficult emotions washed over him. He would do anything for her, anything. But, how could she love him and ask him to walk away from this project? "Not without a good reason," he protested as he stood up, but he did not touch her. His hands remained rigid at his sides. She continued to keep her back to him and her obstinance worried him. "Why? Is that what you're asking me to do?"

"It scares me," she said. "You know that, yet you're going ahead anyway."

"Why does it frighten you, Bekah? Did your grandmother tell you I was going to die working on this project?"

"No."

"Did she say that I would be maimed for life and become a vegetable?"

"No."

"Someone in a wheelchair, perhaps?"

"No."

"Then what?"

"Haven't you asked God?" she wondered.

"I have," he confessed.

"What did he say?" came her stubborn question.

"I'm not sure I understood what His answer was."

"So he didn't answer you."

"Yes, he answered, but my mind was so wrapped up in other things that I was past feeling."

"What does that mean?"

He ran his hands through his brown-black hair as he exhaled sharply. She turned and faced him once again. Finally, he said, "It's an expression we use to indicate that we weren't sufficiently prepared for the answers, so when they came we didn't recognize them."

"Then you don't really want to know," she accused. "Why should I explain my fears when you have no interest in what they are? Otherwise, you would have prepared for the answers God gave you."

"I'm not perfect," he protested. "And I don't pretend to hear God every time he speaks to me. Most people can't really claim to be that in tune that they hear him every time He talks to them. I'm out of practice. It's been a long time and I've only just begun to come back into the gospel myself."

"Then maybe you're not who I thought you were," she said, her lips trembling as she did so. "Maybe you're not the one my grandmother dreamed about."

"If you believe that," he said as he swallowed a lump that grew thickly in his throat, "you'll return the ring and call the engagement off."

When she didn't respond, he turned away and walked to the door. With his hand on the knob he said, "Goodnight, Bekah. I'll call you tomorrow night from the project."

"You're going back there, tomorrow?" she asked as he opened the door.

"Yes. Right after the press conference."

"You didn't tell me," she accused.

He lifted and lowered his shoulders. "I just did."

She turned her back on him and folded her arms.

Abbot had no trouble reading her body language. "Goodnight," he whispered. "I love you." Then, he turned and went down the hall to the elevator.

Within a few minutes he was driving the Bronco back across Fremont bridge toward Westlake Avenue. When he was finally at the parking lot, he set the brake, locked the Bronco and headed toward the steep stairs leading to the dock. He had no idea how he'd driven home. His mind was a complete blank.

For some strange reason he kept looking at his hands to see if there was an engagement ring in one of them. But, she hadn't given him back the ring. No, she would probably give it to her brother and ask him to return it tomorrow morning at the press conference.

He didn't need a cold shower tonight, hot would suit him fine.

After he set the alarm, Abbot climbed wearily into bed, forgetting to say his prayers. When he finally remembered, Hans had already returned and was snoring in the salon on the port settee. Sitting up, he debated whether or not he really wanted to say them at all.

Bekah had given him a bold declaration, revealing where his true alliance lay. He didn't want her to feel that unkindly about him. The desire in his heart to be a better man for Bekah had not diminished, though his estimation of how long their engagement would last had been whittled down considerably.

Abbot knelt on top of the v-berth, bumping his head in the process. The only way he could pray was to bend over so that he was laying atop his knees as they bent under him, but since he wanted absolute privacy, this position was the only possible solution. Then he poured out his thoughts to his Father in Heaven.

When he was finished praying, Abbot was astonished by the prompting and the inspiration that he'd been given. Now, he was frightened, just like Bekah. It couldn't possibly be true. The Lord surely wouldn't ask him to do that now. It was too late, he was too old, he had too many other things that were pressing upon him, demanding his attention.

Certain he had misunderstood, he began another prayer. This time he pleaded with the Lord not to place upon him such a heavy burden. It was more than any father would ask of his son. Surely, Abbot could do the same thing right there in Seattle, part-time, working in a stake calling. But again, the answer came so clearly he could not deny the feelings.

Anger flooded over him. His third prayer was not exactly the kind a man in his position should utter. He begged God not to require that he carry such a heavy cross, for the weight of it was impossible to bear. He explained all the reasons why he could not, would not, be able to do as God had asked. For the third time, the impressions came to him with such clarity and force that he fell over and trembled, consumed with anguish.

Finally, he refused to pray any longer.

Completely disregarding the Lord's request, he climbed back under the covers and said aloud, "You can't possibly know what you're asking, God! Nor could you even care about me . . . and certainly not about Bekah." He pulled the blanket over his head and tried to sleep, ignoring all the feelings and tumult going through him. It was a useless effort. He tossed and turned all night, but he certainly didn't sleep.

Chapter Fourteen

"*D*id you have a rough night?" Hans asked as Abbot ate a dry cracker and took a couple of antacids.

Abbot nodded.

"I hope you'll look better after you clean up. The press conference is in two hours and you're as pale and clabbered looking as the spoiled milk I threw away last night. Do you plan on buying groceries anytime soon, or would you like me to?"

Abbot shook his head. He felt miserable, and he knew the aching in his chest would not be eased by all the antacids in the world. Having recently gone back on the promise he'd made God two and a half weeks ago, he didn't know if there was anything else that could happen to him, at this point, that could possibly cause him more anguish than he was already suffering.

"Not too talkative," Hans observed. "That should glean lots of favor with the press today."

"Will you please shut up?" Abbot asked. "I'm not in the mood to spar with you today."

Hans frowned, but he did not revolt.

He had to give Hans credit for having patience, a virtue Abbot had never garnered. When he couldn't stand the silent treatment any longer, he said, "I'm sorry, Hans. I'm a little irritable."

"An understatement," said Hans, "but you're forgiven. What's the matter with you anyway?"

"I told God no last night." *There! I've admitted it!*

"What could He possibly ask you to do that would cause you to give Him that kind of an answer?" Hans questioned, lifting an eyebrow in surprise.

"It isn't important what He asked. The thing is, I can't do it and I told Him I couldn't do it. End of story."

"How did He take your refusal?" came the query.

"How would I know? I stopped listening after I gave Him my answer."

Hans hesitated and Abbot knew he was choosing his words wisely. It was a habit with Hans when he felt his responses or questions might have some eternal consequence. Finally he said, "Do you think that was wise?"

Abbot glared. "Do you think it's wise of God to take away everything from me? And I do mean everything: Bekah, the project, my career, everything?"

"He wants you to give up all these things?"

"Yes, He does."

"Oh." Hans was obviously perplexed.

"See! Even you can't go for that one, can you?" Abbot demanded. "Well, neither can I! If it was just my career, I could probably find a job somewhere else. If it was the project, that's a little tougher. I'm on the line for the project, you've invested money in it to acquire the property and my name is on the contract as the executive officer. If I gave that up, Dr. Hamilton could take over, but he's retiring, so you may lose a bundle and the project would lose its viability, it may even be lost completely. But Bekah? I'm not giving up my Bekah. I won't do it. She's the best thing that ever happened to me!"

"I can see that you're upset," said Hans.

"Don't give me 'I' messages!" Abbot barked. "I took that psyche class in college, and I don't need it!"

"Back off!" Hans jutted out his chin in defiance. "I'm trying to be understanding, so don't pick up my empathy and beat me to death with it!"

Abbot glared, but Hans glared back. Finally, they both gave in and apologized.

When Abbot finished showering, he was in better humor. They drove to the governor's mansion in Hans' Cherokee and parked. The building was austere and powerful, but since they'd already been there the day before, it had lost a little of its intimidation.

Ryan, Gail, Cody and Bekah were waiting for them when they arrived.

Abbot was surprised to see his fiancée. Part of him wanted to pull her into his arms and kiss her until she had no choice but to forgive him. However, he'd left the ring on her finger, it wasn't the other way around. Whatever happened to their relationship now was up to her. Somehow he would have to tell her that she didn't need to be frightened anymore. He had no intention of doing what the Lord had asked of him.

Cody was dressed in a pair of black pants and a forest green shirt that made his red hair even more attractive. He was definitely going to grow into a handsome young man.

After twenty minutes of coaching, they were finally ready. Ryan, Gail and Bekah waited in the background, then they were escorted into the press room, where they were given front row seats, as was Hans.

The Governor addressed a few other matters before getting to the project. When he did, his words carried hope into Abbot's heart, hope for himself, hope for Cody, hope for the project. "It gives me great pleasure to announce the formation of a new entity today, the Cody Owen Stevens Antiquities Trust, spearheaded by the assistant administrator of the museum, Mr. Abbot Sparkleman. The organization was established recently to provide protection for an area of archaeological discovery that I'm sure he's anxious to share with you. Mr. Sparkleman."

Cameras flashed, microphones squealed and were adjusted immediately, as Abbot stepped up to them. "Thank you, ladies and gentlemen of the press. I appreciate Governor Jannes inviting me here this morning. He's been most gracious in his comments, but I assure you that this project, like any that happens in the archaeological arena, had a more humble beginning. A young man set out on an expedition to find a special cave he'd heard about in a Native American legend handed down from generation to generation in his family. I've brought him with me today so that he can share his story with you."

As Cody stepped up onto the stool behind the platform, his smile was so wide it was contagious. "Hi!" he said with that inherent precociousness in his voice. "I'm Cody Stevens. I found a strange looking rock with some funny squiggles and marks on it when I was looking for the cave of Chief Taquinna. After I told Abbot about it, he took me back there and said the stone was pretty important. It's like a box that has a lid sealed on it and it's the kind that Native Americans used to store their special records in. Abbot says if it contains some family's history, it could be one of the greatest discoveries in this century." Then, veering from the way that Cody had been coached, he said, "I figured out that we've only been in this century a few years, so maybe there'll be more better discoveries later on. But right now, the box we found is gonna' be examined by specialists. That's those guys who know what to do with old stuff, like that. Anyway, that's what happened.

"Where is the box now?" "Where did you find it?" Questions were thrown out at Cody with rapid-fire succession.

"One at a time, please," Abbot said.

In a more civilized manner, the questions were then asked of Cody: "Where is the box now?"

Cody beamed. "In a safe place."

"Where did you find it?"

"In the forest along the coast."

"Can you give us an exact location?"

"No, ma'am. I couldn't memorize it because I'm just a kid."

Everyone laughed.

"Were there any other artifacts in the area?"

Cody dug in his pocket. "I found this here stone. Abbot says it might have been used as a weight for a fishing line." He displayed his stone proudly as cameras zoomed in on him.

"Who will fund the investigation of the site and the box?"

The Governor stepped forward. "I've given approval for thirty percent of the expenses to be paid by state funds, while Mr. Randall Hamilton, administrator of the museum, has generously agreed to match the state's share. The rest, we hope, will come from donations."

"Yeah," said Cody quickly. "Because this is really important stuff that Abbot's doing and he's gotta buy shovels and safety gear and junk like that."

"Young Master Cody," said one gregarious woman in front. "Do you plan on helping with the excavation at the site?"

"No ma'am. I'm just a kid. But, if it takes a long time, like that old mud slide at Ozette, I'm gonna' grow up. Maybe I can help Abbot then."

When the press conference concluded, the governor joined them back inside the main foyer. "I am very impressed, young man," he told Cody. "I think your pitch for donations will help a lot."

Cody took the Governor's hand and pressed three dimes and a nickel into it. "Will you let me donate, too?" he asked. "I would have brought more, but it was kinda' short notice."

The Governor handed the money to an aide standing beside him. "Write young Cody's name down as the very first contributor," he instructed.

"Straight away, Governor Jannes."

"My name's gonna' be the very first one?" Cody asked.

"Yes, Cody, it is."

"Cool! Thanks Mr. Governor."

By the time they were able to break away, it was nearly eleven-thirty. Hans suggested that he buy everyone lunch, but Abbot declined. He was anxious to get back to the boat and finish packing, then head on out to the project.

Being around Bekah had made him uneasy. If she went to lunch with Hans and the others, he would have to tell her goodbye now. He'd hoped she would want to spend some time alone with him before he left, but she'd made no effort to reach out to him and he'd stubbornly done the same.

Knowing in his heart that he couldn't let it end like this, he stepped toward her and whispered in her ear, "I wonder if you would skip the lunch and drive me back to the boat."

She gave him a fleeting smile and nodded her head. Then, she gave Cody a hug and said, "I am so proud of you!"

To Ryan she gave a quick hug. "I'm going to take Abbot down to Lake Union. I'll see you tonight for the missionary discussions."

"It wouldn't hurt for you to apologize," he whispered, loud enough so that Abbot could hear him.

Bekah frowned and turned away. "My car's at the other end of the parking lot," she said, hurrying down the steps in front of Abbot.

He followed behind, almost willing his feet to keep up with her. Evidently, she was still angry with him. Abbot wanted to tell her not to be frightened anymore, but he almost didn't want her to take him back *Bridger's Child*.

For the first several minutes in her caravan, she was silent. Finally, Abbot decided he would have to begin the conversation. Clearing his throat he said, "I have an answer for you now."

She turned long enough to give him what he considered a scalding glare, then turned her attention back to her driving. "Oh?" came her question. Her voice was stiff and cold.

"You wanted to know if I'd asked God why you were frightened and I had. But, I also told you I hadn't understood His answer." Abbot waited, hoping she would respond, but she kept her attention locked firmly on the cars around her as though he wasn't even there. Feeling rejected, he continued. "I asked again when I got home last night and I understand now why you were frightened. What God wants me to do frightens me, as well."

She gave him a guarded expression. It wasn't much, but it was enough to give him hope that she still cared. "I told Him I wouldn't do it," he whispered, disturbing the stillness in the caravan.

Her mouth dropped open and she gasped, "Why?"

"I told Him you couldn't deal with it anymore than I could. And I'm not about to do anything that would drive us farther apart."

She didn't respond right away, but he saw her bottom lip tremble. "I love you, Bekah."

Still, she hesitated. *What is driving her so hard that she ignores me?*

he wondered. "Bekah, we can even get married right away, if that's what you want. I surrender."

And there it was. The fear that he'd seen in her eyes so many times it saddened him and caused his heart to feel sick inside.

"And what of our temple wedding? Will we do that in a year from my baptism?"

"Probably not," he confessed. "I've told God, 'No.' By doing that, I've probably jeopardized all hope of ever receiving His forgiveness. How can I ask for a temple recommend when I've directly disobeyed Him?"

"God is angry with you?" she questioned.

"I'm afraid He is," admitted Abbot. "But what else can I do? If I obey Him, it will destroy my relationship with you and that is something I won't do. Without you, Bekah, I'm nothing."

"And we can never go to the temple to be married?"

"I wouldn't even ask," said Abbot. "Bekah, I just sold my soul to the devil so that I can stay with you. Can't you see that?"

"No. Your scriptures speak of forgiveness and of a kind and wise Father in Heaven who loves us. I can't believe He would never forgive you."

"Telling God no when He's told you three times, with fervor, what He wants you to do, is about the same thing as denying the Holy Ghost, Bekah."

"The unpardonable sin?" she questioned.

"Yes."

"Why would you commit this sin when it can never be forgiven?"

"You've been reading your scriptures, I see," he said ruefully.

"Abbot, why would you do this to us?"

He sighed wearily and shook his head, "If the only way I can keep you is to deny God, then I'm willing to pay the consequences for doing so."

Tears rolled down her cheeks as she turned into the parking lot at Gove's Cove, but he didn't see the love in her eyes that he longed for. Perhaps she, too, was unwilling to forgive him for last night, when he'd foolishly suggested that she give the ring back if she believed he was not the man from her grandmother's dream.

He opened the door and got out. "Thanks for the ride." She wouldn't even look at him. Closing the door, he turned away and walked forlornly toward the steep stairs that led to the docks.

Arriving at *Bridger's Child,* he noticed a seagull had taken liberties with the canvas dodger and mainsail cover once again. He stepped to the end of the dock and uncoiled the hose as he looked up at the Seattle skyline from his viewpoint. Across the lake, he could see Chandler's Cove, where it was perpetually busy, yet always serene. To the north, he noticed how green the grass was at Gas Works Park, refusing to remember how much he'd enjoyed going there the past few weeks. Next week, he would miss the fireworks display over Lake Union for the annual fourth of July celebration, but mostly, he would miss Bekah.

She hadn't given him his ring back yet, and he hoped that was a good sign. His worst fear was that she would send Ryan to do it for her. Having received one engagement ring returned in any man's lifetime was too many. Twice returned would certainly be the complete obliteration of his heart as he now knew it.

"Abbot?" came her timid voice from behind him.

He turned and saw her stepping quickly down the dock. "Bekah?" he asked, fearful that she had decided to do the dirty deed herself. He tried to steady his nerves and brace himself for whatever it was that would bring her racing toward him.

Without warning, she threw herself into his arms. Abbot tried to catch himself, but he tripped over the water hose and fell backwards into the lake, Bekah clinging pitifully to him as though he would save her. The ripple effect caused all the boats at the docks to rock back and forth, making them bump against the fenders protecting them from the dock and strain at their dock lines, but Abbot was oblivious to their plight. Nor had he noticed the coldness of the water.

Bekah was in his arms, kissing his face and hanging onto him as though her life depended on it. As they bobbed up and down in the water, he stretched one arm out and side-stroked toward the end of the dock, bringing her with him. Laughing, his heart suddenly filled with more joy than he thought he could hold. She still loved him and that was all that mattered.

Later, as she shivered in the blanket he'd wrapped around her to keep her warm, he said, "Where's the sun in Seattle when you need it?"

"I don't think I'm shivering from the cold," she responded. "I think I'm still in shock."

"Precisely," he agreed as he toweled his hair dry and sat opposite her on a cockpit bench.

"Emotional shock," she elaborated. "Abbot, how can we love one another yet still allow such a terrible barrier to build up between us?"

"I was trying to break down the barrier in the car," he reminded, hoping his voice sounded as light-hearted as his mood. "You're the stubborn one in our relationship."

She rolled her eyes. "I'm worried about our eternal welfare," she confided. "What you said in the car about never being forgiven, only so you could spend your life with me . . . Abbot, a lifetime isn't very long when it's compared with forever."

"It's not up for debate," he told her seriously. "My decision has already been made."

"Couldn't you tell God you were sorry and do what He wants you to? Wouldn't He forgive you then?" she suggested.

"I already told Him, 'No.'" He crossed over to her side and sat down, then pulled her up onto his lap, where he held her fiercely to him.

"But I want you to be my husband forever," she insisted. "Surely there's some way to do that."

"Bekah, we're not going there again." He nuzzled up against her neck and began kissing her silky smooth skin. "In fact, if you want, we'll go get married today."

"I want a forever wedding," she said.

"Not today." He kissed her forehead and then her lips, lingering for a long time. Finally he withdrew and said, "Or we could just go below and find out what the rest of the world already knows."

"Abbot Isaac Sparkleman!" she scolded, pulling away from him. "I want to get baptized next week."

"Just teasing," he laughed. "I won't jeopardize your eternal future."

"But, I have no such future without you there."

"You'll have me here. Isn't that enough for you?"

She frowned.

"Apparently not," he observed.

"What did the Lord ask you to do?"

"What does it matter when I already said no?"

"Tell me."

"He asked me to go on a mission."

"Where to?"

"I don't know."

"Didn't He tell you where?"

"Look, Bekah. I'm not going, so the question is irrelevant."

"Explain the process to me," she insisted.

Not entirely certain that he understood her motives for asking, he explained, "In order to go on a mission, a man or woman—"

"Women go on missions, too?" she interrupted.

He nodded. "They go to their bishop and ask for a special form to fill out. Then they have examinations by a doctor, an optometrist and a dentist. Their paperwork goes back to the bishop and to the stake president, who sends it into church headquarters. A committee makes a prayerful decision where to send the candidates and they receive a letter in the mail announcing the mission to which they are called."

"That's it?" she asked.

"That's all there is to it," he affirmed.

"Then why did you say no? You could pass a physical, eye and dental exam easily."

"It's not the process that worries me," he explained. "It's the length of time that I would be gone."

"How long?" she asked as a serious frown wrinkled her brow.

"Too long."

"How long?"

"Longer than either one of us could endure." *Especially you!*

"More than six months?"

"Yes."

"More than a year?" came the next inquiry, but he noticed that her bottom lip was trembling again.

Reluctantly, Abbot nodded.

"Eighteen months?"

"Two years," he corrected.

"Two years?" Pouting, tears filled her eyes, but she blinked them back. "How could God possibly expect me to live without you for two full years?"

"That's what I asked Him," he responded.

"No way! I couldn't do it."

"That's what I told Him."

"I won't do it! I can't! One year was going to be bad enough. Two years is a lifetime."

"I knew that's how you'd feel and that's why you don't have to worry about it. I'm not going."

"You're really not?"

"No. I'm not. Now. Do you want to get married today or shall I head on over to the project?"

When Bekah shuddered, he pulled her close, wrapping the blanket around her more firmly. "What is it?" he asked tenderly.

"I don't want you to go"

"I told you I wouldn't."

"No. Out to the Hoh River."

"Why?" he questioned, confused at her request.

"It terrifies me," she answered as her whole body started to tremble.

Snuggling her even closer, he said, "I thought it was just the mission that frightened you. That's what the Lord told me,"

"That's not all," she said. "The site and the mission, they're connected somehow."

"That's impossible," Abbot comforted.

"It's not impossible," she insisted. "Every time I think of your project, or your going back there, I get chills all over me."

"Have you prayed about it?" he asked.

She shook her head. "God doesn't speak to me like he does you."

"God will answer your prayers if you take the time to listen to Him."

Although she nodded, he could see by her expression that she was unconvinced.

"You wanted me to get my answers from God and I trusted Him

to give them to me. If you believe that God lives and loves you, then how could you feel that He wouldn't answer you?"

"You have a special gift that enables you to listen to him."

"Everyone can feel the spirit of the Lord whisper to their heart. You just have to wait for His responses. Try it, Bekah. I feel distressed when I know you're anguishing over something as important as the COSAT project."

When she refused to respond to his continued probing, he shook his head, then helped her off his lap and stood up beside her. "Bekah, I've got to go. It's already one o'clock. I promised Tom I'd be there today and I won't be able to find him in the dark."

"Let me help you pack," she suggested with a sense of hesitancy in her voice.

"You're going to help me pack to go somewhere you don't want me to go?" he questioned.

"It's called love," she answered. "Get used to it."

Chapter Fifteen

Returning to her condo, Bekah picked up the Book of Mormon. She planned to finish reading it that afternoon. The missionaries would be coming again this evening, but Abbot would not be with her. However, many of her cousins, aunts and uncles were joining them.

Bekah had so many questions that she wanted to ask, but she didn't want to do so in front of all her family. Perhaps they would linger for a while. Then, she remembered that they weren't allowed to be alone with a woman in her apartment.

She was so confused by what Abbot had done that her heart felt heavy with sadness. He was willing to give up eternal happiness in order to keep her happy. Her refusal to let him go on a mission made her feel terribly selfish. Perhaps if she'd been less demanding, and more accepting of God's will, Abbot would not have denied God's request, putting his eternal salvation at risk.

But how could she let him go? And what of the ancient ones whom her grandmother had seen in her dreams. The words Grandma Lili had whispered to her, moments before she died, were still etched in Bekah's heart:

> *After you meet him, he will go on a long journey to the*
> *home of the ancient ones. You must be patient and wait*
> *for him.*

In her youth, Bekah had been taught that the home of the ancient ones was where her ancestors lived now, where people go when they die. Abbot would be working with ancient artifacts, perhaps even a family record regarding the ancient ones. Perhaps what he was about to uncover would necessitate the Lord calling him home to them. Perhaps his mission was to teach the gospel to the ancient ones. If that was the case, his going back to the Ruby River was not such a great idea.

Since she'd begun taking the missionary discussions and studying the Book of Mormon, Bekah had learned some important truths pertaining to God's eternal plan. Even though her grandparents were deceased, they could still be married forever by proxy in one of the Lord's temples, and they could be sealed to their parents and they to their ancestors, all the way back to Adam and Eve.

Abbot said that missionaries go away for two years, which was longer than she was willing to let him go at all, but she could survive two years if she knew for certain that's all the longer she'd have to wait for him. Her fears addressed the involvement of where he would be sent when the ancient ones, who were waiting for him, requested that he take his journey to their home.

The terror that settled inside made her heart quiver strangely. Would Abbot be killed or die from an illness if he pursued the records found inside the stone box? If Abbot was going to the home of the ancient ones, she feared that he would have to die to get there.

Abbot's journey to the home of the ancient ones would certainly make grandmother's dream come true, for then Bekah would have to wait a long, long time for him. And their reunion would be predicated upon her willingness to keep the commandments and meet with him after she joined him.

In order to wait for him, she would have to be sealed to him by proxy. The only kind of life she would have left if Abbot died was one of loneliness and sorrow. Yet, if she did give him her blessing regarding his journey to the home of the ancient ones, she would have eternal joy with him after she left her mortal body behind her.

Bekah's thoughts whirled inside her head and her jumbled images frightened her. Unable to concentrate, she put the Book of Mormon down and slipped into her jogging shorts and shirt. Within minutes, she was jogging around Green Lake, hoping to relieve the burden inside her. But after an hour and a half, she realized it was a vain effort. All she had done was exhaust her body.

She walked back toward the condos in a daze. When she saw her cousin's car parked next to the sidewalk, she remembered the missionary discussions. Glancing at her watch, she noticed she was ten minutes late.

Dashing inside, she raced up the stairs, bypassing the elevator entirely. By the time she reached the eighth floor, her legs protested with brutal spasms, but she ignored them. The door to her condo was unlocked and she went inside. The living room was packed with a dozen newcomers, as well as those that were there last night. Some of the investigators she didn't even know.

Elder Daniels was holding up a picture of the Savior and bearing his testimony to them, but her entrance interrupted him.

"I'm sorry," she said, "I lost track of the time."

"I hope you don't mind that we barged in without your permission," said Elder Daniels. "Your brother said you wouldn't mind. Other people haven't arrived yet, as well and we were worried they wouldn't be let in if they buzzed your apartment and no one answered."

"No, that's fine. The more the merrier."

Elder Daniels nodded, then turned his attention to the lesson material while Bekah slipped behind people and sat on a stool near the kitchen counter. As she counted heads, she was amazed to find twenty-seven people, excluding herself, in attendance. Patiently she listened as the elders discussed the importance of prayer and how Joseph Smith's prayer was answered in a sacred grove of trees in Palmyra, New York. Bekah feasted on the sweet spirit that seemed to fill her crowded living and dining rooms.

When the elders were finished, the missionaries opened the meeting to questions, then spent the better part of two hours answering them. Bekah ran out of cookies before everyone left and spent part of the time apologizing, but she felt good about what had occurred in her condo that evening.

After she finally had time on her own, she realized Abbot was right when he told her she should pray about her troubled feelings. A scripture Elder Daniels had quoted earlier that evening had found a secret place within her heart and she brought his words back into her mind, remembering:

> If any of you lack wisdom, let him ask of God, that giveth to all men liberally and upbraideth not; and it shall be given him. [James 1:5]

Bekah recognized her lack of wisdom and this scripture put hope inside her heart that sent her kneeling upon the bedroom carpet where she poured out her feelings to God. When she was finished, her knees ached, but her heart was filled with peace. She knew, like she'd never known before, that God was mindful of her needs and that He was willing to help her work through whatever problems she might face in regards to her eternal salvation . . . especially where Abbot was concerned.

◆§ è◆

Abbot arrived at an old oil road north of the Ruby River shortly before eight that evening, where Tom was waiting for him. Having called ahead and arranged to meet him, he was glad to know that he wouldn't have to pack all the gear in by himself. He'd brought quite a bit with him.

He parked the Bronco well off the road, about two hundred feet into the forest, until it became too dense to go any farther, with Tom directing him every inch of the way. The last thing they needed at the moment was their only vehicle mired in mud.

"Looks like you brought the entire store with you," remarked Tom, giving Abbot a grin.

"I missed you, too," said Abbot, giving his brother a quick handshake.

"Yep," drawled Tom. "I ferget that you were starved fer attention when you were a kid."

"And you got enough to last a lifetime," Abbot teased back.

"How in blazes you expect us to pack all this?" asked his brother.

"On our backs for tonight. In the morning, I expect we'll have a little help."

"In the morning?"

"Sure. Hans is bringing in the Admiral and his crew for a few days. You'll be amazed how quickly the military can set up a base operation."

"I heard Admiral Clark is retired."

"Retired, but not out of commission," Abbot said as he loaded Tom's backpack with everything they would need until the Admiral arrived. Then, he did the same with his own pack.

He lifted the heavy burden onto Tom's shoulders as his brother slipped his arms through the straps.

"You shoulda' brought a pack mule or two," Tom observed dryly.

242   Sherry Ann Miller

"Come on, this isn't too bad. Do you want to make it in one trip or three?"

Tom lifted the second pack and held it while Abbot put his arms through the shoulder straps and adjusted them. Then he released it, letting it tug Abbot backwards a second or two. Bracing himself, Abbot gave his brother a scowl. "We're making only one trip tonight, so we're going to do this if it kills us."

"What I'd like to know," Tom teased, "is who's gonna' rescue you when you fall over backwards and can't get up?"

"You are."

"I doubt that," said Tom. "I'll be too busy laughin' at you."

Abbot bent forward slightly, making the pack a little less likely to topple him backwards. "Let's go," he said, ignoring Tom's joke altogether.

It took them forty minutes to walk three thousand feet, due in part to the energy drops the heavy packs extracted from them. But, Abbot enjoyed every step.

The lush thick forest, with evergreen conifers, Sitka spruce, western hemlock, red cedar and Douglas fir surrounded them. The branches were covered with lichen and mosses in variegated shades of green, from pale yellow-greens, to deep, startling emerald hues, to deeper forest-greens. A few big leaf maples and vine maples were thrown into the scenery for contrast. Tall madrona trees, with their red bark, stood out among the pines beautifully. If anything, the forest seemed denser on the north side of the project site than it was on the south. Abbot decided this was probably due to the slides that had scarred the earth periodically in the southern region.

The moist salt air crept around them in the form of a dense fog. It came up the hill from the Pacific Ocean just a few miles west of them and settled on everything. Assailing his nostrils, the pungent, earthy fragrance of decaying timber and damp mosses mixed with the salt, causing Abbot to sneeze several times as he adapted to the abrupt change in his environment. Licking his lips, Abbot could taste the salt upon them as the salt air slowly moved with the fog and passed him on its journey inland.

The forest became quiet as the sun began to set behind the western horizon. Occasionally, a black-tailed deer, a chattering squirrel, or a jumping mouse would startle the two men, but they were quick to realize the species most frightened were the animals they had scared along their journey toward the project site, and not themselves.

"How have you been building a fire?" asked Abbot when they finally arrived and helped each other remove the heavy packs.

"That's been a trick," said Tom. "But, I been gatherin' driftwood near the beach. If you take it from higher up the beach, it's almost dry. The rainforest, twenty-some miles east of here may git twelve feet of rain a year, but the beach don't git that much, not by a long shot."

"How far is it to the beach?" Abbot asked, pulling a two-man, back-country tent from one of the packs.

As Tom helped him set it up, he said, "I thought it was gonna' be four or five miles. But Saturday night, after the forest hushed down, I heard the breakers down below. Sunday morning, I calculated it to be about a third of a mile, maybe more. It sure ain't any farther than where you parked the Bronco."

Abbot placed the last spring bars into place and spread out both sleeping bags while Tom chipped at some pieces of driftwood with a sharp hatchet, then built a small fire.

"I saved you one of them trout," Tom chuckled. "Keep the fire goin' while I go git it."

"Thanks," said Abbot, realizing that he hadn't eaten since breakfast. By the time Tom returned, Abbot had the second tent set up.

While the trout was roasting over the campfire, Tom asked, "How long you figure this project of yers'll last?"

"If what you told me about the contents of that cave is my measuring stick, I'd say years . . . no, decades."

"I don't suppose there's a place fer me to help out, once the project gits goin'." Tom pulled the sizzling trout off the hand-cut wooden skewer, slid it onto a paper plate and handed it to Abbot.

Detecting a hint of sorrow in Tom's voice, Abbot said, "Tom, you can stay on as long as you like." Then, Abbot forked into the fish hungrily.

"Once the Admiral gits here, I expect he'll have somethin' to say about that."

"You think that because you made one mistake, no one will ever employ you?"

"It's been that way since Pa died. I'm still lookin' fer a decent job. And no woman will give me a second look once they find out about my past."

"Tom, I know that what you did was a terrible thing, but God does forgive you. The fact that you've had your priesthood restored is proof of that. And I . . . well, I forgive you completely. You've more than proven it'll never happen again."

"That's the thing, Abbot. I don't remember it happenin' the first time. I've searched my mind over and over agin' and I ain't found no memories at all. I admit, I was drunk and out of my mind with greed. I went lookin' for the deed to the ranch, thinkin' I could forge Mont's signature and get all the money for it, but I couldn't find it. I got angry and went down to Cooney's Bar and drank myself into a stupor. The next day I thought it was all a nightmare. I kept thinkin' it was Kayla I attacked in a nightmare." He paused and swallowed hard, then continued, "You remember that day Pa threw me in the creek when I got too fresh with Kayla when we were teenagers?"

Abbot nodded. It was old history, but apparently Tom needed to talk about it. He finished off the trout and spooned up a plate of hot beans from a pot near the fire. While he ate, Abbot listened attentively.

"I've had nightmares about it ever since. I ain't never seen Pa so mad as he was that day. It's lucky fer me that all I got was a cold dunk and a couple stitches. Even drunk, Abbot, I swear I'd never do anythin' to make Pa mad like that agin'. Never! But, I guess it had to be me who attacked Morning Sun. Who else is there?" He shrugged, wiped his hands on his pant legs and sighed. "Last thing I remember fer sure, I was down at Cooney's Bar tyin' one on, blabbin' about how I tried to find Mont's deed to the Bar M and sell it to that real estate tycoon. I even remember tellin' my boozin' buddies what an idiot I was to think I could do somethin' like that. But there's nothin' in here," he pointed to his head, "about Morning Sun. Nothin'!" Shaking his head, he continued, " Next thing I knew, Will was shakin' me awake at the cabin. I don't even know how I got there."

"It's over," said Abbot. "Morning Sun refused to identify you as the attacker. She always said she had to go through sorrow in order to get Matthew here. In her mind, he was worth it."

"But, he don't look like my son," Tom insisted. "All this time I been prayin' and askin' God to help me understand how I could 'a done it, but I ain't got a single answer. Not one. Everyone gits miracles, but not me. Guess I just ain't worth nothin'."

"The fact that you gave up drinking is your miracle, Tom. Most alcoholics are incapable of that. And where Morning Sun is concerned, you've repented. You put your trust in God and He pulled you through it. All that really matters now is that you're on the right path."

"I wish the rest of the world could fergive me," he sighed. "They not only can't fergive, they can't ferget. It's a shame I'll carry to my grave."

"Speaking of grave," said Abbot, hoping to lift Tom's spirits by changing the topic, "We only have tonight to do any exploring of that cave. By the time the Admiral's men arrive, it'll be overrun with restrictions. Do you want to go back in and show me what you found?" He tossed his empty plate into the fire.

"It's pitch black out," Tom observed.

"Same color as the inside of that cave, day or night, I'll wager."

A sparkle came into Tom's hazel eyes, and he swept his dusty blonde hair back with his fingers. "I'm game if you are."

Within ten minutes, they stood outside the cave carrying six hundred feet of rope each, headlamps and several large lanterns and flashlights. After they both tied one end of their ropes to a fallen tree outside the cave and one end to their belts, Abbot shimmied in on his belly first, with Tom following close behind.

The air smelled of damp earth and decaying rootstock. Visibility was no better at night than at broad daylight, but their headlamps helped a great deal. They were sliding between two slabs of shale about fourteen inches apart and six feet wide. All they could see was shale and earth and a few straggly roots trying to find an anchoring place around the shale. The narrow space could only be traversed on their bellies, inch by careful inch. As they progressed, the shale seemed to change composition so that they were sandwiched between some kind of natural granite deposit. Several times Abbot felt the sharp edges of rock against his chest and the snagging of roots upon his jacket. After half an hour, they'd progressed to about the same point as Abbot had gone in the first time. "How much farther from here?" he asked.

"You ain't even close."

"You had two hundred feet of rope when you came in before, so we should have plenty this time."

"Just keep goin', little brother. This belly creepin' ain't a smooth ride, you know."

Thirty minutes or more later, Abbot felt a ledge with his fingers. His arms were stretched out above his head, but he couldn't see past his hands yet. "I think I've found your room," he said. "But I can't seem to find a spot to push myself up with my toes and there's no elbow room for pulling myself forward."

"Just a minute and you can use my hand to push off," came the husky reply.

While he was waiting for Tom to catch up, Abbot tried to pull himself forward, but he could only go a half-inch at a time. "You're a whole lot thinner than I am, Tom. There's almost no space between my chest and my back for movement."

"It was tight when I went through, too. Here, I've pulled myself up to yer knees. I'll cup my hand around yer right foot as a lever."

Abbot felt the solid force of his brother's hand and pushed himself forward with the ball of his foot about six inches. Excitement welled within him as he saw the top portion of a room opening up in front of him. "Just a few more inches, Tom. Hurry!"

"Yer about there, I reckon," said his brother, scooting forward himself and giving Abbot another boost.

As Abbot's range of vision increased, he felt a sensation of awe and amazement settle in the pit of his stomach. "Do you realize what this is?" he asked Tom.

"No, but I'm sure you'll tell me."

Abbot reached his right hand out to his side and down toward Tom. "Use my leg as a pulling point until you can reach my hand. I'll try to pull you the rest of the way."

He felt his brother grab his calf, then a slight pressure as Tom pulled himself forward. Soon, Tom found Abbot's hand. Gripping his brother, Abbot pulled for all he was worth. It wasn't long before Tom had the same view Abbot did.

Tom's eyes widened and his mouth dropped open. "I'll be a one-eyed polecat!" he exclaimed. "It's like these folks were buried alive in their own home."

Abbot had the same thoughts. "You may be right," he explained. "Granite is hard to come by this far inland in our time, but who's to say it wasn't a ready commodity for these people. It looks to me like their one-room house was chiseled out of the granite, making it a tomb when a mudslide came and buried them inside it."

"Yep," Tom whispered. "It's horrible."

Feeling completely awe-struck, Abbot made a mental note of the position of the bodies. The skeletal remains of an adult with a child cradled in its arms, their bones and skin petrified by time, lay prone upon a leather bed. Two more children lay beside another adult who had a piece of granite in his hand as though he had been trying to dig them out, to no avail. An open window in the front of the room was filled with old mud that time had long since altered to shale. An opening where a door once stood was blocked with hardened mud, as well.

"These people lived in relative comfort and protection from all the elements," Abbot observed, "until a mudslide buried them, making their home a tomb."

"I've seen enough," said Tom. "This here's sacred ground, Abbot. I'm gittin' out." With this remark, Tom scooted backward.

"I'll be along shortly." Abbot couldn't take his eyes off the scene before him. "Buried alive," he whispered to himself.

Not only had the mudslide sealed the fate of this little family, it had preserved the site in an airtight environment that had withstood the ravages of time. The artifacts that Abbot readily noticed, baskets, pottery, arrows, a bow, fishing gear, pelts and traps: all seemed to be in good condition considering their age and the layers of dust and cobwebs upon them.

In Abbot's heart he couldn't fathom the Lord's goodness in laying such a blessing in his lap. Most archaeologists spend their entire life hoping to find a few simple artifacts, yet before his eyes were dozens of items to be unearthed, documented, studied and preserved. This could become one of the finest dig sites in the world, and he would be a part of it. He wondered if there were other houses similar to this one scattered around the area and if so, how many? A million questions seemed to dart through his mind, all at once, as he considered the possibilities. *This could be the greatest scientific discovery of the century!*

He didn't know how long he stayed there, trapped between two layers of solid rock. After a while, he felt a piece of the ceiling fall down upon his arm. With great curiosity he studied the cave in which he lay and realized that the cave floor was made of granite, but the ceiling was nothing more than loose shale. It was completely unstable. If he hadn't discovered this now, they would have ruined the entire house when they began digging. The unearthing process would have to be carefully evaluated so that falling shale would not destroy the artifacts before they could unearth them.

Cautiously, Abbot backed out, feeling Tom tugging him out as he went. By the time he reached the cave opening, it was nearly dawn.

"It's about time," said Tom. "You've been in there for hours!"

"Just taking it all in," Abbot grinned. "You could have gone back to camp if you'd wanted."

"Sure. And leave my baby brother three hundred feet inside a mountain?"

"I was fine, Tom. I was having a great time."

"Yea, well it's time to turn in, if you ask me."

"Agreed," said Abbot wearily, feeling the shock and grandeur of their discovery sinking into his heart and his mind. His name would be famous the world over, as would Cody's. Not since the dead sea scrolls had something so valuable been discovered by men of science.

Vaguely, he recalled following Tom down the hill to their tents and climbing into a sleeping bag. He wondered if he would ever sleep after all that he'd seen inside the cave. His eyes did close, though, eventually.

It seemed only a few minutes later that they were awakened by a loud, booming voice yelling, "Hello! The camp!"

Abbot bolted upright in his sleeping bag, his head colliding with a lantern hanging from a hook in the tent ceiling. "Who is it?" he called back as he scrambled to crawl out of the tent.

He was just tucking his shirt in, when a man in military fatigues addressed him. "We're looking for Abbot and Thomas Sparkleman," the man said. He was well-muscled and had a rifle on his shoulder.

Finger-combing his black-brown hair, Abbot responded, "You found us, then. I'm Abbot and this is my brother, Tom."

The man reached out and shook Abbot's hand vigorously. "Staff Sergeant Bram Davidson, at your service," he said, saluting.

"At ease, Sergeant," Abbot gave him a wan smile.

"No offense, sir, but this is a military unit. Until outranking officers arrive, you are the designated authority. The men in my unit answer to me and I answer to you, sir."

"No offense taken, Sergeant, but we'll get along better if you remember that I'm only a civilian. The Admiral will be here later, today, and you can resume formalities with him, if it pleases you."

"Sir, the advance unit has arrived. With your permission, we'd like to proceed with the survey. After you're ready to direct us, we can begin sweeping the suspect locations."

"You're the advance unit?"

"Sir, yes, sir."

"We have a lot of valuable equipment in my Bronco a half mile due north of here. Do you have enough men to bring it to camp?"

The Sergeant smiled as Abbot fished the keys out of his pocket and gave them to the him. "The Admiral said you'd be bringing some military issue tents to house the project research lab and for artifact preservation."

"On their way as we speak, sir."

"Good. Proceed, Sergeant. We'll clean up and join you in a few minutes."

As the Sergeant turned and walked toward his men giving orders, Tom swept his dusty-blonde hair back and stuck his Stetson on his head. Then he gave a low whistle and exclaimed, "If that don't beat all!"

"Yep!" Abbot drawled, imitating Tom's expression perfectly.

By three in the afternoon, Admiral Clark had arrived with Hans and an entire platoon. Afterward, everything happened so fast, Abbot scarcely had time to think. Days turned into weeks and the activity around the COSAT project seemed to take on a spirit of its own, one of never-ending discoveries.

The survey was completed, and the entire surface of the property, which was deeded as three-hundred-eighty acres, was swept with a high-powered imaging device that used radio waves to detect anomalies beneath the soil and categorize them not only by location, but by size, shape and possible chemical composition up to a depth of fifty feet.

The images revealed were startling. A small village, perhaps the size of a football field, lay below the surface at least thirty feet, waiting for archaeologists to begin the tedious, time-consuming work of unearthing it. They documented thirty two houses such as the one Abbot and Tom had seen the night before, around the perimeter of the village, with a much larger house at the highest end of the village, probably the living quarters of the leader.

The first artifact removed from its original position and only after laborious, painstaking brushing of the particles of dried mud and soil from around it with fine, medium-length bristles, was the stone box which Cody had discovered. The box, which was video filmed, photographed, and drawn by a professional artist, was about fifteen inches square and nearly two feet tall. X-Ray equipment revealed a stack of thin, rectangular metal leafs inside, held together by three metal rings. It was entirely probable that the metal plates were made of brass or gold.

When the definitive report came back from the carbon dating analysis, the box was estimated to be twenty-one hundred years old. Abbot was ecstatic and he telephoned Cody to tell him that the boy's photograph and story would be printed in newspapers and magazines across the nation and around the world. With Abbot's help, Cody was given a full scholarship fund from the University of Washington for future use.

It would be years before the box and its contents could be analyzed in their entirety, but within the month COSAT applied for permission from the Tribal Council, and the scientific community, to open it.

Interviewing for staff positions, Abbot was tireless in his pursuit for only the best and most qualified personnel. Tom agreed to stay on and supervise the dining hall and prepare the meals with a young man from Forks as his assistant. Having spent a great deal of time learning how to cook for a starving bunch of ranch hands, Tom had the experience and the ability. Besides, next to ranching, fishing and riding a horse, cooking was a favorite pastime. Hans would serve as Abbot's assistant administrator. Security was turned over to an associate of the Admiral's, Corporal Dunbar, who had recently been given an honorable discharge from the U.S. Navy. The Corporal had five assistants equally qualified. A woman from Forks with an exceptional photography portfolio was hired part-time, as was a historian. Two secretaries and a resource manager were part of the original staff, as well. They also had a list, twenty pages thick, with names of volunteer archaeologists, anthropologists and linguists who were willing to donate their time as needed. The COSAT project was beginning to take shape.

Hans' father, Admiral Bridger Clark, sold his estate in California and purchased a waterfront property south of Ruby Beach, about twenty minutes away from COSAT, where he was drawing up plans for a new home. Wanting to participate in some of the actual extraction work, the Admiral wore two hats: financial officer and researcher.

Remarkably, Hans' mother, Sarah Clark, became an efficient PR manager for the entire project. Now that her mother had passed on, Sarah welcomed the opportunity to work alongside her husband. She wanted to contribute something back to society, and managing the press with grace, style and dogged determination was something she relished and accomplished with fervor. Abbot was surprised to learn that the Admiral and Sarah Clark had been baptized last winter, the same day Hans had. Since the COSAT project had received national attention, reporters flocked to the gates like hungry piglets, each trying to get interviews from anyone who would talk. Fortunately, Abbot had selected his staff cautiously. They were indefatigable in their battle to keep the news media from running rampant with undocumented stories. Besides, Sarah Clark would never forgive them if they failed her.

Security guards, under Corporal Dunbar's command, were stationed to guard the site both day and night. Within a few weeks, the entire piece of real estate had been transformed into a closely guarded compound, fenced with twelve-foot chain link fencing and barbed wire spirals placed strategically at the top. Telephone numbers were encrypted and security was tightened.

A road had been carefully carved between the trees, disturbing as little of the natural growth as humanly possible, in an area that had not revealed any anomalies beneath the soil. A research laboratory, two repository tents, one large sleeping tent and a dine-in kitchen had been set up and furnished with military issue bedding, tables, chairs and equipment. Electricity was wired into the property, a water well was approved and dug and a septic system installed. Even more luxurious than these accommodations, a bathroom with hot and cold running water, flush toilets and hot showers had been built behind the sleeping quarters.

The COSAT compound was colorfully decorated in either khaki and brown, or brown and khaki, which wasn't too bad because the greenery surrounding it was still lush and beautiful, if a bit matted in places.

Abbot beamed with pride as he walked around one evening in early August and assessed the COSAT compound. They had far more facilities than Ozette, when it first began, and the financial backing to continue for another thirty years, if need be. It was a dream come true and he knew it. What he had ever done to deserve so many blessings, Abbot had no idea.

The only one who seemed unhappy on the entire project was Hans. His parents were living in a luxurious motor home on their beach front property until their home could be built, while Hans was spending most of his evenings at the compound with the rest of the permanent workers and he didn't like it. The Admiral had offered to purchase a motor home for Hans, but for the first time in his life, Hans had declined the offer. Last summer Hans had given up all the comforts of his 49' Hallberg-Rassey ketch to work on the Bar M ranch for Abbot's brother, Ed. This summer he was doing essentially the same thing, bunking with a group of men in a mountainous area. Hans was weary of it, and Abbot knew it.

After talking it over with Joshua and Kayla, Abbot sprang his surprise on Hans right after supper one warm August evening. "Say, Hans, how would you like a little breathing space?"

"Where?" he asked sullenly.

"I don't know. Why not over at La Push? They've got a great marina there."

"It would take a month to sail *Bridge* up from San Diego," said Hans. "And I can't leave the project that long. Not yet. Maybe next summer."

"I wasn't talking about your boat," Abbot explained. "I was thinking about *Bridger's Child.*"

Hans' bold blue eyes lit up at the idea. "Three days, maybe four from Seattle." Then, his shoulders sagged. "I couldn't boot you out."

"I'm here ninety percent of the time anyway."

"Where would you stay when you go see Bekah?" he asked.

"There are motels," Abbot suggested. "Besides, I think *Bridger's Child* is beginning to show signs of neglect."

A hopeful smile crossed Hans' face. "Do you think Josh would mind?" he asked.

"He said if you take care of it for him from now until then, they'll bring *Bridge* up when they come next summer." Abbot confided.

"You already spoke with them?" Hans asked, his smile deepening.

Nodding, Abbot continued, "I'm going into Seattle early on Saturday for Bekah's baptism. Do you want to go?"

"Of course."

"Afterwards, you and Tom could bring *Bridger's Child* back as far as Clallam Bay. If you'd like, I could meet you there on Wednesday and sail it with you down to La Push. We could all use a little break. What do you say?"

"That's almost a week off," he complained with a serious frown.

"I know but—" Abbot began.

"Gotcha!" exclaimed Hans as his face lit up again. "Have you talked to Tom about it?"

"No. I thought I'd let you handle that department. Since he doesn't know how to swim, he may balk a little. But if he wears a vest and we watch him like a hawk, perhaps he'll survive it."

Hans nodded. "It's relatively smooth waters this time of year. I'll be glad to have your help taking Cape Flattery, though. The ocean can get a little rough."

"As long as we give it a wide berth, we should be fine."

Hans stood up, his features almost animated. "Not that I don't enjoy your company, Abbot, but I've enjoyed my privacy through the years and this place is anything but private. If it wasn't for the importance of the project, I'd have left before it started."

"I know, Hans. I understand."

☙ ❧

Abbot had spoken with Bekah every evening after working in the field and their Sundays were spent together. She had changed her schedule so she could have Sundays off and now, she worked Wednesday through Saturday from six A.M. to six P.M. He drove five hours to Seattle each Sunday, where he spent three hours at church with her, then had supper at her house for an hour or two. Sunday nights he slept aboard *Bridger's Child,* met with Randall Hamilton at the museum each Monday morning, had lunch with Bekah, then faced the grueling drive back to COSAT. But, just seeing Bekah for a few moments was worth any effort.

One of the highlights of the summer was Bekah's baptism. Abbot was finally able to take a few days off and, with Hans and Tom joining him, he headed for Seattle in time to attend the services. Bekah had asked him to perform the ordinance, but he had refused. He felt unworthy of doing so after telling the Lord that he would not go on a mission.

Hoping the Lord would eventually forgive him, Abbot's heart was heavy with grief over his denying the Lord's request. But how could Abbot give up everything that he had going for him? His work, his fiancée, his future and career . . . all combined to hedge up his way.

Besides, he was twenty-seven years old. The years for going on a mission had slipped past him. Now, he was a man fully acquainted with the world who had made some progressive strides since coming to Seattle.

Although the baptism was a crowded affair, it was a special time for Bekah, and he wanted her to know that he supported her decision to step into the waters of baptism and take the Lord's hand in hers. In addition to Bekah, there were thirty-two people being baptized that day, most of whom were her relatives with Native American blood, those who believed her grandmother's dream and had waited for Abbot to come into her life.

Guilt consumed him because he didn't feel worthy of their confidence and trust. He wasn't sure they understood that they were not converting to Abbot or his beliefs, but it was the church to which he belonged.

After saying goodbye to Hans and Tom, who took a cab back to *Bridger's Child*, he joined Bekah for a potluck supper at Green Lake Park with all her family. When the group finally dispersed, Abbot was certain he would never remember all of their names.

Afternoon shadows had faded away as he walked Bekah back to her condo, holding her hand. Her voice was like tinkling music to his ears as she chatted about her work and the patients she cared for, her co-workers and their reactions to her baptism. With her eyes sparkling, she described the surprise baby shower she'd given for her cousin, Robyn, who was having twins in two more weeks. Her cousin's due date was August thirtieth.

The date rang a bell inside his head. August thirtieth was the deadline for giving Mr. Hamilton his answer regarding the appointment to become administrator over the museum when Randall retired.

The summer was nearly over and Abbot was astounded. How had it passed so quickly? It seemed as though he had blinked and six weeks were gone.

Grateful that the worst hours for COSAT were over, it was now time for Abbot and Bekah. COSAT was fully staffed and funded, the unearthing had begun, all the necessary, though temporary, structures were in place. Abbot could begin to relax a little. He needed to unwind from the exhausting sixteen-hour days he'd been working. Now, there was time to marry Bekah and begin the next phase of their lives together.

He hadn't mentioned his plans to Tom and Hans because he felt they wouldn't understand. They both expected a temple wedding from him, but the truth was, Abbot didn't feel as though he deserved such a great blessing. He was still getting indigestion over denying the Lord's request that he go on a mission.

When Abbot had offered to give up his sleeping quarters aboard *Bridger's Child*, it was with the idea in mind that he would be married very soon and living in Bekah's condo until they could buy a home somewhere in Seattle.

Chapter Sixteen

When Abbot grew quiet, Bekah continued talking to him, hoping he was still listening. After a while, she was content just to walk beside him, hold his hand and allow him some time with his own thoughts, without her incessant chatter.

Abbot seemed a little distracted this evening and she hoped he wasn't angry with her for asking him to baptize her. Truthfully, she'd been shocked when he told her he wouldn't do it. Several of her family members, including Ryan and Cody, had wanted Abbot to baptize them as well. But, she had tried to understand his position. He was still agonizing over his guilt from telling the Lord, 'No,' and Bekah realized that he had only done it out of love for her.

How she loved this man beside her! How many times had she wanted to throw herself into his arms and beg him to marry her right that very moment. Now, that was not even a possibility.

When she'd gone for her interview before her baptism, she'd taken her concerns to her bishop and he had treated them with the same respect her father would have. Now that she understood what it meant to be sealed in the new and everlasting covenant, she wanted no other form of marriage, and she would settle for nothing less.

They walked in silent comfort up the eight flights of stairs to her condo, opting to exercise together that way, which they nearly always did, now. He told her he wasn't jogging every day anymore and although his work was physically taxing, it did nothing for his cardiovascular system. He said he was looking forward to the day when he would feel he had COSAT under control and could start taking a little time off, now and then.

When they reached the condo, Bekah unlocked the door and stepped inside. She had left the balcony door open and now a gentle breeze came through the screen, welcoming them home.

"I'll go change," she said, letting his hand go and hating the empty feeling it gave her when she did.

"Sure," he said. He removed his suit coat and tie and laid them over the back of the silver sofa, then wandered into the dining room

Bekah slipped down the hall and changed into a pair of jeans and a cotton blouse. Running a brush though her hair, she walked out into the dining room and wrapped her arms around his waist, snuggling up to his chest, her favorite position.

"You're quiet tonight," she said. "Is something bothering you?"

He sat down on a kitchen chair and pulled her onto his lap. "I've had a lot on my mind."

"Your project?" she asked.

"No," he replied. "I've been thinking about us."

"Us?" She gave him a quirky grin. "What about us?"

"I think it's time we set our wedding date, don't you?"

"Absolutely." She calculated in her mind quickly, having no need to look at the calendar. "Let's see, today's the thirteenth. I guess anytime the week of the fifteenth."

He grinned. "Next week? Are you sure that's not too soon?"

Bekah hesitated. "Next year," she amended.

Abbot's emerald eyes darkened as he looked at her curiously.

She couldn't decipher his expression so she said, "Abbot, I want to get married in the temple."

He shook his head as he scolded, "Bekah, I told you. I don't think I can do that."

"I spoke with my bishop about it. He says a year is more than enough time for you to obtain the Lord's forgiveness."

"You talked with the bishop?" he asked sharply.

"Yes." She gave him a hopeful smile as she added, "I don't know what you're so worried about. Bishop said he saw no reason why we couldn't be married in the temple in a year."

"It's not a question of whether or not the bishop thinks I'm forgiven," he said, his voice cross, as though he was irritated with her. "It's whether or not I can forgive myself."

"I hope you're going to try," she suggested, "because I'm going to marry you in the temple, or I'm not going to marry you at all."

"In one year?" he demanded as he stood up, nearly dumping her onto the floor in the process.

"If you want to marry me," she suggested, turning her back to him. She hoped her tone would not discourage him from the same goal she had, but she needed to convince him that she was serious.

"And if it takes me longer than that to forgive myself?"

Bekah hesitated. She didn't want to give him any leeway. One year was plenty of time for his reconciliation with God. If she gave him an inch, would he want a mile? He may never take her to the temple under those conditions. Finally, she turned back to face him as she said resolutely, "Abbot, I've waited ten years to find you. I'll wait one more year for you to find yourself. If you're not ready to take me to the temple sometime between August fifteenth and August twenty-first next year, I will not wait any longer." Emotions of tenderness welled up inside her, but she pushed them back down. "I . . . I'll look for someone else," she threatened.

The stricken look of anguish on his face revealed more than she imagined and her heart felt heavy with the burden she was placing on him, but she had to help him realize how wrong he was for punishing himself like this.

"Someone else?" he asked as his voice squeaked.

"Eleven years is more than enough time for a woman to wait," she insisted.

"Bekah, the only way I can make amends with God is to obey Him. Yet, if I obey Him, you're saying that I'll lose you."

She shook her head. She certainly didn't see the situation from his point of view. "I'm saying that you're wearing a backless dress and I don't like it. If you love me, you'll not wear it anymore, or you'll alter it so you can."

"My back is fully covered," he argued, his voice becoming strained and raspy. "It's my heart that you want altered! Need I remind you that you were distraught over having to wait one full year to be married? It was your anguish that clouded my judgement when God asked me to make you wait **two** years! Now, you're telling me you'll only wait one year for me to make amends with God, when you know full well He expects two years! How can I ever please both of you under this new ultimatum?"

"The bishop says there are a lot of men who don't go on missions and feel bad about it, but they get over it and do the best they can to build up the kingdom of God where they are," she insisted. "Why can't you do that, too?"

"Because my father taught me that a man always keeps his word, otherwise, he has no honor. God asked me three times to keep my promise to Him and three times I told Him no."

"He'll forgive you," she whispered, unable to prevent the trembling of her lower lip or the moisture from forming in her eyes.

The look he returned was nothing less than absolute defeat. "The first time I told you I loved you and that I wanted to marry you, it was a simple statement of undeniable truth. At the time, your response didn't come with any conditions."

"At the time you said that, you promised I would only have to wait one year after my baptism for us to marry," she insisted.

"So, I have to give you a temple marriage long before I can ever be ready for one, or I can give two years to the Lord and give up all hope of ever marrying you?" he asked, his voice harsh and cold. "It seems to me that our engagement has escalated into nothing more than a bunch of terms and ultimatums. Why don't you admit the truth, Bekah, that neither one of us is ready to commit an eternity to someone who has no honor?"

To her horror, Abbot pivoted around and stomped toward the sofa. Grabbing his suit coat and tie, he left the condo, slamming the door behind him.

What place does honor have in our relationship? she wondered wearily. Was losing it such a terrible thing to Abbot that it would prevent him from marrying her at all? Or, had she jeopardized their eternal companionship because she was unwilling to wait for him any longer than one year from her baptism?

With all these questions circling around in her mind like vultures over a dying prey, Bekah sank onto the floor and wept.

& &

Abbot drove recklessly all the way back to COSAT, his mind racing with thoughts and impressions of his last few minutes with Bekah. That he was angry *and right!* was evident as he passed up slower vehicles, swerving to miss oncoming traffic more than once. It was only by divine intervention that he arrived without causing himself and someone else grave bodily harm. Using the security code to open the gate, he drove down the gravel road and parked just north of the sleeping tent. But, he knew he would not sleep.

Putting on a helmet with a headlamp, he made his way down to the beach where the ocean was hurling itself against the land with a vengeance. His anger was raging as high as the furious tide, but the incessant pounding of salt water against sand did nothing to assuage the feelings within him.

Damp salt air swirled around him, filling his nostrils, cleaning his lungs from the city smog that he'd breathed all day in Seattle. The taste of salt lingered on his lips no matter how often he licked them.

The full moon had a bright ring around it tonight, and appeared like something straight out of heaven, all aglow with shimmering moisture faintly clouding its brilliant edges.

Waves crashed against the beaches with fury, and the roaring sound was almost deafening. Abbot glanced at his watch and noted the illuminated dial indicated it was two-thirty in the morning.

A scripture kept pouring into his mind, regardless how hard he tried to drain it away. It was from the *Doctrine and Covenants*, one that the Lord had given to him nine months ago when he'd finally realized all his errors in his relationship with Alyssa and had wept for the first time over his father, Sparky's, death:

> "*Therefore, they must needs be chastened and tried,*
> *even as Abraham, who was commanded to offer up his*
> *only son. For all those who will not endure chastening,*
> *but deny me, cannot be sanctified.*" [D&C 101:4–5]

Abbot paced back and forth, asking silently over and over again, *Haven't I been chastened enough, Lord? Wasn't losing Mother when I was only four, then losing Pa in the avalanche enough for you? What do you want from me, God? What am I supposed to do now?* His pacing continued until almost four in the morning when he finally acquiesced to his feelings of abject misery. Wearily, he sank onto his knees and took his dilemma vocally to the Lord.

"Heavenly Father, I don't know what to do anymore. I can't please both of you. Either I please Bekah and go to the temple knowing I've denied you, or I please you and accept a mission call knowing I'll fail to meet Bekah's ultimatum. She's already said she won't wait more than a year. And she's stubborn enough to mean it. I can't bear to lose her, Lord. Most young men have gone on missions while their sweethearts have stayed behind and found someone else and she's already told me she'll do just that. I've had my heart broken before and it was terrible. But, without Bekah, I wouldn't have a reason to go on living anymore. What kind of missionary could I possibly be, knowing I'd lost the woman I love because I went on a mission? I need her in my life.

"I'm caught between a rock and hard place, and there's not much breathing room between them. I can't even ask You to tell me what to do, because I already know what You'll say.

"I have to be honest with you, Father, it isn't just Bekah that's preventing me from going. It's fear, and the project, and my career, in almost equal proportions. Most men spend their whole lives trying to stumble into an opportunity like I have without ever doing it. I would be giving up my appointment as administrator at the museum and my executive position here at COSAT. My name is becoming well-known in scientific circles and I'm developing respect in my chosen field. A mission could ruin my reputation as a reliable scientist dedicated to his work. We haven't even begun to unearth the cave Tom and I saw. The archaeological discoveries awaiting us are astronomical in their importance to the world. Not only do I face all these complications, Father, but I would disappoint Cody, who's depending on me to get his box opened and the records within it deciphered. I have a lot of people counting on me down here. You're asking too much for one man to sacrifice.

"But the main reason . . . is Bekah. I love her, Lord. And if I go, I'll lose her. How can I be the man her grandmother dreamed about if You send me away, knowing she won't wait for me? Is that what You really want?"

When he'd closed his prayer, he remained on his knees until the sky began to lighten behind him, but he received no answers because his heart was locked as tightly as his mind.

❧ ❧

While Abbot stood waiting on the beach at Clallam Bay, he wondered what was keeping Hans and Tom. Looking across the Strait of Juan de Fuca, he could see all the way to Vancouver Island in Canada. There wasn't much wind, but it was only morning and that could change quickly. Sailing the strait would be like putting a boat in a bathtub, but the big challenge in his mind would come when they were finally past Cape Flattery and out in the blue Pacific.

The Cabo Rico 38 looked fantastic at anchorage and he could easily see why Joshua and Kayla loved it. But, the inflated dingy tied on behind the sailing vessel was empty, and there was no indication that Hans or Tom were ever coming out of *Bridger's Child's* cabin to pick him up in the tender.

Impatiently, he thought about calling them again to ask what the holdup was, but since they were only five minutes late, he decided to give them another five. He'd promised them last night that he would be at the beach by eight and it was eight-o-five.

Then he saw a head come up out of the companionway, but it wasn't Hans or Tom. Admiral Bridger Clark pulled the dinghy alongside the boat and stepped down the swimming ladder into it. Then, he untied the tether and began rowing the tender toward Abbot.

When he pulled up onto the beach, Abbot tossed his duffel bag into the bottom and pushed them off, then climbed over the starboard side, stepped in and sat down on the inflated gunwale. "I'm surprised to see you, Bridge," said Abbot, using the abbreviated name that Sarah often used when addressing her husband, the one the Admiral said he preferred when he was among good friends. He shook the elder man's hand.

"Sarah took a trip down to San Diego," he explained. "Kayla is having the twins tomorrow, and I'm afraid I'm not very good at helping with those matters."

"She is?" Abbot asked. "That's great! Everything's okay, I hope."

"Splendid," Bridger answered as he began to row.

"Let me do that," Abbot offered.

Bridger shook his head. "No, I need the exercise much more than you do, believe me."

"I'm amazed at the exceptional shape you're in," Abbot said honestly. "You put us younger men to shame."

"Years of practice," Bridger admitted. "Though I have to confess I've slowed down since we moved up here. Until I get my swimming pool constructed, I'm missing my forty laps every morning and it's showing on my mid-section, I'm afraid."

Abbot laughed. "I doubt that!"

When they reached *Bridger's Child*, Abbot tied the tether to a loop on the stern, then walked the boat around to the side with his hands on the lifelines. "After you," he said.

The Admiral climbed aboard and said, "I suppose we'll want the dingy lashed aboard while we're at sea. Let me check with the captain." He slipped down into the cabin.

Abbot slung the duffel bag into the cockpit and climbed aboard the sailing vessel, then hung onto the tether until the Admiral returned.

Within moments Hans and Bridger climbed out of the cabin.

"Good morning," said Hans. "You found us all right, I see."

"Piece of cake. Though I think Dunbar was disappointed he had to stay behind and take the Bronco back to COSAT. He had sailing visions in his eyes when he saw *Bridger's Child* at anchorage earlier. She's like a dream when she's not lashed to a dock."

Bridger smiled as he helped the two men lift the dinghy aboard with a halyard assembly and try to lay it on its belly over the cabin front. But the inflatable raft was too long to fit lengthwise and if they put it on with the nose to starboard and the stern to port, there would be no maneuvering space on deck to reach the anchor or the roller furling in the event of a problem. They finally decided to leave the painter attached and tow it behind them. If it had been a hard-sided craft, they would have had no choice but to leave it on the foredeck and lash it down securely. They debated whether or not to deflate it and stow it, but Abbot wasn't comfortable with that idea, so the inflatable craft was put back over the side and the painter secured to the larger vessel's stern.

When they were done, the three men headed back to the cockpit. Abbot asked Hans, "Why did your grandfather name her *Bridger's Child?*"

Hans gave Abbot a blank stare and shrugged.

"She was my father-in-law's third love," Bridger explained for him. "His first two, of course, were his lovely wife . . . and his daughter, who became my wife."

"Sarah, right?" asked Tom as he poked his head through the companionway.

Bridger nodded. "It took us many years before we had the twins, so he bought it at first to annoy me, I think. But, once the boys were born, he realized that he bought it to take them sailing when I was preoccupied with military maneuvers. Hans is named after him, but I suppose you know that."

"Yep," drawled Tom. "These pancakes are ready if you're hungry."

"Starving," said Hans. "We had to eat my cooking last night."

"A disaster," Bridger whispered to Abbot.

Shortly after breakfast, they hoisted the anchor and pointed the bow northwest, then motored for the first several hours because there was no wind.

Making five nautical miles per hour against the tide and Cape Flattery being thirty miles away it took them six hours to reach it, which they did around four in the afternoon. Their plan was to sail west from the cape about thirty miles out to sea, in order to miss the rocky coastline and the heavier seas that accompanied near-shore waters, then head south another thirty miles through the night. By morning, they'd be able to head west again, reaching La Push in the afternoon. Their prime concern was the sea-stacks and the jagged rocks that could dash any vessel to pieces, and they planned to give the rugged coastline a wide berth to avoid any complications.

By the time they reached Cape Flattery, the wind began to freshen and they were able to hoist the mainsail and the roller furling. The auto pilot kept them on course and with the wind on their starboard side, they were able to sail toward the horizon with no difficulties.

The seas were moderately heavy, with swells to six feet, but the waves weren't curling, which made it relatively easy for the Cabo Rico to roll smoothly over them. When the bow hit a crest too early, the water would part and spray the foredeck with foam. Fortunately, the men had no reason to go forward above deck.

Each of the four men wore Coast Guard approved vests designed to inflate immediately upon immersion. They were light enough not to get in the way and gave a sense of security that Tom, especially, seemed to appreciate.

Since Puget Sound and the Strait of Juan de Fuca were fairly flat and calm on their journey to Clallam Bay, Tom had not experienced any queasiness, but within a few hours of sailing the blue Pacific, he had his head hanging overboard more often than not. He wore a pair of yellow foul-weather bibs and jacket to keep warm, but Tom's skin took on a greenish pallor as he lost lunch and dinner, and everything in between. Sitting on the starboard deck, his legs hanging over the gunwale, a stanchion between them, his arms were slung over the top lifeline and his eyes were fixed upon the horizon, as Hans had instructed. This position enabled him to breathe the fresh air and eliminate his stomach contents at will. Occasionally, he would lay over on his left side, in abject misery. But in this position, a wave of nausea would hit him and he would be forced to sit upright once again and lean his head over the lifeline.

Shortly after eight in the evening, they altered course, heading southwest, which kept them at a better angle to the waves and allowed them to sail with the wind coming off the starboard beam and slightly aft. The adjustment of their sails to accommodate this point of sail made the ride a little smoother. Listening to the weather channel on the VHF, Abbot was shocked to hear that a storm was headed their direction. It was going to be a long night.

As the sun set below the western horizon, Abbot was surprised to note that there was no 'red sky' effect and he recognized a fogbank was moving in toward them. Bridger slipped below and wrote down their coordinates, then flipped a switch that would constantly emit a fog horn blast every three minutes as required by the U.S. Coast Guard regulations. Afterward, he distributed foul weather gear to the rest of them and stuffed the tethers in side pockets below the dodger.

For about fifteen minutes before the fog rolled in, the moon was so bright they didn't need light to see the black ocean slipping past them at four knots. As darkness settled upon them, an occasional wave would crest and break over the bow, but she was a heavy displacement, blue-water cruiser designed to take almost anything the ocean could throw at her. With a sailing vessel this stable, the only problems she would encounter would be the folly of man, or the wrath of God.

With Hans at the helm, Bridger and Abbot rolled up the foresail and lashed it securely, then hoisted a storm sail. Shortening the mainsail to the third reefing point, they hoped the storm wouldn't necessitate their lowering the mainsail entirely. The storm and reefed main gave a good balance to the Cabo Rico, which would give them an edge over incoming seas. When they were finally satisfied that they had taken every possible precaution, they waited and watched. Praying became automatic for Abbot. In his heart he whispered, *Watch over us Lord, protect us and keep us safe.*

Hanging onto the handrails, Abbot made his way out to Tom with a thermos. He sat beside his brother on the deck and looked into his glazed eyes. "Miserable?" He didn't need to ask, the expression on Tom's face told it all.

Tom, so weak he could barely speak, nodded. "Am I gonna' make it?"

"I'm afraid so," Abbot smiled. "You need to keep up your liquids and electrolytes. I've warmed you some Gatorade. Can you drink it?"

"I'll try," said Tom. "It ain't gonna stay down, though."

"I know. But, perhaps your body will absorb some of the electrolytes before it comes back up."

Tom nodded, so Abbot removed the cap and poured some into a cup, then gave it to his brother, helping him steady it as he drank. When he'd finished it, Abbot asked, "More?"

"Later," said Tom.

"Quite a trip," Abbot observed. He didn't know what more he could do to help his brother. Going below would only make the nausea worse. There was nothing like a closed environment rolling back and forth to drive a man to the head. At least this way, Tom had fresh air.

With the fog rolling over them, blanketing them in salty moisture, the entire atmosphere felt stifling, foreboding some great evil that would soon be thrown upon them.

"I ain't never gettin' on another boat as long as I live!" Tom moaned.

Abbot checked Tom's life vest and said, "You're safe enough here. Do you want me to tether you to the lifeline in case it gets rough?"

"You mean it ain't rough yet?" Tom nodded his assent.

"The last weather report was revised. The storm that was headed for Alaska has turned south and we're likely to see it get worse before it gets better." Abbot latched Tom's tether to a lifeline attached between the mast and a winch next to the companionway.

"Why don't we head back?" Tom asked.

"We're thirty miles from Neah Bay and nearly sixty from La Push. That's a minimum of six hours with the risk of being driven onto the rocks at Cape Flattery. The storm will be on us in another four hours. Hans and Bridger both think we're better off heading west until it blows past us.

"Ain't you heard of callin' the Coast Guard for help?" asked Tom, the misery he felt plainly evident. If he hadn't been so sick, Abbot doubted Tom would ever have suggested it.

Abbot tried on a reassuring smile. "Are you willing to put more men's lives at risk, when we've got four of us already to worry about?"

"No," Tom mumbled. "Do you think we'll make it?"

"Hans and Bridger have both handled major storms many times before. Bridger's been in two hurricanes. Hans was in a white squall once. And they tell me that *Bridger's Child* has handled plenty of rough seas."

Tom nodded. "Guess I'll do a heap of prayin', then."

"Good idea," Abbot agreed.

He rubbed Tom's shoulder for a minute, then took the thermos with him back to the cockpit.

"How's he doing?" Hans asked, the worry lines already creasing his forehead.

"Sick, scared, but he's tough. He'll make it."

"The Admiral went below to sleep. He wants to take the next shift."

"That puts him first into the storm," Abbot complained.

"You don't argue with the Admiral," Hans suggested. "It's a losing battle."

Abbot gulped. "That'll put me in the next four hour slot," he reminded. He knew his sailing experience was not proficient enough to pilot any boat through a storm.

Hans shook his head. "Your job is to take care of Tom and keep hot soup in the thermoses for us. I'll get four hours sleep while the Admiral takes the helm, then I'll replace him."

Grudgingly, Abbot nodded. Ashamed at his lack of nautical skills, he knew that Hans and Bridger were only doing what was best for the boat. He'd read some of Joshua's books on safety and seamanship last winter that Josh kept in the starboard shelves. Some of the important points reminded him now that the crew's safety never took precedence over the boat's safety, unless the boat was sinking. This cruel, but absolute reality, made it possible to save the entire crew by first saving the ship. After all, whose lives were at stake if the boat was damaged and was not repaired? Abbot was in total agreement.

Taking a blanket, pillow and the thermos, he went forward once again and made Tom as comfortable as he could, insisting that he drink more warm Gatorade. When he had his brother settled on the starboard deck, he asked Tom, "Are you sure you don't want to go down below?"

"Not yet," Tom replied. "The fresh air seems to help more than anything."

"All right," he said. "But should you change your mind, just wave at me, okay?"

"Yep," came the reply, though it wasn't the husky drawl that Tom usually used. It was a raspy squawk that indicated just how miserable Tom really felt.

Reluctant to leave his brother alone, yet knowing there was no alternative, Abbot went below, down into the dark cabin where he used a flashlight to work. He pulled a pan out of a cupboard, opened up several cans of chicken noodle soup and heated them up. Then, he filled two thermoses with soup and another with hot chocolate, using a funnel and pouring when *Bridger's Child* was in a trough or on the climb.

Searching through the cabin with a flashlight so he wouldn't awaken the Admiral, he gathered blankets and gloves and put them on the quarter berth just below the companionway so they would be readily accessible if needed. When he was satisfied he'd done everything that he could for the warmth and comfort of the crew, he joined Hans in the cockpit.

By midnight, the seas were beginning to build as the wind increased. In thirty knots of wind, Abbot helped Hans lower the mainsail completely and wrap it tight against the boom with tie-downs and shorten the storm sail.

The companionway boards were slid into place and the hatch pulled shut. Abbot thought about asking the Admiral to lock it from the inside, just in case there was a catastrophe topsides, but decided against it.

He checked on Tom, who was huddled into his blanket like a caterpillar in a cocoon. Occasionally, the wind would throw spray over him, but Tom remained steady. His eyes were glazed, and Abbot was beginning to get worried about him. With the wind coming across the starboard beam, Tom was the farthest out of the water of any of them and so far most of the waves had crashed over the bow and washed down the foredeck to port where they dumped back into the sea. Yet, Tom seemed almost unaware of their precarious situation.

"How are you holding up?" Abbot yelled, his voice being lost in the screaming wind.

Tom nodded but didn't answer verbally.

"Do you want to go below?"

His brother shook his head.

"Your blanket is soaked! Are you still dry?"

Tom nodded. "Ain't foul weather gear great?" he asked gruffly.

"You released your tether!" Abbot complained, his voice growing hoarse from yelling.

"If the ship goes down, I ain't goin' with it!" Tom barked.

"It's to keep you from being swept overboard!" Abbot yelled.

"No!" The incoherent look in Tom's eyes worried Abbot as he realized his brother may be too sick to know what he was saying.

"Then, come back into the cockpit with me, so I don't get swept overboard coming out here to check on you!" Abbot demanded.

Tom seemed to consider, then nodded. Abbot helped him to his feet, but had to catch him twice when Tom almost collapsed. When he got him to the cockpit, Abbot grabbed some dry blankets and wedged Tom into a makeshift bed on the port side where he would be the most comfortable and least likely to roll off.

The boat was heeled to port at almost twenty degrees, but the shortened storm sail seemed to be handling the wind well enough. Abbot looked at the wind indicator and was shocked to see the readout at forty-eight knots. *That's a strong, gale force wind!* he recalled from studying the Beaufort scale.

Abbot's prayers became more intense. *Protect us, Father! We are in desperate need of Thy watchful eye and Thy guiding hand!*

Chapter Seventeen

By three in the morning, the black seas were rolling under them at a height of thirty feet, or more. *Bridger's Child* would climb the steep, liquid hill, hesitate at the crest, give a little shudder, then plunge down the other side as if on a roller coaster, dipping her bow in the trough, then rising up as water would pour down her decks like a raging waterfall. Sometimes the inflatable dinghy, still tethered behind them on the painter, would fall faster than the sailing vessel into the trough and slam against the stern, reminding them of its presence. Then the nightmare would repeat itself, over and over again.

Admiral Bridger Clark was at the helm, his eyes fastened on the incoming seas, alert and attentive to every conceivable detail. By now, they had the engine running, as they sailed with the storm sail shortened by two-thirds. They were motor-sailing into heavy seas, trying to keep the boat at a forty-five degree angle from the incoming monster waves.

Abbot had long ago stopped calling these huge walls of ocean 'waves.' The wind blew the tops off the foaming monsters and the towering liquid mountains were difficult to climb and terrifying to slide down. But, the Admiral handled every single one with confidence and with a daring elation that surprised Abbot. Always in charge, that was the Admiral.

Hans had seemed a little less confident when he was piloting the sailing vessel, but Abbot was sure that was only because he lacked the seasoned experience of the Admiral. Now, Hans lay below in the cabin on the port settee, hopefully sleeping. Though whether Hans could sleep or not, Abbot had no idea. The companionway was closed up tight, latched from the inside this time, so that Hans could get out easily in an emergency, but the water couldn't enter.

They'd long since passed the fog, which had swept by them on its way inland, but the moon could not penetrate the thick clouds that swept the storm southeast. With no visible means of seeing where the waves were coming from, the Admiral had turned on the forward deck lights, so he could at least see something that would indicate an incoming monster.

Tom groaned on the port cockpit bench. Abbot helped him sit up and kneel next to the lifeline, where Tom hung his head overboard and expelled what little was left inside him.

Suddenly, the Admiral yelled, "Hang on!"

Another monster had loomed above them unaware and slammed against the starboard beam, broaching the vessel to port, forcing her mast down in the water and dumping a deluge over them that almost turned *Bridger's Child* upside down.

Thrown into the water unexpectedly, Abbot had only enough time to grab the lifelines with one hand, gripping it with all his strength in case the tether broke. Holding his breath underwater, he wondered if the boat would right itself, or lurch clear over on top of him and sink him to the bottom of the sea. His life vest inflated, pushing tight against his cheeks, squeezing oxygen from his lungs.

The ship shuddered like a frightened child and Abbot knew he'd have to let go and swim out from under her if she didn't move soon.

He was out of oxygen and couldn't hold his breath much longer. Visibility was zero and he felt with his feet to see if Tom had been able to hold onto the boat.

To his horror, his brother was gone. A great groaning sound reached his ears and at the same moment he felt the boat rolling back to starboard, the motion lifting him up and slamming his back against the freeboard. Looking for Tom, he saw a yellow shadow in the water behind the boat. He released his tether and let go of the lifeline, yelling, "Man overboard!" Then, he began swimming toward his brother with all the strength within him.

His arm caught something, he wasn't sure what, but when he realized it was the painter to the dinghy, he grabbed onto it and pulled it along with him. When he finally reached Tom, he rolled him onto his back and found him unconscious. He wasn't certain whether Tom was dead or alive. The boisterous storm drowned out any sound Tom might have given if breathing, and the waves hindered Abbot's ability to see if Tom's chest was rising or falling.

Abbot wrapped a leg around the rope and tugged his way, inch by inch toward the dinghy, holding onto Tom at the same time. He felt the waves lift him up like a fishing bobber and drop him down again, as if he were a child's plaything. Yet he didn't lose his grip on his brother, or on the painter.

With all his strength, he managed to reach the dinghy. But, he couldn't push Tom over the inflated hypalon sides. He looked behind him for *Bridger's Child*, but he couldn't see it. The lights had apparently been damaged when she was knocked down. Then he felt something bump him in the back. His worst nightmare, *SHARK!* formed in his mind, but this shark had a voice.

"Let me help."

Abbot was so elated to recognize the Admiral's voice he didn't know whether to hug the man or kiss him! Instead, he smiled and said, "Sure glad you could make it, sir!"

With the Admiral's help, Abbot climbed into the raft and pulled while the Admiral pushed Tom on board. Then Abbot pulled the Admiral up into it with them.

After checking Tom's airway and noting that he was breathing, he felt for a pulse and found it rapid but steady. He breathed a sigh of relief, which only lasted until the Admiral yelled above the pitch of the screaming wind, "I didn't see Hans come on deck! Someone has to go back and secure the ship!"

Torn between helping his brother and saving *Bridger's Child*, which would save all of them, Abbot nodded. "I'll go!" he yelled.

The Admiral winced. "I think my ribs are broken!"

It was the first time the gritty man had indicated anything was wrong with him at all. Abbot noticed for the first time that Bridger's face was pale and his breathing ragged. "Are you going to be all right?"

Bridger nodded, though Abbot could see the pain he suffered by the guarded expression in his eyes.

Abbot wiped the water from his face before he realized the futility of such a gesture. He prepared to go back in the water, but the Admiral put his hand on his arm and stopped him.

"If it's possible, winch the painter in so we can get on board *Bridger's Child!*" he yelled. "It'll be much safer on her than in this dinghy! At least we know she can handle a knock down!"

Nodding, Abbot said, "If anything happens, tell Bekah—"

"Tell her yourself!" the Admiral barked. "Giving up without a fight is not an option!"

Abbot shuddered. He knew the odds they faced at this point.

The Admiral grabbed him by both shoulders. Staring straight into his soul, he shouted, "Put your trust in God and take His hand! That's what He's there for! Now go!"

Without looking back, Abbot dove into the water and grabbed the painter, pulling himself closer, ever closer to *Bridger's Child*. By the time he could finally see the stern, he had managed to bob up thirteen monsters and slide down them again without letting go or getting himself killed in the process.

The big problem facing him would be getting on board, and his best chance was to grab the gunwale and somehow find a way to unfasten the side ladder. The freeboard on the Cabo Rico was more than three feet off the waterline and he doubted his ability to swing himself up freestyle.

When he finally reached the boat, he was exhausted, but he had no time for his own concerns at the moment. Hanging onto the painter, he bounced himself up and down in the water until he was able to grab the toe-rail. Letting go of the line that had aided his progress in rescuing his brother and bringing him back to *Bridger's Child* was like removing his life vest and tossing it into the sea. But, he had no choice. With both hands, he hung from the toe-rail and was bounced around like a toy against the fiberglass; he inched his way around the stern to the port side, hoping he'd be able to reach the ladder.

To his utter amazement he felt two hands on his forearms, and at the same time he heard Hans yelling, "Abbot! I've got you! Just a little farther!"

Then, with one strenuous burst of energy, Hans reached down and grabbed the back strap of Abbot's life vest and pulled him over the toe-rail and onto the deck.

Abbot rolled over, under the lifeline and heaved a sigh of relief.

"Are you all right?" Hans asked, his face red, his eyes glazed with horror.

"Ye—yes," Abbot stammered, his teeth chattering. *Funny,* he thought, *I don't remember it being cold!* His only thought the entire time had been survival, not comfort.

"Dad?" Hans asked, his voice a blend of dismay and horror. "And Tom?"

"They're i–i–in the dinghy," Abbot said, still shaking, almost uncontrollably.

"Thank you, Lord!" exclaimed Hans as he turned his eyes heavenward. "Thank you!"

"We need to winch them in," said Abbot, trying to control his shivering. He sat up, rolled onto a hip and pulled himself into a standing position, hanging onto the hand lifeline as he did so.

By the time he managed to get to the cockpit, Hans was already using the boat hook, attached to a long pole, to snag the painter. When the line was securely tied to a cleat at the stern, they pulled it together until they had it wrapped around a winch.

Bridger's Child, climbing up the waves and sliding down the other side, was still motoring and Abbot noticed Hans had turned on the auto pilot, with the bow headed at a forty-five degree angle to the oncoming waves. The pitching and heavy motion was far more noticeable aboard the boat than it had been when he was out in the water.

Using the winch handle, Hans started cranking the dinghy towards them. Abbot noticed the companionway door was wide open and he knew that if they broached again, the flood of water would flow down below and sink them. *What was Hans thinking?*

Abbot dashed below and saw the cabin askew. Grabbing the flashlight from its secured latch next to the navigation station, he turned it on and noticed the books and equipment scattered every-where. The TV-VCR combo that had been strapped to a starboard shelf lay broken on the cabin sole, next to a pool of blood.

Gasping, Abbot went back out to the cockpit, replaced the

companionway door boards and closed the hatch, then followed the trail of blood over the cockpit floor and on the deck where Hans had helped him on board with the flashlight.

Grabbing Hans by the arm, he spun him around. "You're hurt!" he yelled over the shrieking wind.

"Bumped my head!" Hans answered.

Abbot stopped him. With the flashlight, he saw the blood seeping behind Hans right ear and a wide, gaping wound in his scalp.

"It's jush a li'l bump!" barked Hans.

But the blood was trickling out of it. Looking more closely, he noticed one of Hans' pupils had dilated and his speech was slurred. He opened the hatch and swung his legs up over the boards, found a few towels in the debris below and swung back out to the cockpit, pulling the hatch closed behind him. Pressing the towels against Hans' head he forced him to lie down on the port cockpit bench. "Be still!" he barked, latching Hans' tether to the lifeline.

"Bus—t Dad!" Hans protested.

"Let me worry about Dad or he won't have a son still alive to help him anymore."

"Ish not thash ba—ad!"

"Hans! You're bleeding bad! You can hardly speak clearly. Now lie still. I'll bring the Admiral in." Abbot demanded.

Apparently Hans believed him because he curled up in a fetal position on the bench and rested his injured head upon the towels. Abbot continued to release and return the pressure of the towels against Hans' head, until he noticed that the bleeding began to ease.

Relieved, Abbot turned his attention to the winch. As he began cranking the handle, his mouth dropped open in horror. The painter was no longer attached to the inflated dinghy! The winch handle turned freely, winding up quickly, until only a stub of the painter remained, a stub that had been stretched far too long. It had torn in half, leaving Bridger and Tom adrift, at the mercy of the wind and the waves in a boat no bigger than a thimble.

Terror sank into him as he realized what had happened.

In despair he pushed the hatch open and leaned down inside where he grabbed the VHF microphone and pressed a button. "Mayday! Mayday! Mayday! This is *Bridger's Child*, calling Mayday!"

After several tries with no response, Abbot looked at the VHF display. Their lifeline with the outside world was turned on, but it wasn't working. He looked up at the mast, but he couldn't see if the antenna was attached or not, it was too dark. It may have been destroyed when *Bridger's Child* was knocked down.

The boat began to broach again and Abbot yanked on the steering wheel to bring the bow into the wave just in time. A great shudder went through *Bridger's Child* as she crested, then slipped down the other side of another monster.

With his hand on the wheel, Abbot realized that the auto pilot was stuck in position. At least *this* came as no surprise. The ancient piece of equipment had been working oddly when they'd brought her south from Friday Harbor to Seattle, last fall.

Although a malfunctioning auto pilot did not shock Abbot, it was the proverbial straw that broke the camel's back. Now he was angry. He lashed the wheel with the broken painter to hold *Bridger's Chile* in a heave-to position, backed the storm sail, then cast his eyes heavenward.

With his voice loud enough that God would hear him above the terrible storm, Abbot screamed, "When does it stop, Lord? How many lives will you take this time before you help us? How many more tests, God?"

Looking down at Hans, he noticed his eyes flutter for a moment, then close again as he slipped into unconsciousness.

Abbot had been pushed over the edge, emotionally. With his hair dripping around his face he stepped out onto the deck and walked forward as he conversed with God, though it wasn't a conversation. "How many more tests, Father?" he demanded. "First you use me as your puppet to introduce Alyssa to Ed! Then you give me Bekah only to ask me to give her up. You set Tom and Bridge adrift in a dinghy not a fraction as stable as this broaching vessel! You allow Hans to be injured so badly I don't know that he'll ever recover. And now you disable the auto-pilot?!"

Spreading his arms wide, disregarding the wall of water growing in front of him, Abbot yelled, "You took Pa and Mont away from me. You took my mother when I was too young to remember her!" Tears formed in his eyes and dripped down his face, but he was oblivious of them.

The boat climbed the monster and hesitated at the crest, then slipped down into the trough. Abbot was thrown back by the ocean coming aboard over the bow. He stood up and grabbed the lifeline with one hand.

Unfinished with his stormy conversation, he yelled, "You take Tom and Bridge from me! And likely Hans! Do you want it all? Everyone I ever cared about? Everything good in my life? All right . . . all right!"

In desperation, Abbot dug beneath the foul-weather jacket that he wore and felt the silver chain with his mother's ring upon it. Without stopping to think what he was doing he removed it, held it up and yelled. "You've taken everything I ever cared about, God! All because you're angry with me! But, you can stop now! I'll go on a mission! I'll give up Bekah, my career, everything! My life if I have to! I'll do everything you ask, God! Here! You can have everything I am and everything I own!" He threw the silver chain with his mother's ring overboard and watched in horror as it was buried by the black, angry sea. "That's all I have to give. Take it. Just spare my friend, Hans!

Spare Tom and Bridge. I'll do what you want." he sank to his knees and wept bitterly. "If that's not enough, then take me," he begged. "Take my life. Don't take theirs. I'm the one you're angry with. Take me."

Finally, Abbot collapsed on the forward deck. A heavy weariness overcame him and his eyes closed voluntarily. He found unconsciousness as comforting as a deep and peaceful sleep.

Chapter Eighteen

It seemed that he had been in their presence for several hours, asking questions and receiving answers. How long had they been beside him, conversing with him? Abbot wondered.

"So you see, Son" Sparky said, "there are many things you need to do yet."

Abbot's mother held his hand to her lips and kissed it gently. He looked at her tenderly, remembering another time when she had visited him from across the veil. "What about Bekah?" he asked her.

"Life is a trial, son," she answered. "And Bekah has her free agency."

"What about my career, Pa?"

Sparky squeezed Abbot's arm affectionately. "Your career will fail entirely without your mission," he said. "You must understand that."

"Can you hear me?" came a familiar male voice, interrupting his conversation with his parents.

"But Pa!" Abbot exclaimed. "Don't go—"

"He's still hallucinating," said another voice.

"I ain't never seen him like this," Tom's husky voice said. "You think we should move him down below?"

Abbot opened his eyes. Standing over him were Tom, Hans and Bridger. He blinked. Then, he looked again. All three men surrounded him and he sat up quickly. "You're all right?" he asked. "How?"

"Aw, he'll be all right," Tom told them. "His color's returning."

"What happened?" he asked as they helped him to his feet.

It was daylight, a little foggy, but visibility was at least a half mile. *Bridger's Child* was sitting on a sea of flat, calm water as smooth as glass, in a still, almost ethereal world where the sun was making every effort to drive the fog back out to sea and succeeding.

The first thing Abbot looked at was the mast. The antenna was gone completely, as was the wind indicator. But otherwise, the mast seemed to be intact.

He looked in amazement at his best friend. "How did you find them?" he asked Hans, noting that Hans' chestnut hair was matted on the side from dry, caked blood, but his eyes were a clear, bright blue and the pupils were completely normal. The wound that had seemed life-threatening last night was now grown shut, as though the hand of God had repaired it without stitches.

"I didn't. I must have passed out sometime after bringing you on board. I don't remember anything beyond that," Hans answered.

"Tom, Bridge, how did you get here?"

"You must have done it," said Tom. "Afterward, you must have fainted 'cause we found you here, knocked out colder than a wedge."

Bridge interrupted. "I remember my chest hurting so bad I could hardly breathe. I thought I died and went to heaven."

"But the raft," Abbot insisted. "The line broke. How did you find us without the painter?"

"The dinghy's still tied on," said Tom.

"No, the painter broke in two. I winched it up and the dinghy was gone. You were both gone." Abbot insisted.

He walked aft, past them, where he grabbed the boat hook and latched onto the dinghy's painter. Then, Abbot pulled it in. About fifteen feet before the dinghy reached the stern, he found a knot tied in the painter where it had broken last night. Stunned, he almost fell backwards, but Tom and Hans both caught him before he could. Abbot sank down onto the starboard cockpit bench. "It was broken, I swear. I never tied it, how could I have?"

Bridger's voice sounded raspy as he said, "I thought it was a dream."

"What, Dad?" asked Hans.

Abbot thought it was one of the few times he'd ever heard Hans address his father as anything other than Admiral.

"I dreamed your grandfather tied the line, then took the helm and sailed *Bridger's Child*," he explained.

"Grandpa Hansen?" Hans' mouth dropped open and his eyes widened in surprise.

"There were two other people, too," Bridger remembered, looking straight at Abbot and Tom. "Your father, Sparky. I recognized him from the funeral. He was dressed in a white suit and a woman was with him. I assumed she was your mother. They spoke with Tom in the raft for a while, then they talked to Abbot while Grandpa Hansen sailed us out of the storm."

"That's impossible," said Hans. "Miracles only happen to women, like Kayla and Alyssa."

"No!" Bridger exclaimed. "God is just as mindful of us males as He is of the gentler sex. At first I thought it was just a dream. But now? How will we ever prove it was real?"

Abbot was astounded, as were all of them. For several minutes they just sat in the cockpit, awestruck and filled with wonder.

Then, as though he'd just thought of something Bridger said to Abbot, "Just before he spoke with you, your father had something in his hand . . . a chain! And he slid it onto—" Bridger stopped and gasped as his eyes settled upon the helm. Reaching out he lifted a silver chain off the throttle.

"This!" he said triumphantly. Then Bridger added, "Sparky looked right at me when the boat was safe and said, 'Give this back to Abbot.'"

With a trembling hand, Abbot reached out and took the familiar silver chain. Dangling from it was an exquisitely beautiful silver and jade ring with tiny leaves in a filigree pattern. Tears filled his eyes, but he was unashamed. He remembered his parents conversation with him during his dream, and he nodded as he slipped the chain back over his head. Looking up at them, he explained, "I threw it away during the storm. I was angry and I threw it into the depths of the sea."

When the men finally recognized the many miracles that had come upon them and how gracious the Lord had been in sending them assistance, they were speechless. Except for Tom, who whispered, "We're all worthy of a miracle . . . even me. Git on yer knees, men, while I offer a word of prayer."

Chapter Nineteen

On August thirtieth, Abbot stood outside the museum. What he was about to do would make the scientific world laugh and scorn him. After all that had happened in his life, he had no choice. Emotionally, he was still a wreck over what he was doing to his career and his life. But, his spirit was calm and filled with resolve and that was all that mattered. His life was straight with God, let the consequences fall where they may. With the envelope in his hand, he went inside, across the foyer to Randall Hamilton's office and knocked briskly. When he heard the older man's voice inviting him in, he opened the door. Stepping across the floor, Abbot gulped, knowing that he was about to throw his entire career away, but he was a man of his word and God could trust him. Abbot would never again give up his honor. He placed the envelope on Randall's desk and said, "This is my answer to your request, sir."

"In writing?" Randall asked. "A verbal would have been satisfactory, Abbot."

"It's my resignation, sir."

Randall didn't seem the least bit surprised. "I'm not in the market for resignations," he said. "I'm afraid I can't accept it."

"I'm leaving in the next month or two to fill a mission for the Church of Jesus Christ of Latter Day Saints," Abbot said. "I'll be gone for two years. You'll have to get someone else to fill your shoes, Randall. I'm not your man."

"I have an envelope for you, young man," said Randall, completely unfazed. "Though I have to admit that Admiral Clark's request surprised me, I actually found myself quite excited about assisting him during your absence."

"You spoke with Bridge?" Abbot asked. He was surprised, but knowing the Admiral, perhaps he shouldn't have been.

"We had lunch last week and he is most persuasive." Randall pulled an envelope from a desk drawer and handed it to Abbot. Then, as though he was ready to dismiss him, he said, "It's a tenure contract, effective as soon as you leave on your mission. You'll retain your title at COSAT with my assistance, and when you return, if you still want the position of administrator, it will be yours. My wife doesn't quite understand why I want to give the museum two more years, but I wasn't ready to retire yet, anyway."

Abbot beamed. "Thank you, sir."

"Now, don't 'sir' me, I'm still Randall. I think you've been around the Admiral too much!"

Laughing, Abbot took the envelope and shook Randall's hand vigorously.

Leaving Randall Hamilton's office a few minutes later, Abbot realized that the greatest trial of his life awaited him. His date with Bekah. They hadn't spoken since the night he'd stormed away, seventeen days ago. He wasn't even sure she would see him, because she wasn't answering his telephone calls; he'd left her several messages, but she hadn't returned any of them. Finally, he'd phoned her on Sunday, two days ago and left this message:

"Bekah, I apologize for what I said when I left the night of your baptism. It's clear that you don't want to talk to me, but I have to see you. I'm going to be in town on Tuesday, the thirtieth. I'll stop by your condo at three in the afternoon. If I don't hear from you by then, I'll assume it's all right. If I get there and you still won't see me, then I'll assume the engagement is over and I won't bother you again. But I honestly believe, with all my heart, that we're meant to be together forever. If you believe that, too, then be there. Tuesday, three o'clock."

Abbot looked at his watch. Fifteen minutes and he would know whether the engagement was over or not. He drove the Bronco carefully. This was not the time to get in an accident. If she was willing to see him and he was delayed because of his recklessness, then it would be over. She'd think he stood her up.

Soon, he was back on Green Lake Avenue, headed toward her condo. When he saw the building, his heart started pounding and sweat beaded up on his forehead. He wiped it away with his hand. *Fresh courage take! She's either going to break it off now, or never.* It was the never part that scared the life out of him.

He parked the Bronco out front and looked up at her balcony window. He didn't see her watching for him and that wasn't a good sign. Walking over to the front door he looked at his watch. *Two minutes early.* Pacing back and forth, he waited until it was exactly three o'clock before he pressed the button marked 'eighty-six.'

When he heard her voice say, "I'll be right down," he couldn't believe how incredible she sounded.

But she didn't want him to come up, which wasn't a good sign, either. *Too impersonal this way. Less familiar.* Why was she driving him so crazy?!!

When she opened the front door, she gave him a timid smile, and he felt his heart flip over inside his chest.

"Hi," she said.

"You look great!" he exclaimed. *Down boy! Don't scare her off now!*

"Ditto."

He finally pushed his tongue out of the way and asked, "Is there someplace you'd like to go where we can talk?"

"Shall we walk over to Green Lake? It's so stuffy in my apartment. I'm debating on whether or not to install an air conditioner, but it's hard to justify the expense when I would only use it one or two months a year."

"Sure," he said, taking her hand in his. She didn't pull away and that gave him hope.

Then, he remembered what she'd said once about 'last dates' and how she tried to make the time especially memorable for the man she was dumping at the moment. His heart sank.

He listened to her talk about how well Cody was doing in soccer ball and how progress was coming on Ryan and Gail's new home. They would be moving in next week and Gail was already ordering nursery stock for her garden.

But, he wasn't certain that he remembered everything she'd said by the time they reached a park bench that overlooked Green Lake and sat down. His heart was pounding so loudly he almost couldn't hear anything else. In a few moments on the bench, however, he felt his heart slow down a little and that seemed to help.

He was still holding her hand and he noticed that she was still wearing the engagement ring. It sparkled in the afternoon sun, and he liked the way it looked on her delicate hand.

When he realized she'd stopped talking and was waiting for him to contribute something to the conversation, he coughed a moment then turned towards her and studied her lovely, oval face. Her tan was even darker now that they'd had a few weeks of sunshine and her brown eyes glistened. A faint sprinkling of freckles across the bridge of her nose reminded him how much he'd loved looking at them that first day he met her and she fell asleep on his shoulder at the University of Washington Medical Center.

He lifted a hand up and swept his fingers into her thick, auburn curls and smiled at her, then bent his head to kiss her, but she stiffened, so he backed off immediately. Alarms went off in his head and he realized that their moment of reckoning had arrived.

"Bekah," he said, "I love you more than I can say. I'm sorry we quarreled and I'm sorry that I left in such a huff."

She lowered her long eyelashes and looked down at his hands. "I'm sorry, too," she responded.

"Does that mean I'm forgiven?" he asked.

"Yes," she said, but he also heard some hesitancy in her voice and it worried him. *Forgiven but not forgotten?* he wondered.

"Good," he said. "Then I need to tell you something that will probably make you mad at me again, but—?

She interrupted with, "I have something equally important to tell you."

"I'd like to be first," he told her. "I need to get it out in the open, right now and see how you're going to take it."

"Abbot, you can be first if you want, but I assure you, in the end you would rather hear what I have to say first."

He gulped. Was she telling him that he would have no need to tell her anything after she was done because she was going to tell him goodbye before he did any groveling? "All right," he finally agreed.

"When I got your message Sunday, I decided right away that I wouldn't see you," she began. "But something happened Sunday night that changed my mind."

"Oh?"

"I had a dream. I think it was the same dream Grandmother Lili had ten years ago. The only difference was that Grandma was my escort in the dream. I was walking in a beautiful garden that overlooked Lake Washington. I saw all my cousins there, and a lot of other people, too. I was dressed in a beautiful white gown and you were wearing your tuxedo. We had just come from the temple in Bellevue, where we were sealed for time and all eternity and it was our wedding reception."

Hope began to build within him, but he didn't say anything, he just studied the serene and peaceful look upon her face as she spoke to him.

"Gail was just starting to show a round belly and Grandma said, 'she's having a girl around Christmas.' Then we saw Robyn and she had a young child in her arms. He must have been almost a year old. I said to her, 'I see you had your twins. She pointed toward two young children playing and said, 'Those are my twins. This is Daniel, my third child.' I was so astounded because the twins appeared to be at least two years old."

Abbot smiled. Perhaps his news wasn't going to upset her as much as he'd thought. *Thank you, Lord! Thank you!*

Bekah looked into his eyes and said tenderly, "The day Grandmother Lili died, she asked me to her bedside and recited something to me that I have never forgotten. I was the last person she ever talked to, but I wanted to believe that part of what she said couldn't be true. I wanted to believe that part of her dream had been wrong because I was afraid that she meant you were going to be taken away from me, to the home of the ancient ones. In my youth, that place always meant the spirit world where we go after we die. I thought that you were going to die and go teach the ancient ones the gospel. I thought that the box

Cody found would somehow be instrumental in your death. But I was wrong.

"In my dream, Grandmother repeated her words and I finally understood what she meant. What she said to me was,

> *The man you are to marry will know God, and will talk with the spirits. They will whisper to him and he will listen to them. He will pray mighty prayers and they will be answered. After you meet him, he will go on a long journey to the home of the ancient ones. You must be patient and wait for him. When he returns, he will marry you in a lofty, white mansion where a man with a gold trumpet stands on a tall pinnacle. Together, you and your tyee will preserve the unity of our namima .'*

"Do you understand why I was so frightened?" she asked.

Abbot nodded. "You thought I was going to die. Do you understand now what she was really trying to tell you?"

Bekah moved over onto Abbot's lap and laid her head upon his shoulder. Loving the closeness, Abbot marveled at how quickly all the barriers that had been keeping them apart came tumbling down.

Whispering against his ear, Bekah said, "Grandmother was telling me that you would be called on a mission to a land where our ancient ones came from when they lived here on the earth. And when you return, we will be sealed in the temple. Together, we will do research and find my ancestors, so that they can be sealed to one another as well. By doing this, our namima will be preserved forever."

Abbot pulled her close. "I gave my bishop the papers for my mission last Sunday. He told me that I should know in a few weeks where the Lord will send me. Now that you've told me this, I suspect my mission will be somewhere in South America."

She lifted her head. "Not in the northwest, or British Columbia."

He smiled. "Have you read all of the Book of Mormon?" he asked.

"Yes, of course. I'm starting through it again."

"Do you recall the story of Hagoth?"

"No, I don't."

"He built a ship fifty-some years before the Savior was born and sailed north. In the Book of Mormon, it says he may have drowned in the sea. But, it was never really known what happened to him."

"You think this Hagoth came to the northwest?" she asked quickly.

"Perhaps not Hagoth, but the Book of Mormon says others went away by sea also. Perhaps the COSAT site will tell us who," came his firm reply.

They held each other for a long time, neither one needing to say a word and when he kissed her, she melted against him, surprising and delighting him.

Finally he worked up enough courage to say, "Bekah, I don't have the right to ask you to wait two years for me. And if you can't, I'll understand."

"I'm waiting," she murmured.

Relief flooded over him and he pushed her back just enough to get his hands around his neck. Removing the silver chain, he told her how he threw it away in a moment of desperation and how his father gave it back. She expressed her astonishment at the miracles God had wrought in his behalf, yet she believed him with a child-like faith, never doubting.

Placing the chain around her neck, he said, "This ring belongs to our first daughter. Will you keep it for me until I get home? I won't be allowed to take it with me and I'm certain you understand how priceless it is to me."

"I do," she agreed. "When you return, I will give it back. When I do, you will know that I have waited faithfully for you." As she admired the silver and jade ring, she said. "And our first daughter shall be named Bekah Taquinna Lili Sparkleman, if that suits you."

He beamed. "It suits her just fine,"

"And our first boy should be named Abbot," she suggested.

"No," he snuggled her closer. " I was thinking about Cody Taquinna Sparkleman and calling him 'Sparky' to avoid confusion."

Her accepting smile lit up his world. "I love it," she whispered.

"I'm sorry I didn't baptize you, or any of the others. I don't know if you can ever forgive me for that, I doubt that I'll ever be able to forgive myself. I should have been stronger and trusted the Lord to make everything else in my life work out. If I had only listened to Him earlier, I could have spared everyone a lot of anguish."

"I did not trust God, either," she admitted. "I misunderstood His intentions and I reacted poorly. Can you forgive me?"

"I already have." He smiled as she studied his face and searched the depths of his eyes. "What?" he finally asked.

"Your place as the tyee of Taquinna's namima has already been earned," she whispered. "It is my duty to obey you, O Wise One. Who you would have me marry?"

"You are God's gift to this tyee, Bekah. I follow the Lord, but I believe He has agreed that you will marry me."

"In two years?"

"In two years."

She pouted momentarily, but he put his forehead against hers and whispered, "But in two years, you will marry me forever."

"Forever," Bekah sighed. "I like the sound of that."

Epilogue:

Abbot read from Second Nephi 29:11 & 12 . . . *For I command all men, both in the east and in the west, and in the north, and in the south, and in the islands of the sea, that they shall write the words which I speak unto them; for out of the books which shall be written I will judge the world, every man according to their works, according to that which is written. For behold, I shall speak unto the Jews and they shall write it; and I shall also speak unto the Nephites and they shall write it; and I shall also speak unto the other tribes of the house of Israel, which I have led away, and they shall write it; and I shall also speak unto all nations of the earth and they shall write it.* These scriptures had more meaning to him now than at any other time, and he looked over at his two sleeping, Brazilian companions and smiled.

"Habla Ingles, Senor?" asked the stewardess, interrupting his thoughts.

Abbot turned to face her. "Yes, I do."

"I'm glad. Spanish isn't my strong suit. I noticed you were talking to these two men in Spanish and I need a translator for another passenger. Do you mind?"

"Not at all."

He wandered back and learned that the woman only wanted to

know how long before the plane would arrive in Seattle. After telling her, he returned to his seat and the two sleeping companions he had brought with him.

Putting his scriptures aside, Abbot opened the photo album Bekah had sent him last summer. He was still amazed at how the COSAT compound had been transformed. Instead of tents, there were two large buildings: the research laboratory was already complete, and the second, a visitor's center and museum, was under construction. Another picture gave an aerial view of the dig site. The cave had been unearthed and the family's living quarters opened for the public to view, after all the artifacts and remains had been removed. Seven such houses had been uncovered so far. Other photos gave him an idea how much Cody had grown, and there was Robyn's third child, a son she named Daniel, now nearing a year old.

The photo he most admired, however, was the one of Bekah standing outside the temple at Bellevue. She was wearing an aqua-marine dress, very modest, and sporting a stake missionary tag. She was also holding a big sign that read, *Color me hopeful.*

Now that his mission was over, he understood why the Lord wanted him to go, and he was grateful that he'd finally listened. The two Brazilians sitting beside him were living proof of God's generous blessings. Abbot and his junior companion had found them while tracting, a few months ago. The two men were driving some oxen through the tropical city of Ojalajara, a tiny little village in the jungles of Brazil. Only after they had accepted the gospel and been baptized did he learn that they had knowledge of an ancient language found in no other region of South America. They had learned this language from the tradition of their grandfathers and had studied hieroglyphics depicting it, etched in some caves near their homes. This language was similar to that found on metallic plates found inside Cody's mortared stone box; a language that, up until his friends had been found, no one seemed to know. The Lord had sent him to Ojalajara to find these two, convert them and arrange for them to come back with him to Seattle, where they would be put to work right away on the linguistic challenges found inside that box. Abbot had been teaching them English in the interim and though they were getting quite good at it, they often reverted back to Spanish whenever they could.

Abbot smiled and looked at the photo of Bekah, once again. Now just one thing remained: Seeing if he and Bekah still loved each other as much as when he left. For his part, he knew he loved her more. Her weekly letters had sustained him and had given him insights into her personality that he would never have guessed just by verbal communications, alone. Sometimes people open up their hearts when they write letters, and Bekah was no exception. He was astounded at her goodness and moral character. The mission had been good for their relationship because he now understood her better than he thought he ever could.

Would she feel the same towards him? She had been very careful to sign all of her letters, "Your sister in the gospel," and she hadn't written about how terribly she missed him, or that she was counting down the hours until he came home. He was glad she hadn't because if she'd written those words even once, he would have been tempted to quit and fly home. By keeping her letters busy with things she and her family were doing, then telling him at the end of each one that she was proud of him and asking him to continue in the faith, she had enabled him to stay in the mission field.

Now, he would see her and find out for sure. The only evidence that he had regarding her feelings was that one photograph of her standing in front of the temple with her little sign, *Color me hopeful.*

Finally, the plane landed at Seatac International Airport and Abbot waited for his two companions to exit in front of him. Seeing Bekah's smiling face as he joined her little group quickened his heart and he felt his palms sweating. Bekah gave him a quick hug, then he shook hands with Randall Hamilton and the Admiral, who were there to greet Manuel and Jose Sanchez and take them both to a hotel, where they would unwind, today and be taken to COSAT, tomorrow. When the pleasantries of protocol were completed, he waved goodbye to them and turned his attention to Bekah.

Her hair had grown a little since he last saw her, but the curls were just as silky and her eyes were filled with at least as much love as when he'd said goodbye. His heart was spilling over with love so fast he was afraid he would drown in it.

Pulling her close to him, he held her in his arms and felt much like a man who had been dying of dehydration in a desolate desert and had just wandered upon an oasis. It had been a long, dry season.

Suddenly, he felt her sobbing against him and he tilted her head back and gazed down at her. "I love you," he said softly.

As soon as he said the words, she pulled back, removed the silver chain from around her neck and placed it over his. "I made you a promise," she said. "And I'm a woman with honor. This ring is for our first daughter, my tyee. Will you wear it until she arrives?"

Abbot nodded, but when no words of gratitude would come to him, he pulled her into his arms and kissed her as though he could never get enough of her. And when he did, he found that words were no longer necessary.

Other Books by Sherry Ann Miller

One Last Gift

First in the five-book Gift Series, *One Last Gift* revolves around Kayla, who gave up religion ten years earlier to pursue a lifestyle completely foreign to her upbringing. When she receives a disturbing telephone call from her father, Mont, she reluctantly leaves her fiancée, her sailboat, and her challenging career in San Diego, and hastens to her childhood home high in the Uinta Mountains. Her return stirs up questions from her past she thought she'd buried years before: Why does Mont tenaciously cling to his faith, regardless of his daughter's rejection of it? Isn't God just a crutch people use when they don't understand science? Does her mother really live in the Spirit World, as Mont insists? Kayla conquers one issue after another until she faces the greatest obstacle of her life in a desperate race for survival. Will tragedy turn Kayla's analytical heart back to God, or will it take a miracle? *One Last Gift* placed third in the national "2000 First Coast Beacon Awards" for published authors. Now available from your favorite bookstore. If they don't have it, please ask them to order directly from Granite Publishing & Distribution (800) 574-5779. ISBN# 1-930980-01-9.

Gardenia Sunrise

Frightened by the drastic measures it will take to provide even the remotest hope for a cure to her cancer, Brandje flees to her villa on the west coast of France where she hopes to prepare herself emotionally and spiritually to meet God. Her plans are interrupted when Nathan, an American with a hot temper, arrives for his annual holiday at the villa, unaware that his reservation has been canceled. Brandje's remarkable journey of spiritual and romantic discovery touches the soul with enlightenment, hope and inspiration. *Gardenia Sunrise* is a powerful conversion story that will linger in your heart forever. Now available from your favorite bookstore. If they don't have it, please ask them to order directly from Granite Publishing & Distribution (800) 574-5779. ISBN# 1-930980-33-7.

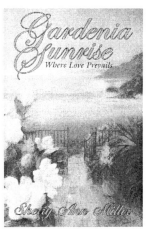

An Angel's Gift

While *One Last Gift* dwelt on Kayla's conversion, *An Angel's Gift* answers the question she left behind: What about Ed? When Alyssa drops in at the Bar M Ranch (literally!), she disrupts the life of the ranch foreman, Ed Sparkleman, and keeps him jumping hoops almost beyond what he can endure . . . *what a hero!* Along the way, Alyssa's confidence is shaken, and she must learn to trust God once again, but not until after a desperate sacrifice and the miraculous trial of her faith. *An Angel's Gift* placed first in the national "2003 Write Touch Readers' Award" in Wisconsin, tied for first place in the national "2003 First Coast Beacon Awards" in Florida, and placed fourth in the Utah "Heart of the West" competition (2002). *An Angel's Gift* is installment two in the five-book Gift Series. Now available from your favorite bookstore. If they don't have it, please ask them to order directly from Granite Publishing & Distribution (800) 574-5779. ISBN# 1-930980-98-1.

Search for the Bark Warwick

Beginning with the stowaway who interrupts and changes John's life forever, and concluding with John's desperate search for his captive son, Thomas, *Search for the Bark Warwick* is a stirring tale of surprise, compassion, love and tenacious devotion to family. The story of a true hero in 1630's England, *Search for the Bark Warwick* will keep you on the edge of your seat, and leave you begging for more. Featured in *48 Degrees North*, the premiere sailing magazine for the Pacific Northwest, in their November 2004 issue, Low Tide Book Review by *Don Boone*: ". . . *Search for the Bark Warwick* is a good book to have aboard . . . Sherry Ann Miller, the author, has a good way with words. Not only does she let you see her characters, but she brings the time of old to mind, and of the surroundings during those times." *Search for the Bark Warwick* is the first of a two-book saga, and is now available from your favorite bookstore. If they don't have it, please ask them to order directly from Granite Publishing & Distribution (800) 574-5779. ISBN# 1-932280-33-2.

Search for the Warwick II

The sequel to *Search for the Bark Warwick* is currently written and awaiting publication, perhaps it will be released by Christmas 2005.

"It will take all our skill and cunning to deceive the hundred-thousand pirates, infiltrate their vast and populous city, locate Thomas and buy him, or steal him, away from his captors, and sail home with him. Other than that, we should expect very few problems." John Dunton's light-hearted words to the men who committed themselves to sailing with him to Algeria prove *almost* true . . . for locating and rescuing Thomas isn't impossible. But, *keeping him,* that will be the true challenge! As the *Warwick II* sets sail for Algeria, John underestimates the pirates, not knowing that they now blame John for the invasion of the Salé Fleet against Morocco, a year earlier. A generous reward for John's capture drives the pirates' greed to extreme measures. Now, John Dunton must not only find his son, he must avoid his own recapture, *and* keep Thomas safe, while he and his devoted crew attempt to outsail and outmaneuver a horde of pirates who have sworn vengeance against him. Rescuing Thomas and returning him to his mother, Rebecca, becomes John's and his crew's only purpose. Nothing else matters to them, not even their own lives.

Charity's Gift

Hans' story, the fourth book in the Gift series, takes place in the Pacific Ocean, on Cocos Island and in Costa Rica. Charity Perez Blake's touching story of love and redemption begins with Hans and Tom sailing to Cocos Island, where Charity works for the Costa Rica Island Preservation Society. She lives with her mother and younger brother in San Jose, Costa Rica. Her LDS military father either died or abandoned his family when Charity was still a child, during the invasion of Nicaragua. Her mother thinks that he died in battle, but Charity is certain that he is still alive, and living in comfort in the United States, perhaps with another family. When she meets up with handsome, intelligent Hans Bridger Clark, who is attracted to Charity and attempts to learn more about her, he triggers her deep-rooted fear that all men have a "love them and leave them" attitude. After all, Hans is well into his thirties, rich and single, with plenty of academic credentials, and absolutely zero career goals. He's a live-aboard, sailing the oceans for the sheer pleasure of the experience. *A vagabond, really!* she thinks. *And a rich American, just like my father!* Is there nothing Hans can do to persuade her otherwise? Charity certainly does not think so! But she underestimates Hans' devotion. **Charity's Gift** is currently in progress.

The fifth and final book in the Gift series, as yet unnamed, will include the ultimate gift for Tom Sparkleman, a man who let liquor nearly destroy his life five years ago. What miracles the Lord has in store for him, Tom can only dream about, for Tom does not believe he will ever find a woman who will love him regardless of his past. The miracle, for Tom, will exceed his wildest expectations, and will thrill the Sparkleman and Clark Clans for generations still unborn.

Readers' Comments

Sherry Ann Miller loves to hear from her readers! All readers whose comments appear in the back of this novel will receive a free, autographed copy of it. **YOU CAN RECEIVE A FREE NOVEL, TOO!!!** Simply e-mail Sherry at Sherry@sherryannmiller.com, putting the title of the book in the subject line, and your comments in the body. Be sure to include your full name, current e-mail and postal addresses, and a statement saying that Sherry Ann Miller has your permission to use your comments. If your comments are selected for inclusion in one of Sherry's books, you'll get your own autographed copy of that book, and a personal note from the author. Read what other readers are saying about Sherry Ann's novels:

I loved **An Angels Gift**! I read **One Last Gift** and I couldn't put it down! I had to know what would happen to Kayla. When I found out there was a sequel, I couldn't wait to read it. Once again, I couldn't put it down and I cried through at least half of it. I can't wait until the third book comes out and I look forward to reading it.   ~ Breeann Law

I went to see my grandkids in Utah and Idaho and got your book, **Search for the Bark Warwick**, and had to write and tell you how much I LOVED it. It only took me a few days to read because it was hard to put down. I'm so happy there is a sequel, the only bad thing is it isn't out yet! I didn't know there was a sequel to **One last Gift** until I was in our bookstore in Houston, Texas. As I was browsing, I saw your name on **An Angel's Gift**, I read the back and was so excited to see the story would go on. Now that I've read it, I can't wait to see what's going to happen next. I love how you write about our loved ones who have passed, showing how very close they still are to us. In **One Last Gift** I was crying so hard. Then, **An Angel's Gift** was so special it made me happy!
~ Jackie Arnold

Just finished reading **Search for the Bark Warwick** this morning, what a fantastic book! From the first pages till the ending, I just didn't want to put it down! You've outdone yourself, girl!!! Can't wait for the sequel . . . hope it's coming soon. :-) I really enjoyed the notes at the end, too, referencing the historical aspects and those that were fictional. Glad you did that. I came to love John Dunton almost instantly for his integrity and kind heart and your Rebecca is perfectly matched with him. What can I say? I LOVE this book!!!!

~ Margie Kawamoto

I read **Search for the Bark Warwick** & LOVED it!!! I can't wait for the sequel to see if John Dunton finds his son.   ~ Jenny Manlove

Thank you so much for autographing my copy of **Search for the Bark Warwick**. What a treasure! My sister read it to me over the phone for more than an hour, and I thoroughly enjoyed it. Once I got my copy, I started reading and didn't stop until it was finished. I read aloud to my husband a good part of the book and we both agreed this is our new favorite book. I've been telling all my friends and family about it. The only disappointment is book 2 isn't out yet! I am anxiously waiting so please hurry! Thanks again and may heaven smile down upon you.   ~ Lora McLaughlin

Sherry Ann's response:

The sequel, **Search for the Warwick II**, *is written and currently with my publisher. Hopefully, it will be ready for Christmas 2005. In the meantime, I hope you enjoy your copy of* **The Tyee's Gift**, *the third installment in the five-book Gift Series.*

~ Sherry Ann

Congratulations Sherry Ann! When I received your book, **Search for the Bark Warwick**, I put down the book I was reading and read your book in two sittings. I had a hard time putting it down. It is one of my very favorites of all time. I can't wait for the sequel(s). I hope there is more than one. Too bad you can't put out 2 books a week to keep me going. I can't wait to find out what happened to Thomas. Let me know when I can get a copy. They should make a movie of it! You really embarrassed me, by the way. I was reading it on the train with tears streaming down my cheeks. Can you imagine what my engineer (*my boss*) was thinking about me? Once the word gets out about **Search for the Bark Warwick**, you will have no peace. I can actually see this one on the New York Times #1 best seller list.   ~ Roarke Stone

I wanted to tell you that I finished **Search for the Bark Warwick**, and loved every page of it! For much of it, my heart was pounding so hard, that I had to remind myself to breathe, and couldn't wait to turn each page, as I was so caught up in the characters, I felt as though I was living each adventure with them. I can hardly wait for the sequel! I decided to re-read your other books again, while my eye sight holds out, so I'm well into **Gardenia Sunrise** again, and enjoying it as much the second time.   ~ Diane Anglesey

While *The Tyee's Gift* still leaves these questions, "What about Hans?" and "What about Tom?", their stories are in progress. The five novel Gift Series is designed so that each novel can be read out of sequence, and still be a satisfying "stand-alone" experience, each with its own merits. If you enjoyed *The Tyee's Gift*, please feel free to read *One Last Gift*, which contains Kayla's conversion story, and *An Angel's Gift*, first-place winner of both the Write Touch Readers' Award and First Coast Beacon Award, which details Ed Sparkleman's romance with Alyssa Mae. All novels in the Gift Series are filled equally with their share of miraculous adventures!

Sherry Ann Miller
a.k.a.
Writer of Miracles

Beginning with her birth and up to the present day, Sherry Ann Miller has lived from miracle to miracle. For this reason, Sherry Ann chooses to write miracles into her novels. She is a firm believer that "nothing is too difficult for the Lord." Many people dismiss miracles as science or fantasy. Sherry Ann hopes to change this way of thinking for anyone who reads her novels. A rosebud opening its petals for the first time is recognized for its intricate design. So, too, is the human heart, which beats without any conscious effort. Both are miracles, yet scientists do not classify them as such. To Sherry Ann's eyes, everything is a miracle. This attitude leads her to accept God's love and the beauty of His world more fully.

Visit Sherry Ann online at www.sherryannmiller.com or email her at Sherry@sherryannmiller.com

For Sherry Ann, one of the most amazing miracles of all, is the thinness of the veil that clouds our view of the Spirit World. She states, "When we are fully in tune with our Father in Heaven, we will see that our loved ones, those who've gone before us, are not far from us. They, along with our Father in Heaven and Jesus Christ, want us to succeed! Thousands of our departed ancestors, together with the Godhead, make up an entire cheering section across the veil! They encourage us upon the righteous path of life, inspiring us to hold fast to the word of God. On the other side of the playing field, angry and fathering discontent, Lucifer beseeches us to choose *any other path* that will lead us away from God. The miracle of this over-balanced game of conscience is that we, alone, will choose how well we play the game."

It is Sherry Ann's hope that her readers will begin to see that everything good in this life is a miracle, from the tiniest blade of grass, to the hearty pumpkin patch, to the majestic order of all creation. Occasionally, God throws in some unexpected twists that seemingly defy us and make us stretch beyond what we believe we're capable of, but He is always there to take our hand and lead us to success. Sherry is not alone in receiving some of the Lord's bigger challenges. It is at those times of greatest opposition that God works some of His most remarkable miracles. Sherry Ann is living proof that this philosophy is true.